Shane Connaughton, after working on farms, in factories and City offices, trained as an actor at the Bristol Old Vic Theatre School. He has written plays for the Victoria Theatre, Stoke on Trent, Half Moon Theatre National Theatre, London.

His wrote the scripts for *Every Picture Tells* The Run of the Country, O Mary This Long

He has won the George Devine Award, T Irish Post Award. *A Border Station*, his first novel, was short-listed for The Guinness Peat Literary Award and for *My Left Foot* he was nominated for an Academy Award.

Fiction
A Border Station
The Run of the Country
A Border Diary

Plays
Lily
I Do Like To Be
George Davis is Innocent, OK?
Sir Is Winning
A Wicked Hoor

BIG
PAI

By Shane Connaughton

The Muswell Press Ltd
www.muswell-press.co.uk

Big Parts by Shane Connaughton
Text copyright © Shane Connaughton 2009

© Muswell Press Ltd 2009

First published in Great Britain, February 2009
by The Muswell Press Ltd.
PO BOX 56946
London N10 9AH

ISBN 978-0-9547959-6-2

"I won't Let You Down" & "Sugarolly Mountains" kind permission Jim Diamond.

A CIP record of this book is available from The British Library.

Book design by This Is Studio / www.thisisstudio.com
Printed by Short Run Press Ltd.

The Muswell Press Ltd
www.muswell-press.co.uk

A Border Station

'With its sparse yet melodic prose it is a skilful tribute to a way of life that is as uncompromising as it is unchanging.' The Evening Standard.

'Comparison with work by JohnMcGahern and Patrick Kavanagh is inevitable....it is a tribute to Connaughton that his child's view of life holds its own with those two giants.' Irish Times.

'Wonderful...vivid...beautifully wrought.' Daily Telegraph.

'Emotionally powerful.' Booklist

'Brilliant....Any story here can stand proudly beside those of Frank O'Connor.' Cleveland Plain Dealer.

'Immensely readabe....Each story is a gem.' United Press International.

The Run of the Country

'What is most profound in this wise, unsentimental and wonderfully poignant work is Connaughton's lament for the exorbitant price the human heart must pay.' Washington Post

'Connaughton leaves you in no doubt of his talent as a writer.' Irish Times

'Connaughton does wonders...surprising us with sudden revelations of character and curiously twisted events.' Chicago Tribune

'There may never be a better description of how it felt to be seventeen.' Ruth Rendell, Daily Telegraph.

A Border Diary

'Observant, funny and politically astute.' Gillian Freeman, Hampstead & Highgate Express.

'An ebullient, good-humoured, nostalgic and astute commentary.' Times Literary Supplement.

'Hypnotic as a camera, the diary has images just as remarkable as any film could supply'. Eugene McCabe, Irish Times.

'Its richness lies in its interweaving of the unreality of making a film with the reality of people whose lives are pervaded by violence or the threat of violence.' Roy Greenslade, The Times.

A Sunday. After the roast beef and Yorkshire, apple pie and tea, we cleared the dishes and clambered onto the kitchen table. We poured Moet et Chandon over each other. I wanted to raise our basement lives to decadent heights.

A flash of camel hair went past the window. My wife scrambling from the table, grabbed her clothes and fled to the bedroom. A second later the glass door rattled with coin raps. I couldn't find my trousers. The door opened.

'Anyone at home?'

I grabbed the apple pie.

Wearing a duffel coat and brown Oxfords, the elderly gentleman who lived on the top floor came in. Staring with stately unblinking chin-up arrogance, leonine head thick with long steel-grey hair, he stood massively four-square. Our small kitchen seemed even smaller. His shiny forehead had a skim of flaky skin and the thin lashes round his watery eyes were old man gummy. Stern, silent, petulant lips twitching, it seemed he was waiting for his brain to deliver a message. After about twenty seconds it arrived deep and plummy.

'You do know we are being decanted?'

Did he really not notice I was naked save for the remains of an apple pie? Crabbing sideways, I sat in at the end of the table, the pie now on my lap. Normally we'd hear him tramping up and down the communal stairs, his great shoes welting the treads.

The house was a warren of rooms, the tenants on the cranky side of life.

'Have you received the letter? Are you being decanted? Or is this a plot reserved for April and me? The sods!'

His Home Counties tone was his shield. I slipped the apple pie onto the table.

'Care for a slice? It hasn't been seriously molested.'

'Oh yes, rather.'

He didn't seem to mind I was short a cloth or two.

'The whole country is corrupt. Rotten. You know I address young men?'

'Stamp them as well do you?'

His lips frogged alarmingly.

'What, what? They hang on my every word. Fabulous. You do know me, yes? Freddie. Freddie Parts. Top floor. You've seen me with April, no?'

'Is she your wife?'

'Good Lord, no. Buggered by her father from an early age. Isn't Croydon a beastly place?'

From the deep pockets of his duffel coat he produced a letter. From the landlords. He thrust it at me..."Fabric of house in such a state urgent repairs must be put in train immediately...Re-wiring essential...Rising damp of such...It will be necessary to decant both yourself and Miss Fard..."

Rising damp on the top floor?

'Decanting us as if we were cheap plonk. Decant? It's eviction by another name. Nowadays people treat the language like a sewer. They go down into the filth and God knows what they come up with. Delicious pie. We need a new leader.'

His false teeth gleamed like chunky earthenware on an oak dresser. His upper lip was dictator deep. His barrel chest stretched the horny toggles on his duffle and when he adjusted his trousers, tugging the creases along his thighs, I glimpsed his ankles. They were sturdy as newel posts. He was a dusty piece of Victorian furniture, mislaid in a corner of the twenty-first century.

'To be a leader you must have vast experience. You must know how to entice the sheep through the gap. I'd like you to read a novel I wrote last evening. I need a cogent response. You appear literate.'

'How do you spell that?'

With an irritable gesture he brushed pastry from his mouth.

'You jest?'

'You wrote a novel in an evening?'

'Good Lord no! It took me all week. I finished it last night. I read to April. She's an avid listener.'

'Are you published?'

'I may execute an internet launch this time. Direct to the public.'

'Is it pornographic?'

'I fear it's not pornographic at all. Did you see the Telegraph yesterday? There's a musical opening shortly in which the entire cast sing and dance, got up as dildos!'

'Sounds like a good night out.'

'The entire country is plunging.'

He laughed a hopeless sort of laugh, spluttering the table with bits of pie. He had undoubted force. Static hopped off him.

'Plunging? In what way?'

'Water - I know water. You know about the water-table, yes? Words are like that. We're full of them. You only have to lower the bucket.'

By the time he trudged out of the kitchen, I was cold and my wife fast asleep. A colour supplement lay open on the bed. Someone had invented underwear to give would-be rapists an electric shock. In the event of attack the victim's heartbeat would activate a charge severe enough to frazzle a donkey. The marital bedroom would be a dangerous place indeed.

I dressed and went out for cigarettes. Two men wandered along our street. One wore a T-shirt and jeans tucked into boxing boots. His mate wore trousers, a shirt and tie and across his arm a jacket. Like he was strolling along on a hot day. It was raining. His socks were red, his black shoes muddy. Boxing Boots sported a brass ear ring dangling from a smaller silver one.

BIG PARTS

His left boot had the lace knotted in a floppy bow. The right lace was undone. It snaked about, causing him to lift his foot unnaturally high as he walked. Red Socks was arguing with Boxing Boots.

'Everything comes from the earth. That car comes from metal. Metal comes from coal. Coal comes from the earth. Everything comes from the fucking earth.'

Rain was invented for Sundays. Religious weather to dampen hearts.

The streets were full of wanderers. There were more barking humans out than dogs. They howled in doorways, on park benches, standing outside the shut Post Office, walking in the rain, beer cans in hand. The Chaos In the Community policy came with matching weather. Decanting weather.

As darkness fell, curtains were rarely closed. You could see right into the wealthy houses. The ground floor through-rooms all looked alike. Plush new sofas, tasselled lamp standards, anodised aluminium desk lights, walls covered with oil paintings and cartoons. Or tapestries. Kitchen units and cookers with more knobs and dials than an aeroplane cockpit.

From a gleaming kitchen with shaker units, zink tops, hidden lighting, a woman waved out to me. Lady Hannah, wife of Sir Neville Earthy. I went round the side entrance and into the lobby.

She groped me below the equator. As we rolled along a wall of theatre posters, over her shoulder I read,

"Magnificent! Emotionally rich. You must see this."

I wandered my hand up her long dress.

'Just testing that your knickers aren't plugged to your heartbeat.'

'I'm not wearing any.'

The glass in most of the poster frames was cracked. She'd rolled a lot of blokes along that wall. The claims on the posters were quite ridiculous.

"A pioneering work of theatrical reportage." I'd never heard of the piece.

Hannah was a drinker, Neville a theatre director. 'A dram and a pill gets you over the hill.'

Her long hair had been chopped boyish fashion. It made her strong face even stronger. Her greeny-brown eyes sat large as Kiwi fruit. Previously a redhead, now she was blonde.

Music played in the sitting-room...Jim Diamond singing Hi Ho Silver.

'Neville will be out ages. There's been a break-in at the office. Haven't seen you in months.'

'Have you discovered the meaning of life?'

'I don't know the meaning. I think I know the purpose.'

A door clicked. Zoe, her four year old daughter, stepped into the hallway. Thumb rammed in her mouth, puzzled, she stared at us.

'What is it, Zoe?'

There was enough confusion in the child's face to last forever. I left at once.

Back in the rain, Boxing Boots and Red Socks were fading in the distance. Walking into air. Dreaming their way.

Some days we disappear from ourselves. Some mornings I couldn't find myself in the mirror. That morning I'd nuzzled my wife awake, told her I was scared of death. She told me to relax.

'We don't remember before we were born, why should it be any different after we're gone?'

I propped myself up on the pillow. There I was in the mirror okay. Looking at myself looking at myself. Tousled, pale and puzzled. If you came from the Midlands you were pale.

My wife had hot flesh everywhere. Even her elbows were warm.

I went into Muzie's shop and bought two packets of cigs. Muzie was better known as Miss Jackpot. Standing in his doorway out of the rain, I lit up. A man walked past, a mobile phone pressed to his ear. Like a folk singer concentrating on a song. Or someone listening to a sea shell.

A matronly woman patted my wrist.

'You really want lung cancer?'

She was married to Dr. Tripp, the specialist bum doctor. Couldn't have been easy for her - him coming home every evening having spent the day looking up rectums. Piles of them. Still, where there's muck there's brass. I liked the touch of her unfamiliar fingers. Insect fingers. Drizzle fingers. The light from Muzie's window washed her face yellow. She went off smiling. A stout woman in sensible flat-heeled shoes, brown woollen stockings, a blue kagool. I imagined her a dumpy tuning-fork. Everybody had a few notes in them. We just need striking the right way.

Two middle-aged men stood at the bus stop. They wore plastic macs buttoned to the chin, the collars turned up. One of them ate fish and chips.

' Ted Seegar,' he said, munching, ' I saw him play. A few years ago. In goal.'

' I thought he wur in Preston?'

' No, he wur goalkeeper.'

' You couldn't have. He quit yonks ago.'

' I did, I saw him.'

He swallowed a nip of fish, licked his thumb and added -

' In goal. He wur a small man.'

' That's right. Because he kept a pub in Macclesfield after.'

Ted Seegar was small, therefore he kept a pub in Macclesfield?

The brian could rattle off down a wayward track, crash through linguistic signals, upend language and logic without you even realising it.

Muzie came out of his shop.

'Today I Miss Jackpot. I 'ave all bloomin' eight hawses, the bet vos placed, yeah? Ve-well the dawkit vos ritten out an' everting an' I have to place bet by 2 p.m. o'clock...'

Muzie was Indian, his dirge unchanging. Only the bookie loved him. His face was sallow, his brown eyes tired. His spectacles jockeyed up on his caterpillar eyebrows. His mustard-coloured cardigan hung open. He wore leather sandals.

'...I 'ave late night and I set the clock bee-side my ear to go off the bloomin' ting at heh quarter to the hour so I go to Ladbroke at right time enough...'

The traffic lights turned green. A massive flat-faced transporter lurched forward, its two sloping tiers bearing nine cars. They looked like an orgy of frogs.

'But for some ree-saun the bloomin' clock do no go off until 2 p.m. o'clock and I race a-roun' to Ladbroke...'

A bluebottle bumped into his wiry hair. It buzzed excitedly. Muzie raised a weary hand to send it on its way.

'My bloomin' luck is so out I caunnot understan' eet. Why?'

His ritualised suffering was somewhere between neurosis and religion. The phone rang at the back of the shop. The place was a jumble of newspapers and magazines. Displayed on a top shelf were the mucky ones.

I noticed a CCTV camera newly erected in the High Road. Paranoia was spreading like flu.

I was worried about being decanted. I'd have to get all the tenants together and plan a campaign. It was hard to pin them down. Despite Boards of Management, Tenants' Forums, Housing Officers, Maintenance Departments, the Landlords were a faceless crew. Tenants were a disparate bunch. Our street was a lovely street. Once out would they let us back in?

The clock on Freddie's mantelpiece was solid as himself. It had an erratic tick-tock, as if the innards were in atrial fibrillation. Whirring to a dusty wheeze immediately before striking, it marked the hours as if coughing. You expected blood on the dial.

Freddie's flat was in the attic. A large painting of a cardinal dominated the room. The red Vatican costume on the enthroned figure surged to the floor. Two golden slippers peeped out from under this billowing cassock. On his head was a red biretta. The face had the thinnest of skins, the bony structure of the skull beneath, stretching it almost to breaking. A hand, delicately fingering a dangling crucifix, displayed a diamond ring on every knuckle. The other hand was partially obscured by a copious sleeve. When you noticed it, the skeletal bones shocked. A sly effect. In a lower corner of the canvas, a young woman, oddly sexual in Salvation Army uniform, cowered obediently. The corpse-toothed cardinal leered at her from his dominating position on the high-backed throne. There was a skull almost hidden by the golden slippers. It was the last detail you noticed. The whole thing was a mixture of Renaissance camp and modern baroque. It was meant to disturb. Freddie cackled.

'Do you know the Newman painting by Millais? I've sent that up. The Vatican is pure Disney you see.'

'You don't have to believe in Mickey Mouse.'

'In Disneyland you do. Religion is the fangs in man's skull. That's what the painting is saying.'

'Why don't you paint a caterpillar?'

'Don't be absurd.'

The double bed in the room was covered with a faded red eiderdown. On the floor was a pile of Daily Telegraphs. Freddie rested on the bed, his back propped against a mound of velvet cushions. He fingered through a pornographic magazine.

'It's important for anatomical accuracy. And cheaper than models. Bare flesh is harder to paint than costume.'

'It's easier to wear though.'

By the window was a wicker table just big enough for his Adler Electric 21D and a few sheets of paper, pens, rubbers, pencils. And most outdated of all - a prickly rubber thimble page-turner. On a shelf stood a solid phalanx of manuscripts. The flimsy carbon copy spines looked vulnerable. The top copies were out doing the rounds of publishers. Like missing parents they'd probably never be seen again. Covered with a strip of cling film was an Apple Mac laptop.

'If I'm writing an historical, I use me Adler. Modern I accomplish on Apple. My room is my scriptorium.'

'Paper never refuses words. Nor screens screeds.'

'What? If the subject matter is moral, they won't publish. You do know that, don't you? The whole country is a cesspit. I fear we're bumping along on the bottom.'

'Can be rather fun. Depending on the bottom of course.'

'What, what? Nowadays, to be English is to be impotent.'

This he addressed to a technicoloured pudenda on a magazine cover.

New Building Trust were our landlords. In a recess by the gas fire was an Edwardian wardrobe, hand-painted in gold and blue. The fire was wall-mounted, cheapo-cheapo. Typical Trust. Everything in the room was dusty, the tattered carpet decidedly so. I surreptitiously wiped my finger along the edge of the mantelpiece. Talcum powder. Why talcum powder? Freddie lay back, breathing heavily, lips frogging in and out. His red ears were big as an oilman's gloves.

'"Because" would be a good title for a book.'

His eyebrows shot up some inches.

'You say the strangest things, boy. Because? Caterpillars?'

On the pile of newspapers was an empty toothpaste tube. The brand name and lettering had been removed. The tube was slit lengthways and widened out. Beside it was black crepe hair and a piece of red velvet.

'I have written a play. Could you give it to that dreadful chap you know? Fanny.'

'I don't know any chap called Fanny.'

'No, no. Fanny by Gaslight. My play. The chap along the street. Earthy. You know his wife don't you?' He cackled knowingly.

'I received another decanting letter today. They mean business.'

Resting a weary hand on his scaly forehead, he hung his head. His thick gunmetal hair fell forward. His shirt collar was dandruffy with talc. Or talcy with dandruff.

Out the window I could see the back garden way below. My wife and I had exclusive use. She filled it with flowers and shrubs and waged a war against the bindweed. The Trust gardeners planted the bindweed. It's cheap. They pretend it's a flower.

It started raining. As each drop hit a leaf, the colours exploded. I'd worked in a furniture factory paint shop, in Bromley-By-Bow. A gas bottle exploded right beside me, taking a dozen paint drums with it. Lying on the floor, through the multi-coloured pain and flame, I saw rainbows bleeding. Since that day, grey reality came a poor second. To celebrate coming out of hospital, we went to Epping Forest and from a mossy clearing where we lay, uprooted a silver birch sapling and brought it home. There it was four floors below, tall now, swaying in the wind, a tree of love and kisses.

'Trees are the planet's pubic hair, don't you think?'

'This decanting business, boy. I do have a bloody good legal firm behind me, you do know that, don't you? We must fight them.'

'Who?'

'The Trust. You silly sod. Where would we go? April adores here.'

'I'll call a meeting of all the tenants.'

The demented clock baroinged eleven, though the time read ten to ten. Freddie's attic was traditionally English. It had at least one resident lunatic.

The door creaked open. A blue cup on a red saucer appeared, hovering three feet from the floor, as if afloat in an abstract painting. A thumb and fingers gripped the saucer. Tea trembled over the lip of the cup.

'Come along, my dear. Do come, sweet.'

April Fard was a wraith in a white summer frock and blue plastic sandals. Pink doll clips pinioned her hair. Her bare arms were dusty with talc. As she came towards me, the tea divided itself between cup and saucer. There was as much in one as the other. The tea was lukewarm and pale as her skin. She was dressed like a schoolgirl, though she looked in her late thirties. Her upper lip and nose were oddly tilted.

'You know April, don't you?'

'Yes, comes after March.'

'What? No, her name.'

'Hello April.'

Her upper lip wasn't a hare-lip exactly. But the tip of her nose turning up, pulled the lip with it, raising it enough to reveal where teeth and gum met. A village idiot look. Had she been a ghost she couldn't have exerted less pressure on air or eye. It was clear she was the woman in the painting. On canvas, her introverted Renaissance physiognomy disconcertingly angled at the viewer, she had substance. But standing beside me in her girlish summer frock, she was less than flesh and blood. Her eyes were without light. I didn't exist in them. Freddie watched amused, at the discordant world over which he presided.

'Lovely tea, April,' I lied.

She headed for the door, her feet fluttering across the tattered, powdered, carpet. In Trust flats, sound-proofing was squares of hardboard, faced with foam, then copydexed to the floor. The squares imprinted themselves through the carpet and made walking a spongy adventure.

'She has such a lovely wardrobe. She adores frocks. No tights for her. She's a suspender belt gel through and through. A real lady. You can tell that, can't you?'

April's room was next to Freddie's. She began to torture a piano.

'You do know April is my model? Oh yes. Her bosom is all her own.'

The flat was full of pictures. Her bosom was in most of them. Freddie was eighty at least. She was no more than forty.

'What do you think of this Iraq business? It used to have a flat "a". Now the BBC pronounce it "Irawke." '

'I'll call the tenants together. In my place, Freddie. I'll let you know.'

'Why your place?'

'Because.'

'I hate that word. It is full of deceit.'

I went out onto the landing. April's door ajar, I could see her sitting at the piano, fingers frozen above the keys. The room was painted pink. The bed clothes were pink. The carpet pink. The armchair had pink cushions. The small ornamental china clock on top of the pink piano was pink. Practically everything was pink and liberally sprinkled with talcum powder. The tassels on the lamp shade were pink. Even the black piano keys were painted pink.

He followed me out.

'Do you know much about water?'

'It leaks?'

'I was Parting the Waters. I topped the bill all over the country. You do know I'm an engineer by profession? Oh yes. I was huge. You should have seen my spouts. Water is art. Television killed me. I'm convinced there is a new audience waiting.'

The nation was treasure island. Every head a map marked X.

Pasted to the landing wall was a faded photograph culled from an actor's directory. Vastly younger but recognizable and sporting a cravat, Freddie smiled coyly, his chin tucked into his shoulder.

"FREDDIE PARTS Currently Booking PARTING THE WATERS. Now recovered from Broken Leg."

'Did you write it?'

'Write? What?'

'Broken Leg.'

'Christ! It wasn't a play. I broke my leg in Blackpool. The stage couldn't support my machinery. Have you any idea the weight of water? An ordinary person would have been killed. The doctors said I wasn't human.'

'You took it as a compliment?'

He still did. Head back, delighting in the memory, he howled with laughter. He sneezed with such ferocity, his upper teeth shot out, landing in a tin bucket under an old sink. Such was the clatter he might have been dumping a saggar of broken ware.

'Damn dentures. Everything goes in the end.'

The landing smelled of damp. The wallpaper barely clung to the wall - most of the paste had been eaten by silver fish. Up in the corner were worrying cracks in the plaster and brickwork. The putty in the landing window had perished. The frame, particularly along the bottom, was rotten beyond repair. In older properties like ours, long-term neglect seemed a tactic. Every month we were sent glossy brochures with wonderful stuff about reactive maintenance, community news and tough new policies to deal with anti-social behaviour. But basically, tenants were left to fester. By the time the rain seeped in through the walls you had to be decanted.

Freddie, fishing his teeth from the bucket, stropped them on his sleeve, then rammed them back in his mouth.

A painting hung above the stair-well. The colours were cheerful greens, yellows, reds, pinks, white, a few dots of blue. A table bulked large in the foreground but stretched to disappearance in a narrowly distant horizon. Assorted animals sat at the table, all leering at a female figure serving tea. This girly-woman held a brown teapot in her right hand, her left index finger pressing on the lid knob. It was the Mad Hatter's tea party as a sticky-bun wonderland of pubescent sex.

The Alice figure, a hare, a white rabbit, a cat, a snail, even the tea pot - they all had in common a lift of upper lip revealing slightly protruding teeth. Alice was April. April was everything.

Our other tree was a pear. My wife had green fingers. Especially when it came to nail varnish. Green nails matched champagne. Holding a glass of bubbly, she'd often saunter, barefooted, round the garden, admiring her flowers. One evening she decided the pear tree needed pruning. It had she said, too many useless shoots. She hired a girl she met in the street. This tree-punk, when she turned up, wore steel-capped boots, torn black stockings, jeans, a kilt, a blue cardigan, red and green hair, fingerless gloves and something metal hanging from her lower lip. Armed with a rusty handsaw she climbed up into the tree. Her objective was to cut it in two. Once the top half was sawn off, further pruning would be unnecessary.

Every half hour my wife gave her tea. Sitting on a branch, hugging the half-sawn trunk with one arm whilst she drank from an expensive china cup and saucer, induced vertigo. In me. My wife, glass of champagne in hand, talked up to her as if it was the most natural thing in the world.

Job eventually done - it took hours - my wife parted with a hundred quid.

'She's not a gardener. She's a drug addict. How could you have fallen for her story?'

'I fell for yours, didn't I?'

The pear tree, without its top half, looked half dead. I was convinced winter would kill it off completely. But spring came and one morning I noticed tiny silvery buds. A few rainy days later the buds burst open. They developed into fluffy balls, each one green with a white tip. There were as many as eight balls a cluster. When the wind blew, it fanned them to blossom. The tree shimmered as if caught in white flame. When the wind dropped, the tree, entranced, stood dead still. To look was to be part of a vision. A week later the vision became a reality of white petals. We'd have fruit come autumn. The tree, half murdered, had renewed itself.

'See, darling? There's a moral there somewhere.'

'In every Eden there's a serpent. Usually ourselves.'

My wife had a good job. I didn't even have a bad one. I stayed in the house or sat in the garden reading the newspaper. One day, a neighbour - May was her name - stuck her head over the fence. Breathless with excitement, she had just disturbed a burglar and had called the police. She was in her forties. She was a regular in the local pub. Students drank there. It was thirsty work trying to pin down even the weediest brain box. But by the end of the night she'd have more often than not managed to get one of them into the corner by the juke box. They called her the Praying Mantis. I liked her. She wanted something out of life. And she never tried to get me into the corner.

Her description of the burglar had more to do with fashion and passion than forensics.

'He was ever such a nice looking feller. Ever so nice looking. He'd on a lovely cashmere wot's it. And Armani jeans and them nice Reebok Classics. Blonde hair. Only about twenty. White and all.'

She was wearing leopard skin hot-pants and patent leather knee-length bed-me boots. Her mouth was raddled with red lipstick.

She'd fallen in love with a young electric meter reader. But the meter reader left her after two days and she had to return to her husband who hadn't even noticed she'd gone.

We went out to the street. Toby Turfe, our community policeman, ambled up. May invited him in for a cuppa.

'No thanks. Duty calls.'

Freddie came out. Seeing May, his big red ears twitched and his lips frogged as if testing sugar.

'Halloo, my dear, hm-hm, ha-hah, I SAY, what, eh? Hm? Ha-hah, what?'

He brazenly stared into her cleavage.

In his hat, old double-breasted brown suit, brown Oxfords, leaning on a black brolly, he looked the model citizen. May loathed him. He was over eighty with a leer for every year and a sexual sneer to demean a Mayfair tart.

'I was wondering, would you care to sit for me, my dear? There would be a payment of course.'

'Sit for him?' said PC Turfe.

'He's a painter,' I said.

'Well, he wants to paint the front of the house.'

Under his constabulary gaze our house looked shabby indeed. The paint-work peeling, brickwork crumbling, cement work cracking, it looked more in need of a face-lift than May. Or Freddie for that matter.

'Council?' Toby inquired, with not much fear of contradiction.

'New Building Trust.'

'Same difference.'

'Same indifference.'

I phoned the brain-sifter. He was father of a girl who went to university with my wife. He liked my wife. He liked me too. So he said. He told me to visit him any time I felt unduly worried. What he was exactly I never worked out. Therapist? Analyst? Psychiatrist? Psychologist? It was good puzzling things out with him. Was it all really random? Was it pre-ordained? But this time when I phoned him, he wasn't pleased. He told me not to phone him again. Other than to make an appointment in the normal manner.

'Normal?'

'Yes.'

'Forgive me.'

'We must learn to forgive ourselves.'

The local paper, from time to time, carried stories about tenants being decanted to inferior accommodation; their house done up; then let to completely different tenants. Or worse - sold to a property company. The Trust did a good job. It gave a roof to people, many of them with mental and social problems. But the bigger it got, the more houses it owned, the further the gap grew between the office and the tenants. Organising the people in our house would be my cause. My mission. My wife was my heart. Home was where my heart was.

Freddie and April lived in the attic. Wally, a black Londoner, lived in one room below them. Wally came from a broken background. He was supposed to take tablets every day. He was in his thirties. Phil and Rosa Gibbs were pensioners. They had little left but dreams. They lived above us. There were seven of us in all.

My wife had money. Her father was wealthy. She worked in Whitehall. I was Stoke-On-Trent. She was Staffordshire. I loved her.

'I adore you.'

'I window you.'

Miss Chats was our rent officer. She arranged to meet me in the Electric caff. It was called the Electric after the electric pole outside the door. It was owned by a Turk, worked by Bosnians, frequented mostly by assorted refugees from all over Eastern Europe. Hit by the fallout from exploding bombs and imploding currencies, the Electric once utterly Cockney, with a cheery greasy cuisine, had become a political phenomenon.

Few locals used the place anymore. It was no longer the same. A scrap of decoration, thumb-tacked in a corner of the ceiling, was all that was left of a forgotten Christmas.

For Freddie the place was a Foreign Office insult to the national psyche. Simply put it was the borough's take-up of people bombed out by government. By the time the Electric caff loomed up it didn't much matter which government.

The new waitresses were a plus in anyone's language. Especially the girl with big brown eyes, loose summer frock and a holiday smile would perk a flat battery.

Miss Chats was waiting for me at the table by the street window. She had a gap between her top front teeth.

'Legendarily, a gap like that is sexy.'

It was an inappropriate comment. Her look confirmed it.

'We have a number of properties to which you can be decanted.'

'I have to consult.'

'Who?'

'My fellow rent boys and girls. Of an accumulated number of years worthy of Methuselah.'

'I will arrange a meeting. In the former school - St. Mary's. Inform the other people in your house. The sooner we sort you all out, the better. It's a building in desperate need of structural repair. And decoration.'

'St. Mary's?'

'No. The house you live in.'

'What age are you, Miss Chats? If you don't mind me asking. You have one of those faces - you could be twenty, you could be thirty. Could have something to do with your crew-cut hairdo. Why do you wear black? Even your necklace is black.'

'Black - there is no confusion with black.'

Under the table our knees touched. I got a jolt of static. She was good enough to plug into the National Grid.

'If there isn't a score of men fighting for your soul, London is on the way down.'

'I will let you know date and time. Of the meeting.'

She left me to my too pale tea and a jammy bun.

St. Mary's was behind our house. They'd shut it down. It had a reputation for poor standards for poor students.

The meeting turned out not to be about our house at all. Miss Chats was there with some people from the Town Hall and a New Labour chap. Freddie and April turned up and about a dozen locals. Wally, who lived above us, was there as well. The meeting was about plans to turn the school into a dormitory for refugees from the Balkans. Miss Chats opened proceedings.

'These refugees will bring much diversity. A vibrant culture and a work ethic to be envied.'

Freddie steamed in dragon fury. April sat beside him as if she were dead.

May, wearing a mini skirt and red ankle socks, sat with her husband, Jim. Big Julia, a native of the street we lived in, wheezed loudly. She was a perpetual cadge – 'Git us a pyeper 'nd a pecket of Anadeens'.

The schoolroom was cold, barren. Huddled in overcoats, people sat smoking, despite a poster proclaiming a health warning. At the back of the meeting was a scattering of young drunks and drug addicts. They'd been dragged in by the Town Hall to show they had their fingers on a youthful subterranean pulse. Some of them were recognisable from begging outside the Post Office or making half-hearted attempts to wipe your windscreen at traffic lights. They were always accompanied by a three-legged dog.

'Hands up who'd like to start the ball rolling,' Miss Chats said,'come on, don't be shy. This is a consultation process after all.'

Freddie, lips frogging, breathing heavily, cheeks puffing in and out, looked like a gigantic marsh toad ready to explode.

'We will not be decanted!'

The Town Hall people looked to Miss Chats.

'Oh, Mr. Parts. Welcome. Thank you. That matter is of no concern to this particular forum. But thank you.'

'Right,' said the smartly dressed, good looking New Labourite,' this is just to do with our refugee friends. We are here to listen to you. We want what is best.'

His tone was smooth as old Tory. His blue suit cost three times the national average monthly wage. So did mine.

Miss Chats was trained to stonewall. Private desire had to come second to public concern. Her blank-as-slate face was hard to stare down. The X-ray eyes would shiver anyone's timbers. The gap between her top front teeth and the baldy haircut gave her a fierce, sexy look.

'The consultative process is on-going. Management use their best endeavours to keep everyone informed. Any queries on related matters, Mr. Parts, contact C.S.I.'

C.S.I. - Customer Services Info.

Freddie groaned as if stabbed.

'Christ! The country is a sewer. And the turds have come to the top.'

The three-legged dog barked.

A druggie at the back of the meeting muttered,

'How long's this gonna take, fuck's sake, you know?'

Last time I saw him he was running out of the Oxfam shop in Brondesbury with an armful of clothes and an electric kettle.

Whilst Miss Chats and her group put their heads together, Wally stood up.

'Scuse, Miss, yo!'

Instead of swallowing his pills, Wally chewed them. This explained the powdery dribble at the corner of his mouth.

'I'm concerned I am abaht these people. I can't sleep nights sometime. Howsabaht the noise factor? Bozzies go nicking. Be fair.'

Wally hardly had a visitor from one end of the year to the other. Apart from me. So long as Social Security paid his rent, he wasn't on Miss Chats' radar. He went up and down the stairs through the night, checking the front door was locked. He regularly loitered on the landing, having imagined hostile knocking. Or he stood there claiming he'd heard loud music. He threatened to kill the person he imagined was the cause of it all. He accidentally flooded our flat several times. Pills were all that sewed him together.

His fat smile was boyish, endearing. He was hard to dislike.

Miss Chats couldn't turn her political guns on him. He was an ethnic minority.

'We have been given the task of helping our Eastern European friends and that's what we intend doing. This country has always opened its heart to the persecuted.'

'I'm persecuted, Miss.' He sat down.

True. And there was no answer to it. If we hadn't bombed them in the first place they wouldn't have come here.

'War is like sex. It starts out cheap but ends up dear.' I sat down.

'Can we keep sex out of it?' Miss Chats said quietly.

Mr. Stavrou, an elderly Greek Cypriot, came into the meeting. He was going blind. He could just see enough by tilting his head to the light. He was a dapper man with a hooked nose and a massive moustache. Rooted on his left temple was a clump of red moles and grey warts. His beautiful eyes were blue as wild cornflower. In Cyprus he had been a sheriff in the police. When the Turks invaded in 1974, he fled to England. To his son who ran a shop in the High Road. He was a long time smiling, a long time going blind, a long time waiting for Justice.

His moustache was as big as a squirrel's tail. How come you never saw a moustache like that on all those Greek statues?

You could tile a Sultan's palace with eyes as blue as Mr. Stavrou's.

Freddie, leaning forward on his brolly, and now the perfect gent, in his rich, deep voice, declared sadly to Miss Chats,

'England's epic story has come to an end, I'm afraid. Does it belong to us anymore?'

The three-legged dog barked, lowered its head to the bare floor again, bopped its tail a few times.

'I have a feeling, Miss Chats, we do not want to be decanted.' I sat down.

She edged her tongue into the gap of her teeth whilst deciding what to do.

'It was a good meeting,' she said, 'very helpful indeed. Definitely. Understand your concerns. Know your worries. Wish to do what's best. Take your considerations on board before any final decision is made. Thank you. Mr. Shand, here, my colleague in the Town Hall, is always open to suggestions.'

'Reg Shand,' said Mr. Reg Shand, tapping his hat down tight on his head. 'Just ask for Reg.'

'Good God,' Freddie erupted, 'the cunning! "Understand your concerns. Know your worries." Are they orders? Or a deliberate elision of the personal pronoun? You do know,' he declared to the meeting, 'corruption breeds corrupt language.'

Miss Chats stared at him, then at April. April, in private agony, opened her mouth wide, then closed it tight, as if shouting hopelessly in nightmare.

Big Julia, heaving to her feet, tottered towards Miss Chats.

'Git us a pyeper 'nd a pecket of anadeens, will yah, love?'

'No,' said Miss Chats, curtly. People laughed.

'Fock you darlin', said Julia.

Freddie roared. The dog staggered barking to his three legs. The meeting was over.

Outside we stood under a rusty moon. You could never pin it down. All you could do was bark up at it.

I'd get on with calling my own meeting. My wife called it wasting time.

'The poor have the time to waste it.'

Though we lived in the basement our post was delivered upstairs. We had a peculiar dark stairway leading up to a door giving access to the main hallway. The house was a warren of rooms, partitions, stairs, half-landings. My wife had expensively trendied up our bit but the rest of the house hadn't seen a paint brush in years. Sadness is sadder with peeling wallpaper.

I was in the hallway the morning after the meeting, collecting the post, when Freddie came in, laden with shopping.

'My play. I told you about it. Will you give it to Earthy? Bastard.'

'Why? What have I done?'

'Not you. Earthy. Fanny by Gaslight. I've got an essential that goes with it. Come upstairs.'

He trudged up the several flights, counting each step as he went.

'...Four, five, six...bastard...seven...Christ...eight...'

All the way to the attic door was a track worn in the lino.

In the narrow stair foot area of the attic entrance, he put down his bags and banging the door shut, lowered an anti-intruder device of his own invention. This length of wood, calculated to a nicety, rammed tight against the door. It looked more substantial than the door itself, which was New Building Trust cheapo-cheapo.

Climbing the last eight steps to the stair head landing, he paused on each one, coaxing his legs to further effort -

'Come on, sods! One more! Christ. There's no justice.'

Had he toppled backwards I'd have been crushed to death. April's door was open. She sat staring at the window. A bluebottle on the net curtain, tilting forward, wiped one back leg against the other.

'It's only us, lovely one, sweetie pie.'

In the kitchen he unpacked tins of tuna, salmon, sardines, spaghetti rings, carrots, pears, cat food, baked beans, golden syrup, Ovaltine. He didn't have a cat.

Holding up a piece of beef in Union Jack wrapper, he observed it in the manner of Hamlet perusing Yorick's skull.

'I know meat. The French smuggle in theirs and pretend it's ours! French butchers are evil; you do know that, don't you?'

April came in and, like an animal that had never before set eyes on a human, looked right through me.

'Fuckoffbackeroll. Backofffuckeroll.'

'Tush. Go to your room,' Freddie commanded. Then turning to me, said,

'Do come along, come in.'

The clock groaned seven times, tried for an eighth, gave up. Freddie sighed.

'Good Lord, where is it? Why does everything have to...? Ah, there you are!'

'I've been here all the time.'

'Not you. Fanny.'

'Oh. I thought her name was April?'

'What? No. My play. Fanny by Gaslight. You have a most irritating habit of misunderstanding one.'

He held up some kind of object. Vaguely phallic, about six inches long, it was the paint tube I'd seen last time I was in his room. Definitely a paint tube. With the neck cut off. About six inches in circumference, it was covered in velvet. The open end was rimmed with a thick frizz of artificial hair - the stuff used by theatricals for beards and moustaches. There seemed to be something inside the tube. Freddie was looking at me triumphantly, as if I surely must recognise genius. He picked up a wodge of typed manuscript. 'There was a melodrama, titled Gaslight. Of no moral consequence whatever. You see my play is all about morals. The corruption of young gels. My main character is Fanny. You see the double entendre? Hm? Hah-ha. She's being pursued by a lecherous sod of a man. 'bout your age. He thinks her innocence is a green light for disgusting immorality. You see, I have deliberately subverted the genre.'

Vigorously slapping the manuscript, powder puffed from between the pages.

'I am convinced it will make a fortune. It's perfect for Shaftesbury Avenue. It has always been my ambition to return to Mayfair. April and I will decant ourselves.'

Pausing magisterially, waving the thick manuscript in the air, he added,

'I shall tell Miss Chats where to stick it!'

'It will certainly cause her fundamental injury.'

'What, what? I speak in metaphor. Are you so unaware of linguistic tergiversation? Or do you play dumb for evil ends? I must know.'

'What is that?'

'This? This is the essential. It goes with the script.'

Holding the velvet tube out to me, I peered in the open end. There was a mechanism of some kind inside the tube. Why was it covered with red velvet, rimmed with crepe hair? Foolishly wiggling my finger inside the tube, I activated a spring-loaded trap. As I jumped in pained shock, Freddie howled with the maniacal laughter of a pantomime

23

villain. The contraption was some kind of cunning mousetrap.

'Why didn't you warn me? It's bloody dangerous. What has this got to do with you wanting me to give your play to Earthy?'

'Hah-ha. You see, our lecherous friend advances on our heroine. Fanny. Instructed by her kindly generous old uncle, 'bout my age, she plays along. Our syphilitic adventurer produces his member and prepares to ram home. The essential is carefully concealed 'twixt her legs. Imagine his surprise and the triumph of virtue over evil, when the fanny trap springs into action, catching him by the cock, his full wickedness exposed for the world to see. The police are called and yet another of Satan's toffs sent down. And our heroine, divine gel, saved. Hm? Yes, what? Hah-ha. What do you think?'

I should have made my excuses and left. The warm red velvet, the frizz, the inviting canal - how could I not have noticed? In the big canvas above the fireplace, the Baconian cardinal smiled. The place smelled of talcum, decadence and maybe death.

'Give Earthy both my script and the essential.'

'The essential as well as the script? A bit risqué isn't it?'

'If it wasn't it wouldn't be art.'

'Well, supposing he puts the play on, how will the chap playing the lecherous role, 'bout my age, survive the first night? Assuming the essential hasn't rendered him incapable in rehearsal?'

'Why so prosaic? The actor will not actually get his appendage trapped. The audience will think he has. That is the magic of theatre.'

'So why go to all the trouble of actually making this, ah, this ah...essential. Fanny trap. In full and dangerous working order?'

'Are you suggesting my purpose is not of the highest moral bent?'

'A tad bent is exactly what it might seem to the likes of Sir Neville Earthy. How many plays do you think he gets in the post with props included? Especially such a pubic extravaganza as this...essential.'

'The essential shows the force of the script. The essential is essential.'

'I can't see Earthy joining your moral crusade, Freddie.'

'He will if it's profitable so to do. April is my inspiration. Innocence must be promulgated and protected.'

He lowered himself to his bed and sat there, ears glowing, his old eyes weeping resin. I looked up at the painting of the Cardinal.

'Where's the innocence in that?'

'The Cardinal is a mask. You can see his skeleton, barely hidden by a web of flesh. We have our skeletons inside. The crab has his on the outside. Likewise the lobster. You see? You see? If it could be defeated - what triumph!'

'Defeat a lobster?'

He walloped a pile of pornography with the back of his hand.

'No, no. Death, you fool! The stuff that kills life. Death. You must take cognisance of my engineering background. The essential I devised from a toothpaste tube. An old one. Have you noticed they use a plastic substance nowadays? Impossible to roll up. So you can't extract the last gobbet of paste. Bastards. Society stinks. The masses are leaderless. It was a simple matter inserting the sprung bolt.'

April sat by the gas fire. I hadn't heard her come in. She sat still as an inanimate object. Her frock gathered up between her bare legs, a good deal of her fleshy inner thigh was visible. Pale as mild cheddar. She scratched at her shoulder with her chin. Like she was trying to shake out tormenting voices in her head.

Freddie handed me the script. And the essential.

'What's that in your hand?'

'A microcassette tape recorder.'

Whilst waiting for my wife in the Electric caff I read snatches of the play. It seemed to have a gaggle of Lords and Ladies wandering round Soho, when not hanging with intent outside suburban convent schools. The heroine, Fanny, a sacred innocent in uniform, nevertheless possessed an array of underwear to tempt a saint. A mere mortal stood no chance. Especially the dubiously named Lord Crotch.

I somehow couldn't see Sir Neville Earthy going for it. Jacobean drama was his thing, not horny melodrama. And he never ventured without a knight or dame on board. However senile, I couldn't see any of them lining up to play Lord Crotch, Lady Gusset, Sir Roger Cocker, Dame Barbara Nobra, Canon Bishoprick.

Could Freddie be for real? Did he actually believe his sexual farrago would be taken seriously? And what would Earthy make of the essential - now sitting on the table beside my baked beans on toast?

Turkey, the proprietor/waiter, picking it up, examined it from every angle. He got it straight away.

'Heh, bladdy good. Who do it, eh? You an artist, innit? Who use it?'

'It's ah…it's for a play. You know - theatre? Do you have theatre in Turkey?'

'Leave it aat! We got everting. Futball, seaside, pedestrian crosses, the lot, innit? Dis bladdy play, I like to see dis play, yeah?'

He held the essential up to his Bosnian staff. They laughed. Audiences went for the most amazing stuff. Piles of bricks, calves in tanks, elephant dung, men waving their pricks about on stage, women talking about their vaginas. I was the one behind the times. But maybe Freddie was so far behind he had looped the loop and was now out ahead.

My wife came in.

'You look fucking gorgeous!'

'Thank you, darling.'

I slipped the essential in my pocket. I told her about Freddie and Fanny by Gaslight. It all went in her disbelieving big brown eyes.

'Why do you indulge him?'

'Keep him sweet 'til this decanting business is solved. We got to stick together. If they get us out, maybe they won't let us back in again.'

'Nonsense. Miss Chats is an honourable person.'

Though she worked in Whitehall, everything seemed above board to her. She shone with certainty. I wouldn't like to lose her, that was a fact.

Out the Electric windows, heavy clouds hustled over the roof tops. Sooty, brutal tempered, churning, ready to heave. A malicious wind whipped low along the pavements, driving skirts between legs, sticking trousers to bony ankles, turning umbrellas inside out, raising a forest of windscreen wipers.

Rain soon arrowed into the street, as if attacking it. A loaded gutter sagged. The old-fashioned metal span dangled dangerously. A spume of liquid filth sploshed down onto a news vendor's evening papers. A pigeon, dirty as a dishcloth, flopped from under the railway bridge onto the road. It didn't move. It was dead.

As in a vision, I imagined the street a lost city of the Incas, the buildings covered in dripping vegetation and big insects. The memory of past inhabitants long since wiped. Above all was the only god for certain there's ever been - the covered sun. No rabbi, priest, vicar, imam and their various bags of tricks would ever convince otherwise.

'Dis cauntree wettest in world.' Turkey said, putting cups of coffee on the table.

'Dat's why dey rich. Peepel 'ave to do sometink. You got sun, who wanna work, innit?'

My wife smiled to him. 'Sweet person.'

'That Lady Hannah come in 'ere ask for you udder day. She got deh hots for you, brudder.'

He went back behind the counter, laughing.

My wife stared at me. I held her warm hand. Flesh-eating Time refuses bone. Flesh rots quicker than peach. You got to grab it while it's there. My wife knew Lady Hannah. And Earthy. They all knew one another. The classes stuck together. The best thing to do was decide what you had was what you wanted. Then hang onto it. I held her tight.

'Have you been seeing that dreadful old wrinkled drunk? Hannah Earthy?'

'Do us a favour!'

'I see - you have.'

'You're the diamond. Not Mrs. Earthy. You're the gem. The bit of fallen heaven. The gold standard. The dew on the grass. The juice in the glass. I wouldn't swop you for a

copy of the First Folio signed by the author.'
'The First Folio dates from 1623. Shakespeare died in 1616.'
'Cos it'd be a forgery.'
'Did you work out the 'because'? The two men I told you about.'
'It was just a normal desultory exchange between two minds, one of them at least, imprecise. Ted Seegar the goalkeeper was confused with Preston, the geographical entity. You don't have to be a Schopenhauer or Wittengenstein to get it.'
' Who did they play for?'
' You're such a child at times.'
The rain stopped, the wind fell, the Bosnian waitress put two more cups of coffee on our table. She and my wife exchanged female smiles of understanding.

A few tears from her eyes and I'd want to crucify myself from guilt. My wife's eyes. Every time I saw her naked, and that was every day, I'd wonder how come I was so lucky to be so close. I was reasonably sane until we shacked up together. This wasn't magazine stuff. This wasn't first-love sincerity. Lady Di lie. The pretty lass filling your in-tray. The attractive nurse round the Health Centre. This was Zeta-Jones, Paltrow, Eddie Izzard all rolled into one. I learned the meaning of entrancement.

I'd jump on her as if trying to eat her. I was relieved when she turned the light out at night. I could recover in the dark.

Come mornings she wouldn't move until I brought her a cuppa and marmaladed toast. Then on with the Paris underwear, Calvin Klein trouser suit, Ferragamo shoes, jewellery, Rolex and off to work she'd go, the entire ensemble worth more than a mortgage. For fun she sometimes wore a bejewelled corset affair and stockings. A Bengal Lancer from North London calling himself Mr. T. Choolup designed the corset. He designed only for the rich. The only thing she ever got cheap was me.

I met her first in Hanley. It was the annual warm day. She was wearing a dress so neat and tight it looked like it was spray-painted on. She was twenty-one. And so china fine you could almost see the sun pass through her. We walked down a narrow street, the only one in town with cobble stones. Gentrification in the Potteries was just beginning. A smart wind blew up.

'Isn't that a charming breeze?'
'A charming breeze with a licence to roam.'
The elements were always at her. Tickling her, nibbling her, playing shadows on her face, landing diamonds in her hair, testing her to see was she for real? Could anyone be that beautiful and living in Stoke?

Her father, a Staffordshire farmer and racehorse trainer, was gobsmacked when he met me. My ambitions were beyond articulation. By the time I wrecked a few tractors, toppled his combine harvester in a ditch, drove his horses to Uttoxeter racecourse, lugged his drunken body home from the boozer a few times, he got quite fond of me and was prepared to forget I'd spent time in prison. The day I married his daughter, outside the church after the brief ceremony, he said to me,

'Never went emptier pockets up to the rails.'

He was a bluff old bugger whom you couldn't bluff for long.

'Come come, old chap, it's not just a father's pride makes me say it. You got by far the better part of the bargain.'

He'd even paid for my wedding suit.

The moment waiting at the altar for her high heels to hit the tiles was the loneliest moment of my life. I couldn't help feeling a bit of a fraudster. Like I was taking part in some sort of emotional swindle. I didn't turn my face until the frou-frouing of the longest white dress ever whispered to a stop. When I looked at last into her smiling happiness, I knew I'd never do the Lottery again. I'd just won it.

Her father sold all his cattle just before the BSE bomb exploded. Made a killing. Concentrating on grain and the Stock Exchange he made further piles. As a lucrative sideline, he set up a chemical company selling sprays and fertilisers. My wife was his only child. I'd landed on my feet alright. I didn't have to make money. Other than love and tea I didn't have to make anything at all.

But that was then and this was the Electric caff.

Noticing Freddie's script, she flicked through it, quickly pronouncing it porn.

'It's meant to be a moral play. That's what he said.'

'Mr. Parts is an old fascist. Political porn and plain porn are twins.'

She opened the racing pages of the Evening Standard. Her father's horse - Five Towns - was tipped to win the following day. She'd ridden the nag some years before at Uttoxeter.

Her enthusiasm when talking horses was almost touching.

'Dear old thing. We all had heaps on him. A cert. He clipped the last and we were exceedingly lucky to finish a game third.'

'Yeah, clipped the last with his head!'

'Shut up, darling, you wouldn't know. It was that moment when sport and philosophy merge. When the jockey becomes Wittgenstein in silks.'

'Metamorphosis? Like when the caterpillar becomes a butterfly?'

'We're talking horses, not caterpillars. If you don't mind.'

'Black ones walk quicker than green ones. White ones are worse in nightmare. They crawl down your throat if you sleep with your mouth open and if you are having a particular bad dose of imagination they come out your navel. Most of them you cannot easily tell front from rear. Can you imagine if people were like that?'

'Some people are, darling.'

Turkey laughed.

'A caterpillar has a leg for every hair on its back. And each leg has a load of hooks.

There's about one hundred thousand different ones.'

'Hooks?'

'No. Caterpillars. Everyone looks like a caterpillar. Right now you look like a Puss Moth, in threat posture.'

'Who? Me?'

'No. Turkey. You're not a caterpillar. You're a butterfly in a part of the jungle where no man has yet set foot.'

'Except presumably you. Anyway, you're interrupting. From the moment he clipped the last, I've never believed anything is certain for long. Nor, as you know, have I wagered since. Bad luck is like bad breath. Hard to get rid.'

'If a brown caterpillar spat on you it could burn a hole in your ankle.'

'Absolute cock.'

She'd look at me in such a way my heart slurped. Long legs prancing towards you, hair bouncing, a fourteen upper teeth smile, torching eyes, you'd not see a like apparition outside the parade ring at Ascot. One night, when she gently flicked the strap of her bra from her shoulder, I fainted. She gave me mouth to mouth resuscitation. You couldn't tire looking at her. But you paid a price. Like looking at a Rembrandt self-portrait. The complete honesty of the face turned your gaze inwards.

She sometimes lay naked on the sofa in characteristic pose...An arm raised, the back of her head on her hand, other hand on her tummy, legs apart, knees slightly bent, nipples raised like her lips, eyes shut, resting at complete ease, still as the forest floor...

Underneath she was fruity as a five-tier wedding cake. Beauty IS skin deep. What other way could it be?

Her father had lost a leg in the Battle of Crete.

'I gave the chaps a tot of rum, then charged. You could hardly see from the dawn mist over the airstrip. It was bayonet to bayonet stuff. A bugger came at me with a butcher's chopper. One swish and my leg was in serious disarray. A Maori plugged him. At least I came back wedding tackle intact. Very pleased.'

His daughter, when a child, wasn't scared of her father's amputation. But in her adolescence it took on a phallic intensity. She called it *The Cretan Stump*.

We finished our coffee and toast. Turkey hovered round the table. My wife indicated the cups and plates.

'Please remove them, like a good fellow.'

The tone was relaxed imperial impeccable. Whole nations hopped to it one time. Before they were partitioned.

She paid the bill, left a handsome tip, strode out. I hurried after her.

As we turned into our street, Sir Neville Earthy was getting out of a taxi. Tall and sleek as an Afghan hound, he wore shag-haired moonboots and a white hairy-hippy sheepskin coat. He looked like something out of his own modern production of As You Like It. His blonde hair was tied in a pigtail. Aged fifty - it said so in the press - blue-eyed, high cheekbones, tight lips, Oxford educated, he was the full Anglo-Saxon shilling. Another one with the knack of being able to stare at you without feeling the need to speak.

'Sir Neville! Just the geezer I want to see.'

I gave him Freddie's script and essential. In front of my wife he wanted to appear magnanimous. A nice person.

'He comes round to Hannah, when neither of us are there.'

'If neither of you are there, where is the problem?'

'When I'm not there. And you're not there. Do you see?'

My wife did see. She turned to me, her eyes waiting for truth. I held my hands out wide, shrugged.

He examined the essential, turning it over and back, genuinely puzzled. The crepe hair was familiar, the red velvet... He was convinced I was setting him up.

'No, no. Freddie says it's a fanny trap. The main character gets his Cretan Stump caught in it. I think it's a first in the history of theatre. Which is why it may appeal to you.'

He looked to my wife. Deep into her eyes. A pained expression. He expected her to be on his side.

I had my tape recorder in my pocket. I pressed the record button and held it towards Neville. With moonboot smoothness, he abruptly walked away. A dignified stalk like the ghost in Hamlet. No way was I going to tape his words. Like he was any crackpot in the streets.

Recently when I went to the brain-sifter, the brain-riddler, our psychiatrist friend, as he pulled out his tape recorder, I pulled out mine. A battle of the buttons ensued. Neither of us said much that day.

I alienated men like Earthy. Why? Because. I'd go out of my way for any old toerag but not for someone remotely respectable. The sifter told me, deep down, I hated authority. Who doesn't? Sir Neville was constantly in the papers. Attending a first night, a showbiz wedding or funeral, the Queen's garden party. Just a day or two before I'd seen a poster advertising a lecture.

"My Life In The Theatre. Sir Neville Earthy. Senate Building, Gower Street, Thursday, 1 p.m. sharp."

That had to be where he was coming from. He wore the moonboots for the students. Slumming for the Wittenberg brigade. With them he was Hamlet. With the politicians however, a suited Polonius.

Dr. Tripp, the bum hole expert who lived along the street, was another man I needlessly annoyed. In a hypochondriacal frenzy, I'd convinced my wife there was something the matter with my stomach. She arranged for Tripp to examine me. He invited me round to his house and after ramming his finger up my bum declared,

'Prostate absolutely normal.'

To be absolutely certain he arranged a sigmoidoscopy.

'It'll cost you five hundred.'

'500 what?'

'Pounds! Sterling.'

Money cures imagination. I instantly felt better. But I kept the appointment at his hospital. A nurse shot some fast-acting laxative up me. I managed to make it to the loo and got rid of every morsel I'd eaten for the previous two years. Tripp was quite witty. When he was ready for me, he euphemistically asked,

'Did you have a delivery?'

The sigmoidoscope couldn't see through faeces which was why the bowel had to be empty. I was wearing a skimpy white robe revealing all below my navel and lay in such a position that, as Tripp probed with the instrument (it had a tiny camera on the end), I could observe on a TV monitor the inside of my colon. A red with a touch of blue world, the colour of ripe plum.

'Have you been on television before? You're giving a great performance.'

I could have been watching a documentary on outer space. Any moment I expected to see an astronaut float past. I knew nothing about my own body. The thing I walked around in every day. That raw colon was me. My blubbing heart, sweating liver, bellowing lungs - all me. We lived inside a machine. But where exactly was the me?

Not in my body. Somewhere in my brain. In behind my eyes someplace. Nothing was of much consequence. Except making love. The moment of sexual explosion blew the brains. For a few seconds. Maybe one day we'd evolve from bodies and float around as flecks of sense. No bones, no blood, no flesh. But where would the pleasure be? And would we even float about? As bits of pure thought, we'd cloud eternity, out-thinking each other. Thought out-thinking itself. Wouldn't be much fun, would it?

'You'll be pleased to know you are absolutely in the clear. No growths, blemishes, whatever. Good.'

Next day I dropped a note in his letter box.

"Dear Dr. Tripp, Thank you. Your face and my posterior are a perfect match, don't you think? Regards to Mrs. Tripp."

Flipping raging, he came rushing round, waving the note in my face. My wife was on his side. I was on his side. Why did I do it?

'It's your head needs examining! Are you schizoid? Do you hear voices?'

'Yes.'

'Yes? What do they tell you?'
'They tell me to shut up, I'm driving them mad.'

I went to Freddie a number of times, trying to arrange our decanting meeting. He'd start hounding me for news of his play. I couldn't pin him down to a time.

Miss Chats wrote to me wondering, had we decided what we wanted to do?

I phoned her and asked her out to lunch. She asked had I my wife's permission? No lunch. No progress. She wrote to me again. "...our legal department will soon become involved..."

That was a threat. I was getting tangled up in problems. Pressure.

One night I heard Freddie coming down the stairs. I knew he wanted to see me. I nipped out and stood in the public gardens opposite our house. Leaning against a London plane, I waited until he retreated back up to his room. Eventually, I saw his shape bulking about the attic and April, like a demented moth, flitting in and out. It was like watching a shadow play. She tore at her hair, her cries curdling the night.

'Fuckoffbackeroll. Backofffuckeroll.'

He roared,

'Enough! Sleep! Sleep!'

'Backofffuckeroll. Fuckoffbackeroll.'

'I have no option but to restrain you.'

Their powerful shadows wrestled as he shackled her to an armchair.

A cat came to my feet, the moon splattering its tiger grin. An eye gleamed up at me, pinpoint bright as a doctor's torch. Its life was trapped inside fur and silly whiskers and claws. Trapped in skin and blood, we're bound in miles of buried brain coil.

I was afraid of night. Of unseen grabbing hands. Glad hands, sad hands. Dormitory hands. Police hands. Hands with surgical gloves. Inky fingers. Prison fists. Outstretched hands at job interviews.

After university and jobs of no desire, I returned home. It was the usual not bad usual atmosphere. I lay in bed a lot - just like university - and surfacing late, stood at the door looking up and down the street.

One afternoon I saw a coach parked near our house, half up on the pavement. The door was open. It looked empty of passengers. Ambling over, I went up the steps and in. It seemed to me to be a snug place with the possibility of flight without actually having to flee. The key was in the ignition. The driver had popped off somewhere. I decided to try his seat. I had no intention of driving anywhere. Even were I capable. Seated behind the steering wheel, I fiddled with the key, pressed every button, pulled every knob, displaced every lever, pressed every pedal...until eventually I was lurching from the pavement onto the road and almost without realising, down the street.

A sense of abandon fused through my brain like a hot whiskey. There was a CD sticking out of the radio cassette. I pressed it home. Warm music tanked out - guitars, bass, drums, keyboard, accordion, a mellifluous voice...

"I won't let you down, won't let you down again."

Such was my happy delusion, I actually thought I might apply to the bus company for a job. The same company whose bus I was now stealing. Even a rapidly looming T-junction, failed to impinge on my anaesthetised version of reality. I ploughed straight into the traffic-flow, making a hash of a white van ferrying stray dogs to the local pound. The road turned barking mad. Dogs ran everywhere and all in my way. I had to keep moving. I had to get to wherever it was I was going. My name was Ben Hur. Address Toad Hall. There was a coffee bar in Hanley with nice Greek cakes. I'd park the bus somewhere nearby. I began to hear a series of crashing bumps.

Bump-bump-bump-bump-bosh-bosh-wham-wham-clang-clang-klangety-klang-whack-whack-oh-fuck! Oh no!

In as many seconds I'd hit fifteen parked cars. A lamppost finally brought me to a halt. Not a very well made lamppost. Most of it snapped off and went crashing through the window of 'Man About Town Menswear With a Difference'. There was more broken glass about than you'd see at a Bentilee wedding. A crowd gathered. And eventually the police.

They thought I was high on drugs. I told them I'd seen a caterpillar crawling along the top of the rear-view mirror. In court the magistrate refused to take this into account. When he asked why I did what I did, I replied,

"I played a quite important game of rugger one day..."

The local rag carried the report....

"Magistrate: Can't hear you. Speak up, please.

Defendant: I scored the only try and converted it myself. I remembered the conversion but I couldn't remember the try.

Magistrate: What relevance has this?

Defendant: Everyone congratulated me but I couldn't remember crossing the line. They told me I'd run the length of the pitch on my own. I must have momentarily fallen down through a hole in my brain. For eighty yards reality didn't exist. I went missing. This coach business must have been the same. I meant no harm. When I get excited maybe the blood to my coils (sic) rushes at such a rate, it blocks out sense. The sight of a woman's naked...thigh say, could similarly strike home.

Magistrate: Come again?

Defendant: If you ask a caterpillar which leg it moves first, you'll knock it off its leaf of logic."

I received a custodial sentence.

A prison officer gave me chewing gum every day. And a newspaper. He also tortured me by coming into my cell and playing Mozart's Requiem which wasn't wholly by Mozart at all. The tenor was George Shirley. The P.O. had a thing about George Shirley.

'He's best tenor in world. Better than Pavarwotsit.'

'Is he?'

'Tek my word for it.'

As well as music he had a thing about philosophy.

'The world outside is an open prison. Each person is a lump of stone. Inside every stone is blackness. But you open the stone and the light floods in. Understand?'

'Thank you.'

'Do you understand?'

'Yes. I think so. Thank you.'

'Don't despair, lad.'

A few months later I was free. I made straight for the scene of my crime. Hanley. I wanted that coffee and cake. As luck would have it, summer had arrived. Super sunny beams streamed in the coffee shop window and along with them came my future wife. Her white summer dress couldn't hide a heartbeat. And I was bare as a live wire. When she sat at the next table I spoke to her.

Boarding that bus - what if I hadn't? Your number's in the revolving drum and the hidden hand will pull it out.

Our faces change with the weather. Our hearts stay the same.

Miss Chats sent me an epistle, threatening immediate decanting. I replied straightaway.

"Dear Miss Chats,

What is you marital status? I have not so far seen you wear a ring. I would like to play Santa Claus in Selfridges. If you know anyone there, will you put in a kind word for me?

Our hearts are sitting tenants.

Best wishes always..."

She replied three times.

"As previously stated, damage to the property is such, major repairs can only be carried out in an otherwise empty house."

"You will be transferred to a suitable property whilst programme of works is being carried out."

"We feel the consultative process has by now gone on long enough. The sooner you decant, the quicker this phase of the works will be completed."

It was all serious stuff.

I didn't want us to be buggered about all over the borough. Refugees in our own country.

I bumped into Freddie and April in the supermarket. She gripped a parasol to her chest. He had two plastic bags laden with tins and a stick of French bread.

'Ah, there you are,' he boomed in the crowded aisle, 'anything favourable as yet?'

'Yes. Some cheap Chilean wine over there.'

'No, no! My play! Has Earthy got back?'

'I didn't even know he was away.'

'What? No. You gave my work to him, did you not? Have you had a response?'

'I'm seeing him today,' I lied, 'I'll let you know at once.'

April stood in her own abstracted silence. She wore a blue girlish frock, yellow sandals, long white lace gloves. Her talcumed hair, in two plaits, dangled over her ears, the ends resting on her shoulders in bizarre epaulettes. Freddie wore his immaculate ancient double-breasted suit and Oxfords. Against the background of laden shelves, clacking registers, crashing trolleys, oestrogen-driven queues, they might have been two specimens from an Edwardian past.

'Freddie, I'd like you and April to come and see me. We must stop this decanting business.'

'Decanting is not at this moment on the agenda! Are you hiding anything? Have you seen Earthy?'

'Oh yes. Often. I gave him your play, didn't I?'

He let out such a howl of rage people shot away. There are more nuts in supermarket aisles than the ones from Brazil.

'Am I in the hands of a secret imbecile?'

A tin fell off a shelf. No one had touched it.

'Oh, I see, so sorry, I'm on my way to see him. Earthy. I told you. I'll report back straight away.'

The lie necessary.

'I hope no one tries anything slimy. I'll sue, you realise that, don't you? I don't care who or what you or they are!'

Such paranoia was attractive. He was hard to dislike.

Outside the supermarket, Filfy Wilfy - the human skunk - with outstretched hand and familiar, cranky, inveigling voice, tapped me up.

'Got a quid for me, Guv? Cuppatea?'

His thumb rubbed two fingers in rapacious circles. His nails were so incredibly long they clicked together like knitting needles. Outside the bookie's, next to the supermarket, was a favourite spot. To avoid arrest he pretended he was advising the public on matters of mutual interest.

'Cayful of the twaffic, love, mind that bus, cuppatea? Gordbless yah. Cuppatea? Who wants the winner 3.30 Goodwood? Cuppatea? Got a quid for me, Guv?.'

A slow lava of urine and excrement oozed out over his shoe onto the pavement. The fork and leg of his flannel trousers were saturated. He seemed pleased.

'Gorblimey. Lookatit. Cuppatea, Guv?'

He had a sly, sideways, cocked expression, suitable for rejection or grateful thanks.

'It's not tea you want Wilfy, it's an operation.'

'Can't 'elp it, mate. Shit. Piss. Eighteen times today. Thirty one pisses! Whaddayafink's the matter wif me? CystitisColitisArthritisMastitisGastroenteritisHepatitisDermatitisDiverticulitis?Clotting?Rotting?Kidneys maybe?'

He rattled the words out proud. He never noticed the microcassette in my hand.

He couldn't smell worse had he been two weeks dead. Though his eyebrows were dandruffy, his forehead scabby, skin pasty, tongue puce, the way his grey hair swept back onto his black overcoat collar and the cravat he wore with a once white open-necked shirt, somehow gave him a dapper look. You could tell from the twinkle in his eye, the cocked challenging gaze, the gushing patter, he was no fool. Upwind, you could imagine him a painter, a poet maybe, brought low by lack of favour. Upwind. Downwind he was a monstrous dung-beetle. Even his nails looked unhealthy. He grew them long because he had a lot of scratching to do. If you were dying of the itch you wouldn't let him near you. Though his pitch was beside the bookie's he was barred from entering. It wasn't just the stench. His earnings from tapping were all in pennies and his bets never straightforward. They were mainly cunning, confusing multiples of two penny accumulators. He was a master of paranoid arithmetic and shifty bet hedging.

'There see look, 2p each way, each way, The Hitman. 10p on whatsit... 'ucking 'ell where's it gorn? that's it, "My Old Man's A Dustman..." yah double up Cock Robin 6p on the nose...'

Public lavatories barred him. He'd hog the cubicle for hours, studying form and exercising his extraordinary bowel. He blocked the plumbing in Euston using fifteen toilet rolls and three copies of Thursday's Guardian.

'Heah, come 'eah, don't go way, Guv! Mad Cow Disease, I know wot causes it, mate! They won't listen. They won't 'ucking listen. Supposin', supposin' you never did you know, howsyourfahver wif your lady wife...Supposin' you gives her artificial insema'uckingnation instead, then when her sprog gets born, you whips it away from her arter a few days, she'd soon go bonkers, wouldn't she? Same with them 'ucking cows. That's wots happenin', mate. They're driven' 'ucking mad they are. Calf whipped away from 'em soon as it's born! Nuffing to do wif 'ucking feed and all that. Stands to reason. And it's going the same way, mate, wif humans an' all!'

As if to emphasise his agricultural insights, a gush of urine ran over his shoes and across the pavement into the gutter.

His mind free-ranged over anything current. Philosophers and dossers had time to think.

'I saw you talkin' to old Partsy.'

'Who?'

'Freddie Parts. They say he was my bruvver. Leave it aht! He ain't my bruvver, is he? He's not Tufnell Park, is he?'

They did look a bit alike.

Lowering his head for a moment like a sulking dog, he then looked straight into my face.

'Wot would you do if you were me?'

His rhythmic ramblings invariably ended with that clincher. I walked away. What indeed? If I were you and you were who?

The way he said 'Thirty one pisses' - numeral and noun, all five syllables, soared from a hollow of despair to a crest of indignation. A shriek. The plaguing of his body he cudgelled with words. His native Cockney was a flag bravely flying in an ill wind.

The prophets, sages, soothsayers were in the street. The stay away from me closer brigade. We sailed along in a cargo of offal. Out the port holes there was beauty enough to block the smell.

'Oh my love there is always a yes in your eyes.'

I went round to Earthy's. A television broadcast truck was parked outside the house. Thick cables snaked up the steps and in the front door. Hannah was alone in the kitchen. The BBC were upstairs interviewing Sir Neville in his study. They were doing a series on great actors of the past. Lady Hannah, in the kitchen, reached for a bottle and two glasses. To her chestnut hair were added streaks of colour - green, yellow, black.

'You're seeing a West Indian!'

'Don't be ridiculous!'

'Anything interesting on underneath?'

'None of your business.'

'A hairdresser told me girls are dyeing their pubic hair. Could that be true?'

'If a hairdresser told you it must be ex cathedra.'

'Any chance of a squint? Just to check.'

She laughed.

'I don't think so.'

So cavalier with the life of a significant other, perhaps, maybe, you never knew, some other was being equally cavalier with insignificant me.

'Actually, the reason I'm here, I need to see Neville. Old Freddie wants to know has he read his play?'

She gave a golden whiskey, chuckle. Drink for some was as good as sex when you weren't having sex. Her aging face had a handsome, lived-in wholesomeness. She was a bit of an upmarket gypsy; with strong cheekbones, a blunt nose damped down with powder, an elfin grin and tumbles of hair when she allowed it to grow.

Sir Neville, she said, was so genuinely revolted by the play he considered calling the police.

A young man rushed in, frantically tapping his lips with his index finger.

'Sssh! Quiet!'

'We're only laughing.'

'We're picking it up. Please. We're nearly there. It's going well Lady Hannah. Sir Neville's wonderful.'

Shooting a professional smile bright as a flash from a speed camera, he gently closed the door after him. You could be certain he'd end up running a chunk of the country.

'Why don't you bring your formidable wife round sometime? I'd like to meet her more often.'

'Bring my wife round? More often? What for? What for? And how can you tell she's formidable?'

'Anyone wears knickers costing a hundred smackeroonies is formidable in my book. I happened to be in Simon Pool's in Knightsbridge and saw her there. She bought two pairs. I couldn't afford bejewelled boxers.'

'Women will be mugged for their drawers.'

She slammed the table, guffawing like a mule. The entire television crew followed by Sir Neville, clattered down the stairs and in on top of us.

'What the hell's going on? You nearly ruined the last take.'

He wore a Boss suit and an open-necked Gieves and Hawkes shirt. Prada shoes. This was Earthy, responsible pundit. The licence payer's headmaster. The man who knew how Burbage burped. Lady Hannah ghosted the whiskey into a cupboard and plugged in the kettle. She was scared of him, that much was clear.

'I came round to find out how you liked Freddie's play. He's getting a bit anxious. Was it your cup of tea?'

He dug the script from a waste-paper basket and flung it at me.

'You can tell him, his play, apart from being perverted drivel, would have been old fashioned in 1938!'

'Oh. Really? Are you sure? He won't be pleased.'

'Do I care? It's full of cheap tricks. Banging into imaginary doors, tripping over the carpet, putting four spoons of sugar into a cup of tea - it went out with the Ark.'

'Maybe you don't get his sense of humour.'

'Sense of what? Get out! Get out before I stiff you.'

He sounded oddly impressive. What if he took kung fu lessons?

'I learned in jail how to stop folk stiffing me.'

I was well outnumbered by the TV crew. I had no wish to get beaten up by a bunch of ex-Newnham girls in hand-painted Doc Martens.

A British Rail platform clock clunked the time. The black minute hand dropped through thirty seconds of space. Suspended above it were two signal box switch levers. Folk memory. Reminders how our grandfathers had to work for their living. I got up to go. Earthy stopped me.

'No, wait. Stay a mo', old chap.'

Lady Hannah look worried. I'm sure I did too.

'Listen to this, just listen to this.'

Grabbing Freddie's script from my hands, he grubbed through a kerfuffle of pages.

'A random sample. Right. This is one Lord Crotch speaking. I kid you not. Crotch. Take a seat everyone. Just because I happen to be in charge of a well-known theatrical enterprise, every third-rate scribbler in the country thinks I'm fair game.'

The Russell Hobbs kettle, shiny as the F.A. cup, began to steam. Hannah slid to turn it off. She was wearing Turkish slippers turned up at the toes.

Holding Freddie's play high, whilst adopting a bent, drooly-lipped, dirty-old-Lord Crotch pose, Earthy began,

' "Oh, Fanny sweet-sweety..." Fanny is the leading lady by the way..." I have a teenyweeny secret. You see, Fanny, Nature has endowed me, why no doctor knows, with a parcel of such elephantine proportions, the Gods themselves are jealous. It's a glandular peculiarity according to some, to others, particularly of the gentle sex, a priceless gift, for sharing only with those who love me." '

The crew were more indulgent than canned laughter. Earthy did it well. But after a few more lines, he suddenly looked depressed. The crew, reading his mood, stopped braying. The bloke who'd told Hannah and me to be quiet, grinned from ear to ear and winked, as if he knew it was really me who'd written it.

An embarrassed silence descended. The crew were ashamed. They knew their raucous laughter had been somewhat sycophantic. Hannah rattled out cups and saucers.

'Well, think me a silly-billy but it sounds a winner to me.'

Earthy glared at her in wounded surprise.

'And to me,' I said. 'Innocence corrupted. It's classic stuff, no?'

Hannah's slippers now looked green. Caterpillar green. How could that be? They were red before.

'There is no such thing as innocence anymore,' the Beeb bloke said. 'Kids are smoking pot on the way to school, shooting up on the way home.'

SHANE CONNAUGHTON

His tone had conviction beyond contradiction. He'd probably done the documentary. His big red bovver boots proclaimed his street-cred.

Earthy was right. Fanny by Gaslight was a pile of tosh. So what?

Writing it had kept death at bay. What else were words for?

Earthy's fair quiff fell across his right eye. Hannah tenderly fingered it back. He was out eighteen hours a day playing at grown-ups. She was at home taking her consolations from bottles and the odd interloper. It was better than voluntary work in the East End.

'Is it true Shakespeare added black currant juice to his sperm and used it for ink?'

Fair face clouding, index finger already raised, Earthy searched for angry words.

'Okay, forget Shakespeare. The essential, Neville, what did you think of the essential? Freddie wants it back. You didn't like the essential?'

Young Zoe came in. Silently she leaned against her father's knee. A child could calm a storm.

'You come in here with that tape recorder and brazenly use it! Do you think we don't notice?'

'There's no in your nose. But yes in your eyes.'

'Why did you ask Miss Chats for a job as Santa Claus? Don't deny it - she told me.'

'To waste her time. Like I waste my own.'

'That Freddie came down looking for his play. He hammered at the door. He's very angry.'

We were in the pub. On the table Freddie's script was a beer mat for my pint. I needed him on my side. But how precisely were we going to resist being decanted? Barricade ourselves in when they came to evict us? Pour buckets of water down on top of them? Acid? Petrol? Chain ourselves to the radiators? And how about his play? Would I destroy his illusions? Even at eighty-four years of age, fuming with unfilled political, artistic and probably sexual desire, he could work up a storm to sink an oil tanker. He was a Prospero marooned in a London attic.

We strolled home, arm in arm, hand in hand behind our backs. Nearing the house we could hear Prospero roar. Head sticking out April's window he was roaring for me.

'Come up at once, damn boy! I'll be fobbed off no longer! Where's my script? Have you seen Earthy?'

My wife didn't want me to go near him.

Rosa Gibbs was standing on the main steps up to the hall door. She was a tiny, frizzy-haired, seventy-year old, wearing a short skirt, a woolly jumper and fur-lined bootees. She looked like she'd just come from the Poodle Parlour. Her husband Phil wasn't well. They lived above us.

"e's gorn dahn agin, can you 'elp git 'im ahp? Rrroarring like a pig 'e is.'

'Your husband?'

She cocked a twinkly dismissive eye at my wife. She had no use for women.

'Not you. It's a man I need.'

Freddie would have to wait. I followed her up the steps and into the bedroom of a tiny flat off the main hallway.

'There 'e is, silly bleeder.'

Phil Gibbs, naked save for a short vest and tartan cap, lay on the floor. He'd fallen out of bed. The flat was dampy-mouldy-smelly-tatty. The walls were lined with woodchip to camouflage bad plastering. Because the house was Trust, tradesmen couldn't care less. One fellow sent to plaster over rising damp in our flat, mixed the finish in a bucket used for carrying sand. The result was an epidemic of pocks and pimples so bad I had to remove the lining paper, sand the wall and hang new paper. Another time I heard a decorator saying to his mate,

'Slap it on. It's only Trust. They won't know.'

Tenants, old or mentally handicapped, were powerless.

'Phil, are you okay?'

'Git 'im up!' Rosa said. She looked like a fat mouse.

There was a Pisa pile of newspapers stacked at the end of the bed. An unconcerned cat lay sleeping on top. A cheerless mound of unwashed clothing obscured a three-legged armchair. On the floor beside the bed was a plastic milk bottle full of urine.

Falling out of bed was a regular occurrence for Phil.

''allo mate. Sorry 'bout this.'

'Ynah Gibbs, dontcher? Everrrrybody nahs Gibbs.'

Rosa roly-polyed her r's. She rarely used her husband's Christian name.

'The docter tol' 'im not to git aht a bed. 'E won't stay put!'

'No need to shout, woman. I have to pee, don't I. You can't, you know, angle it into a bottle when you're lying down.'

His body was white as snow. The angle of his face and shoulder into the tattered carpet, body twisted behind, made it look as if he'd crash-landed from a great height. He tried to get up but there was no power in the frail legs. He didn't seem embarrassed about his nakedness. Predicament normal. Kneeling beside him I rested my hand on his lukewarm flesh. Another's flesh was the only contact worth a damn. That beating heart within.

'Get me under the arms and just heave, mate.'

I managed to haul him, dead legs dragging, onto the edge of the bed. As if I'd pulled him from the sea.

'Ta, mate. Ever so grateful.'

His pubic hair was grey. That was a bit of a shock. The cat on the paper Pisa awoke and, wary of underfoot conditions, uncoiled gingerly, ready to spring onto something firmer. Rosa swiped at it with a distant hand. I had seen Gibbs and Rosa only a year before, round the pub on a Friday evening, singing lustily,

'Rrrrooll aht the barrrelll, let's 'ave a barrrelll of FUN...' as if they were in the pay of English Heritage.

'e's 'ad a stroke, you know that doncha? Cuppa tea?'

Scorn or humour nibbled her lips. She and Gibbs had a son but he'd fled. Blood was a knot. But who wanted to live in knots? The sheets on Phil's bed, grey as old hair, hadn't been washed in ages. The plastic rose, through which the bulb cable disappeared into the ceiling, was coming away. The bared positive and negative wires were visible.

'They're trrrying to git us aht, yah know? The Trust.'

I told her I was having a meeting and that she must come to it.

'Cover yersel' ahp!' she shouted at Gibbs, as if he'd only just revealed himself.

'I don't care,' he replied simply. Beaten.

They'd rolled out the barrel and now it was empty.

'I've got to go. I have to nip up to see Freddie.'

''im? Satan he is. Bleeder. And she's mad.'

The bare partition wall vibrated as Freddie shouldered against it, descending. His pounding feet shook each step. When he reached the door I could hear him fumbling around with his anti-burglar device. It took him longer to get out than a burglar to get in.

'Drat! Come on! Open! Are you still there?'

'Let's hope you never have a fire, Freddie.'

He enjoyed my shock. He was wearing a woman's dress. A vast loose brown and red number down to his ankles. It looked as if he'd wrapped himself in a roll of Indian restaurant wall-paper.

'You never told me you were transvestite.'

'Good Lord. Ha-hah. I find it cool. Gives ease of movement indoors. Is Earthy doing it?'

'Wearing a dress?'

'What? My play. Fanny. Come up at once. Have you the essential?'

'Ah, he's ah, kept it.'

'He likes it? Oh good. Come.'

He trudged, swearing, all the way up.

'Christ. Two, three...Agh...damn steps! Bastard. Who the...? Why? Seven! God.'

Turning onto the landing, April peeped out her door. She was making a kind of fish noise in her throat. Oily and sighy. Like a pike being clubbed to death.

'Fuckoffbackeroll. Backofffuckeroll.'

'Sweet-sweety, you know who this is, do bring in tea, there's a sweet-sweety.'

· Sitting on the edge of his bed, he adjusted the dress about his widespread knees. The span of material was of prima donna proportions. A Mrsblouse big lady High Street special. Looking utterly relaxed, he twinkled mischievously, knowing I was somewhat bamboozled by the sight of him. How could I seriously discuss Earthy's reaction, the author sitting there like he'd just won the Turner prize? I handed over the script. He stared at it.

'Disgusting.'

'That's what Sir Neville thinks.'

How did he know?

'It's obvious. You were in the pub and used it as a beer mat. I can see the ring, clearly. My frontis-page is stained irredeemably.'

'Oh, sorry.'

'Does he want rewrites? I hope not. Rewrites are the demands of bureaucrats.'

I would have to, somehow, shoot it to him straight.

'Well, Freddie...The news is not, ah, what you'd call...good.'

His jaw stiffened. The cardinal above the mantle looked threatening. Next door April clawed the piano keys.

'Don't get me, ah, wrong, Mr. Parts. Freddie. It's not bad news. Far from it. Sir Neville loved it. He did. The play. Good old Earthy. Ah, er.'

Face thawing, sulking lower lip melting, he adjusted the dress about his bosom as if plucking it.

'Earthy, Sir Neville Earthy, our greatest living and ah, dead director...he told me...he said it straight to my face...'

'Out with it.'

'...that Fanny by Gaslight, your play...he said to me...he said in all the years of ah, endeavouring to remove filth from the stage ...the great classics, he said, Neville did, has now been added a work of such compelling authority, yes, that's the word he used, Freddie. And.'

His face shimmied between pleasure, outrage, puzzlement. Lips frogging, chin jutting, chest swelling, the buttons down the front of his dress looked ready to pop.

'Speak! Explain. "In all the years of endeavouring to remove filth from the stage... the great classics..." What is that? It seems to me an incomplete conjunction of utter confusion. I see no sense. Is the man mad? Or, I seriously fear, are you?'

April stepped in and back out again. If she was making tea, what was she doing with a spoon big enough to baste a turkey?

'And. And. Sir Neville was mad, indeed, yes. And. Very. But. He ah, said, Lord Crotch, about your age, was the kind of part only a great actor could play. It. Someone like

Lord Olivier himself. Unfortunately he was...deadish. And therefore your play could not be performed in his lifetime. How sad.'

'Whose lifetime? Olivier's or Earthy's? It's rather important which.'

'Both, perhaps. Neither, maybe.'

'What? What? Continue.'

The ecclesiastical clobber in the painting above the mantelpiece was a bit like Freddie's dress. And with as many buttons. I imagined the smell of incense. In her room April was fighting with ghosts.

'Goway! Backofffuckeroll! Fuckofffbackeroll!'

The sounds came out as if she were wrestling a dog. Freddie shouted, 'Quiet! Shackles!' She obeyed.

'Are shackles appropriate?'

Reclining on the bed with plutocratic ease, all angst about his play now seemed forgotten.

'She needs restraining occasionally. The shackles I invented. An anti-mad device. On the manacle principal. It could make a fortune. Much simpler than a strait-jacket. It allows unhindered movement for a specific distance. In a strait-jacket that's impossible. I've contacts in the Patent Office you know. Oh yes. Rather.'

The weirdos on the streets were weirder indoors. Freddie, in his big dress and brogues, looked a mixture of coal-heaver, charwoman, academic.

'This country has plumbed the depths. We are up to our necks in ordure.'

He had in common with Filfy Wilfy the ability to hit words with idiosyncratic emphasis.

'You know that bloke, Filfy Wilfy? The human skunk? Are you his brother?'

'Certainly not.'

'I have to go, Freddie.'

'Earthy is a sod.'

'My wife is waiting for me.'

'Democracy is the election of the cunning by the ignorant. You can no longer buy a decent enema. Men's prostates are ignored.'

Anyone who could mix democracy, enemas and prostates was hard to dislike.

'See you.'

'Would it help were I to reveal my full name on the title page?'

'Come again?'

'Parts hyphen Rinser. Fanny by Gaslight by F. Parts-Rinser.'

'Parts rinser? You mean like a bidet?'

'What, what? Parts-Rinser. I'm double-barrelled.'

'Earthy didn't criticise your name. Were a play to be turned down on account of the author's name, most new plays would go unperformed.'

'Most plays are unperformed. I've got ten of them sitting there on that shelf.'

'The name is okay. He likes your name.'

'He thinks my name good?'

'Your name with Earthy is a big hit. He feels he's half way there as far as that's concerned.'

'It's a very old name, you know. I have connections in the aristocracy. The King was a mamma's boy. Edward. You do know that, don't you? Oh yes. When one was young, about your age, Navy types often phoned me in the small hours. Looking for engagement. "Are you free for engagement?" Oh yes.'

'And were you free?'

'I took up boxing. I was rather handsome then. I had a number of fights. I scored two knockouts in Blackfriars. When they knew I packed a punch they kept away from me.'

'Did you wear a dress in those days?'

'Did I hear you talking to those dreadful nonentities on your way up here?'

He meant Phil and Rosa.

'To be perfectly honest, Earthy thought your play disgusting. The essential even worse. He wouldn't touch it with a Dyno-rod. He thinks the whole thing out of date. Drab. Dead.'

He lay back on a mound of pillows. The hem of the dress by now was nearer his thighs than his ankles.

'Disgusting? Why, how did they give him the job of running theatre? Did you not explain the essential is merely a device, which transmuted by imagination, becomes art? This is the universal struggle. This country is truly sunk when fools like Earthy run it. We can cut the essential. Do without it.'

'The essential is inessential?'

'What? Are you in the Secret Service? Or have you spent time in a home for the mentally challenged? You heard what I said. I am willing to cut the essential.'

The clock began to wheeze. It managed a series of clacks bearing little reference to the real hour. A reminder that time was an accident that didn't have to wait to happen. Time was purposefully chaotic and dusty with talcum. Time was a concertina player. Too short and too long at the same time.

'Freddie, I have tried to be honest. Earthy, Sir Neville Earthy, our greatest living and ah, dead director, is not going to do it. Put it aside, until fashion catches up, eh?'

Springing at me with alarming speed, towering over me, hair spilling forward, I could smell his anger.

'Christ, boy, I survived war. I did the Blackpool Tower Circus. Do you think I'm afraid of Earthy's opinion? Or yours? April loves my play. I have tea regularly in the Inns of Court. I don't need Earthy. I've just written a novel. Heine & Logan, the best new publishers in

England, have accepted it. Yes. Yes.'

Getting a massive tome from a shelf, he plonked it on me, inviting me to read it and report to him next day. It was thicker than Yellow Pages. The word processor had made it all possible. No wonder postmen were issued with trollies. There were so many manuscripts going to and fro they couldn't possibly carry them without risking hernias.

I looked at the title, Hare's Rural Rides by F. Parts-Rinser.

He was already scrutinising my face for the slightest sign of acceptance or rejection. I flicked the pages. First thing caught my eye was something about two young ladies in gym slips, enticed into a bath by an elderly bawd.

'What's it about?'

'Hare invites two gels down to the country. There to use them for evil ends.'

'Animal Farm with sex?'

'Hare is an Estate Agent, operating round the West End and Guildford, for the Duke of Porchester. A knave of course. On the surface.'

'The Duke?'

'No. Hare. The Duke is too old for normal engagement. He needs excessive stimulation. His wife's a seamstress.'

'The Duke's wife?'

'No. Hare's. She makes perfumed underwear for the elite and calls it haute couture.'

'And Heine & Logan are going to publish it?'

'When I popped a copy into them, the Receptionist, a charming gel, about your age, told me it sounded like their kind of thing all right.'

Slamming a fist into a cupped hand, he then shook it at the world, as if certain triumph were his. Despite years of failure he still believed. Faith without miracles was faith indeed. Impervious to critical frost, he was a caterpillar forever on the brink of turning into a flying success. Longing to circle the scorching flame.

'Can you let me know what you think. Say this time tomorrow?'

By the fire, a six inch nail stuck out of the floor, a hammer beside it.

'Ha-hah. Hm-hm. The chappie somewhere below us, when he makes a dreadful racket with his jungle music, I hammer on the nail until he stops. Oh yes. It usually works.'

'I'm having a decanting meeting day after tomorrow. In the evening. It's important we get your input, Freddie. I'll have this read by then.'

Out on the landing, the crack high up on the gable wall looked wider. The house was not built on rock. It stood on rubble and rattling dreams and the Bakerloo Line. In every rotten brick was the still potent nightmare of German bombs. Only fantasy kept us standing.

BIG PARTS

'What's that in your hand?'

'My tape recorder.'

'Why do you do it?'

'In time to come they can't say we weren't real. We were true. We existed.'

On the way down I knocked on Wally's door.

He opened the door the width of his face. His lips dribbled white powder. The big money was in legal drugs. The only complete piece of furniture he possessed was a television. His bed was a mattress on the floor. Beside it a coffee table with three legs and a pile of books compensating for the missing one.

'Wally, day after tomorrow, evening in my place. A meeting. If we don't do something about this decanting caper, we might find ourselves exiled in a sink estate somewhere.'

The palms of his hands were the same colour as my own. Skin really was only skin deep.

'My sink is blocked as it 'appens. I'm let down by it.'

His kitchen was wet, bleak. Along one wall a white tea-stained laminated worktop puckered from neglect and lack of heat. Under the lifting plastic a woodlouse lurked. Frantic pale legs gaining an edge, it emerged to take a bumpy scuttle across the surface. Reaching a spot from which the laminate had been ripped, it buried itself in the pulpy wood. On the soaking floor, tiles lifted. The walls bulged, the plaster cancerous. Spanning the strip of wall above the window, as if hung out to dry, were veils of cobweb thick as snot. A cupboard door hung on one hinge. The filthy sink was blocked with grease and tea bags.

'Any hot water, Wally?'

'It's broken or somefing. I'm let down by it.'

'Let's boil some in the kettle.'

'The element is gorn in the kettle. I've reported it.'

With a bread knife I gouged away the blockage. Running the cold tap, the water just managed to slobber down the plug-hole. The floor was soaking wet. The only food in the place was crisps, twiglets, peanuts...the bags open, the contents half eaten.

His jeans, white shirt and shoes were clean as new. Giro day, he was always first up in the house. Soon as the brown envelope hit the hallway you'd hear him hurrying down.

'Freddie says you play your music too loud.'

'I ain't got music. He hits the floor with a hammer. It does my 'ead in, mate.'

I could see a ghetto blaster half-hidden under a towel.

Our basement flat was paradise compared. I greeted my wife like we hadn't seen each other for months. She was trying on underwear and a new skirt and jacket. Absorbed. There wasn't anything or anyone in the world but her and her mirror. Her pubic hair was dense as a bale of tobacco.

I phoned the Health Centre. I wanted help for Rosa and Gibbs. The phone buzzed and buzzed, then clicked to an unobtainable sound. I tried again, gave up.

My wife's flesh was warm as honey in the sun.

'Keep an eye on the time.'

'It keeps an eye on us.'

She examined her breasts in the mirror.

'Can you feel anything there? Tell me honestly.'

Lying on the old sofa in her arms I was head over heels.

I postponed our decanting meeting. That day she was taking me with her to an Oxford encaenia. She was meeting her father there. He gave money to her college.

On the train from Paddington I read aloud bits of Freddie's latest, Hare's Rural Rides. We laughed so much the ticket inspector thought we were druggies.

Hare, a randy estate agent, organised a party for the Duke of Porchester, to which only men over seventy were invited. Apart from two fifteen year old girls in school uniform. One hundred men, two girls. After Hare's elderly sister, an old bawd, worked on the girls, they'd be sold for the night to the highest bidder. Opening bid five thousand.

"Old Porchester lay beside his naked wife, watching as she, younger than he, casually examined her thighs, her torso, for signs of aging. Sighing, she said, "Not bad for an old wrinkly."

"Not bad at all, juicebox," echoed Porchester.

"No," said his wife, "you're the old wrinkly and I'm not bad for you."

A bloke in a seat near us laughed so immoderately he had to be drunk. An academic of some kind, he corrected essays as he listened, burping occasionally.

A middle-aged lady politely asked me to stop reading.

'Pornography is a poor substitute for a buffet car.'

It was well we just then trundled into Oxford.

The town was dressed for summer and summer didn't let her down. The streets rattled with bicycles, most of the saddle-swampers simply corking. The dreaming spires were wide awake and warm.

My wife was buzzing. This had been her second home. She wore red high heels, a gorgeous white frock, priceless pearls, a cashmere cardigan draped about her shoulders. The Raybans wedged up on her forehead added a Riviera touch. Walking beside her through the gifted masses, I felt pleased as a spaniel with a duck.

The randy sun licked a stone wall russet.

We walked into her college under a noble archway. It reminded me of Stafford

BIG PARTS

Gaol.

The place was full of men in sober suits getting legless. The waiters seemed to be army lower ranks doing catering on the side. They had tight haircuts, thread-thin moustaches, pectoral muscles bulging their white jackets. I whipped a glass from a passing tray and managed to grab a full bottle of champers as well. A hell of a lot of the suits were round my wife. Outside, young things lay on manicured grass. Smoking it too. The waiter from whom I grabbed the bottle came over. He had a head so round and solid, it could have been a stone ball borrowed from the top of a pillar entrance to a stately home. A corporal if ever there was one.

'How did you get in here, Scobie?'

'I'm the Vice-Chancellor's boyfriend.'

Instead of Scobie, he now called me Guvnah. My wife queened over to the door. Her father had arrived.

He gave the college City Bibles every year. That's what he called money. Money was the only good book. An empty wallet was a bad read. A lot of hands reached out to him - Master, fellows, dons, doctors, profs. My wife kissed him fondly, delighted he'd arrived.

A formal fine figure of a begowned man spoke to me.

'The ceremony is due to commence shortly. I advise you contemplate making your way to The Sheldonian.'

I don't think he approved of my snazzy tieless shirt and suit. And the way I slugged from the champagne bottle.

My wife, looking across the crowded room, flashed a smile. She came over, her adoring father with her.

'How the devil are you, you young reprobate?'

'Just because you're in Oxford for the day, doesn't mean you have to use big words.'

He gave me the boyish look he always gave when pretending hurt. In the bookish surrounds, he stood out in his brown tweed suit - leather patches at elbows - and oiled hair combed back tight on his head. Like a fifties footballer. His healthy, weather-beaten face, rude vigour, marked him out from the chalkies lining up to shake his big raw hand. He was in Oxford to spread the gospel - dispensing City Bibles. And all because his lovely daughter had been a student there. He loved her. She was his only child.

I held up my bottle of champagne, by way of cheer, by way of toasting him and, thumb on the neck, shook it well. The result was a spume of champers hit him slap in the face. I hadn't meant it at all. I really hadn't. But hell, anarchism and slapstick are close aligned. I tried genuine desperate apology. The waiter lit on me and, despite appeals on my behalf, expertly marched me right out to the street. He did it well. He was a pro okay. I flung the champagne bottle after him. It bounced off his head. I took to my heels, scattering an impressive procession of academics I'd not seen coming. They were heading for The Sheldonian. I headed for the railway station.

A few hours later I was safely back in London.

Going round the side of our house, I saw an earthworm wriggling in the middle of the path. It was exactly the same colour as wet nylon. I flicked at it with the toe of my shoe until it fell down through the drain grille. Then I noticed another one, sticking out from a hole in the rotten brickwork, at ground level. Probably popped out to see where its mate had gotten to. I'd broken up a happy home. A worm is the same colour as the inside of your lip. The worm is reddish because of haemoglobin. We have haemoglobin. We share genes with worms, caterpillars, plants. The world is one. Could a worm therefore feel loss?

I went out to get cigarettes. An ambulance, lights flashing, siren sounding, tore down the High Road and round into a street by the Greek church. I followed after it. It pulled up outside a house and by the time I arrived they were carrying a man out on a stretcher. I got a hell of a fright. Must have been the drink. The man lying under the blanket appeared to be myself. His eyes were open. He was looking at the sky. They were my eyes. So I thought. That was my face. Then I bent right over him and went to put my hand out to touch him, to tell him not to worry, I'd be okay.

One of the ambulance men told me to clear off.

'But, but, that's...me.' Even as I said it I knew it was ludicrous. Perhaps I was looking for a cataclysmic event to make an excuse for mucking up in Oxford.

I went home. The sky was clear blue. It was there all the time. Over us. Was ever. Would always. The big top under which we took part in the circus.

Was I turning sociopath? No, no way. I didn't love to hate myself that much. Or anyone else either. At the very least I had been reckless. Every fool knows - shake a bottle of champagne and the stuff comes like a whale. Did I sub-consciously want to drown my wife in it? She was so easily, glamorously queen of that ancient room. At one point I heard her say to an adoring circle,

'If we want the classics to survive, then we must fight for them. The vandals are already inside the doors.'

I waited for her to come home.

I was the kind of bloke who shouldn't drink. Because I couldn't. Drink went straight to my head. The influence. The sea fog smell of a cork instantly wafted across my brain. The taste engulfed sense. Pity. Because I loved it.

I phoned Freddie. I told him I'd read his novel and I now proposed coming up and telling him what I thought. He was surprised me ringing at such a late hour.

50

'I thought it was some sod looking for engagement. Hm-hmm. Give me five. Ha-ha.'

Surprisingly, when I reached his door, it was open. I called his name. No reply. I called April's name. Definitely no reply.

In the darkness I felt conquered. When I went into his room, for a second I thought I was sleep-walking. The light was darkish red. Enough to reveal April sitting by the glowing gas fire. I could make out her blue frock, slippers, her hair in girlish ringlets. The cardinal, trapped in the canvas, evil as ever, looked down through the episcopal gloom. He seemed to be alive - an effect cast by a flickering candle stuck in a wine bottle on the mantelpiece. The clock was doing its one-legged tock.

Standing by the bed were Freddie and a woman in cruel embrace. His body was tense as he forced her backwards in his masterful arms. He wore a black dinner jacket, striped trousers and some kind of small hat on the side of his head. He had one arm round her waist. She had an arm round his neck. Or was it round his throat? She wore an evening gown. I couldn't see her face, just the dress either side of his legs. Her arm was strong, a big silver bangle on the wrist. April sat by the fire, oblivious. Freddie turned, glared at me and in menacing, acid tone said,

'The bitch is on heat!'

He meant the woman in his arms.

Executing a sudden pirouette, he spun her round so now I could see her. The gown was a full, formal, ruched, green satin affair. Round her neck was a string of red jewels. She tried to pull his hand from her waist. They stood incredibly close. A symbiotic attachment too confusing to decipher immediately.

She sang in a shrieking soprano tone.

'Unhand me, cruel man
I must be treated kind
Your lips disturb my soul
Your passion makes you blind.'

A fat fold of flesh hung out under her arm. It wasn't a tit. They were cupped in a decorative shield. She appeared to be Freddie's age. Her hand began to grope at the dress, slowly pulling it up her leg, revealing frilly underwear, suspender and stocking. The leg was formidably strong.

Freddie toppled her onto the bed and straddled her. They looked ridiculous. Why were they behaving like this in front of me?

'Do you think I care about your feelings? What about mine?'

He spat the words out with terrible, mincing, cruelty. I looked to April. She stared at the fire, her curious hare-lipped grimace unchanging.

Freddie now kissed the woman, pressing her head deep into the pillow with his mouth, as if trying to suffocate her. Kissing her to death. She moved her leg hopelessly, vainly attempting to escape from under his weight. Her foot squirmed in revulsion. The shoe - a high-heeled slipper - fell off.

They sat up, all tension gone from their bodies. He howled laughing. Demented as Satan. I scrambled for the light switch by the door.

Freddie, grotesque male-female, bowed as if taking applause. He had fooled me rotten. His costume, I could see now, was half gents suit, half ladies dress, cunningly sewn together. Even the bow tie had one wing only. And the red jewels just went round the 'female' side of his neck.

Reason was unreason. Half what you saw was unreal. His act looked a throw-back from recondite Edwardian nights. Removing the hat, which had been held in place by an elastic band running under his chin, he pulled off a tuft of wig from the other side of his head. The elaborate costume had taken much thought and execution, but as he slumped down on the side of the bed, bubbles of perspiration on his forehead, he and it looked tawdry, ridiculous and faintly repulsive. Under it all he was wearing frilly drawers and at least half a suspender belt. Was he hermaphrodite or was the division psychic? He tore off the velcroed shield cupping what I'd thought was a breast. Covered with sequins it was an item neatly wrought.

'I created the entire assemblage. The peplum I attached at the waist to disguise the male posterior. I used petersham inside the dress hem to add weight, so it hangs properly. The flounce is perfect. When she sings soprano, I can reply in tenor. Oh yes. The underwear is vital for the feeling. Women have been known to faint when bumping into me backstage. Ha-hah.'

His face had been painted and powdered to bank down gender. It gave him the blank asexual look of a clown. Like a priest signalling the end of ceremony, with finger and thumb he quenched the candle stuck in the wine bottle on the mantelpiece. Savagely, bored even, he ripped off the costume. The inside of the trouser leg unzipped the whole way down. Up on a stage I couldn't imagine anyone being really gulled. But in the shadowy room, the cardinal, the candle, April by the fire, truth was shaky.

He stood bare-chested. One of his legs was still in its stocking. The hairs were visible through the sheer nylon. His pectoral muscles, collapsed with age, were the droopy tits of a crone. He stood for a moment breathing heavily. He pulled off false, red-painted nails, and tossed them into a tin box.

He cleaned his face with a cloth. He looked like a beached whale whose chances of getting back to water were nil. He might have been one of those aquatic animals both male and female at the same time...or are neither...and ten million years old. A creature capable of mating with itself.

Getting up and making a barely audible whinny, April tiptoed out over the creaking floor. A ghost walking.

'Television killed us. What's badly needed today is an elevating artistry. When the morals of a nation are corrupted one must try to shock them to sense. All these foreigners - if they knew how we really felt, they wouldn't stay. This, this is the pain of archangels.'

Television killed him before he killed it.

He was a fearsome sight. A crusader emerged from a septic tank, cross intact and dripping. Lord Crotch, the Duke of Porchester, with pants down.

'They call it globalization. They want us covered in the same universal ash. Did you bring your tape recorder?'

'It's been on since I came in.'

'What did you think of my novel?'

'Oh. Well...Ah what a, what a, what a read! What a read! What? It will get you your just rewards?'

'You think so?'

'I took it to Oxford with me today. My wife and I. I read extracts to her. She can't wait to buy two copies. So she can read it twice. Yes.'

'Good Lord. My background is engineering you know. Oh yes. Christ. You don't notice 'em piling up. Until they've piled up. The years. The years, dear boy. You didn't think the scene outside the brothel was too naughty?'

'Pitch perfect, Freddie. Now, how about this decanting meeting?'

He stared at the pages, his plucked eyebrows shooting up and down.

'Is there something the matter with you? Fanny you returned with rings of beer. This is even worse. You have mangled, soaked, jumbled the order beyond recognition! Do you read in public houses only? It's stained irredeemably. The truth! I hate liars.'

'Actually, I must confess, I did spill some champagne. My wife and I were toasting you. Champers is sperm of the Gods, don't you think?'

Wearing half a panty sewed to half a suspender belt, he looked a fat old pike, newly hooked, lying stunned on the bottom of a boat.

It was late. As I went back downstairs, all the way down through the house, from behind every door, came groans and snoring.

My wife arrived home in the early hours. She'd taken a mini-cab the whole way from Oxford. She collapsed into an armchair, crying her soul out. Head slumped, face wreathed in her hair, Raybans in her hand, one red shoe on, the other kicked off, knees touching, legs splayed, she was heartbreak in a crumpled dress. Gulping for air, tears spilling to her lips, falling into her lap, she managed to sob out,

'You-u've ru-u-uined everything!'

I tried to pin the blame for my behaviour on the waiter. The army corporal.

She screamed protestation. In the dead hour of night, it sounded scary as hell.

'He wasn't army. That was a senior proctor. Idiot.'

I made for the door. She stuck her arm straight out across me, her fingers urgently beckoning me to touch. In an instant I was on my knees, head buried in her lap, kissing her wildly, holding her tighter than barrel hoops, trying my best to sob, to show my apologies were deep and true. Her desperate act of forgiveness was overwhelming. It always was. Why did she do it? The first gesture of the arm sticking out, stopping me, was girlish. It had real sorrow but also a playful edge. Like a child. Whatever, for the moment I was the child and buried in her warmth.

'I love you. Because I don't know an alternative.'

'Why, why do you do these things, darling, why? I'm so, so tired.'

'At odd times, certainly when drunk, I lose control. I show off my feelings. I don't care about anything then. Or I care too much.'

Eventually we managed to get to bed.

I lay beside her, the tape recorder switched on. I was hoping she'd say something about love. I was like someone collecting evidence for a crime that hadn't as yet been committed.

'Daddy said - no more money until I leave you. I love you. Now go to sleep. I'm dead. We have to leave this place. It's the sensible thing to do.'

I set the decanting meeting for eight o'clock. First to arrive was Wally. Not wanting to get in the way, he sat on the floor in a corner by the piano. He wore a fresh tartan shirt, clean jeans, well-polished shoes. He looked a shiny, contented, black Buddha.

My wife had arrived home with a bag of goodies from Fortnum & Mason. Assorted delicacies of a fishy nature. Expertly arranging them on trivial biscuits the size of postage stamps, she offered some to Wally. He took what looked like a sardine's tail on a coin-sized cracker.

Next to arrive was Rosa. Though not having to leave the house to get to us, for public show, she wore a heavy fur coat. She peeped out of it like a mouse peeping out of an empty sack. Sitting back on the sofa her short legs didn't reach the carpet.

'How is your husband, I understand he's not well?' inquired my Lady Bountiful, proffering her tray of F & M anorexic feastings.

Rosa, with utter contempt for her husband and my wife, replied,

'He'd be better orf dead!'

Her frizzy hair, eyes and upper lip, were all you could see above the collar of her coat.

Wriggling her nose at the tray of tosspottery, she dismissed them with a flick of a hand, just about visible up a furry sleeve.

'"e's gorn dahn agin!' This she addressed to me.

'Oh dear. Shall I go and...?'

'Leave 'im. Serve the bleeder right. 'e won't do wot 'e's told!'

My wife, retreating into the kitchen with the tray, Rosa nodded in her direction.

'I 'ad all that stuff when I worked for Mrs. Gamm. I didn't like it then neiver.'

Big Julia, the lady who pestered passersby to get her a paper and pills, arrived. Stomping into the room on her walking stick, without ceremony, she plonked herself down on the sofa beside Rosa. The sofa which, at a pinch could seat four adults, now looked too small for one and a half. The last of the natives owning her own house, Julia was not a Trust tenant.

'I'm sorry, Julia, this meeting is a tenants meeting only. This house only. Why have you come?'

'I 'eard it was to do wif the Bozzies. I'll go if you want me to go, but you'll 'ave to give me five minits to git me bref back. Sorry.'

My wife, gracious as ever, came in once more with her tray of Fortnum & Mason vol-au-vent bilge.

Julia regarded them as a whale might. She didn't know what they were exactly but they certainly didn't add up to much. She pounced on about nine items, quickly ramming them into her raw girlish face.

The meeting was pointless without Freddie. Whilst we waited, I put on the television. Wally wanted to see a much talked about heavyweight boxing match.

Julia wiped her greasy lips with her fingers, then wiped them on the armrest of the sofa.

The white heavyweight was a vastly overweight target. His opponent landed so few blows on him, he must have been blind. They looked less threatening than Rosa 'The Pocket Rocket' Gibbs and Julia 'Thunder Drawers' Smith who were now giving each other pre-fight stares and vicious verbal insults.

'I gives you an overcoat. Given me by Mrs. Gamm. You never wore it once.'

'Shut your mouf. Pipsqueak. Mrs. Gamm was a old tart.'

My wife mimed to Wally to sit between them. He jumped to it, squeezing onto the edge of the sofa. Rosa peeked at him.

'Gorblimey. You're black, ain'tcher?'

'I fink he'll knock 'im out in the next round,' Wally said quietly, trying to be the peacemaker.

'How much room does a body need?' Julia growled, piling up elfin dainties from the tray of nonsense-nibbles.

'Fuckyah! And doublefuckyah! If it's a row you're lookin' for!' Rosa said in a mini-mouse screech.

My wife was never so delighted by the arrival of Freddie.

Wearing his double-breasted brown suit, carrying a walking cane, kid gloves in hand, he looked not only immaculate but powerful. April was with him. She wore long white gloves, a yellow frock, glass beads round her neck, brown sandals. She stood dutifully by him as he surveyed the company. Hugely unimpressed, he withheld any word of greeting.

My wife carried in two chairs. Freddie, uncaring of others, sat bang in the middle of the room, bolt upright. His two-tone shoes gleamed. His cravat was held in place by a brilliant gold pin. Only the night before I'd seen him ridiculously accoutred in underpants and suspender. April seemed hypnotised by the grunting bruisers on the telly.

She then spoke the only articulate sentence I'd ever heard her utter.

'He's got the body of an old man.'

My tape recorder was on top of the piano just out of sight behind a vase. She'd spoken the words deep and slow.

'He's got the body of an old man.'

There was dumb surprise in the intonation. Did it remind her of another old body, closer to home?

Freddie laughed. Unconvincingly.

'Neiver of 'em could box eggs,' Big Julia opined with the sure-sounding sagacity of Ring magazine.

I declared the meeting open.

'That this house needs attention, is beyond question. We all know this. Rising damp down here. And most alarmingly, rising damp upstairs. Re-plastering is required everywhere - inside and out. Structural work outside needs to be carried out as well. The brickwork needs re-pointing. The whole house needs re-wiring. Switching on an electric kettle is often a dodgy undertaking. One wonders why we want to carry on living here at all. Why? Well, because it's home. Home is where your pillow is. The point is, can they do what is necessary without decanting us? I believe they can. It will be uncomfortable for us and admittedly awkward for the firm doing it. Messrs Cackhand & Bindweed. There'll be dust everywhere - it'll be like living in a building site. But! If we leave, would you bet on getting back in? This is a nice up-market street. The Trust gets money from Government. But naturally, they spend it as they think fit. The Trust if you ask me could become, in time, a private organisation. Funded but private. Dealing more and more in new property only. Why would they want to bother with all the hassle of an old building like this? They might want us out in order to sell it. I think we should dig in and refuse to budge. Let them work around us. We won't mind, will we?'

They didn't respond. They looked settled in for an evening of telly and snackettes.

'I don't know what you're complaining about, this place you got is bloody lovely. You got no worries, mate. You landed on the pigs back.'

Big Julia was right. Her beady eyes roamed over every object in the room. She shuffled her feet on the thick Wilton, checking its comfortably thick pile. My wife had furnished the place from Harrods and Heals and Lisson Grove.

The fight on the telly climaxed. A lucky punch had somehow landed, with the extra detonating power of complete surprise.

"e's gorn an' knocked 'im out,' Rosa said, feinting an uppercut to illustrate the bleeding obvious.

Heap Big White Belly lay upended on the canvas and was duly counted out. His opponent fell over with relief. I turned the telly off.

'If they, wotsit? Give some money for movin'. Know wot I'm sayin'?'

'Julia, you're not a tenant, remember? You own your own home. The Trust will not be giving you anything.'

'Beg pardon, course. It's upsettin' though, 'n'it? Could still do with a few quid, mind.'

Freddie, ramrod straight on his chair, raised his cane, looking as if he were about to demolish someone - anyone would do.

'Unless we...'

That was as far as he got. He'd noticed something outside on the patio. Others were arriving. A voice called out,

'Can we come in?'

It was May from next door and along with her Sam Tripp, the bum doctor's son, and Muzie/Miss Jackpot.

My wife, her teeth shining like a string of 100 watt bulbs, greeted them.

'Do make yourselves at home. You're most welcome. Nice to see you, Sam.'

'Hi,' said Sam, raising his hand shyly. His hair was Mohican, the middle section dyed green. His ears, lower lip, right eyebrow, were fashionably in the grip of horse-shoe nails.

'I'll make some tea, shall I?' my wife enthused.

Wearing a stunning black and silver silk blouse, combat trousers and green high-heels with a diamante clasp, she looked a million dollars. I couldn't help gawping at her myself. We looked shabby in her light.

May, when I asked her why she'd come, said she was representing tenants in other households. They were in the same situation as ourselves. Muzie was a special friend of hers. He wanted information on a horse running the following day at Stratford and believed my wife could help him in the matter. Sam, she explained, was a - 'particular good friend.' That could only mean one thing.

'Oh, really?'

'He's ever such a nice boy. He's waiting to get into - where is it, Sam?'

'Balliol. Yea, right. I've done nine months in a mental home.'

'Oh dear. Are you all right now?'

'Work experience! Dumbo! My gap year.'

'Sorry,' I said.

'Sam and me are going out together,' May said.

My wife halted mid-stride. May was old enough to be Sam's mother's older sister. He sat on the floor, head bowed, tugging at the nail in his eyebrow. He rubbed his index fingers together. It was some kind of habit.

Freddie was doing double-takes by the dozen. Rosa lit a cigarette and once lit, never removed it from her pout. With each puff, the end, almost hidden in the parapet of her fur collar, glowed like a third eye.

'Good Lord! Ha-hah. Hm-hm. All sorts here. You do know the Indian is a coloured Jew.'

With curious humour, he had addressed this to Muzie. My wife looked furiously at him. Then at me as if I could shut him up.

'In India the natives couldn't run out of your way. Here they make fortunes.'

'Muzie come here with a fortune, I'll have you know! His family were Matterahgies!' May said.

Muzie, unaware he was the subject of hostilities, cut to the chase.

'The hawse is Coyney Girl. I am ready for change of luck. Bloomin' luck so out I had all eight hawses, the bet vos placed, yeah?'

'Give it a rest, Jackpot. Just ask her what you want, go on.'

Saying this May hit him a playful slap on the arm.

'Is Coyney Girl vwinner? I mus' know. He your father, yes, I am put her on dawkit wit seven other I fancy. I need to know form please an' dis an' dat.'

'Certainly,' my wife said, 'let me phone Paps.'

Swiping her mobile from the top of the piano, she headed for the kitchen, already dialling.

Freddie addressed us.

'I want to know - do I have your support? I am prepared to lead but I must have back-up. When I look you in the nostrils, I want to see fight. You can all see it. You can all smell it. We are up to our necks in it. I for one say, "Stop! No more!" England will be saved by those who love her. Will you vote for me if I stand? If I lead, will you follow? Democracy stinks because Westminster is a sludge farm. It will take a massive enema to clean it out. The newspapers are full of breast cancer, oh yes. But when is the last time you've seen a prostate mentioned? We have plunged. Miss Chats, who is in charge of this house, is quite frankly, a frostie minge. They will stop us singing Christmas Carols. Mark my words, next thing they forbid will be Guy Fawkes. The Bishop of Sedgefield and the Texan preacher man are the twin towers of evil. They must be stopped. England is ours. Young men, now is your chance. Join me. Now. It will be hard. Very hard. But what fun! The harder the better, I say. You know where I am. Come up anytime for advice.'

Enunciation perfect, his words jabbed out like punches. The coop went silent as if a hawk hung overhead.

Rosa's fur collar had turned grey beard with cigarette ash.

'I've seen you abaht, ain't I?'

She chuckled this conspiratorially, implying she knew the great man personally, wishing to impress the others. Freddie slowly bared his dentures. Hers was one vote he would not be soliciting.

I wondered what young Sam thought. Sam had brains. Sam was the future.

My wife came in from the kitchen.

'What he say, please?' Muzie, interested only in horsey matters, inquired.

She went to the window and opened it to let in some air.

'Paps informs me they had coughing in the stables but the Girl is fine, touchwood. It's worth an each way bet.'

'I do only accumulator. She one in a chain. My bloomin' luck gotta turn. Coyney Girl is it maybe, and dis and dat.'

Sam stood up, and going to the mirror, which was all part of our elaborate antique pine and marble fireplace, studied his reflection. Gripping the point of his chin with the fingers of one hand, he gently stroked it as if he had a goatee.

'No matter which end it comes out,' he said quietly, crap is still crap.'

May rewarded his insight with a raucous laugh. Freddie turned quickly on her and sneered right into her soul.

'You keep your mouth and legs shut, deary.'

Sam, without farewell, went out.

'You wouldn't 'appen to 'ave anyfing strong in the 'ouse missus, would you?' Julia asked.

'Apart from my husband? No.'

'Here's what I think,' I said. 'I'm not going to be decanted. Let's stick together. Rosa, how could they decant you and your husband? He's a sick man, right? You don't want to go either, do you, Wally? My wife's put a lot into this place. That garden out there was an overgrown wilderness until she took it in hand. I like it here better than any place I've ever been. And that includes prison. How can we resist them? Threaten them with publicity? What big firm hasn't something to hide? They're not saints, are they? Any one agree?'

My speech had considerably less impact than Freddie's. Why did I bother? Let them be decanted. They weren't even looking at me. They were positively avoiding my eyes. Acting weird.

I couldn't believe it. Filfy Wilfy. He was outside on the patio. How the hell had he found us? He didn't know where I lived. But there he was, crouching down, the better to look in the half-open window. He had the usual wodge of newspaper in his left hand, the cadging rodent right sticking into the room, nails clicking.

Who told him about our meeting?

'Pardon my pardons I did say him outside bookie your wife father had hawse.' Muzie.

Filfy, crouching, stared in at us, perfectly framed in the proscenium arch of the open window.

'Cuppatea?'

'I know you yah rotten crow! Get off! Go way! Filfy toerag!'

Rosa's insults made no impact.

'Hallo Partsy. Long time no see.'

Freddie, leaning on his cane, angrily chomped his dentures.

'I am not your brother!'

The rest of us immediately thought he might be. If they weren't actual brothers, Wilfy looked as if he might have crawled from his subconscious.

I surreptitiously changed over the cassette in my recorder.

'I know you, Rosa. Wery true. I've done it all. Women's clothes. Tights. Bras, panties, stockings, the lot. I've done all that. All them film stars, film stars, all them stars are bent. Wotsit was a hairpin, old wotsit. All them intelligent ones are hairpins. Fifty times a day. Fifty 'ucking times. Shit. Pissing ninety. Utopianism. Liberalism. Conservatism. Socialism. Radicalism. Communism. Anarchism. Syndicalism. Trotskyism. Catholicism. Protestantism - it's no longer a religion, that one. They're all hairpins. The Pope and all. Hail Queen of Heaven. I washed cars for Mrs. Gamm, didn't I? A lot of money, them days. Wash and wax. Every Sat'day I filled her kettle, Mrs. Gamm. Mrs. Gamm's kettle. My bruvver did nuffing. A 'ucking nutter. E's a NUT-TER. He died last...a year ago me bruvver died. Haemrige. Right to the brain. Right up to the 'ucking brain. Eighty six he was. Jack. That's right. No, tell a lie. George. That's me twin. Me sister - Dolly. She never did a stroke in her life. Good luck to her. Right, Partsy?'

Freddie, a picture of loathing, sat subdued.

Filfy turned his attention to me.

'What height are you? Six foot eight? Your lovely muvver still alive? Or did the cancer get her an' all?'

Six foot eight? Was he looking for heroes to defend him? My lovely mother? His ridiculous flattery was delivered with a shifty sideways glance and the trace of a derisive smile.

I'd never seen my wife so ill at ease. She was convinced I'd arranged the whole thing.

'Are we having a meeting about being decanted or are we not?'

She rummaged under the stairs, emerging with an air freshener. She went about the room spraying scented chemical. She shot several clouds in the direction of the window. Wilfy, impervious to this napalming, smiled in at her.

'Filfy old toerag! Ruining a lovely evening he is,' Rosa said.

'Is it going to 'ucking win, Missus, is it? Is it?'

In an uncertain world words had to battle putrefaction.

'You can't make money unless you got a fifteen horse accumulator. You listening? You 'ucking listening? You want a hundred each way accumulator to pick any money up. You got, you got Run Up The Flag, you got Stretch It, put them two in a single to be on the safe side. Put in Coyney Girl in the last. Put ten p each way on The Caterpillar, I'm tellin' you. If The Caterpillar don't run go for Boothen Boy. B-O-O-T-H-E-N, that's it. B-O....are you 'ucking listening? He's worth a ten p, to be on the safe side. I 'aven't eaten proper food, drink, sex, sleep, a proper shit for thirty years. What's causing it? What would you do if you were me?'

Under prompting from my wife, I reluctantly suggested it was time for him to be on his way. And if he'd left anything of a farmyard nature behind, to take it with him. Like a coffin exiting through the cream curtains, he vanished. My wife immediately went out the kitchen door to inspect the patio.

'Nothing. Thank God for that,' she said, a hand to her relieved heart.

Like Freddie, Wilfy had tremendous rage. When he challenged you his register instantly sharpened. Most of the time he adopted a chatty tone. But if he thought you weren't paying attention, his emotions surged, words shooting out, blasting you, his face flooding with red rage. When he considered you were brought to heel, he as quickly calmed down. When he'd said his brother was a "ucking nutter,' he sounded quite reasonable. But in the blink of an eye the rage boiling over in him, the...."e's a NUT-TER'...was articulated with such scathing contempt, the repressed never forgotten loathing of a lifetime was clear. Having gotten it off his chest, his next sentence was a calm mutter, accompanied with a truculent schoolboy scowl.

In the wilderness of the city the crying voices are completely indifferent to anything said back to them. To all but personal demons their ears are dumb. Like Freddie, Wilfy's self-immersion was total. The one knew what was wrong with the world, the other how to put it right.

My wife, smiling warm as ice, suggested they might all like to start thinking about going home. Wally gave me a hand hauling Julia to her feet.

Freddie stood and surveyed the room. He looked at me as if I ought to know what was on his mind.

'I've had good news. Heine & Logan want to see me immediately. Could you possibly accompany me? We could celebrate afterwards in Woffington's. My club. I'm a life member.'

He looked about the other faces as if expecting drooling envy. Prouder than Lucifer, a peacock compared was a plucked chicken.

I agreed to witness his moment of triumph. Woffington's was in the West End. 'And afterwards,' said my wife, 'you can buy a new suit.'

Rosa, rocking herself forward a few times, managed to hop off the sofa. The ash in her collar snowed down the front of her coat.

'Toerag! I knew 'im all right! Mrs. Gamm was a lady. He'll be asleep on the bleedin' floor when I gets in now. Gibbs. Go'nigh'.'

When they'd all gone my wife slammed the window shut. She ripped into me. It was the same in Oxford. Nothing I did was accidental. I sprayed her father with champagne because that is what I'd set out to do. The decanting business I was using for my own diversion. I had no interest in the others per se - I was just out to cause trouble for Miss Chats and the Trust.

'Why would I do that?'

'To pass the time!'

'Wouldn't it pass anyway?'

'So would a bus. You don't have to get into the driver's cab and crash it into a lamp-post.'

She was going to buy a house in South Kensington. If I didn't behave.

'And get yourself a job!'

'Oh, come on! There's enough people working. Why should I add to the traffic jams?'

Snorting derision better than Filfy Wilfy, she ordered me to bed.

'Forgive me all my sins.'

I woke in the night to hear music coming from the back of the house. I went out and down the garden, climbed the shed, then mounted the high wall separating us from the ex-school. From there I would be able to see what the asylum-seekers were up to. The Bosnians. Settled there by Miss Chats and the Town Hall.

Above the playground a crescent moon hung on a necklace of stars. Children skipped about, dancing. Buttery light fell from an upstairs window. In shadow, watching, I could make out the waitress from the Electric. Fata. The night air tucked at her petticoat. A man played wild music on a violin. A mad exciting tune. The children had abandoned themselves to it and, helpless in its power, were bubbles on a breeze. Gypsy music. From somewhere in Europe. Romanian probably. Was it the Eastern moon sucked them out onto that square of London tarmac? That banana moon. In those midnight moments watching from the wall, I knew I wanted kids. Kids. This time do everything right. Turn back the wheel. Laugh instead of cry.

I got back into bed...very quietly. My wife hated being disturbed. She dived deeper into featherland than any one I ever knew.

'Where the hell have you been?'

'Looking at the moon.'

'ucking NUT-TER,' she said.

Sometimes I kneeled beside my wife as, trowel in hand, she worked in the garden combating the bindweed. I loved watching her skill, calm energy, above all, her patience. Bindweed spread and choked like ivy on speed. Its root system seemed endless. It was impossible to eradicate. My wife dug it out or painted its leaves with poison. Nothing worked for long. She never got into a temper or cursed. Like me. She had something inside her personifying goodness. She didn't rant. She explained.

'Bindweed is part of the convolvulus family. It has to root and twine or die. It's from the Latin - convolvere. If you don't want to be decanted - become like the bindweed.'

'We have rooted. All the tenants have. Twine? We cling on, right?'

'Right. But please - no more silly letters to Miss Chats.'

Bindweed was love itself.

For Freddie to be summoned to the West End by Heine & Logan was pure bliss. Immaculate in dark blue suit, black and white shoes, dangling cane, he could have been an advert for Savile Row. Hair carefully combed, powder on his face, liner and mascara on his eyes, old bones swaggering, the world was a Garden of Eden and he was back in it. What could be better than that?

I was impressed. Heine & Logan had obviously taken leave of their senses but that's what you had to do in the market place. Take a chance.

On the bus into town a middle-aged couple sat in front of us. They didn't speak for quite a while. Then the wife said,

'Will we have the tablets now? Or will we take them when we get home?'

Her grumpy husband eventually replied,

'Let's take them when we get home. It's better.'

Freddie, elbowing me in the ribs, took this exchange as portending decline.

'You see. Man as a species is dying.'

Above the city, the clouds were low and black. A spit of rain splatted the bus window.

'Have you got them on you?' the grumpy husband glumly inquired.

'No. They're at home.'

They got off at the next stop, the man foozling with a golf umbrella, people avoiding his widespread efforts. The wife must have known the tablets were at home. If he'd answered in the affirmative the first question, she surely would have had to tell him she didn't have them. So why did she ask?

'That's why I refuse pills, dear boy. Once you take them, they become your life. You talk and think nothing but pills! "Oh, time for my pill." I always avoided the pill.'

'And you never became pregnant?'

'What, what? Do you know, for instance, if you've got hair on your chest, it first goes grey around the nipples. That's a fact.'

'I readily confess I did not know that. Thank you.'

'Don't mention it.'

'I won't.'

The clouds parting, we drove into a pool of sun covering Trafalgar Square from Admiralty Arch to St. Martin-In-The-Fields. Freddie flapped a florid pink handkerchief about his face, returning it to his breast pocket with plunging finger and thumb. He'd known all along Hare's Rural Rides was a winner. At last, at last, after years and years of midnight toil, he had struck black lubricant and could see the spouting gush drown his enemies.

'Bastards. Yes. At last.'

Walking up St. Martin's Lane he had a stiff-backed lordly strut. He was amazed at the traffic. The road was so jammed even he was moving faster than the cars. On the pavements slow-moving clumps of tourists clogged every corner. Girls loaded with backpacks, airline tags still in place, had all the time in the world to get annoyingly between him and destiny.

A queue had formed outside a theatre. There was a girl at the front wearing thick-soled boots, ankle-socks, canvas shorts. She was sandwiched between a huge backpack and a frontpack round her belly just as big. She had quite a small head and wore spectacles. She looked like a giant turtle balancing on its hind legs. Freddie stood transfixed.

'The female you see - very strong. Look at those muscles.'

Her legs were gym-knobbly from tourist-trotting the planet.

Plastered all over the front of the theatre were massive words on vast posters. Freddie was foxed by the name of the play.

'"My..." what? Clematis? What's it saying?'

'That's the name of the play, Freddie.'

A blow-up of a favourable review stated the show was truly ground-breaking. Hence the hefty queue.

'Is it about flowers? My Clematis.'

'No, no. Clitoris. My Clitoris Sings. It's a big hit.'

'Good Lord. Surely not? My Clitoris Sings?'

'Yours as well?'

'What, what?'

The girl had an Oz emblem on her rucksack. She'd come twelve thousand miles to join in the chorus.

Freddie's reactions amused the queue. He was as good as a busker.

'This Government has finally killed off morality. My Clitoris Sings. How can it? Is it a ventriloquist show?'

'No, Freddie. It's all girls. A gender counter-blast to Tricks With Dicks. That was all blokes on stage waving their pricks around. Honestly.'

'Never!'

The queue erupted.

'Actually, there's a show on at the moment...It starts with an actress coming on stage with a biro stuck up her...inkwell. I'm not kidding, Freddie. It's Spanish. She proceeds to draw pictures which are flashed on a big screen. Then she defecates, the camera giving the audience a close up.'

'Good Lord! Where does one book?'

The queue was convinced we were a double-act.

'Makes Fanny by Gaslight seem an innocent romp.'

'I blame the Bishop of Sedgefield. The more pious they pretend the more corrupt their rule. You see now why the sod won't do it?'

'Who? The Prime Minister?'

'No. Earthy.'

'Lady Hannah assures me he does it at least once a month.'

'What, what? Christ. No. Fanny by Gaslight. The moral drive of the work in this present atmosphere of corruption renders it unperformable. The fall of the Roman Empire, you see? When something is corrupt, an apple, a government - it falls.'

Two policemen, chatting, cradling machine guns, ambled past.

A sheet of newspaper lying in the gutter, perked by a sudden blast of wind, sped ghoulishly along the pavement. Swirling about as if going down a whirlpool, it gusted over to Freddie, wrapping itself about his cane. Holding it in place with his foot, he prodded it flat. The front page of a broadsheet, it had a coloured photo of the Queen. She was greeting an African High Commissioner at Buckingham Palace. He was dressed in what seemed to be a three-quarter length pink and white petticoat, a red bath hat, grey ankle-socks and matching loafers. Round his shoulders was a more authentic looking jazzy homespun tribal shawl. He looked bizarrely matronly.

'How can she keep a straight face shaking hands with that?'

'Look what she's wearing. A Mrsblouse floral dress if ever there was one.'

'She's trying to make him feel at home.'

'Maybe he was trying to make her feel at home.'

People poured down Leicester Square tube and as many bubbled up. Quite a few glanced at Freddie. He had that unmistakable dictatorial je ne sais quoi. Venerable old age in an abdication suit and eyes that looked through you. Presence.

As we proceeded up Long Acre, someone tapped me on the shoulder. It was the bright spark who'd been in charge of the filming at Sir Neville's house. He was wearing his big red bovver boots. He asked me, smiling, had anything happened to Fanny by Gaslight?

Freddie was all ears.

'Who is this?'

'He works for BBC TV. This is Freddie Parts. He wrote the play.'

'You've read my play? Will the BBC do it? It's not evil.'

'The name's George S. Drake.'

'We're on our way to Heine & Logan. They've bought Freddie's novel - Hare's Rural Rides.

Freddie chopped his dentures.

'Really? Congratulations. Is Hare like Cobbet?'

'No,' I replied, 'this is different territory.'

George S. Drake smiled.

'I knew your wife at Oxford. Lady Hannah mentioned her. That's how I...give her my best.'

'You're best ain't good enough, mate.'

Making a sound with his tongue as if geeing up a horse, winking at the same time, he turned and bounced off in his big red Doc Martens. I felt weakened. Jealousy did that.

'Oh. I was about to invite him to Woffington's,' Freddie said huffily.

Why could I never hide my feelings?

A young girl dressed as a butterfly flitted by us. Her scolding mother marched ahead.

'Do come along Vanessa!'

'I am coming along, Mummy!'

She was a Red Admiral. She followed her mother with elegant playfulness. We shared genes with insects. They had a one way pumping system. Ours was a two cycle system. We shared cellulose. Maybe we shared dreams.

We came to a kebab place. In the window was a turning spit of greasy lamb. It reminded me of my father-in-law's stump.

A few weeks after I first met my wife, he demanded I present myself. Boarding a single-decker country bus, I ended up miles out in the Staffordshire country. The stop was close to the estate entrance with its massive iron gates and long driveway. This was the real thing okay. Like a guard of honour, trees edged the drive. There were acres of parkland and oak. In the misty distance was a Tudor postcard dream. My future wife waited before the massive doors.

Her father was in the swimming pool and would like to chat to me alone. I walked round to the stables - a rectangular yard of boxes, a horse head sticking out of each one. The swimming pool was for the horses. There was a black horse in the water, on a rein, being guided around by a jockey-sized man standing on a bridge affair reaching out over the pool. The goggle-eyed beast, snorting with effort, looked as if at any moment it was going to drown. But it must have been enjoying the experience, otherwise it would hardly have stayed in. After a few circuits it was led up a slope and out into the yard.

'Hallo there!'

Her father. He was naked, poised on the edge of the pool, ready to dive. Balanced on one leg. The other one was short a foot and a goodly portion of ankle.

Diving in he swam furious circuits in an aggressive crawl. Hauling himself out, perched on the side, he shook my hand, dried himself with an outsize fluffy white towel. When he got to the abbreviated limb he touched it tenderly, caressing the end with his hand, plucking at the skin, as if feeling between his toes; except there weren't any.

He told me about Crete and how lucky he'd been. His leg and knee shattered in combat, the battlefield surgeon, too busy to deal with it, instructed a young doctor to do a quick and neat job by amputating above the knee. The doctor, pity his guide, severed and stitched five inches below. The shattered knee healed and with five inches of tibia the limb, when fitted with a prosthetic, had adaptability nearer the norm than would have been the case had the surgeon operated.

The German soldier had the butcher's chopper hidden down his jackboot and had whipped it out as a last resort in the desperate hand-to-hand fighting.

'All's fair in farming and war.'

'What about love?'

'There's no future for you with me daughter. I must be blunt.'

'You are.'

Apart from a dead wife and a foot, he had everything. I had nothing. Except his daughter.

...The turning spit of lamb kebab turned him in my mind. Freddie tapped sharply on my leg with his cane.

'Boy, you've been there for the last five minutes. Is something the matter?'

We carried with us the people who meant something. All the time they were blipping electric pulses in the brain. Imagination could not be stopped. I stared at Freddie.

Why was I walking through the West End with this man? To hoist him on his mule and hand him his lance?

He halted outside a corner premises. It must, in a former life, have been a pub. It had two curving plate-glass windows and narrow double doors above which was a fascia board, the paint flaking. A man wearing peculiar footwear darted out. For the few seconds the door was open I got a glimpse of a stout, middle-aged woman wearing stern glasses and more make-up than clothes.

'My club, Freddie said proudly, Woffington's.'

The Garrick it wasn't. And maybe the woman was a man.

'Have you been here recently?'

'I was resident artist for years,' he replied cryptically.

We eventually managed to find Heine & Logan, the best new publishers in England. It was up a side street in Covent Garden. The reception area had black leather sofas, a glass-topped table, shelves of books, flowers, a 'No Smoking' warning in red and a large, flat, coloured television on a wall. On. At first I thought it was a painting. The bare floor boards were old oak. Loads of the stuff had been imported cheap from a collapsing Eastern Europe. The building, gutted and modernised, was now supported on pre-stressed concrete pillars. One of them stood bang-slap in the middle of the space and had to be avoided to reach the receptionist. She was very definitely about my age. Snug behind a self-contained desk unit, she was busy taking phone calls, buzzing the door intercom, twitching smiles, addressing envelopes - all at the same time. Black cropped hair, blackberry eyes, a swan white bosom to live and die for... On the desk were ominous piles of padded envelopes, some of them nearly as thick as Hare's Rural Rides.

Freddie, as was his habit, waited for the receptionist to speak as if she should have instantly recognised him and more importantly, known what was on his great mind. He was a beat behind the world, though his desire way ahead. I moved to calm his burgeoning tantrum.

'Good afternoon. This is Mr. Parts. Author. Hare's Rural Rides? I'm his amanuensis. Would you care to join us for lunch in Woffington's after our meeting?'

'Parts-Rinser. Parts hyphen Rinser.'

The nonplussed receptionist temporarily ignored her blipping phones. There was a book open on her desk. Chekhov. A translation by yet another chancer who hadn't a word of Russian. Perhaps, one day, there'd be a queue of Siberians lining up to do versions of Fanny by Gaslight, the little matter of not having a word of English no impediment at all. The girl's eyes were fruity, deep and dark. I did my best to dive into them. Freddie rapped the desk with his cane.

'Appointment!'

'I beg your pardon?'

'By the way - lavatory?'

Chin resting on cocked thumb, she stared at him.

'Round the corner. First on the right.'

With geriatric swagger, narrowly avoiding the concrete pillar, he disappeared. This was his second visit to the loo since we'd left home.

'Have you had lunch? Bit early I suppose.'

'I saw you being ejected. In Oxford. I know your wife. I don't envy her.' Her tone was flat, dismissive.

Spooky or what? I could tell from her face my heart was hardening quick as plaster.

'Sorr-eee!' she said, trying for a light tone.

'Why? Why don't you envy her? You don't know me, do you?'

My words were guttural, low, laden with intent...doomed.

'I said I was sorry!'

'Sorry? Like contrite? As in remorse? Are you really?'

She knew my wife - so what? George S. Drake knew her - so what? A coincidence, that's all!

'Look, I'll call security.'

Reality was a rotten brick wall. You could easily push the bricks aside, make a hole and scramble through into the garden called madness. It was as if you were having an epileptic fit without the fit. I concentrated on my tape recorder. I was smiling now, giving her the full normal, pretending I'd been kidding.

'Do you mind me recording your foot tapping against the desk?'

She stopped doing it. Freddie came back from the loo. She was more relieved than he was.

She manhandled a package, big as a concrete block, onto the desk. It could only be Hare's Rural Rides. I could see the writing on the wall -

"For collection by Mr. Parts-Rinser."

'When do you intend publishing, my dear?'

Her tone when she addressed him was both seductive and blunt as a boot.

'Thank you for popping in. And for letting us see it first. It is not for Heine & Logan. There are firms who publish pornography but we are not one of them. Mr. Letts actually read it. He was particularly pleased to know you were coming to collect. Sending such material through the post, he felt, was to risk a criminal offence. The paedophiliac content he found extremely worrying. I'm sorry I cannot be more encouraging.'

Freddie's great barrel chest heaved. She'd gotten through to him okay. A stonking blow. His gluey face was so frozen he could have been embalmed.

He staggered back against the concrete pillar. Perhaps the architect had in mind moments like this when designing it. 'You can't dissect morals wearing rubber gloves, don't you see? The fate of this land is my sole concern. She must be washed clean. Lord Crotch is England, you see.'

She didn't see. And Freddie himself had lost the plot.

'Crotch is Fanny by Gaslight, isn't it?' Do you mean The Duke of Porchester?'

He had one plot only - innocence debauched; one character only - himself. Lord Crotch/Porchester were pseudonymously interchangeable.

He whacked the desk with his cane.

'I warned you not to interrupt, boy! It is not your place.'

He'd arranged to pick up his manuscript personally if rejected. He could fantasise when summoned to do so, not about rejection, but acceptance. A pipe-dream without a pipe.

The receptionist stared at me, eager to see me gone.

'What is your name?' I asked her.

'Kate Drake.'

She flashed a necklace of teeth to do a Hollywood starlet proud. Except hers were her own.

George S. had to be her brother. He'd rung her after meeting us in Long Acre. They'd had a good laugh. Freddie and I were a pair of fools. He an ostrich, head so high he couldn't even see the sand. I an ostrich feather.

Pausing as he prepared a spectacular exit, lips frogging, Freddie picked up his rejected work. Swivelling proudly he stormed out - straight into the concrete pillar.

'Christ! Why? Why? Who placed such here?'

That was his strength. He could always spot another windmill bigger than the one had just knocked him flat.

On the swish television someone was hauling a massive tuna from the sea, its mouth round as a beer keg, its fins big as wellies. A whale appeared. The whale had lungs, a nose, bones in its flippers like hands. We were all one.

In silence, we walked through Covent Garden. There were at least two tourists per cobblestone. Freddie managed to avoid seventy per cent of them. A young woman got out of a car. Another young woman rushed up to her. They hugged, kissed and such was their enthusiasm, they almost ended up on the car bonnet. A young man got out of the car and there were more kisses, hugs and handshakes. Freddie, observing the scene, had insight peculiarly his own.

'Good Lord. Good Lord. Did you see? Two lesbians. Oh yes. One got the other and worked her on the bonnet of the motorcar. In full view. Good Lord. Good Lord.'

The flavour he gave to 'worked' was original and offensive.

It was impossible to tell what was going on in his mind. Life was a circus performed in an abattoir. And he was ringmaster.

'George S. Drake - did you notice the look he gave me?'

'What do you expect with that tape recorder in your hand all the sodding time?'

'I want to have proof we exist.'

'You think me an old bugger. All these young people here - I was the very same.'

He peered about at the regiment of youth.

'My water still works you know. I still have all my machinery intact. I'd like you to take a look.'

'I'm not a urologist, Freddie. I have no wish to look at your water. I've glimpsed enough already.'

The memory of his stockinged leg the night he was half man, half woman, would not easily be erased.

'It's in a warehouse. You could help me get it up and running. I'm not dead yet! The wheel has come full circle. I feel it. The time is right. Can't you tell?'

Holding his hand towards the rooftops, a visionary gleam in his eyes, he saw the future, feet planted firmly in the past.

'PARTING THE WATERS. GIGANTIC WATER SCENA. SENSATIONAL DANCING WATERS. PARTS PRESENTS...HIS WATER ORGAN.'

He'd just been rejected, yet here he was a few minutes later, taking huge bites into what had to be yet more sky pie.

The Gigantic Water Scena was, apparently, a water show. A demonstration of the artistic possibilities of the wet stuff, common in pre-war Vienna. Fountains, spumes, jets of water were made to sprout in time to Strauss. The blue Danube dancing to the Blue Danube. The water was stored in tanks and forced out various nozzles to spectacular effect. The Viennese went in for it big time. Londoners? Freddie had tried it on them, but modern times or television, or some other curse, finished it off.

Who would want to watch arty rain? Water belonged in grannie's whiskey.

We sat at a table in a roped off area outside a cafe. The wrapped Hare's Rural Rides left little room on the table. On the edge of a frail, modern, shiny metal chair, leaning forward on his cane, wanting as little contact with the place as possible, he ruminated.

'Little jets, big jets, I could get laughs, you know, from water. I'd give them a little jet and then - phumph! Thump them up the arse with the full panoply! The audience roared!'

He roared. Laughter mocking the gullibility of customers past, present and to come.

'In Manchester, they tried to put on a flying act during my act. A trapeze. Right over my organ. "Look here," I said, "they'll be impaled on me equipment!" Bloody fools.'

Sexual innuendo was as natural to him as breathing. From a Music Hall age, his was an innocence so naturally bawdy it was beyond moral censure. The perversions of Lord Crotch came with bowler-hat, trouserless pin-stripe, shirt, black shoes and black socks, held up by suspenders. To get from that to political respectability just add the trousers. The language of the one world seeped easily into the other.

Near the entrance to the Opera House a West Indian busker sang Bob Marley. He had a fine voice and listening to him I was happy sitting in the sun, believing everything was indeed going to be all right. Freddie bristled. He didn't even like the cobbled piazza. It looked far too European.

'We live in a peculiar time in our history, boy. They can't sing as well as pretended on their behalf. I presented my organ at the Royalty, in Holborn. A troupe of them was singing there. Do you know, there were white girls off-stage, singing into microphones, giving them vocal strength and respectability! One more minstrel myth exploded. We've got to get the truth out. The Gogs are using them to pollute our country, so they and the Jocks and Rocks can divide and conquer.

'Gogs?

'As in synagogue.'

'Rocks?'

'As in shamrocks.'

No one was safe, no one passed his test - not even the Royal Family. At core, they were about as English as Germans, Greeks...Bosnians.

In the packed piazza no one looked more respectable.

'You talk like Filfy Wilfy looks.'

The pair of armed policeman we'd seen earlier strolled into view. The black bullet-proof vests made them stand out even more.

'You're young. Therefore you're sentimental. Wilfy is scum. I knew Mrs. Gamm. She asked me to marry her. She loved my taste in cars. I was a fabulous driver.'

He held up his bunched fingers.

'I could make the water jet out like flowers. My convolvulvia, I called them. The Blackpool Tower wanted to put dancing girls in front of my waters. "They'll tear you apart, if you do," I said. "Who?" he said. "The fucking audience," I said. They loved me. That's where I met April.'

His big mottled hand gripping the knob of his cane, he shifted it about as if moving a gear lever. Engine engaged at last, he managed to get to his feet.

'I want your help. I need it.'

Instinctively, I took his elbow. Amused, he guffawed, dismissing my presumption. It wasn't the help one gave the aged he needed. He was young. It was the world had grown old.

'No. With me machinery.'

We headed towards Long Acre. On reaching Woffington's he didn't even glance at the place. Hare's Rural Rides wedged under his oxter, face grim, cane tapping his stride, he seemed to know where he was going. His face was shiny from pampering with lotions, creams, powder. A dried blob of shaving cream obliterated an ear lobe. His double-breasted suit must have been sixty years old. I doubt the one I was going to buy would last as long.

'The Government's literacy programme - it's merely to teach them how to read the instructions on the medicine bottle.'

We came along the Strand. Turning right, we walked across Waterloo Bridge, stopping when half way over. Down river the beehive bulk of St. Paul's basked in a shaft of sun. Beneath us the wide Thames water was the colour of Freddie's hair - sweeping gunmetal grey. Over on the right bank of the river were the concrete abattoirs of culture.

Freddie set down Hare's Rural Rides on the bridge parapet.

'There will come a time!'

I flicked my finger. The manuscript went plummeting through the air at thirty two seconds per pornographic second before hitting the river far below with a considerable sexy splash. A heavier parcel of soul-dandruff never drowned in mud. Gripping the parapet, a captain on his bridge, he looked down. He had no regrets. He thought he'd done it. To the waters consigned great treasure. All who rejected him, who refused all his life to share his vision, he'd finally show them. He was already charging towards the next windmill.

'We'll set it up. Invite television. Replace violence with excitement. I will show them a weapon of mass entertainment.'

'I'll arrange to be elsewhere that night.'

He waxed lyrically about pulling rusting tanks and pumps into the light of day. I would be his right-hand man.

Packed buses, folk on bikes, taxis by the dozen, traversed Waterloo Bridge.

Who were we all? Stalking loons, murderers out to strangle kids, citizens longing for the Cretan Stump, religious smarmies who knew why countries had to fall, could you believe a word out of anyone's mouth?

With Freddie you could.

'Hm-ha. Ha-hah. I met a girl once, you know. Had her several times. She was the only female I met who could grip or eject a man's prick with her cunt muscles. She'd been done at twelve by an older man. He'd picked her up outside school. Oh yes. Never did her any harm at all. She liked it. All this child-abuse fuss. Nonsense.'

'An older man, about your age?'

'Cost me fifty thousand! A lot of money then. Lost everything. I was lonely. It was a lonely life.'

'Were you imprisoned?'

'What? No. My lorry. My tanks. My equipment. The banks closed me down. I could lift pumps single-handed four men together couldn't. In Manchester I heard the stagehands say, "Ee by gum, gaffer n't human." '

His tone demeaned the men. He didn't like people. He just wanted to lead them.

'I told Billy Kantor I wanted equal billing. I'm a showman. If a showman doesn't get publicity he dies.'

'You've lived a long time without it.'

Turning his back on St. Paul's, he faced Westminster. Under his chin the wattle tightened. He looked a cock turkey mad enough to pluck itself. Big Ben donged one.

'Who will defend our corner? Who will save us? Us. Not them. England. Who?'

His pain seemed genuine. That was the scary thing. I'd keep in with him until the decanting business was sorted. I walked away.

In the Strand just ahead of me a blob of rain hit the pavement. Like someone had walked on a spider. The sky darkened. It was going to bucket. I stood in a shop doorway. Splat. Another crushed spider. Another grey inkblot. And another. People walked faster. Traffic lights, car head-lamps, bled. The noble buildings, theatres, shops, buses, lost any colour they had. Everything looked scared as the wind picked up. Pigeons squatted on high window sills for shelter. An Agincourt of arrows showered down. In seconds the gutters ran full. An oily spectrum skimmed the road like a piece of rainbow had fallen. Colour itself was cowed, drained of light. An unseen hand had drawn a black canvas across the city. Every shop door was wedged with people desperate for cover. A few brave souls, under umbrellas, scuttled in front of the hounding rain. Not Freddie. He came walking slowly along, head erect, disdain incarnate and soaking. Soaking to the skin. Cane tapping, hair hanging, he wasn't going to hurry and certainly wasn't going to shelter with the common herd. Suit wringing wet, he looked as if he'd just emerged from the Thames. I hid behind a bunch of be-tartaned Japanese.

The rain stopped, the clouds disappeared, the pavements swarmed with people. The two armed policemen came ambling along, cradling their guns. Dry as bone. On the political barometer the needle was stuck on fear. Fear had a government subsidy. On the streets of London fear was medieval, like the fear of hell.

But not all the money in the city could cast a shadow like that first drop of rain.

I went to an Asian tailor round the back of Regent Street. Having the universal access of a doctor's stethoscope, soon one end of his tape was at my groin. The shop floor was covered in hard, green, bumpy-lumpy lino. Suits smelling of wool and textiles dangled everywhere. I looked at myself in the full mirror. How could I spend so much money when African women were scrambling on dusty roads for a tiny bag of rice? The tailor told me he was closing down in two days time.

'I am going into food and drink. People have to eat. You happy - you spend on drink. You sad - you eat. I am out of this. Congestion charges? Who dreamed that one up? Political situation here now is impossible. The M.P's - they bonking all the time. How they do that? Bonk, bonk, bonking. Why vote for man who bonking all the time? Bonk, bonk. They all bonkers.'

'It's the ones who don't bonk you got to watch.'

'Bonking is full time job. But it never advertised at Labour Exchange.'

I told him my wife was paying for the suit as I handed him a wad thick as the new testament.

'You have very rich wife? That is good that is bad. That is bad that is good.'

After blowing this verbal dandelion, he laughed and shook goodbye.

'Maybe you my last customer.'

'Maybe you my last outfitter.'

I'd bought a new suit for no purpose at all. It wasn't like I needed it for a job interview. I'd changed the fig leaf.

There was a crowd outside Hamley's toy shop. Excited children looked at the window displays. On the edge of the crowd was a woman in a burkha. It was expensive black material, trimmed and criss-crossed with white. Covered from head to foot, as if wearing a tent, only her eyes were visible. Her eyes were naked. Seeing me look at her, she hurried away. I had looked in her light. What had she seen in mine?

I wandered round the West End enjoying the anonymity of the streets. As long as you didn't come from a place, you were free. No parents to weigh you down. No bulb burning, awaiting your return. In the streets you were more on your own than in a prison cell.

On my way home I met Miss Jackpot - Muzie. The horse he'd mentioned to my wife at the decanting meeting hadn't won. Coyney Girl. He was angry. As if it was my fault. He followed me along the street.

'If you'd saved all the money you've lost you'd be rich.'

When I reached home Miss Chats and some Town Hall types were outside looking at the building. And making notes. Miss Chats said they'd be able to move us out very soon. She said it in a confidential, smiling way, as if including me in a great secret. She wore a dark blue dress and dark blue high-heels. I could smell her lilac perfume. They waited for me to say something.

'Care for a boiled egg, Miss Chats?'

I dodged past them and slammed the side door behind me.

My wife was waiting. Freddie had been down, accusing me of throwing his book in the Thames. He demanded apology and compensation, without which he'd have no alternative but the law.

'Not guilty, your honour. He threw it in himself.'

'He says you did.'

'Maybe. Come on, I'll try on the suit.'

She liked it. Now she was all smiles.

'Why don't we have a baby?'

'A baby? Just one? Like in China? I want half a dozen.' I did.

Before she met me, a horse-box load of Hurrah Henrys had driven to her door. All of them in a state of social grace. What swung it for me, I think, was a trip up Park Hall Hills. There was an old blackthorn and ivy tree I remembered from childhood. I climbed it, silent as could be, and with infinite delicacy, parting branch and leaf, I found a sleeping tawny owl. She climbed up beside me. We stared at the owl, at its big moth face, shared its stillness. It was a moment stolen from normal. We kissed.

Back on earth we kissed again. She told me she could love me. If I could love her. That was it.

We heard a loud knocking at our door. It had to be Freddie. She wanted me to ignore him but I was determined to confront him.

It was Rosa Gibbs, clutching a bottle of Lucozade.

'I can't get no bleeder to open this.'

She'd been wandering the street looking for someone to unscrew the top. That could happen in a city. She was no bigger than a fat mouse. A nutmeg. A button. A boil. A pimple. An apple seed. Her hair was frizzy as wire wool. Despite the worries of the world, her sallow hangmouse face twinkled gameness.

'He's gorn dahn agin. Can you git 'im up?'

Gibbs was on the floor in a remarkably similar position and posture to last time. As if he crash-landed, face first, in exactly the same way, on the same spot, every time he fell out of bed. Lying so still, he was like a work in progress; a china clay figure, abandoned for the moment on the floor. His bare chest was white as cigarette paper. The Pisa pile of newspapers at the end of the bed was even higher. The bed was littered with lottery tickets and play slips. The only thing could get Rosa and Gibbs out of here was the jackpot. Or the coffin. Unless, of course, we were all decanted.

''allo, mate. Ta again.'

I lifted him under the shoulders. He seemed heavier than last time.

'No, no, not the bed. Put me standing by me Zimmer.'

I had to lower him to the floor again - the Zimmer frame was behind me.

'Fuck yah. And double fuck yah,' Rosa squeaked angrily.

'That's enough, Rosa! Make the tea.'

He was cold to the touch. How long had he been lying there? They couldn't afford to turn the central heating on. Gripping him under the arms again, I managed to lug him to the Zimmer. He grabbed at it and, with sheer arm strength, held himself up. His legs were knackered. However dire his predicament, it couldn't get the better of his ego.

'Did I tell you I taught judo to the Police? The Chief-Inspector asked me. My fighting weight, incidentally, was 10 st. 3 lbs. I won every contest. I retired undefeated.'

At that precise moment - as if it were a comedy routine - his pyjama bottoms fell down. Naked to the ankles, he clung to the Zimmer, like a man on a trapeze. His bum was pale as moon. Rosa poured herself a glass of Lucozade. I lifted the pyjamas up his legs and he managed to get a hold on them. Unphased, as if what had happened was a mildly interesting occurrence, he commented,

'Ah, no wonder - button missing. I've got a spare. A good soldier always has back-up.'

'Gorblimey. You need your ears boxing!' Rosa exclaimed, as if she were about to do it there and then.

I grabbed him from behind and lugged him to the bed. He lay back on the pillows, his mousey peeking out from its grey nest.

'What's it like out?' he asked, in a tone of humdrum ordinariness.

'The weather you mean?' He was sharp enough to grin as he scrabbled with his hand to cover up.

Even if the weather was lovely out, what possible benefit could he extract from the information? The world was a bloody extraordinary place to be. To cope, you had to pretend it was utterly normal. What if the cat on the pile of papers, the peeling wallpaper, the plastic bottle by the bed, the Zimmer frame, became my existence?

'Don't look so worried, matey chum. I want you to do something for me. Two things as a matter of fact.'

He pointed at a blanket thrown across something along the wall. He wanted me to remove it. I did so, revealing a very old bicycle.

A sturdy, post-war model, it had a stout bell, a lamp (badly corroded), a saddle made from black leather, thick as army boots and, hanging from the back of the saddle, a leather case for a puncture repair kit. The tyres were flat and frayed. Spider webs strung the front wheel spokes. A cocooned pupa dangled from the crossbar. The whole thing was rotting with rust. It must have been a hell of a time since Gibbs last rode it. I'd be happy to dump it for him in some skip or other.

This was not what he had in mind at all. What he wanted was resurrection. Would I build some kind of structure to support the bicycle and make it free-standing, the back wheel off the floor? He would then be able to mount it. Daily exercise would restore him. Once his legs were back in full working order, he'd be right as rain.

Only minutes before he could barely stand at the Zimmer frame. In the kitchen Rosa rattled cups.

'Get the power in me legs back - bingo! See what I mean? If all goes well. There's no reason why it shouldn't, is there? You'll be able to do it for me, won't you?'

If it proved a botch-up, would the fault be mine? Rosa scurried in from the kitchen.

'Who'll pick you up? Who'll pick you up offa the floor? You're going nowhere, Gibbs. Unless you grow new legs. Do what you're told or I'll box your bleeding ears!'

'That's enough, Rosa.'

'What? What did you say?'

'Show some politeness.'

'A box on the ears, that's what you'll get.'

'It'll make no difference to me.'

'Nah. 'cos you're 'ead is full of sawdust!'

'So much for sympathy.'

The exchange was well-worn ritual. A path hacked through the jungle of days. Life was a death sentence. With no appeal.

What he was asking me to do was build a Zimmer frame for the bicycle. A dicey task. He wouldn't hear of me buying him an exercise bike.

We could hear Wally below in his room, singing.

'Give me the shoelace

Give me the yam

You got the car

But I got the phone. Ring-ring.'

He could only have made it up himself.

We were all like the owl up that tree. We thought we were safe in the branches. But the ivy was choking the tree. And sooner or later someone was going to shift us. Remove us from our roosts.

Hearing Freddie's descending footsteps, I whipped out to confront him in the hallway. Gibbs shouted at me to come back.

I was a tad scared. But we had to stick together. I wanted to confront him.

He was taken aback to see me - arms folded, legs crossed, leaning against the wall.

'What's all this about me throwing your book in the river? Apparently you told my wife. Was it not you yourself knocked it off the bridge?'

He was wearing slippers, black trousers and a big brown, polo-neck woollen jumper. The jumper was spattered with paint low on the left side. He smiled at me first but then his forehead went red. In orotund voice he fiercely declaimed,

'You do realise you have put yourself in such a position I can sue? It is regrettable you make me feel it necessary to do so. Your indifference to the discomfort of others appears obvious. A very mean attitude. What alternative do you leave but an injunction in the High Court? Woofington's legal team are mine too. Your wife, incidentally, agrees with me.'

'Agrees with what?'

The hallway immediately outside his door was covered with dust, brought down on his feet every time he descended.

'That book was my crowning glory.'

'Your glory is drowned. I'm the only friend you got. Why sue me? And leave my wife out of it.'

'Hm-hm. Hah-ha. Guilty mind.'

'What do you mean?'

'We know so little about you. Who you are, what you are. Your family. For instance what's your name?'

'Joey.'

'Joey? Really? Joey? It's a clown's name. A good old slosher's name.'

Slosh was a circus term. In between acts, the clown put on diverting antics - slosh. Every ringmaster needed a clown.

As I leaned against the wall I felt the damp on my shoulder. I could taste it in the back of my throat. Like I'd bitten a weed. Out on the return roof, the expansion tank was open to the elements and the birds.

On the strength of the name Joey, his demeanour changed.

'Could you hire a rather large van, Joey? We'll inspect the equipment first, of course. We'll need somewhere to exhibit. Any ideas, Joey?'

'Are you still going to sue me?'

'I'd rather not, Joey. Membership of Woffington's will be yours. If you help me.'

'Is Woffington's a transvestite place?'

I was thinking of the man we saw rushing out as we passed on our way to Heine & Logan. He'd worn a brown herring-bone overcoat, obscuring all but the hem of what looked suspiciously like a petticoat. His golden footwear was decidedly ambiguous. And why was he darting away from the place quick as a kestrel?

'I painted the main picture over the dining room fireplace. You'll see. We dined with royalty there. Before the war. Mrs. Whats-her-name, she was a man, you do know that, don't you?'

'Mrs. Gamm?'

'What? No. Simpson. And he, bless him, hunted in puff sewers. In Woffington's we were all in the know.'

The more shocking a picture he painted of England the more urgent her need of rescue. He was still the only man could do it.

'I have to go now.'

'Really, Joey? Where?'

'I do have a life of my own. I think.'

'Earthy! He's no artist who fears risk.'

'He's no artist who cuts his throat in public.'

'Fanny by Gaslight is my Twelfth Night. Lord Crotch, my King Lear. Let him crawl to the grave via his bank accounts. He will never sit at my table.'

'Who - Lord Crotch?'

'No. Earthy. A silly Joey gets a whipping you know. Be warned.'

Tramping back up his stairs, feet thumping the treads, the frail partitioning separating the stair-case from the rest of the house, shook as if about to fall.

'...Two, three...Christ!...Four...Why? Why?..Five...Joey.'

Did I really knock his manuscript off Waterloo Bridge? I remembered his hands on the parapet. Claw hands. Owl hands. I shouted up after him,

'Freddie, I take it you are no longer interested in Miss Chats getting us out?'

He'd reached his landing. I could hear him panting.

'What, what? Chats bitch? If they want me out - they'll have to carry me. In a wooden box.'

That would be one heavy coffin.

I didn't bandy my name around. In a city you didn't have to. I was called after my grandfather. He'd been a coal miner. For every hour he spent underground at the coal-face, he made sure to spend an hour overground. In fresh air. He fished along the Trent & Mersey canal. In Etruria. One day round our house, someone asked him about the state of his chest after years as a miner. There was a fire - newspaper, sticks, coal - set in the open fireplace but not yet lit. He looked at it and said,

'If I spat on that lot, I'd kindle it.'

His words were as graphic as his big, black and blue hands. My father was a teacher. He always referred to the classroom as the chalk-face. As if trying to link himself to his father. He too spent hours along the canal. In Etruria. Same spot always. Sitting for ages, especially at weekends. He had all the gear - rods, a special canvas seat, a big umbrella, tins of writhing worms, any amount of hooks, various nets. And me. He insisted I came with him all the time. It was boring and usually cold. Spaced along on both sides of the canal sat dozens of men. All after the same fish. No one ever seemed to catch it.

One day he slipped away to get cigarettes and left me in charge of his line. There was an old boot lying along the towpath. I hooked it on and cast it into the water. When he returned with the ciggies, he fell for it hook, line and sinker. The other anglers enjoyed the joke. But such was his vile temper, he chased me the whole way home. His rage spilled over onto my mother. She tried to defend me. He said I'd shamed him in public. Made a fool of him. He'd break my neck if I did the like again. I was very scared.

'He's a moody man, your dad. A weak man. You shouldn't have done that, Joey.'

I heeded her. I lived a wary life.

Rosa Gibbs asked me to post a letter. First person I saw in the Post Office was Filfy Wilfy. He sat studying a racing paper. His bumble bee eyebrows were laden with dandruff. An elderly woman sat beside him. Her husband was doing the lotto. She shuddered, startled, when Filfy peered at her over the top of his paper.

'New York? Like to go there? New York?'

The more ingratiating he was, the more effeminate he sounded. She was afraid to say anything in case she upset him. His grin was sinister. He had more teeth than a

BIG PARTS

hen. Two rows of pins.

'All them muggins! Central Park! Terrrrible. Terrrrible.'

He moved seamlessly to even more profound matters.

'They can do all sorts nowadays. Clone sheep. Grow bodily parts. Kidney. Lung. Heart. They've grown an ear on the back of a mouse. Next thing you'll see policemen with ears on the back of their 'eads. What's to stop 'em growing the male member? Who'll need a man as such? They gonna come up with a penis. It'll be in control of the Government. Any woman wants a baby will have to fill in a form. Apply for a poke from the national prick. Men will be redundant. It'll be totally unfair.'

Indignant at the prospect, he flapped his newspaper. The elderly lady, without waiting for her husband, waddled out to the safety of the street. Wilfy buried his head back in the paper.

He reminded me of my father. He had total concentration, head at a slight angle, lips pursed, chalky skin. Then a sudden challenging look at you.

People were like snowflakes. But only in the general drift.

What did I fear? Being decanted. I'd try to make the bicycle contraption for Gibbs. I'd run errands for Rosa. I'd keep an eye on Wally. I'd help Freddie with his water exhibition.

You had to live out of your head or out of your blood.

Did I really flick Hare's Rural Rides into the Thames? My wife believed I craved attention whilst obliterating my attempts to achieve it. I therefore suffered from excessive ego, balanced by excessive guilt. When I was a kid I saw guilt as cold grease on a frying pan.

Rosa had said of Gibbs, 'He'd be better off dead!' The woman in the house next door ate cat food. My father-in-law had his foot chopped off on Crete.

There were objects so big in outer space, light couldn't escape from them. They were there but couldn't be seen. April was a big object with no light shining at all. Her imagined world sucked it dry. Was beauty synonymous with goodness? Hardly. And love didn't confer ownership. But without it marriage was feudal.

You had to be lucky. I was lucky. I loved dodging about the streets. A good life was doing nothing. Doing nothing was doing something. Doing a little was doing a lot.

'Rum-tum-tum-tum-tardyum
From Cookshill Green to Carser cum
Me mother cum fetch me father whome
Me father's drunk an' wunna cum home
Rum-tum-tum-tum-tardyum."

My wife took a shower at least once a day or lay in the bath, her face plastered with white clay. It was supposed to purge the pores of dirt, excess oils, while "firming, refining, moisturizing."

We had no end of hot water. Until the Trust decided we needed a new water pump. Everyone was going to get one. Our tank and pump were in a cupboard under the stairs. There was nothing wrong with the old pump. I phoned Miss Chats and asked her what was the point of putting in a new pump when we were about to be decanted and the place pulled apart?

'The programme of works calls for it. The plumbers will arrange a mutually convenient time.'

From the moment they put in the new pump we had nothing but trouble. The controlling switch mechanism was so state of the art it hardly ever worked. We had a spate of plumbers round trying to fix it.

One geezer came in with more tools than a troop of monkeys. A fag in the corner of his mouth, he stood staring for ages at a mural my wife had painted on the wall. It was three staves of music meticulously draughted - treble clef and treble clef and base, complete with notation. She didn't write down the words of the particular ditty. She'd done it to cheer up an otherwise drab hallway. Only someone capable of reading music, with a rare ear and preferably from Stoke, could work out the tune. Many tried. It was a chant peculiar to a particular part of North Staffordshire. The plumber decided to have a go. About thirty, lank fair hair, blue jeans, desert boots, T-shirt, he faced the music, moving the fag in his mouth from side to side. He asked, did I know what it was? I pretended not. Gripping the fag in his teeth, he nodded his head a few times.

'That there, you know what it is? I fink it's Mozart. It is. It's Mozart. You can tell by looking at it. My whole family was musical. Me dad was a great listener. To brass bands. Not military bands like. Means he 'ad a great ear.'

'So did Van Gogh.'

Dropping the remains of his cigarette straight from his lips to the floor, he squirmed it with his desert boot. Getting down on his knees, he stuck his head in the cupboard containing the hot tank and pump.

Five minutes later he hadn't moved. He could have been praying.

'Oi,' he grunted, turning round, 'can you do us a favour?'

'Sure,' I said, thinking he wanted me to help in some way.

'Can you not watch while I'm working? It does me 'ead in. Standin' behind me like. Lookin' over me shoulder. Drives me fucking mad.'

'Oh. I was just checking. I thought you were dead.'

'What?'

'Pardon?'

Next day we privately hired a self-employed plumber. He was in and out in an hour, new pump installed, job done, hot water restored, my wife happy. Two days later

'Mozart' came back with a mate. I didn't tell them they were surplus to requirement. The two of them put their heads into the cupboard.

'I can't odds it,' said the mate, 'ain't nuffing wrong 'ere. They musta sent us to the wrong ad-dress.'

'Nah, nah,' said 'Mozart', 'ang on. It's only Trust, this place, right? Take that new one out, stick in this one I got here in me bag. Bosh.'

I emerged from the kitchen.

'Sorry to look over your shoulder, Wolfgang, but this particular engagement has been cancelled, by order of the Archbishop of Salzburg. Fuck off!'

Utterly matter-of-fact, they picked up their tool bags and, without a word, left. As if the charade was a daily occurrence.

A few hours later, Miss Chats phoned me. She'd had a complaint from the plumbers. Had I verbally abused them? If so, I had broken the tenancy agreement. It was a serious matter.

'Miss Chats, what colour underwear, if any, are you wearing today? I'm doing a survey on the hidden chromatics of London. We'd appreciate your co-operation. This call may be recorded for training purposes.'

She hung up.

Freddie's equipment was stored in a lock-up just off the High Road, under what was the Bedford to Brighton railway. There were a number of these caverns. Originally a series of arches, they were erected solely to support the railway as it spanned the busy road below. When the city crushed up closer to the tracks, the arches were bricked up at one end. With the addition of doors they made excellent storage spaces, garages, workshops. Freddie signed a lease for his arch in 1960 and, able to afford the rent, held on to it through the shaky metamorphosis of the public company into a private one.

Once a year, he poured oil into and over the padlock but never ventured inside.

That was about to change. I watched as he fumbled with the key. The hinges, sick with rust, the door had to be shouldered in. Foul dank air immediately engulfed us. Stabs of daylight made little impact on a solid wall of blackness. A garage mechanic from the next door space ran us out an extension lead.

The bulb's cheesy light spread thinly over bulky shapes thick with dust. Brick walls arched up to a high vaulted roof space. The place was cold as a ruined church. The black bricks fanning gracefully upwards were a monument to the skills of tradesmen dead for a hundred and thirty years. The place was flagged with hanging cobwebs - dull regimental colours of death and years. A giant snail-trail of water glistened down the back wall. Overall though, the place seemed remarkably water-tight. A train rumbled overhead.

I began to make sense of the bulky shapes sitting on the floor. Tanks. Five in all. Water tanks. Four of them measuring six by six and four feet deep. Beside them on the ground were fire-engine type hoses, mostly uncoiled, as if dumped in a hurry. Assorted valves, jets and spouts were scattered all over the place. Some of these were ringed on metal tubing, others separate. Piles of them. Bumping against a mound of black drapes, I knocked over a sheet of tin. In a choking cloud of dust, it hit the concrete floor with a tremendous clatter.

'Ha-hah. Thunder-sheet. It commenced with a bang. Grabbed their attention right away. Then the music. Then the lights. Then - my water.'

'All that just to have a pee?'

'What?'

There were spotlights stored in one of the tanks. In another were old box loudspeakers. I pulled a spotlight out. Inches of congealing dust and rust almost obscured its form.

'And you haven't been in here since 1960, Freddie?'

'Came off the road then. See there - that's a generator pump, diesel-driven. Oh yes. I could lift that just by myself. Rather. Oh yes. Oh yes.'

Our footsteps were visible on the floor, so deep was the dust. Black snow. My throat clogged on the foul air. I shifted the light closer to Freddie. His face gleamed. He could have been an archaeologist in a pyramidic tomb laden with treasure. Or a general surveying the rusted weaponry of his greatest ever triumph. His huge shadow spread across the back wall, right up to the roof. He brooded massively. A ghost come back to haunt itself. Could he resurrect by willpower alone? He stared at the heap of drapes. Bending down he picked something up. It was a plastic daffodil. He beat dust from it with his hand.

'Made this myself. Some of the towns didn't have fresh flowers, can you believe that? She was so young, so innocent, so beautiful.'

Shivering at the memory, he hummed a tune, then tossed the flower onto the drapes.

'Who?'

'April.'

Behind him, a shaft of sun stole shyly in. Intensifying, it forced the dark to step aside. A golden river of light now ran across the floor. The toe-caps of Freddie's brogues dipped the edge. Dust swam into the beam and revolved smooth as goldfish in a tank of water.

In the farthest corner I noticed a rather large object. It looked like a bed with maybe a wardrobe dumped on it. Going closer, the bulb held before me, my perceptions sharpened. It wasn't furniture. It was a motor car. Slowly, its outline emerged from a cloak of dust, rust and grime. Fuzzy with cobwebbed age, it was hard to pin down to a firm image. There must have been three inches of congealed black dust on the roof. From the vaulted brickwork way above, a drop of water fell. It fell right through the car. It was then I noticed the hole. Rust and water had eaten through the roof. Probably from the day the car had been abandoned, a drip-drop drilled slowly through the metal. Time and bitter cold had made the drop diamond sharp. The hole was big enough to dangle the bulb down through it. The car filled with misty light. The leather seats, carpet, chassis, were all rotted. It could have been a ship wreck at the bottom of the sea.

The front bumper hung off. Damp had eaten through the holding screws. The car was metal. What hope flesh?

'What was is it, Freddie?'

'Auntie Rover. P4 saloon. We drove to Brighton. April loved the sea. Ha-hah! She adored speed. Boot to the floor. Oh yes. Rather!'

Over by the entrance, in a ray of sunlight, the dust in Brownian movement turned and turned.

'April - I did it all for her. She was the innocent victim of an incestuous parent, I told you that, did I not? I took her with me. How could I leave her behind?'

'A nice behind isn't easy to leave.'

'What? What?'

Anger puffed his face. His chest, even his shadow, swelled.

'You need treatment, Joey. You load language like a politician. You sicken it. I am tired of you all. If I die, bury me in here and turn the key.'

If? Only if?

His plan was to drag the tanks and all the other assorted equipment into the light of day, and restore them to working order. Hoses were to be inspected for leaks, the black drapes repaired where moth-eaten, the diesel-driven pumps restarted. I would be his linchpin. I was to engage help, he would pay. Eventually, we'd move the entire shebang to a suitable venue where he'd re-create his dancing waters for a select audience of television producers.

'Men of discernment, taste, courage.'

'What about women?'

'Gender is immaterial to me. You know that.'

It was my job to find the venue. I was to spend as much money as needed. Within reason. That sounded like I'd better not spend too much. Another impossible task.

He particularly wanted me to get a roll of canvas. This he would turn into a banner to be hung above the action.

"Parting the Waters. Gigantic Water Scena. Sensational Dancing Waters. Parts Presents His Water Organ."

'What is a water organ? Nothing extremely personal, is it?'

'I'm no longer in possession of mine. The bailiffs seized it. Sods. No wonder England hit the buffers. Why kick a man when he's down?'

'In case he gets up again?'

There were a few lengths of timber lying around outside an archway used by a carpenter. It was all I needed to build the bike-steadying contraption for Phil Gibbs.

'Today, to believe in God, is to be a class traitor. April and I are the only people in the street who go to church. Have you noticed?'

'Were you to address the multitude, what would you say?'

'My name is Freddie Parts-Rinser. I have come to save you.'

Jesus walked on water and turned it into wine. Freddie could make the water dance.

'Canterbury no longer believes in the Resurrection. At root that is the truth. That's why the theatre is dead.'

Freddie went home. He was an Adam trying to re-enter Eden, having surely evicted himself.

I decided to see Miss Chats.

At Reception there was an Indian woman, clip-board in hand, vetting people. She wore a badge - "Fat Is An Issue." She must have weighed twenty stone.

The top floor had a series of offices - Housing Admin. Housing Management. Programme Manager, Property Services (Planned). Housing Officers. Income Recovery Office. Rents & Housing Administrator (Ms. Polly Sting). Tenants Forum. Tenant Initiatives Officer. Assistant Director (Property Services). Maintenance & Repairs. Chitchat - tenants' newsletter. Housing Services Director (Miss Chats). Cyclical Decoration Contracts Dept.

I was in the heart of an expanding empire. I went straight into Miss Chat's office. She was busy at her cluttered desk. Her baldy hairstyle revealed cranial bumps and bulges. Her brown leather jacket matched her leather chair. On a wall were graphs, calendars, planners and a big memo - "MEMO TO GOVERNMENT". On another wall hung a poster of Madonna, a dumb-bell in each hand, biceps looking hard as grain-fed rats.

'May I call you Samantha, Miss Chats? The reason I came to see you is this. Why don't we buy the house? My wife and I. That would save you a lot of bother. I'd look after the others. We'd pay the market price.'

'No.'

'Why not?'

'We are a registered charity. Tenants have not been given the legal right to buy. Our stock of houses is for the underprivileged. Can you really say you are underprivileged?'

'I'm from Stoke-On-Trent.'

'If your wife can afford to buy, she can buy in the private market. We have finalised plans to decant you. You will be able to view the alternative accommodation very soon. We will assist with removal.'

'This office reeks of sex and you are its source. You should be very proud of that.'

'There's an available house over in Thatch Lane. Public transport is excellent.'

'You have seducer's eyes. Tenants of all ages, some of them very ill, are willing to die for you.'

'When vacating, all flats must be completely emptied of furniture, carpets and personal effects.'

'If you ever attempted to seduce your tenants I can't imagine anyone objecting. May I call you Miss Chats, Samantha?'

'We will arrange to have the electricity and gas meters read. And the phone disconnected.'

'Mr. Parts-Rinser, Freddie, living on the top floor, yeah? He may be embarking on a series of nudes and I just wonder would you pose for him? The nudes are on biblical themes. I'll only agree to be Adam, if you agree to be Eve.'

'Don't come here again without an appointment.'

'The local paper is interested in an in-depth article on your hegemony here. You're way more powerful than a private landlord. They are amenable to the law. You are the law.'

'Silly Man. Go away.'

She dialled a number. I fled.

I wondered how I'd actually do the job for Gibbs. My effort would probably make a New Building Trust carpenter look like Chippendale. Some kind of frame was required to support the back wheel...I'd cut two lengths of wood and nail the two pieces together to form the frame's base... The other bits of wood were three by two's. I'd cut two of them an inch higher than the back axel...nick out slots at the top to hold the axel...nail the other ends to the planks. Bingo.

'Oh no. Oh no. Sorry. Sorry. Whoops. Oh no. Sorry. Agh. Jesus. This bloody saw is useless. Not again! Sorry. Don't worry about the sawdust - I'll sweep it up. Agh. Sorry darling. Oh no.'

I was making the frame to support Gibbs and his bike. Manipulating a six foot plank in a small kitchen, you couldn't avoid whacking the sink unit, the cupboards, the dresser. I was Laurel and Hardy rolled into one.

When my wife was really angry, she'd sing a few lines from her old school song. Bluntly cutting across your stupidity.

"Founded on truth our school endures

Firm buttressed with deep loyalty
Stafford's meadows, hills and vales..."
She'd usually break off at that point; the song no longer able to contain her temper.
She could never understand why the world wasn't as uncomplicated as she was. Why
I wasn't. But deep down, actually not that deep, she had her own complications.

Her father's severed leg shadowed her life. She dreamed of going to Crete and
searching for it. The morning after dreaming she'd wake up unsettled. Her father never
tried to hide the reality. Sometimes, when the end of the stump irritated, he'd remove
the prosthesis and, in front of the open fire, gin and tonic in one hand, soothing cream
in the other, cosset himself.

That image from childhood remained powerfully in her mind. There were all too
many fleshy reminders. Fellatio for instance was always a risky entertainment. Dipping
the Member for Eden in Bollinger and tying a ribbon and bells round it did help. A
little.

Sawing timber troubled her too. If I was the one doing the sawing.

' "Founded on truth our school endures.

Firm buttressed with deep loyalty..." '

'I'm sorry, but I promised Gibbs, I'd...Agh!'

I'd cut my hand. Not badly but deep enough for blood. She shrieked. I nailed two
lengths of the plank together. She could no longer bear to watch. She lurked in the
sitting room, singing in mock opera,

'BotchBotchBotchBotchBotchBotchBotchBotchBotch...à la Eine Kleine Nachtmusik.

Using a hand saw required smooth power and grace. You had to let the teeth do
the cutting. Effing and blinding aren't teeth.

'BotchBotchBotchBotchBotchBotchBotchBotchBotch.'

I knocked a cup clean off the sink draining board.

Bashing on regardless, I cut two lengths of three by two, each fifteen inches long.
These I'd nail to my sandwiched planks. First though, I had to cut out V-shaped slots,
which would take the bike's back-axel. This was a tricky operation. I decided to get
up on the table and kneel on the lengths, the better to secure them as I sawed. Not
having the ends far enough out over the table edge, when the teeth nibbled through
the wood, they also nibbled into the table. An oak table. It had been her mother's.

'You stupid plonker, get out! Give me, give me that! Get out! That cup was
Wedgwood. Look, look at it! Mummy's table! You totally unreconstructed botching
nutcase! Cackhand! Plonker! Caterpillar! Phil Gibbs has had a whole series of strokes.
He's beyond help. You also went to the office and talked dirty to Samantha. Don't try
and deny it. She phoned me.'

Saw, hammer, nails, planks, V-slotted lengths - she dumped the lot out on the patio.
She then thumped me out after them. And bolted the door.

I'd wait for the storm to blow itself out. I'd gotten away fairly lightly in the circumstances. Miss Chats had spilled my beans, which was not very sporting of her.

Banished to the patio I nailed the V-slots on either side of my plank sandwich. Was there a carpenter's word for two short planks? Plankety-plank? A blob of blood seeped into the timber. I'd wrecked the kitchen, strained further my wife's tolerance but at least, at last, the job was done.

I went round the side of the house, up the front steps, and rang Rosa's bell.

'Gibbs is waitin' on yer. He didn't fink you was goin' to show.'

Gibbs, when he saw me come into the room, with surprising energy flung the bed clothes aside. He watched excitedly as I centred my turbo-trainer on the only uncluttered piece of floor-space available - between the wardrobe and the Pisa tower of newspaper. The cat, as usual, snoozed on top of the pile.

By the bed, on the floor, the plastic milk bottle was full. Those bottles with their screw-on tops were just the job.

I lifted the battered bicycle away from the wall. Grains of rust rattled inside the frame. The bell was about the only thing that appeared as if it might still be in some kind of working order. The tyres were flat as pancakes. The bike was little more than a rusty ghost. As if reading my thoughts, Gibbs said,

'It don't matter about the tyres, mate. I'm not going nowhere, at the moment, just yet, am I? I got a pump. Somewhere. Rosa? Where's my pump?'

'Shut up.'

Out in the middle of the room the bike looked even worse than in its customary position by the wall. A pedal rubber fell off.

Rosa with little enthusiasm swished at cobwebs with a rolled up newspaper. Then she rammed the newspaper in under the bed.

'It won't work, how could it? You wasted the man's time.'

The wardrobe had a mirror, cloudy with dust. Gibbs glanced at his dim reflection. The bike was in the glass too. He watched as I placed the back wheel between my strips of wood. There was too much clearance between wood and axel. My plankety-plank was six inches wide. The axel was only four. Gingerly pressing the strips together, I raised the wheel and lowered the axel into the V's. It fitted perfectly. The bike was now free-standing. I turned a pedal with my hand. The chain needed oiling; but no major problem - the back wheel was actually revolving. You beauty. I'd done it. My contraption worked. Could anything be simpler? Gibbs was eager to take control.

'I raced Reg Harris. On the Bath road.'

'Who?'

'Who? Did you hear that, Rosa? He asked me who? The best cyclist this country ever produced. That's who. Fixed wheel.'

'The wheel IS fixed. I've fixed it in the V slots.'

'No. Reg Harris. Fixed wheel sprinter. Without compare.'

Rosa sat on a three-legged stool by the door. As if taking up her corner in a boxing ring.

The moment had come when Gibbs had to prove himself. Adjusting his tartan cap, determined, he reached out for his Zimmer frame and skittery-legged, managed to stand. Rosa, a cigarette in the corner of her mouth, smoke streaming up past her eye, stared at him.

'Gordelpus.'

Now that Gibbs was on his feet, my wooden frame didn't seem quite so roadworthy. He weighed about ten stone and didn't look as if he could stand without the aid of the Zimmer. He was a sick man. How was I going to transfer him from Zimmer to bike?

The man who outpaced Reg Harris on the Bath Road wasn't about to back down. He must have been a tough bugger in his heyday. Small, wide-shouldered, strong-armed, for a dying man he was still in good nick. But only down to his navel. His legs were wasted hairpins, white as snow. There was more meat on a chicken wish-bone. I held the bike by the handlebars, my legs either side of the front wheel. If he wasn't able to transfer his hands from the Zimmer to the bike, the experiment was over.

Casually he asked -

'What's the weather like?'

'Makes no difference what it's like. You ain't going nowhere!'

Rosa leaned nervously forward on her stool as he grabbed a handlebar with his right hand. His other hand was still on the Zimmer frame. Somehow, he flopped his arm over, grabbed the handlebar with his left hand and, very wobbly, righted himself. All his weight was now leaning on the handles. But how was he going to get his leg over the cross bar? He'd hardly done anything yet and already he was breathing hard.

'They don't make 'em like this anymore,' he said, addressing the rust-eaten mirage.

'Think you can do it?' I asked him.

'Get me legs in working order and I can get out into Epping Forest again. I did photography one time. Still do as a matter of fact. One day I photographed a ghost in Epping. I got it on film. Rosa will tell you. I was snapping a tree. When I developed it, there it was, a spectral figure. No explanation. Where is it? Search that drawer, Rosa, will you please.'

She didn't move. The crafty cat hopping down from the pile of newspapers, took up a safer position by a chest of drawers heaped with clothes and sheets. The drawers were all pulled out, contents bulging, spilling. I doubted they would ever be shoved back in again. Somewhere amongst all the dunnage was the picture of a ghost.

On the wall above the drawers was a calendar three years out of date. They didn't need a current one. Each day was the same.

Did they have an income? A pension? Welfare? Whatever they had, it was the minimum. Was it lack of money frayed the soul?

Gibbs began to grunt as he tried to will his leg, his sapless right leg, over the crossbar. The only movement I could detect was in his big toe. It had a long shiny, convex nail.

'What if I just, you know, lift you on, Phil? Until you get the hang.'

'Think you can manage?'

'Do yer want a nand?'

'No ta, Rosa.' I said.

'Course yer don't! Yer a man!'

The belittling edge was aimed at her husband.

Only the end of the street away cars were going up and down the High Road. Buses packed with people headed home. I could hear kids laughing as they ran round the gardens. In the sky, an aeroplane rumbling smoothly, tilted for Heathrow. I took Gibbs - man-baby - in my arms, raised him up, then plonked him down on the saddle.

'Gordelpus,' Rosa croaked.

I didn't let go until I was sure he was securely in place.

Axel firmly in the slots, the wooden struts creaked under his weight but miraculously held. He managed to take a grip on the sit-up-and-beg handlebars. His legs though couldn't engage the pedals in any meaningful way. They were limp as straw. I held onto him, steadying him.

'Chrrrist Almighty,' Rosa groaned,' 'ow's 'e goin' to get on when you ain't 'ere?'

'A horse never jumps a fence until he gets to it, Rosa! Okay, mate - let go, go on. Let go!'

The moment had come. I let go. He was on his own.

As soon as I stepped back I became shockingly aware how creaky my structure was. The back wheel really needed stays, supports, side-bars, stabilisers of some kind. It was too late now though. Gibbs, in his tartan cap, pyjama bottoms, off-white vest, was in the saddle and looking horribly brave. An amateur jockey at the start of the Grand National on the five hundred-to-one outsider. Don Quixote compared was a hard nosed pessimist, with the whole of Spain for tilting. Gibbs was confined to a deadly bedroom in which he couldn't swing his traitorous green-eyed cat. I was full of Sancho Panza moments. What if it all went crash? What if something went so badly wrong, Gibbs died? Could I be charged with attempted murder?

Instinctively, Gibbs crouched as if sprinting to a finish along the Bath Road. I crouched too, ready to spring to his aid.

Rosa, two hands to her face, in agonised suspense, was a mousey version of the Munch Scream, plus cigarette.

Were it any older, the bike would have been a penny-farthing.

Above the bed was a painting of a girl tending geese. The kind of Victorian item you'd pick up at an auction. Girl and geese seemed to pause in their advance to a nearby pond, so taken were they with Gibbs the trick-cyclist.

He was breathing hard but his legs refused to move or had forgotten how. Face reddening, constipated, I think he was trying to press down on the right pedal.

'That's enough for one day,' Rosa said, 'get down. Or I'm leaving.'

'You'll do worse than that. You'll come back.'

His tongue still worked.

Leaning over the handlebars, he willed himself to action. The cat darted to the door. The effort to pedal was beginning to produce a definite sideways sag. I was sweating snow. The decisive moment had been reached. Gibbs and my frame versus Newtonian law.

In slow-motion, through the eternity of a second, he began to topple. The Pisa tower of newspapers at the end of the bed saved him. But only for a blink. No foundation in anything other than dead fact and fib, they quickly gave way, Gibbs plunging after them to the floor. As if in cinematic slow-motion, I failed hopelessly to catch him.

He hit the floor so hard, his face and neck seemed to flatten out. I was sure I heard his shoulder splinter. He and the bike, in the space of a nanosecond, had become a tangled disaster. My struts having failed, the back wheel buckled. He looked dead. How could I have condoned, aided and abetted, his fantasy?

Rosa stayed on her stool.

'He'll be all right.' She sounded disappointed.

I began the unravelling of his legs from the spokes.

'I'm so sorry, Phil, I'm so sorry, God I'm so sorry.'

'Leave it a mo', mate, I'm okay.'

I was astounded he could speak. The newspapers had cushioned his fall. The tartan cap was still on his skull. My bits of flimsy wood had come apart. My wife was right. BotchBotchBotch...Cackhand & Bindweed, tradesmen to the Trust, could not have done worse. The back wheel, squashed to a rusty figure of eight, with Gibbs' foot and big toenail interlaced in the twisted spokes, was a piece of modern sculpture.

Managing to disentangle him, I cradled him in my arms. Man-baby looked at me, chin tilted, eyes gleaming.

'Did you notice the way I took the fall?'

From total failure he'd extracted triumph.

I laid him on the bed. He was able to raise himself to the pillows. I sweated contrition.

'I'm so sorry, Phil.'

'Judo black belt, see. You ask Sergeant Spencer. I gave him his first lesson.'

'A normal man would have broke his neck.' Rosa said.

Raising her frustrated eyes to the peeling ceiling, she got up and pussyfooted to the kitchen.

Icarus, crashing to earth a singed chicken, had little humour in it. Besides, it was a myth. Gibbs was for real. His vanity was on a different scale. Such belief was heroic.

The out of date calendar on the wall had a picture over December. Fields of snow, a church spire, a frozen lake, two skating lovers in pirouetting bliss.

A dream had to be tested. Phil Gibbs failed his. He was a sick man. I was nuts. What sort of reality was an old Raleigh bike and my wafer struts?

Gibbs rubbed his elbow, adjusted his cap, scratched under his vest.

'We just need stouter bits of wood next time,' he said.

The frailer the person, the stronger the dream. I knelt and kissed his foot.

'Hand me that plastic bottle, will you, matey chum?'

He peed. I lifted the bike, went out and dumped it by the bins. The clatter was good. I got my tape recorder, set it up on the wall, and did it again.

Clangclugclattclang. Ding. That was the bell falling off.

My wife insisted I go to the brain-riddler. Inside every person was a shaft of sense. To have done what I did with Gibbs I must have fallen down the shaft. To keep the peace, I made an appointment. Mr. J.O. Ronnoc, Therapist.

He met me, a pipe in his hand which he wedged with tobacco throughout the session.

'I still haven't found the meaning of life. Have you? Don't muck about if you have. Just tell me.'

'What you should be looking for is the secret of life.'

'What is the secret of life?'

'If I told you it wouldn't be a secret, would it?'

'I'm not paying for that.'

'It's like asking a caterpillar what's the meaning of butterfly. We don't know the next stage, my friend. If there is one. A disposition to live each moment fully is all we can aspire to. Forget the imago.'

'Moments don't match. I might want something right now you don't.'

'That's all right. Intensity is all right. With responsibility. The caterpillar eats and eats and eats. It is propelled by its destiny. Now if you don't mind - I'm busy.'

'That's outrageous. I'm definitely telling my wife not to pay you.'

'It would be better for you if you had to pay. The constant paying out of money is to be in a permanent state of self-analysis. Do you love your wife? Love conquers all. True love that is. Love simple. Love true. I saw you in the High Road recently. You were hopping along on one leg. Why was that?'

'Oh, probably just imagining something. Amusing myself.'

'People had to get out of your way. Just remember what I told you about inappropriate behaviour, hm? You know what a sociopath is, don't you? We don't want to go there, do we?'

By the time I left him, he was still thumb-grinding tobacco on his palm. He was very good at his job. I always went home feeling glad not to be him.

My wife suggested we go to Brighton. A spin. Tender moments in the open air. The planet was full of wonders. The sea was one of them.

We lay on the beach, a blanket softening the stones. The apple moon showered silver into the rioting waves. Stars were pin-pricks in the tented sky. A fishy-chippy sea smell oiled the air. In a cocoon of lullaby sounds, we folded into one. O foaming love and dreams.

Schishhclishhcleeehewhooshhbooshhdrishhvoomboomahahschishh.

Constabulary boots crunched towards us. Brighton. We moved on.

Heading back to London, we zoomed around towards Epping. On the forest floor we lay the blanket down. The moon had travelled with us. It skittered through the trees. Haunted. Damp dripped from every leaf. The wood was full of lovers. Gibbs and Rosa had moments here when they were young. Gibbs had photographed a ghost.

'Why did I kiss his foot?'

'You were so relieved you hadn't killed him.'

On the way back into town, our headlights pushed the night aside. At eighty miles an endless hour.

I never wanted to say no to anyone. Tatty dreams impressed me. I signed on with Freddie and engaged young Sam Tripp and Wally. I bought overalls for them. Wally's was too tight, Sam's too big. Sam rolled up the legs and arms, which made him look more comical still. And over all of Wally his overall couldn't go. His ankles and wrists stuck out, and when he raised his arms, a seam ripped.

When we opened the door of railway arch No.441, the damp, dark, putrid fug swirled out over us.

'Bloody hell, man.'

We quickly dragged the nearest tank into the open. It was completely covered in dust and rust. We went at it with wire hand-brushes. Wally volunteered to go inside the tank. Sam's style of brushing was more suitable for painting than hard brushing. He dabbed rhythmically as if gently playing drums. Sometimes he'd peer very closely at the tank to see what effect he was having. Not much. Wally brushed with a heavy hand, pounding the sides, as if he were beating the tank up.

'I found thermodynamics neither hot nor dynamic. I told him that.'

'You talking to us, Sam?'

Dirt and dust from his hands gradually transferred to his face. He was soon nearly as black as Wally.

Wally was singing,

'I got the brush

You got the shekels

Sing me some blues man

Paint me up your mush.'

Inside the tank, his voice reverberated. When he finished singing he paused, then shouted, testing for an echo.

'Yo Blair! Yo! Yo-yo.'

We laughed. He seemed surprised.

He pounded away with the wire brush, knocking jagged bits of rust tinkling to the tank floor.

Sam sunk into himself. Every so often he'd look up and remember he was in company.

'Okay, Sam? I bet May is hot and dynamic.'

'The second law states, heat transfers from a hot body to a cold. It can't go from a cold to a hot. I've got to concentrate on getting into Balliol. I think I told you, right?'

'I bet May was hot and dynamic.'

'She likes holding me down. It doesn't make one feel empowered.'

The next tank we tackled had a hole low down on one side. We dragged it back in again, dragged another one out. The West Indian in the next door garage poked his head out a few times, wondering what we were really up to.

'I thought maybe you was loading drugs. Guy busted down here only a week ago.'

'Loading drugs with wire brushes?' Sam reflected aloud.

'Can I have a dekko?'

He was a paint-sprayer from head to toe. Lovely crusty scabs of paint congealed his boots. His hands were dotted with all the colours of the rainbow and then some. His face looked as if he was suffering from multi-coloured chickenpox. Even his hair was splattered.

He circled the old Rover car, bending to peer inside.

Under the remaining paintwork were spider webs of rust. The tyres were perished, the front number plate had come away, the fog lamp drooped, there was the hole in the rust-eaten roof. It barely held its shape. The drip-drop of water fell constantly from the depths of darkness clean through to the floor. Forty years of water torture.

'Wow! Wow! Instrument dials - they all got rectangle faces. Nice. Nice. British

Leyland.'

Taking hold of the driver's door handle, he yanked hard.

Instantly, like a planet imploding, time crashed into space. As the door broke from the rotted hinges, the entire car disintegrated. The roof, bonnet and boot collapsed inwards, the rust making a grating sound like sugar being walked on. The whole thing looked like a heap of cinders and ash. Under the pressure of light and eyes it had finally caved in. Time had taken its time softening it up and, the moment right, devoured it at a gulp. The windscreen keeled back and smashed on the steering wheel. The four wheels were still intact, so too the engine and most of the chassis. But what, a few seconds before, was the venerable image of a stately car, now looked like the remains of a burn-out.

'I did nuffing. You saw. I just opened it. I did nuffing, mate.'

He still held onto the driver's door. Even that began to crumble.

The front bumper, which had been half hanging on, fell to the ground. Time was a monster. Everything ended up in its belly.

Freddie and April had breezed down to Brighton in that car.

Wally climbed into the tank we were working on. Balanced on the edge, like a snooker player playing a difficult shot, he clung on for a moment, before falling in with a heavy thud.

'It's not funny, Sam.'

'How many gallons of water will these tanks hold, Sam?'

'The one with the hole in it won't hold any.'

'Smart arse.'

'The smallest tank is six by four by two. 48 cubic feet. One gallon is 277.274 cubic inches. So you work it out.'

'How long would it take to fill?'

'Depends on the size of the pipe. A half inch pipe, the flow ...two gallons a minute. A two inch - sixty gallons. Three inches - one hundred and seventy.'

'Full - how much would a tank weigh?'

'The six by four by two, full, would weigh one ton and a third.'

Off a side street off the High Road, the railway arches were a warren of workshops with people coming and going all the time. Filfy Wilfy, no matter how habitually hostile the reception, never went by without trying his luck.

'Cuppatea?'

Filfy Wilfy in his black overcoat, brown cardigan, white shirt, flannel trousers, grey socks, came bobbing along like an old pigeon.

'Cuppatea, guv?'

Bits of dandruff, big as insect eggs, clung to his eyebrows.

My tape running, I stood close to him.

BIG PARTS

'I've worn ladies under-garments you know. Stockings, belt, high heels. Have you?'
Wally ducked down inside the tank.
Wilfy flashed a ratty smile at Sam.
'You ever wore a bra? Panties?'
Sam raised his nailed right eyebrow. Wilfy turned to me. He did look like my father. He did have something of Freddie about him. It was an Everyman look.

'I get a war pension, ear trouble see, for me ears. Eleven o'clock Mondays I pick it up. Italy, North Africa, Austria an' all. Alongside the guns. Old age nowadays is about ninety-eight, ninety-four; 'ucking 'ell. See? See the piss? I'm pissing now.'
The front of his trousers dampened and soon a stream ran over his shoe and onto the cobbles. Sam stared unbelievingly.

'In Monte Cassino you 'ad the lot. You 'ad seven, seven and a half million in Italy. That's big innit? Army, Navy, Airforce. 38th German Division. German army, Fifth Army. Five armies. Popskie's private army, blowing the ammunition dumps. 1st Army. 8th Army. American Army. Five hundred pound bombs going in. German 88's opening up on the Italian farm lands. The Infantry, I saw the Infantry go in, go up, go up, go forward. Go right up the lines. Goin' right up to Death. Marvellous innit? I come through all that, I come through all that. I done eight year washing cars ah'ter all that. Mr. Gamm's car number was CYO 556. Mrs. Gamm. I filled her kettle often. She wouldn't let any, any of the uvvers fill her kettle. Her, wots'ername, rahnd your 'ouse, Rosa Gibbs, she was trouble. Mrs. Gamm wouldn't give her no more clothes. Frocks, coats. She was too small to wear 'em proper. Mrs. Gamm gave 'em to me then. She admired my turn of ankle. I used wash eight cars for Mr. Gamm, two, three for meself, keep that money see, a quid here, there. It was a lot of money them days. I come across Rosa one evening. She weren't wearing nuffing under the fur. I was fillin' Mrs. Gamm's kettle at the time, as it happens. Right out of order, right out of order. Cuppatea, guv?'
The 'Guv' in question was a bloke looking out from his workshop.
'Piss off. Go on. Git out of it. Filfy old toerag.'
Wilfy glanced over his shoulder in a split second pretence it was someone else being addressed.
'It's a free country.'
He watched Sam and Wally working, a cynical smile at the corner of his mouth. Even the tufts of hair sticking out from his ears had dandruff.
Viciously he said,
'They don't know where Italy is. They don't know all the towns in Italy. They don't want to know. Over fifty, sixty year ago that was. Monte Cassino. They never 'ucking 'eard of it. Eighty thousand didn't come back from Monte Cassino. I used dig all the slits and gun pits and put all the wotsaname in and then help the Infantry out. You had the Ghurkhas. Very good, the Ghurkhas. They used go in over the top and cut the German

97

ears off.'

'Pity they didn't cut your bollocks off!' someone shouted from inside an arch.
Wilfy paused.

'See what I mean? Jealousy and spite. Why? Two o'clock in the mornin' waitin' to go in. Waitin' to attack. Sleepy Time Girl, they was playing. Alexander was me guvnor. Not Montgomery. Alexander. Very good. Heard he was a hairpin - Montgomery. Is that true? All the film stars all fuckin' one another's arseholes. The more clever you are, the more intelligent, the more bent you are, you're a hairpin. All them directors, all hairpins, all them directors. Action, lights, all that, yeah. Listen, listen, Dodge City, no listen to me, Dodge City was the greatest film ever made. Dodge City. That was real, Laramie, Wyoming, that was the real old West. Kansas. Punch-ups, running on top of the trains, punch-ups, wotsanames...Real city Dodge City, real. Boot Hill. 1931 I saw that one, thruppence, thruppence it was. Not there now the cinema, it's gone. Dodge City, that was, that was the best 'ucking film ever seen. Boot Hill. What do you fink my trouble is? Prostate? Cuppatea? Everyone's going to 'ave a chip inserted in their 'eads. They'll be able to see your thoughts in Scotland Yard on a screen. They'll be able to read us like maps. Stands to reason, don't it? Nine o'clock tomorrow, no Monday, eleven o'clock, no ten, I get me money. Me war pension. I'm retired, aren't I? Stomick, heartburn, burning all the time, farting all the time, farted it out. Then I get the stomick pain, crapping, pissing all the time, pissing and crapping all the time, it's got to come out see. What would you do if you were me?'

I gave him a few quid. He scuttled off. His words were a familiar patter but they were his whole life. His words lived his life. They came out of his mouth livid wasps. They fell from his lips like rotten fruit. Suppurating words were the map and disease of his being. They kept him going long after he should have been dead. When he spoke about Dodge City he cocked his index finger and thumb as if holding a six-shooter. Monte Cassino, Dodge City - the odds against you were great. But it was only in peacetime you wet your pants in public. His head was full of ghosts. As he went about the streets, people fled from him. He was the ghost of the ghosts.

I had him word for word.

When we'd finished the rest of the tanks, we headed for the Electric caff. We ate a heap of food. In silence. Like we hadn't eaten for days. Fata, the waitress, smelled of perfume and pepper. When she laughed, her head went back, so she was lit for a moment by a strip light. Her neck would have roused a cob.

Wally munched a tablet round his mouth before swallowing it.

'Sam, do you think they'll ever come up with a tablet to cure death?'

'I'm working on it.'

The brain-sifter looked at me across his kitchen table. He nursed the bowl of his pipe in cupped hands, the stem pointing directly at me. As if he were fishing with an invisible line.

'When I was a kid, I was frightened when my mother cried. She'd be upset by my father. I'm in bits at the sight of female tears. They wash me away. Is that why I dive down, in my mind, to escape problems?'

'Come up. The sun is always shining. Especially above the clouds.'

'Is that it? How much you charging for that?'

My wife worked in Westminster. She knew powerful people. Some of them on the verge of being caught out.

'They'd wipe the floor with you, buster. Get a job, then you can talk.'

'I want to be like the Royal Family.'

'The Royal Family get out and about. You rarely go further than the High Road.'

'I've got everything I want round here. That's the great thing about it. The High Road is the world.'

'Do you not see love has rules?'

'Marriage has rules. Love hasn't. I hate rules.'

'Oh, so the world can go hang?'

'It was hung billions of years ago. Around the sun.'

'Go and wash your hair. The feeling of hair is important to me. It just is. And don't go round turning the radiators off. Don't fiddle with the heating.'

'Sorry. I know how you feel.'

'That's another thing - you don't know how I feel. So stop saying you do. You're not my father. And when I give you my clothes to hang out on the line, you hang them like rags. You can't even hang your own socks properly. I give them to you in pairs, you bring them back in odd. You can't even hang a sheet properly. You bundle it across the line like it's a dead body. Ironing is hell for Mrs. Clay.'

'Mrs. Clay is a semi-inebriate, with one leg in the gutter.'

'You're not the only one with lost causes.'

'Yeah? Right. I know.'

'You don't know! Got that? You don't know.'

'Mini-cab to Calvary, quick. And don't worry - I'll nail myself up.'

'See? You never take anything seriously. And stop criticising Daddy's horses.'

'Big up for Daddy's horses. Let's hear it for the nags. Sorry. No, seriously, sorry. If you weren't you, I wouldn't be me. You mean everything. I love you.'

'Show it, don't say it.'

'Can't you see it? Look in my eyes. Look in my light.'

'This house is bats. Perhaps we should move.'
'This house is my mission. It can save my soul. The sun is always shining. Especially above the clouds.'
'Words are cheap.'
'Expensive. Ask the brain-sifter.'

I reported to Freddie. He fumed. As if I were a menial, he the Managing Director of a major enterprise.

'I insist on daily bulletin. How am I to gauge progress otherwise? We have agreed terms. I am of a mind to rescind. Do you understand? Why are you wearing one glove?'

'I've been varnishing a chair.'

There weren't any terms.

He wore an immaculate green tweed suit. His gunmetal hair swept back from his forehead, ending in a straight line just above the collar. His forehead was a tad flaky and scrubbed red - that trace of pityriasis he had in common with Filfy Wilfy. His cheeks, lips, sparse eyelashes, were raddled and rouged in an attempt to dock the years. There was a lot of wool in the double-breasted suit. That great strength took some covering.

The tatty carpet was so dusty, I wondered had he freshly shaken talcum over it? Perhaps April had. The bed was strewn with copies of The Financial Times. The canvas cardinal above the mantle was as real as Freddie himself. The sardonic leer deliberately threatened and demeaned living flesh. A portrait from the other side of death.

April came into the room wearing full Salvation Army uniform - black shoes, black stockings, skirt, jacket, a hat perched on her scraped-up hair. In her gloved hands she clutched a Bible. Because of her turned-up nose and raised upper lip, you could never tell if she was sneering or trying to smile. Her eyes were vague as holes in mist. She stood without pressure. As if she didn't exist. Like a thief in a crowd. There and not there. Creepy.

The clock reminded us time in Freddie's attic passed but had little in common with the stuff they brewed in Greenwich. Baroingggg-wheezing, clatter-grinding, doi-donking, it generously marked the half hour seven times. Freddie saw I was intrigued by April's uniform. They were going to Church.

'You do know April is vital in the community? Oh yes. She has followed the band. She has served in the Old Folks Home. The Salvationists adore her. She has had to do terrible things. They asked her recently to hand cups of tea to blacks.'

My microcassette recorder was hidden inside my glove.

'Ready to go, are we sweet-sweetie?'

A vague breathy consonant, wispy as cotton, was her answer.

'Splendid. Mustn't keep God waiting. Are you a churchgoer, Joey?'

'You can't bandage Time. I prefer to have my voodoo with the Sunday papers.'

'They can't bandage Time either. Without religion, law has no basis.'

'Well, you should be pleased with all these foreigners coming in. They bring God with them.'

'We must fight their God with our God. This time the crusade will be conducted at home.'

As he walked off to church, wielding his black brolly, he looked stern and utterly respectable. I followed them, keeping a distance, just to see where exactly it was they were going.

Off the High Road there was a nondescript church hall. Over the years it had housed many hues of Christianity. Mostly of the tub-thumping variety. A torn poster proclaimed,

"The Lord's Supper. HE is in here."

A chunky middle-aged man, in a dark terylene suit and pork-pie hat, stood before the door, declaiming,

'Holistic Christian message inside. Full English breakfast free to over seventies on production of I.D. Jesus died for our sins.'

I got a glimpse of the set-up, as a West Indian man and a young girl dressed in white hurried inside. Rows of chairs in an otherwise bare hall...A preacher standing on a stage at the far end...Freddie sitting stiff-backed, April beside him...A definite smell of bacon frying. The man at the door was Reg Shand, the Town Hall comrade of Miss Chats.

'You're welcome to come in and pray, but we want no mucking about.'

'Is this a private venue? Or Town Hall?'

'It's private when hired.'

'So it's Town Hall?'

'Holistic Christian message inside. Full English breakfast free to over seventies on production of I.D. Jesus died for our sins.'

'I'd like to hire it. Who do I see? Do I see you?'

'What for? This has nothing to do with the Town Hall.'

I explained about Freddie's dancing waters. He wasn't impressed. I told him we could slip him a good few quid.

'Holistic Christian message inside. Come and get it. Phone me at the Town Hall. Full English breakfast free to over seventies.'

'We'd need it for a Friday evening. All day Saturday and Sunday morning.'

'On production of I.D. Jesus died for our sins. You'd have to be out by twelve noon

101

on the Sunday. Nothing gets in the way of the Lord's Supper.'

I could hear a Salvation Army Band.

'Onward Christian Soldiers marching as to war...'

They turned the corner and halted outside the hall. Their conductor dramatically raised his hands.

'Can you play Don't cry for me Argentina?'

'Piss off!' Reg said to me, quietly and fiercely.

I went round to the railway arch and in the damp blackness removed some of the copper piping - circular lengths fitted with various nozzles, jets, spouts. I lugged the lot back to the house and left it on the landing by Freddie's door.

Rosa, in a panic, opened her door. Gibbs wanted to see me. She muttered something about a bomb.

Gibbs was standing by the open window leaning on his Zimmer, looking out at something.

'It's down there, see? A bomb. The police are on the way.'

He was pointing at something by the dustbins at the front of the house.

'I heard the motorbike pull away. After they planted it. See? There! Get your wife out of the house immediately. Go into the back garden. Rosa and I will stay here. Do not go out the front. It doesn't matter about us, we're older than you two.'

There were three bins at the front. And a number of black plastic bags.

'Who'd want to plant a bomb round here?'

'The A-rabs will plant 'em anywhere. Believe me. I heard it ticking. Tick-tick-tick. Away, mate, go, quick, please! Go!'

Was it possible bin Laden had irony enough to plant a bomb in an actual bin? Gibbs looked adamant. Rosa hopped anxiously about in tiny circles. The pile of newspapers had been reassembled, the cat once more firmly in place. The plastic milk bottle was down by the bed - half full.

Maybe the bomb was meant for the gentleman we called Nigerian Ore. He lived next door but one! Terrorists often got the wrong address. NO was rich enough to have enemies by the dozen.

Belting downstairs I alerted my wife who, understandably, was reluctant to budge, reclining as she was in a hot bath. Her hands were in glamour gloves and a good deal of her flesh was covered with thick green lotion. But such was my genuine alarm, I persuaded her to grab a towel and leave instantly.

We fled out the kitchen door and down the end of the garden. There was a low brick wall, part of a semi-circular decorative feature in the corner. Wrapped in the towel, she edgily sat herself down. She looked a rare sight with her wet hair, bare arms, long naked legs, green shoulders, glamour-gloved green hands. A Botticellian Venus for the twenty-first century. Crossing the wall dividing us from next door, I made my way out to the street. Supposing it was a bomb and the bloody thing went off? We'd be decanted and no mistake. Was it a plot to get us out? My paranoia didn't stretch that far.

A lone policeman arrived in a car. I pointed out the bins and the black bags. Cautiously he approached them, then stood stock still, head cocked, listening. He glanced at the privet hedge in front of our house. This high hedge augmented the wall along the pavement. All the houses in the street had hedges. I'd clipped our hedge the day before. The clippings I wodged into a bin and two plastic bags.

The policeman relaxed by the second. Coming from inside the bags was the unmistakable sound of ticking. It had to be the clippings unravelling against the plastic. Gibbs stared down at us from his window.

'Was it you phoned us, mate?'

'No. It was old Phil there.'

'Not to worry, mate. Better safe than sorry.'

He shouted up to Gibbs,

'It's only bits of privet unkinking, mate. In the bags, mate. Okay? Ta ra.'

He got into his car and drove away. It started raining. I went back up to Gibbs. He was neither ashamed nor apologetic.

'I like to shove my head out the window, get some fresh air. I saw a motorbike pull away. Then I heard the ticking.'

'Not to worry, Phil. False alarm, thank goodness.'

'And the trouble is you see, I no longer have my bomb defusing equipment.'

This he said with a vainglorious nonchalance. On the Home Front during the war he'd belonged to a bomb-defusing unit. But for the lack of this equipment, he'd have been out at the bins defusing bin Laden's best. To Gibbs, the man who photographed a ghost; Gibbs, the man who rode against Reg Harris on the Bath Road; Gibbs, the man who taught judo to the police was now added Gibbs the bomb squad!

'Search the drawers will you, Rosa? I want to show him my shells.'

'Gord Almighty, 'ow long do I 'ave to suffer this?'.'

'I'll come back later, Phil.'

'No wait a mo'. They're in here. Last time I looked.'

He tugged at an open drawer but couldn't budge it. Maybe he had a horde of ammunition stashed away since 1945. An alarming thought.

'I'm a well known conchologist. My sea shells were famous.'

Though he'd made an utter fool of himself, he'd gone seamlessly from the non-existent bomb, the war, to conchology, in a matter-of-fact delivery without flourish or apology. A minimalist adventurer, the antithesis of Freddie, he was like his chest of drawers - spilling with quaint odds and ends. Small treasure abandoned.

He made his way back to the bed. His face was greyer than his vest. He and Rosa lay down in that bed. The sheets hadn't been changed in months. The pillow-cases were grey as the blankets. They had lived all their lives in our street. They had survived the Blitz. Time had him in sight and would soon pull the trigger. By the time you were Zimmer-framed, it was too late to do anything about it. It was subtle and maddening. One fell stroke was all it took.

Outside fangs of rain bit the road.

I suddenly remembered my wife. My wife. Jesus. Surely she wasn't still down the bottom of the garden?

Practically nude, she sat dutifully on the small wall, wetter than when she'd lain in the bath. I tried explaining, apologising. It had all been a false alarm...The police had checked it out...Blame old Gibbs...My only concern had been her safety...Gibbs imagined it all...

Calmly she stood up, removed the glamour gloves, then whipped them across my face. Twice.

'Plonker! Plonker!'

It was like getting slapped with cabbage leaves. I laughed.

'Think it's funny, do you? It's raining. I'm cold.'

Covered in green mud, towel tossed aside, like a naked cave-woman she came at me from all angles. Her bare feet imprinting the grass, wet hair swishing angrily, thighs spring-loaded for action, fists swinging, she was utterly angry and fearless.

'You silly bastard. Plonker. Prat. Dickspan. Poxbrain.'

Eyes blazing, the veins on her breasts neon strips, she ran full at me, expertly raising her leg to hard-heel me in the chest. I hit the ground, rolled away, made a dash for the wall, jumped up on it and climbed into the pear tree. She stormed into the house. There was no shelter in the pear tree since the tree-punk cut it in two. The rain pelted down.

My wife was normally placid. But when she took the notion she could be moody as winter. You couldn't shift her. Warm, cold, sexy or sad, she gave the moment everything. Only two weeks before, when visiting her father in Staffordshire, we went out at night to look at some of the horses in the paddock. The strange pre-historic shapes in the dark were wonderfully scary. Those massive dreamy heads, slabby necks, long legs, gurgling bellies, had power and mystery. She suggested we take our clothes off and mount one. Make a three-backed beast. Soon, she had a horse nuzzling her hand.

Naked as the melon moon we got aboard. I faced backwards. Tucking into me, an arm either side, she took fist-fulls of mane for steering and erotic purchase. A click of her tongue and round the paddock we rumpy-pumped at a gentle trot. It wasn't comfortable but I wasn't complaining. This was the life - if you could get a willing horse. A light flicked in her father's bedroom.

'What the ruddy hell's going on out there?'

'It's all right, Daddy, it's only us.'

He couldn't see what we were up to. The horse's racing name was Clayhanger. Two days later he was running at Uttoxeter. To avoid the price collapsing, I laid a hundred pounds on him in different bookies round the Potteries. My wife bet a hundred each way on the Tote.

We were there to see him romp home at 20/1. When we told her father about our midnight ride he was absolutely furious. We could have ruined the animal. It could have gotten injured. Gone mad even.

But it was the only winner he'd had for a long time.

He drove the horse box home, the two of us in the cab with him. We headed for the Red House in Caverswall. The brakes weren't good. To make sure we came to a stop, he expertly drifted the horse box along the wall outside the pub, gently scraping to a halt. He was pleased with this caper. Pints poured down throats. His 20/1 outsider had creamed it and a lot of the locals had lapped it up.

'Rum-tum-tum-tum-tardyum

From Cookshill Green to Carser cum...'

At home, before we parted for what was left of the night, he staggered against me at the bottom of the stairs. One hand hanging onto my shirt front, the other on the goblin-topped newel post, very fervently, drunkenly, he said up to my face,

'You're a good lad, youth. But I don't see you ever ending up in charge of the country.'

Plonking down on the bottom step he removed his artificial leg, then dragging it after him by the strap, crawled up to bed, helpless as a baby. A big old drunken baby with a foot missing.

By the dying embers in the drawing-room fire, my wife and I counted our winnings and our blessings. Love was a beatitude. And money wasn't far behind.

' "Founded on truth our school endures.

Firm buttressed with deep loyalty..." '

I eventually came down from the pear tree. She was in the bath - singing. I felt it safe to go in. Her glamour gloves were filled with - according to the blurb on the tube - 'Time-correcting gel'. Just what Gibbs and Rosa needed. Something to fox the clock. A pluperfect wind-back.

She stopped singing. I could see me die a little in her eyes.

I asked her had she slept with George S. Drake at university? She wouldn't speak to me. I tried really hard to get round her - wrestled her onto the bed and everything. She shouted I was raping her.

'We love each other. How could it be rape?'

'I danced with him at the May Ball. Okay? He puked on me. As in vomit all down my gown.'

For a teeny-weeny second, I admired George S. Drake. How did he escape? 'Do you think you could ask him and Neville Earthy to come along to Freddie's extravaganza? George could bring telly people, Earthy theatre producers. Butter them up. They won't refuse you. Come on, you're in Public Relations.'

'Right now it's private relations I'm worried about.'

'How about pubic relations?'

'Don't be juvenile.'

I thought she'd perked up somewhat when I mentioned Earthy.

Freddie and April arrived home. We could hear him pounding the stairs. I nipped up to him.

April sat by the fire in her Sally Army uniform. He sat on the bed, a ring of copper between his knees. He pricked at the series of holes with a pin.

'Water must get out. Block it in - it will get very angry. It must be channelled. People are the same, you do know that, don't you? They want to be led.'

'What is Holistic Christianity?'

'A catch-cry to entice the impressionable. The free breakfast attracts the old. Religion is a river on which the powerful sail. That Reg Shand is a limp idiot. Why is he alive? He stopped me from addressing the congregation. England is a noble beast. Artificial manure is no match for the real stuff. The streets, when I was your age, were full of it. Our gardens full of roses. The decline of the horse has oddly paralleled England's fall.'

Changed out of Sunday best, he wore his matronly dress.

'The rabbi, the imam, the vicar, the priest, they line out with the politicians. They scare me. So do caterpillars. The brain-shifter told me it's an affectation.'

'Have you ever seen an army of caterpillars? Well then. Don't be absurd. If it can't carry a gun, no harm can be done. The air sucks leaders to the fore in times of need. We must be ready. The streets are filling with Muslim women spying on us from inside billowing sheets. Men with silly beards and head rags. Ghastly. We must strike while the iron's hot. Have you found me a stage yet?'

I told him I was negotiating with Reg Shand for the use of the Bible hall.

'I tried hiring Drury Lane but they're booked up years ahead. And the Royal Opera House won't consider dancing water. However artistic.'

'Won't consider? I read where they put on a ballet with full orchestra and conductor, but the orchestra wasn't actually allowed to play a note! Is the world gone that mad? In my day to be a pansy was illegal. Now it's the other way about. Sex maniacs, such as yourself, are out of date. My work comes up against such prejudice. It's all Jocks, Rocks, Cocks, Wogs, Gogs, Asians, Vegans. They hate the tweed suit. We have to stop them. The people are like water. If they are not stirred, they stagnate. If the sword isn't used, it rusts.'

Thoughts smacked into one another like wagons in a marshalling yard. 'Take this very house. How like England. We don't own it. We're not council tenants. We haven't got a landlord as such. In the traditional sense. We've got a quango over us. We are shadows, boy. We may as well be dead. Maybe we are. Ever thought of that?'

'Yes.'

He dismissed caterpillars. But they had a system pumping life through them. Like ourselves. They had genes. So did we. They didn't look like us. But looks were deceptive. I am you and you are me and she is he and he is me.

The double-bed, the small wicker writing table, the chairs, the low armchair April sat in, the tattered carpet - none of it would be ending up at Sothebys. A tasselled lamp shade was the most exotic thing in the room. The tassels were yellow, the rest of it black. An Edwardian wardrobe was daubed blue and gold. Daily Telegraphs, porn and art books, were scattered everywhere. The mad clock was spattered with talcum.

'Why all the talcum powder? If it is talcum powder.'

'April is a stickler for cleanliness. Do you find her attractive?'

Did I what? He awaited my answer, ready to be affronted. She stared just above my head. Her wide apart legs tensed her tight skirt.

'Attractive? Like a hare looking at the moon. Words beyond both of them.'

'I have told you, haven't I, immaculate conception is possible? Penetration is not necessary at all.'

I never had an inkling what he was going to say next.

'Really? Well, this is the age of test tube babies. Artificial Insemination and whatnot.'

'No, no. The semen must be passed bodily. I speak of miracles.'

As he pricked at the holes in the copper piping, bits of dirt fell into his lap.

'A hare looking at the moon? Whatever do you mean?'

Turning her chin to her left shoulder, she shouted violently at the something invisible perched there.

'Fuckoffbackeroll. Backofffuckerroll.'

The guttural intensity, the sheer agony, chilled the blood.

She rose slowly from the chair, unaware I think, she'd said anything at all.

She was in pain. The voices were driving her mad. They had exploded her personality to genetic smithereens. She was walking debris. Freddie was the only one could shout her voices down. His voice was stronger than all hers.

'Quiet. Enough. Go to your room. Change into your house-coat.'

She obeyed. How could he live with such craziness?

'You do see why she has to be restrained? She's very strong you know. Her father was a scoundrel. I beat him up. Anyone hits a female, even a dyke, deserves whipping.'

'She's lesbian? April.'

'What? April? No,no.'

'You're not her father?'

'What, what? Ha-hah. Is that what you thought?'

'Are you Filfy Wilfy's brother?'

'My mother's womb, of course was the ultimate jungle. One just wouldn't know. In Parting The Waters, she entered stage right, holding the flower.'

'Your mother did?'

'What? No. April. There wasn't a dry eye in the house. If we can reproduce that moment for the television people! My dancing waters.'

'What was your mother like?'

'A caterpillar, actually. Never once saw my show. Ghastly creature.'

As he sat on the bed pricking the holes in the copper rings, his concentration was immense.

There was more dignity in his attic than in an institution. He looked after April. I'd keep an eye on Rosa and Gibbs. On Wally as well. Perhaps there was method in the Trust's madness. But what would happen to April when Freddie died?

Below us, Wally started shouting,

'Leave it out! The noise is driving me mad. Twenty-four hours a day. You people! Noise! It's driving me mad! You people! You people!'

People talking or laughing together made him angry.

April came in with a packet of digestive biscuits and a cup and saucer. Trembling, she handed them to me. The cup was empty. As she left the room, the spongy under-carpet sound-proofing deflated under her foot for a moment, before swelling to normal again.

Every village had an idiot. In the city every street had two. You and the other one.

'Society is a forest. Creatures are bumping into one another constantly. You don't bring order by chopping down the trees. Someone must crack the whip.'

He held a circle of piping against his chest as he pricked at the rusty holes. It looked like he was tuning a medieval musical instrument. He loved England. What was the point of loving anything if it didn't love you back?

'Corruption is the first thing must go. The City stinks. Too many of them are fiscally and therefore sexually rotten. The cock is order. The cunt disorder. Putting the one into the other is disastrous.'

'It's vice versa, isn't it? If it's anything.'

'Don't interrupt. How dare you! You have not the knowledge to contradict! What do you know of metaphysics? I speak of purity. Man must re-discover absolute purity. You take on this decanting business, as if you alone speak for the whole house. I will not have it. You are buttressed by your wife's money. Your flat is done up as if private. It is

April and I who suffer most. We now have a leak. There's a slate loose somewhere.'

There he was, in his Mrsblouse dress, convinced he should be in charge of the world. I didn't tell him modern dictators had to be younger by at least thirty years. World leaders of his vintage, when they weren't killing people, were very sentimental and loved babies and old 78's. Freddie had records in stacks along one wall.

Immortal Strauss. Love Me As Though There Were No Tomorrow - Malcolm Vaughan. 'Charlie Kunz Piano Medley'. In A Monastery Garden - Peter Dawson. Ai Nostril Monty Ritornereemo - Florence Austral and Browning Mummery. Liebeslieder Walzer. Down In The Forest - Ronalde - Whistling Solo. I counted ninety at least - all produced by His Master's Voice, Decca and Brunswick.

'I understand you visit a psychologist? Are you a spy?'

'A spy of what?'

'Each street has a spy. You don't seem to work. Yet you're always moving about. From house to house. Flat to flat. Bed to bed. They have people in the newspapers spying out letters to the Editor of a political nature. They're forwarded to Scotland Yard. The internet is their newest device for entrapment. People like you, you can be used, you know? Has any policeman made approaches to you recently?'

'I'm rarely on church property.'

'Woofington's is full of policemen and psychiatrists. We live in an age which pretends to be modern. But you can still be arrested for your very thoughts! Why? Why? Christ! Psychiatry is a training-ground for espionage, you do know that, don't you? We no longer have a culture. Do you even know what culture is?'

'Culture is a cannibal.'

He gave me fifty pounds to pay Reg Shand for the hire of the hall. A taster. More would follow.

'I want for England, what I want for myself. To be left alone.'

'Reg is a friend of Miss Chats. Perhaps I can get them to leave us alone. Not decant us.'

There were two kinds of people. People who needed looking after. And the people who did the looking after. It couldn't be denied Freddie was the latter. His attic was prison and paradise.

April had given me a cup with no tea in it. Had she imagined it full?

Life is an accident. You don't see it coming.

The Town Hall foyer was full of citizens. Borough bees in their bonnets, they were directed to various gubernatorial hives by a uniformed commissionaire, sitting on a tall stool in a glassed-off cubicle near the entrance.

The spacious black and white tiled foyer had oak-panelled walls. At the far end was an impressive marble-stepped staircase, with French-polished handrails and decorated iron railings. Above, was a heavily corniced ceiling and a large stained-glass window. Architecturally, it was a mix of railway hotel and Victorian Gothic. A John Betjeman wet dream. Young men and women with bundles of red tape hurried in and out of doors. Each office was a deadly world of word processors.

The commissionaire's right hand had two thumbs. Each thumb about half the thickness of an ordinary thumb. He ran the thumbs down an appointment sheet. As if making sure you noticed the disfigurement.

"He stuck in his thumb and pulled out two plums."

Reg Shand's office was down the end of a corridor lined with people queuing for parking permits. May, Sam's lover, sat amongst a group of Indian women and their handsome, shiny-haired children. The Indians wore saris. May wore black and white striped tights, high heels, a green and white striped shirt and a red plastic bolero jacket. She looked like something from Venetian carnival. She'd bought a car for herself and Sam. Probably a ploy to keep him. How could he ever reduce that rampant libido, that magnificent bosom, to a manageable formula?

The Town Hall was a warren of corridors off corridors off corridors. Eventually I found Reg Shand. He was lurking behind a stout oak door, in a decent sized office, with desk and chairs and a big sash window looking out on the street. On the desk was a telephone, a notepad, a desk calendar, a jar of pens and a thick book sitting on blotting paper. He wore grey flannel trousers, a white shirt, striped tie, a blue blazer with shiny buttons and a porkpie hat.

'Your phone message, I got that, ta. Now about the matter pertaining. Take a seat, Joey.'

'My name isn't Joey.'

'Yes, it is. You're in the computer.

'Who put me in there?'

'Yourself.'

There was a cross on the cover of the big book. A Bible. Perhaps the BoS had ordered town halls to open Departments of God.

'You need the hall for a weekend, right? I won't be soft-soaped by old Parts. He's tried taking over our Bible society. For his own political ends. We know that's at the back of it. Now. Everything must be official, regarding the matter pertaining. Five hundred. Plus damages. If any occurring. Sign here.'

'No.'

I floated five ten's onto the desk. The big book turned out to be a money box in disguise. The black cover with cross, the spine, the gold edged leaves - all tin. Reg lifting the lid, carefully pressed the notes in. The box was about full. Closing the lid, he locked it with a tiny key.

'Deposit accepted in matter pertaining. That's now official. The Town Hall doesn't accept responsibility. This isn't official. Got that?'

'Is there anything you're afraid of, Reg?'

'No. You?'

'Maybe caterpillars. One dropped on my face from a bird's beak, when I was a kid. It inhabits a part of my brain. A tiny part.'

'That right? Yeah, well, every flea has its own way of jumping.'

Above the desk, a cone-shaped lamp shade hung like an upside down Chinaman's hat. A translucent parchment of some kind. A wasp had flown inside the shade and was bumping round and round like a demented wall-of-death rider. Each time it flew upwards it hit the bulb and, stunned, crash-landed to the bottom of the cone. It had flown in, yet couldn't fly out. Panicky flitting got it nowhere. Its dull shadow buzzed desperately. In a garden its sting could kill. Trapped in the shade, bumbling about hopelessly, it reminded me of Gibbs on his Zimmer.

'Switch the light on. By the door.'

Hands resting on his stomach, neck resting on the back of his chair, he looked up at the lamp shade. As if observing the stars.

'They get in the window. The light fixes 'em.'

As the bulb warmed up, the wasp made fewer and feebler attempts to escape. Outside the window, black taxis scuttled in and out the railway station. People hurried along the street, some eating as they went. It was lunch hour. A boy and girl, under a blue and white golf umbrella, weaved through the traffic. The buildings were grey, the light bleak.

All the world's reality TV. We make our lines up as we go. Then someone kicks us out.

Reg contemplated the wasp. Between his Adam's Apple and chin was a beardy tuft spared by the razor. Similar tufts sprouted from his nostrils and his ears.

The wasp at last slipped down into the bottom point of the shade. Toasted.

'Bit cruel, isn't it?'

'God is Life.'

'Does He work in the Town Hall?'

'The balance of the money in the matter pertaining will be collected on the Friday evening. One other vital thing. Miss Chats. We have been in contact. The decanting process has been set in motion. Take my advice, Joey. Leave without fuss.'

The phone rang. He looked at me.

'That's it then. I'll see you then. Goodbye then.'

He didn't want to pick up until I'd gone. I sat on. Annoyed, he butted his head towards the door.

The phone stopped ringing.

'I thank you, Reg, on behalf of Mr. Parts, of Parting The Waters. In the matter pertaining.'

Miss Chats had the Town Hall on her side. They really wanted to decant us.

My wife liked to show how civilised and liberal she was. She and Miss Chats met up. I wasn't in the house at the time. After their cosy tête-à-tête, she spoke to Freddie, April, Wally, Rosa and Phil Gibbs and advised them they should, at the very least, visit the house to which the Trust wanted us to move. See it. They might like it.

I was out-voted, in my absence, by a charmed shower of fools. I was angry. I also had to organise the trip.

The house was way across the borough in Thatch Lane. I hired a mini-cab. My wife - supreme delegator - opting out, left me to it.

Gibbs insisted on coming. So I had to go round to the Health Centre and borrow a wheelchair. Wally, when the time came, helped me wheel him down.

I gripped the handles, Wally took the strain at the front. After three steps he was sweating. Pill dribble stained his lips. We had sixteen steps to negotiate to the landing, six more outside...if we got that far.

Gibbs sat back, dead weight, tartan cap in place, walking stick hooked nonchalantly round his neck, at ease, chatting.

'A fireman's lift - there's a knack to it.'

Freddie and April had already gone down to the cab. So had Rosa. She was wearing a brown overcoat with wide fur lapels and a dead animal of some kind peeping over her shoulder. Mrs. Gamm must have given it to her. For Rosa it was a day out, a beano.

Gibbs, as we eased him from step to step, at one point almost tumbled out of the chair. He started clutching at the banisters, hindering our descent.

Somehow we made it to the communal landing. The tenants were supposed to take turns keeping it clean. Wally didn't own a brush. Freddie was too old, April too ill, Rosa too preoccupied with Gibbs. I did it from time to time. I sorted out the mail as well. They'd leave anything not addressed to them lying on the floor. A hurricane of bills, circulars, fliers, chuckaway newspapers, estate agent bulletins, telephone directories, mini-cab cards, littered the hallway. My wife bought a table but they rarely used it. Occasionally, Freddie might toss an envelope onto it. It was a hallway to depress a sloth.

We wheeled Gibbs through a pile of rubbish inches deep. The six concrete steps outside were easier to deal with. Freddie and April were already sitting in the back of the cab. Rosa was in the front. Gibbs insisted on getting in beside her. Holding onto the open door like it was his Zimmer, he tried to swing his bum down onto the seat.

I tried to assist him. The cab window was wound down. Out of breath, he collapsed through it, and hung like he was draped across a gate. The cab driver, a hugely overweight Welshman covered in dog hair, was no help.

Rosa angrily got hold of Gibbs and pulled him in towards her as I lifted him. My arms wrapped round his waist, his arms round my neck, we looked like we were wrestling.

'Lower your head, Phil,' I gasped.

'Not necessary,' he replied curtly. Clunk.

'Ouch.'

'You was told to lower your 'ead, yah bleeder!'

In the window of the next door house, the elderly American lady, Mrs. Baum, chomped on a pre-cooked mackerel. She hadn't removed the plastic packaging. Mrs. Baum was abandoned. Her daughter lived abroad and didn't want to know. We were Trust. We weren't alone. We were lucky. I remember thinking, not for the first time, organisations like the Trust weren't a bad idea at all. In theory.

In the back of the car Freddie made it clear the standard of transport and passenger were beneath him. April looked out with as much interest as if she were sitting eyes shut in a dark room. She might have been chained in a chest at the bottom of the sea. Wally was beside her, his glasses askew. The fat cabbie sagged behind the wheel, waiting for me to complete the transfer of Gibbs. Somehow I managed to ball him in beside Rosa. I even managed to get the door shut.

There were four of us wedged in the back. As we drove out of the street, people walked along, exercising their dogs, chatting. The overloaded cab with its dislocated temporarily decanted psyches, piloted by a driver reeking of tobacco and onions, car seats covered in dog hair, was a parallel planet, fate unknown.

'Can we have a windahnopen?' Rosa asked.

'I'd rather not,' Freddie growled.

'Sod yah!'

'One more bleddy word, just one more and I'll dump the lot on you right 'ere.'

He sounded serious. His radio crackled a message...

'Anyone near the shopping centre? Have you picked up from the hospital, Dave?'

'Any chance of a drink on the way?' Rosa cheerily inquired.

'I got a bleddy good mind! For two pins. I don't need this. Why should I?'

I could see him in the rear-view mirror. His abundant black hair shone. It was at odds with the considerable unkempt rest of him. It was hard to understand why he was so vexed - we were a good fare.

'I know this part of the borough like the back of my hand,' Gibbs said. 'If we cut down by Bunch Brothers - the demolition firm, we'll be there in two ticks. They sold excellent yard brushes, I seem to remember.'

This extraordinary information silenced us.

The cab roof lining was ripped. The top of the dashboard was ringed with tea/coffee stains and edged with cigarette burns. A St. Christopher medal swung on a safety pin just above the windscreen. A Volvo of some kind. Wally began breathing heavily.

'There's a lot of mud flowing. A lot of mud flowing,' he said.

Were we the mud? Or did he say blood?

Freddie, seething in haughty silence, lips frogging, had taken exception to Gibbs and his arcane remark about yard brushes.

'Yard brushes? Bunch Brothers? There never was a Bunch Brothers.'

'Yes there was. Bunch Brothers. Not far from here. They had a false wheelbarrow outside the shop.'

'A false wheelbarrow? The man's not right in the head.'

'I'll have you know, I'll have you know, the wheel was made out of plywood, to prevent stealing. It was an ornament to advertise. When you saw the wheelbarrow you knew you were there. Bunch Brothers. I know what I'm talking about, Mr. Parts.'

'I do not wish to be addressed by you. My name is for friends only.'

The lofty tone left no room for social doubt.

'Friends? You ain't got any friends.'

Gibbs voice was an octave above normal. He was so angry he burped. A peculiar flattish sick sort of sound.

'You're not going to puke, are you? Gordelpus.'

Furious at Gibbs, Freddie became possessed of an extraordinary intensity. Eyes blazing, ears glowing, skin rage-red, chest a tidal wave of emotion, he was at boiling point. His steel grey hair shifted as if disturbed by a throbbing skull. The driver headed him off.

'There'll be no argy-bargy in my cab. One word and the lot on you are out. And I mean it. They didn't tell me you was all nuts. They didn't say as how you was all dolally merchants.'

His fat tits wobbled in his T-shirt. His fingers were bitten, nicotined stumps, his car a hairy tip. Yet we were nuts, he a perfect specimen.

Freddie vented gallons of air. He didn't dare speak. Angry words would see us abandoned on the side of a multi-ethnic street. It was all Bengali, West Indian, Nigerian in that part of the borough. They would not be impressed by his brown pin-stripe, gleaming Oxfords, the furled brolly. Buses and proper taxis in that part of the borough would be blue moon manifestations. How would he and April get home?

Bengali women billowed along the pavements, laden with shopping and kids. Nigerians swathed in colourful garb stood outside a vegetable shop. Turks sat sipping coffee in a cafe. You could read Freddie's thoughts...The nearest thing to a white man was this Welsh fellow and he was a tricky customer. He'd better stay quiet.

Gibbs was trying not to puke.

The cab swerving round a corner, took us down a side street. Small brick-built Victorian houses. Every roof had slates missing or slates held in place with strips of lead. Asian women stood in doorways. Children, with crow-black hair, dark brown eyes, pausing in their play, turned to stare.

'Christ. We need a leader.'

We turned into Thatch Lane. At the far end was the only three-storied house in the street. That was it. I got out and my foot asleep, almost fell over. After hobbling about to get the circulation going I helped Gibbs. I hung him over the car door whilst I paid the cabbie. Without a word he closed the money in his fist, and as soon as I unhooked Gibbs, executed a speedy three-point turn before driving furiously away as if the get-away car in a bank robbery.

Freddie stared at the house. He had to accept that this indeed was the correct address. Most of the upstairs windows were broken or cracked. There were filthy net curtains in place downstairs so you couldn't peep in. The brickwork had been cemented over. Scabs of it had come away. The top storey showed deep cracks running all the way down to the front door. The lintel over the main downstairs bow-window sagged. The flaking, cheapo-cheapo front door had a letter-box just big enough to receive bills. The doorbell dangled on two loose wires. The tiny front garden was full of litter and bunged black plastic bags.

'There's something missing,' I said.

'Yes,' said Freddie, pointing with his brolly, 'half the sodding roof.'

'No. He's gone with the wheelchair. The cab.'

'Gordalmighy, I told 'im stay at 'ome.' Rosa said, scuttering about like a rowdy mouse. The dead animal on her coat collar, in a previous life I could now see, had been a fox.

I had no idea what to do with Gibbs. His legs were putty. Tight as dancers, his head resting on my chest, I held him up. Helping Gibbs was a mug's game.

'You can let go now, go on, I can stand under my own steam,' he ordered, 'I know this part of London. I know this street.'

As if knowing the street was going to help him stand up in it. Carefully easing my grip, I could feel his legs taking the strain. The feeling lasted the half second it took him to reach the tarmac, where he lay prone.

Wally looked away. I shouted at him. We managed to manhandle Gibbs onto the low garden wall. Gibbs, a bit dazed, felt for the wall on either side of him and, when sure of his bearings, visibly relaxed. He looked up at Freddie and, voice contorted with feeling, cried,

'Bunch Brothers! Yes, Bunch Brothers! You barmy old bugger!'

He collapsed backwards onto the plastic bags, his feeble legs kicking hopelessly. He was completely engulfed in rubbish. The others were so little concerned, he might have been just another sack added to the pile.

'Gord 'elp us! Dig 'im aht quick.'

By now every door in the street was festooned with saris. A group of children had seen Gibbs flip and were hysterical. We were as good as a circus newly arrived in town.

We dragged him, tartan cap still in place, back up onto the wall. I swiped bits of rice, rotten lettuce and a green caterpillar from his lap.

He was a cock with few if any feathers left. It didn't stop him crowing.

'When you've been on the judo mat for as long as I have, on the judo mat, with some of the best in the business, on the judo mat, a backwards roll like that is child's play.'

His cussedness was remarkable.

'I don't know about you lot but I couldn't half do with a stiff drink. Who's for it?'

'No, Rosa, get me home, gel. I seen enough.'

'You ain't seen nuffing at all, mate.'

Groups of Asian women and a few pantalooned beardies chattered excitedly. A family of Romanian gypsies laughed. Two Arab women smothered in blue burkhas looked like ultra-cautious beekeepers.

It was a sobering feeling being the odd ones out. The sore thumbs. The displaced.

'Christ! Why? Why? Multi-culturalism is a lie. If there was such a possibility, do they not see, it would have worked by now?'

'At the bottom of the barrel it is working, Freddie. At the bottom of the barrel we're all equal.'

Rosa wandered off through an alleyway at the end of the street, probably hoping to find a pub. I didn't want her to get lost. The alley led to an open stretch of trodden ground on the far side of which were dilapidated high-rise flats. A few massive West Indian youths rode round on BMX's. A couple of white youths, in hoods, hunkered on the ground.

The high-rises looked wet, stained, unutterably depressing. A concrete jungle in twenty storeys. There was no sign of a pub.

''e's so ill my 'usband, he oughter be dead.'

She was never more wistful, never so lost. We walked back to the others.

The Thatch Lane end of the borough was a designated modern European melting pot, with a mix of old empire tossed in. A reservation for foreigners, beggars, druggies and us. A New Labour sink estate. The only way out - down the plug hole. Political skulduggery had decanted half the world. Freddie flailed around trying to think of a solution. It had to be strange when loads of complete strangers began turning up in your neck of the woods. You couldn't deny that. But this wasn't his neck of the woods.

'Time will sort it all out, Freddie. Eventually. The English weather will soften their suntans.'

Before trying to get a taxi to take us home, I peeked in the house letter-box. The hall was knee-deep in mail. Sitting ominously on the bottom stair-step was a syringe, an empty beer can beside it.

I slumped beside Gibbs on the wall. I could feel it coming over me ...that familiar cloudy sigh wafting through my brain. A sense of foreboding. Something was happening to me. A childhood sensation. There was a crack opening up in the planet...And I was falling through it. Flying into it. A shaft sucking me down. Maybe up. The dead wasp in the town hall buzzed at my ear. Wasps were here before us. When earth was mostly fields. For a million years they flew to their nests in trees or down on the ground. Then obstructions appeared in their path. They carried on flying. Buzzing in through cracks. In windows. Under guttering. They couldn't be stopped. I helped my father-in-law get rid of a nest in the corner of an upper floor. They were getting in under a loose ridge tile. I went up on the roof and watched them zoom in like tiny helicopters. Always from the same direction. You'd see a dark blip in the distance gradually turning amber and there it was - landing on the slate below the ridge tile. A hurried shuffle and in under it would go. Thousands of them. An unstoppable flow. I had a painter's blow torch. I started burning each one as it landed. I killed hundreds. Below in the surrounding fields, fat cattle moved through the chemically fertilised Staffordshire grass. Lorries lumbered along the distant M6. The wasps kept arriving. And leaving. They'd come out from under the tile, as if pushed, then take off, always in the same direction. It was busier than Heathrow. I turned the torch off. The only thing in life was life itself. You couldn't kill it. You could make it miserable but you couldn't get rid of it, so why try? The most you could do was maybe re-direct it. I bedded the tile down and sealed it, using a silicone cartridge gun. In the paddock, the horse on whose back we made love, flicked his tail at flies. He was all black except for the blaze on his forehead and the white sock on a hind leg. I sat astride the ridge tiles, watching him shaking his head, the mane flouncing along his lovely neck. He chopped at the grass, his neck stretching as far as it could, before he'd put a foot forward.

Stopping, he raised his head and stared ruminantly into the distance. As if sensing something, he turned his head and looked right up at me.

I had blocked wasps in, kept others out. Killed hundreds. They'd get their own back. They'd invade my dreams. Maybe April's head was full of them.

...Someone was pulling me. Shouting down at me. Why was he bothering? When I opened my eyes it turned out to be the Welsh mini-cab driver. Realizing he'd driven off with the wheelchair, he'd come back to find the others standing around trying to work out what had happened to me. I was lying on top of the narrow wall, a leg on either side, hands dangling, totally out of it, my head on Gibbs' lap. A marionette whose strings had snapped. Apparently I'd been lying there for half an hour. The cabbie had taken pity on us and come back. He could have dumped the wheelchair outside our house but he didn't. He and Freddie discussed what to do with me. That made me happy. The cabbie tried to get me to my feet but I refused. In a temper he got the others into the cab, even managing Gibbs. Wally looked out the window as they drove away,

'Wossamaherman? Kushdie.'

He looked worried. I couldn't help liking him. They drove off. What kind of crazy apostle was I, lying on that wall? The trip was my wife's bright idea. Her and Miss Chats. I knew full well there wasn't anywhere could match up to home.

I'd take great pleasure telling Miss Chats where to shove it.

But the trap had sprung and once more I'd fallen down. Fallen down inside myself. The foreign-eyed kids gathered round. Some of them laughed. A man spoke,

'Okee, okee?'

'Okay. I'm just sad. But I'm happy too.'

There was Oriental resignation, even understanding, in his eyes. They left me lying there. My back hurt but, to spite myself, I wouldn't shift. I wasn't just testing myself some way or other, I was testing her too. My wife. I wanted to show her the extremes I'd go to shock her. Freddie, as soon as he got back, told her what had happened. Dropping everything, she'd jumped into a taxi and come to get me. I heard it pull up, the confident diesel engine throbbing. I closed my eyes. I knew it was her. I could smell the expensive perfume.

'You're doing this purposely. Because I spoke to Miss Chats. Stop it.'

'What?'

'Pretending you're mad when you're not.'

'Why would anyone pretend? I don't want to fall down. I want to fall up.'

'What are you doing? What do you look like? Get up.'

Black stretch velvet jacket, tight trousers, shoes you could put down as a deposit on any of the surrounding houses.

'Any chance of a fuck?'

'Not here.'

The cabbie got out.

'He pissed?'

'Yes,' she replied, 'but not from alcohol.'

When we got back to our house Gibbs, abandoned, was outside in his wheelchair. He gripped the armrests like he was strapped into an electric chair. There was no one to haul him up the steps and stairs. My wife wondered what we should do.

'I'm going to drag him up, step by step, and you're going to make sure he doesn't spill out.'

'Do you think I should go and get Neville to help?'

'Neville? Earthy? That primrose?'

Why had she mentioned Earthy? I grabbed the handles and, mad as a bull, yanked the wheelchair onto the first step and the second and the third...Gibbs looked as if he was going to slide out. My wife, putting her hand on his head, pushed him back. With each step he seemed to get heavier. Next time he'd weigh as much he'd probably be in a coffin.

We managed to get him inside the house. My wife grabbed the handles and, hardy as a mule, yanked him the rest of the way. Rosa opened the door. We shunted him inside.

''ow did you git up 'ere?' she asked Gibbs.

'How do you think, Madam?' my wife answered.

'No need to get all hoity-toity, deary.'

The cat purred round my wife's ankles.

'What an exquisite pussy!' she enthused. As if she'd wandered in from a Pinter play.

Gibbs wanted to give me something towards the price of the minicab.

'Thank you for your kindness, mate. To me and Rosa. Your wife's a lovely person, by the way.'

In triumph, she switched on her floodlight smile. For a second the tawdry surrounds gleamed. Even Rosa was impressed.

'Cuppatea?'

'No thanks, Mrs. Gibbs, very sweet of you to ask.'

Doing a Lady Bountiful swoop out the door, she hopped down the stairs three at a time and, by the time I caught up with her, was waiting for me in the kitchen, hands on hips like a fishwife.

'There is not a thing the matter with you. You have to be centre stage in your own drama all the time. Falling down inside yourself? Give me a break! You haven't a bipolar disorder. You are not schizophrenic. You are not suffering from clinical depression. Anyone in your family ever have episodes?'

'Yeah. My father. Bad tempered episodes. My mother now. There was something odd about Mum. She drank tea from a china cup with a broken handle. She carried on using it for years and years.'

'A cup with no handle?'

'Right. It was a Hammersley. A clover design. With piping hot tea in it, without its handle, she couldn't hold it with bare fingers. So she wore a glove. A white glove. She called it her tea glove.'

'Oh my God, that is weird. I might never have married you if I'd known your mother wore a tea glove. By the way, I phoned George S. He will attend. The Dancing Waters.'

'You're a pal, pal.'

'A pal is the best thing to be.'

'I see my soul, my spirit, as smoke in which my brain floats. Can bad times, bad vibes, bad events thicken the smoke, so that it acts on the genes? My mother grew up in the fifties. Her family was big and poor. They drank tea from jam jars. In the Potteries! Can poverty stay in the brain? Generation after generation generating naff genes.'

Freddie thudded straight into our kitchen without knocking.

'It was you, wasn't it? You did it. Don't lie. I intend taking this to law. Why did you? Own up.'

My wife gave me a 'the man's a lunatic' look and left us to it.

'I will not be made a fool. This is libellous. You changed the P.'

'The pee? What are you talking about?'

'You know perfectly well. The P.'

'What pee?'

'Above the bell. It's a deliberate act of wilful vandalism.'

He glanced at various objets d'art my wife had purchased over the course of our marriage - Edwardian figurines, silver boxes, Wedgwood plates, Victorian marble items. He couldn't find fault with them. They were his period.

'I have appointed you manager of my imminent display. Is this my thanks, Joey?'

'My name is Sidney.'

'What? You scurrilously changed my P to something which immediately gasifies me.'

'Come again, Squire?'

'You have tampered with my name. By the bell. It is now an F. In biro.'

All our names were by the bells at the main door. Someone had changed the P in Parts to an F.

'You didn't do it yourself, did you?'

'Turn myself into Farts? This will not do. April was particularly upset. She thought she'd come to the wrong house.'

I couldn't help laughing.

We went round to the front of the house and up the steps.

The conventional curve of the P had been interfered with. All but the middle section of the curve and the stem itself had been heavily scored in black biro.

'You see, you see? Is it your handiwork or no?'

'Luckily you have few callers, Freddie.'

His red-rimmed eyes looked angry enough to shatter. He smelled of shoe polish, carbolic soap and sardines.

'Few callers? How dare you, boy! Society knows where I am. Truth seems to you a random notion. That business today - collapsing. Refusing to move. What was that? I am genuinely concerned. What if something similar happened during my display?

Have you an underlying ailment of some kind? You must come clean with me. Would you like a massage?'

'What kind of message?'

'Massage! Massage! I have good hands. Come upstairs, Joey.'

'My name is Howard.'

We stood in the porch - a canopy supported by two pillars. The brick pillars were thinly rendered with cement. Supposed to have two coats of cement, I overheard a foreman tell a plasterer to give them one coat.

'It's only Trust.'

A few months later the rendering crumbled, the bricks once more revealing themselves. The doorstep had a zig-zag stress crack. Every time you looked, it seemed wider. With imperceptible stealth the house was shifting. One day it would tumble. So would we.

'Are we fighting a losing battle, Freddie?'

Over in the public gardens a woman walked her poodle.

'Dogs are evil. Cats are the only animal. Lions love me. Every time I go to the zoo, they crowd the bars to see me.'

'Do you have to buy them all a drink?'

'The cage bars, you silly sod.'

'I was quite upset you leaving me lying on that wall. Going off in the minicab without me.'

'You were beyond reason, dear boy. There is no such thing as mental illness. This world is logical. It spins. It spins according to strict laws. At my age there is no time for passengers.'

His wide upper lip shone hard as an anvil.

'I am counting on you to save us from decanting.'

He gently rubbed his scaly brow. He went in the hall door, shut it. Peeping through the letter-box, I watched him attempt the first flight, his Oxfords sledge-hammering each step.

'One...two...three...Christ. Four...Why? Five...Hm-hm. Hah-hah. Six...Europe? Never! Seven...'

He did catch me one day drawing a circle on the front of the house. With an A inside it. A for Anarchist.

I called through the letter-box, telling him George S. Drake was going to attend Parting the Waters.

'April is very fond of you, you do know that, Sidney? Joey. What is your damn name?'

'Peter.'

The Trust housed a pair of heroin addicts a couple of doors down from us. A husband and wife. And two kids. The place soon became a centre for crack deals. Addicts were like moths. Society was a dress and the moths were eating through it.

Some days April went to Sainsbury's alone. She'd fill a metal basket, take it to a till, hand money over and not say a word. She didn't have to. That was the beauty of supermarkets.

Did she speak to Freddie? Whatever, he was some kind of hero. Maybe he was so lonely he was pleased she was there. Better a crazy mule than no horse.

I followed her one morning. She caught me watching her. Her upper lip snagged on her upper gum, her upper teeth bared, the upturned nose made it seem as if a fully costumed hare had infiltrated the aisles. Flaring with alarm, mouth grimacing wildly, she hurried away from me. Her loneliness had an odd purity. Nothingness. Pure nothingness. She had nothingness in abundance. She had less substance than a shadow on water. Powerful screaming silence.

'Backofffuckeroll. Fuckoffbackeroll.'

Freddie gave me a wad of money to complete the hiring of the hall and pay Sam and Wally for helping.

The plan was simple - get the tanks and equipment in on the Friday evening. Set up all day Saturday. Freddie to present the show that evening. Next morning remove everything and leave the hall exactly as we found it.

The hall was bare except for ten rows of iron-framed, stackable, canvas chairs. It was a barren space, the four foot crucifix hanging above the stage a real chiller.

On the stage itself was a lectern. Freddie wasn't going to let the occasion pass without a scurrilous remark or three about the state of England.

On the Friday afternoon we carried the tanks from the railway arch to the hall, a distance of a hundred and fifty yards. A six by six by four tank, though empty, was still heavy. Sam and Wally took one end, me the other. The weight stretched our arms like chewing gum. Sam and Wally moved awkwardly in their ill-fitting overalls.

'Bloody hell! Can we put it dahn? Cool.'

'Sam, how's May?'

'Sandwiched between April and June.'

'Very funny.'

Filfy Wilfy looming out of a derelict house fell in with us and, beating a dead march with his fist on the side of the tank, kept up a constant spew of observations.

'It's all about oil, course it is. It's not ourn. Oil is for the axel of the planet. It's going to grind to a halt one of these days. Like a rusty wheel.' Boom. Boom. 'What's the point of puttin' men in space? I'll tell you for why. Space is going to be a prison. You commit a crime, rob a bank say, or croak your missus - bosh! On a space ship and off you go. Round and round and round and round. You won't know your arse from your elbow.' Boom. Boom.

He shuffled along beside us, shoes loose, black overcoat flapping, wad of newspapers in his left hand, right hand out cadging when not thumping the side of the tank. He looked as strange a human being as you could clap eyes on. He was a sick man.

'How's your lovely muvver? Still with us is she?' Boom.

When we reached the hall it was too early to get in. We left the tank outside along the side wall.

'They've found water on Mars - so what? There's not enough to boil an 'ucking egg. Lady Di - she didn't die in that car. Her body was placed in it arterwards. Straight up.'

Sam looked at Wilfy, revolted as much by the wild words as the smell.

'You're about ready for burial, my friend.'

Simply said, cold, effective and because Sam was young, it got to Wilfy. He cleared off.

The next tank we carried was the six by four by two. That was a piece of cake.

We were interrupted by Earthy driving out of the supermarket car park in a brand new BMW. We were blocking his path. He assumed we'd immediately move out of his road. I went round to the driver's window, matey as could be.

'Sir Neville, hi. It's a tank for Freddie's show. Parting the Waters, right? My wife says you have agreed to come. Thanks so much.'

Wally, impressed, examined the car.

'Massif. Yeah. Cool. How much did it set you back, Sir Neville?'

Cars were coming up out of the car park like bees. A queue quickly formed. A horn sounded.

'Now if you don't mind.'

Blonde hair covering one eye, Sir Neville's good-looking bland features betrayed no emotion.

The irate driver directly behind him blared his horn again then, leaping out, stormed up to us.

'What the bally hell's going on? We're trying to get out of here.'

He was a solid citizen, well dressed and spoken.

'Sir Neville Earthy here, I have a suspicion he wants to fuck my wife.'

The man's anger quickly deflated. This was the kind of incident that could easily and bloodily evolve to the front page of the local rag. He got back in his car and locked the doors. Clug. Earthy drew his upper teeth over his bottom lip a few times.

'Look, old chap, just move that...tank. Please.'

'Certainly, Neville. Sorry.'

We lifted the tank out of the way and plodded onwards.

'Why do you suspect Neville?'

'One afternoon I met Lady Hannah. She was wearing a familiar pair of green shoes. Stilettos with diamonds. Were they my wife's shoes?'

'Are their feet the same size?'

'My wife's feet are bigger than Hannah's. They're bigger than mine.'

'Neville is a good enough sort.'

'Why are you on his side all of a sudden?'

'He knows the people at Balliol. He's very good on interview technique.'

Miss Jackpot, carrying a net bag of oranges, came round the corner from the open-air fruit and veg market. We could hear a costermonger shouting,

'Gityer oranges. Lahvlee straws. Mush fresh this morning Missus. Mush lovely fresh mush.'

Miss Jackpot looked into the tank. He dabbed his spectacles to the bridge of his nose. Half his finger nail was billiard-ball black.

'Koran say what is this life? an' dis an' dat. Obey God an' love life to its full. As the prophet was getting on his hawse, they ask him, master what is this life? One foot in the stirrup, he swing other leg over hawse, an' answers even before he sit in saddle. Obey God an' love life to its full an' dis an' dat. It only take him second to give it. Obey God and love life.

'We are seashells on a shore. The tide comes in and out. We hope some gentle hand will pick us up and hold us to a lovely ear. Sex, creed, colour measured against the stars don't register. We must rub along, live together or die alone. It's what anarchy means.'

'Yeah, man yeah. Massif.'

Miss Jackpot wandered off. We went into the chippers by the station and bought fish and chips liberally sprinkled with salt and vinegar. We ate outside, squatting down in the doorway of what used to be a record shop. Sam licked his fishy fingers with great concentration.

'Does your wife achieve orgasm on a regular or interim basis?'

He stared hard at me, awaiting answer.

'You sound like a salesman. Why do you want to know?'

'It's just May and myself. She's bought a car. We were on the back seat for quite a while last night. It was desperate stuff. But nothing, as far as I could tell, was achieved. She put her high-heel through the rear window. She was furious.'

'Because nothing was achieved?'

'No. Because of the broken window someone stole the car in the night. She's too old. It's like sleeping with your mother.'

'Have you tried that?'

'I don't live in a Greek drama.'

The expansion tanks out on the flat roof over Rosa's kitchen were housed in a hut made from cheap wood and ply. Hopelessly rotten and falling apart, it was another Cackhand & Bindweed special. The door off its hinges, the insulation blown away, pigeons roosted on the ballcock and crapped in the water.

I checked the tanks from time to time, cleaned them out, wrapped newspapers round the pipes. It was a philosophical exercise. Man was doomed. Therefore we dreamed of escape. The only reason we want to go to Mars - it's free from council housing.

The roof was paved with uneven stone slabs. The rain leaked through into Rosa's and eventually oozed down the walls to us. The slabs were covered with moss and dirt and when Wally wanted to get rid of broken bits of furniture and other rubbish - newspapers, empty boxes, shopping bags - he just dumped them out on the slabs. Every so often I'd clear up. Then I'd lean on the parapet wall and gaze down on our garden and the flowers grown by my wife.

Honeysuckle, hollyhock, peony, lilac, rose, clematis...The brilliant colours, perfumes, in her absence were her ghost. Clematis, the loveliest of them all, didn't have a scent.

How could we leave that garden? Even if Eve didn't mind.

Freddie was in the hallway, by his feet a rolled-up P.V.C. banner. He'd found it at the rear of Sainsbury's. Taking it home, he'd painted a slogan on the reverse side.

Gaudy lettering in reds, blues, greens, yellow, surrounded by theatrical stars and playful water spurts, announced -

"GIGANTIC Water Scena. PARTS Water Organ. Presenting The Sensational Dancing Waters.

The full-stops were perfect round dots in black.

Pleased, as if he'd slain them in the aisles already, he awaited my reaction.

'Seen is spelt wrong. S double E, N.'

'What, what? SCENA! Not seen. S-C-E-N-A. The unfolding dramatic events. SCENA! It's a professional word.'

He pronounced the scena with operatic flourish, inserting an H sound between the C and E.

'Parts should have an apostrophe. The genitive case.'

'There is no room for pedantry in top billing. They know it's my organ.'

'Recognise it, will they?'

'What? No. I no longer have it. I told you. I sold it. A troop of Primitive Brethren in Burslem purchased it. Don't forget to deliver the thunder sheet.'

'What about the old generators? They seem to have disappeared.'

'They are in hand. Dickie Grimes has been working on them this two weeks.'

'Who he?'

'You'll find out. As there isn't a suitable room backstage, see there is space reserved for me off-stage right. With an extra chair for April. Her entrance is glorious. Just wait until you see it!'

'I'd rather not.'

'What, what? Come upstairs, help me choose.'

There was a yellow frock and a brown two-piece suit on his bed. On the floor were two pairs of high-heels, one white, the other green. I looked closely at the green ones - they definitely weren't my wife's. Carefully placed on the pillow was the daffodil he'd made in the distant past, when towns in England couldn't supply fresh ones. It had already picked up a sprinkling of talcum powder.

The cardinal above the mantle screamed death and corruption.

'My masterpiece. Clearly. I'm so glad you like it. If anything ever happens to me, you must sell it. For April. The price will see her through a comfortable old age.'

'What you'd get for that, would it see her to the end of the street, Freddie?'

'Paintings are fetching fabulous prices in Berlin. Sell it there. Or have an exhibition of all my work in Bond Street.'

'Art is elephant dung. Or human blood. Or a dead cat in a jar. Or a stack of panties autographed by the numerous lovers of the owner. Unless you're prepared to operate on your own prostrate in public with a can opener, whilst recording it on video, no one will look twice at you. Art is no longer in a frame.'

'Taste is circular. The public can eat muck only for so long.'

The door opened. April's hand materialised. Her fingers wagged about as if trying to get a purchase on the air. When the rest of her appeared, she looked straight at me. Freddie noticed.

'You see, you see? Ha-hah. Definitely attracted. Rather.'

I could never get used to the dead eyes that looked but never saw. She was wearing a blue house coat and a mop cap under which her hair bulged. I was certain she was naked under the house coat.

'Just before April makes her entrance I will beat the thunder sheet three times. She comes on...the flower...the flower...The Strauss rises to a crescendo. Spouts leap, the water a blue tumult. The moment is heartrending. Before all that you will say, "And now ladies and gentlemen, it gives me great pleasure. To welcome back. The one and still the only man. Ever to put his head. In the lion's mouth. Under water. Mr. Freddie Parts, his protégé Miss April Fard and winner of the Blackpool Tower Circus Souvenir medal, the gorgeous Annette Fischer!" The build-up is important. I've seen people die for the want of an introduction.'

How would the water turn blue? Who was Annette Fischer?

April, hands clasped under her considerable bosom, stood still in the middle of the room, her flesh pale as early morning mushroom. On the small writing table by the word processor was half a loaf, a knife resting on it, a pot of marmalade and butter in its opened wrapper.

'How does the water turn blue?'

'You'll see.'

'Who is Annette Fischer?'

'You'll see.'

He pointed to the clothes on the bed.

'Which do you prefer, dear boy? For April. Be frank, Joey.'

'Okay, you can call me Frank.'

'What? What?'

'The green shoes. The two-piece I think will give her the dignity she deserves, whilst actually enhancing those curvaceous parts for which she is justly famous. In this attic anyway. Her legs, taken together or apart, are outstanding.'

'I beg your pardon?'

'Exactly. I must go. I have arranged with Reg Shand to get into the hall in an hour's time.'

April, a grimace on her face, her neck powdery, stared through me. I bolted out the door.

I waited for my wife to come in from work. When she did, she immediately started changing her clothes, flinging garments all over the flat. She'd been all day in a committee room at Westminster, and proudly told me of a verbal assault she'd made on a grand penitentiary mandarin, whose chief objective was to make it harder for blokes like me to get out, once in. Sometimes she almost boasted I'd been to jail; making it sound as if I'd robbed a bank; whereas all I'd done was crash a bus.

'You know your green high-heels? You haven't given them to April, have you? Or Hannah Earthy?'

'Of course not. I'm wearing them.'

She was. And for the moment nothing else.

'You met Neville outside Sainsbury's.'

'Told you, did he?'

'You ask me to ask him to come to Freddie's water thing or whatever it is, and then you insult him. I mean why?'

'I don't like the way he looks at you. I don't like the way you mention him in a warm tone. He's all success and no talent.'

'And what are you?'

The Earthys were coming to Freddie's show. Also Nigerian Ore. Sam's parents too. May. Julia. She'd told them all. They were coming to extract the urine.

Getting into exquisite casuals she slotted a video into the machine, ready for an evening of ease and olives and gin and tonic. She wasn't pleased I was rushing out.

'Whatever happens between us will be your fault.'

'Between you and Earthy? Or between you and me?'

In silence, she smoothed her face before a mirror.

I called round for Sam.

He was sitting on a tall stool placed on an old weighing scales platform - the type once used for weighing bags of coal or corn. The scales and a few storm lanterns, miners' lamps, a copper kettle and ceramic beer pumps made the kitchen seem like a farmhouse museum. They could have charged admission.

When he saw me come in he rubbed his index fingers on his thighs so hard it wouldn't have surprised had his trousers caught fire.

'I've being accepted by Balliol. I just heard.'

He didn't look half happy enough. His mother beamed proudly.

His father did a world-weary yawn but you could see he was mighty pleased.

At the Bible Hall, Reg Shand was waiting for us. He wasn't pleased when we carted the tanks inside. Up on the stage they bulked large, heavy and dull. It was impossible to imagine how such utilitarian drabness could be part of any dramatic display. Freddie believed in action. Action transformed.

What really irked Reg was my refusing to be decanted to the other end of the borough. What had it to do with him? He didn't work for the Trust. Was he trying to pull a fast one? Empty, our house would be valuable.

'The other tenants would agree, only for you. You're asking for it, pal. And you're going to get it one of these days.'

'Is that right?'

'You're a wind-up merchant. Why, no one knows.'

'We're like clocks. If we're not wound up we stop.'

Removing his pork pie hat, he contemplated it for a moment, before returning it to his head.

'You're a prawn or two short of a cocktail, pal. We'll get you out, don't worry. The place is falling apart, you know that. There's property people involved, I'll be honest. You'll have to push off.'

I took out Freddie's roll of dosh and with a quick furtive back-handed gesture slipped a fifty into his hand. The implication being I knew the money would never see the light of official day. He darted the note down into his breast pocket.

'The matter pertaining is in hand and received with thanks as per.'

'The outstanding amount will be tendered on completion of our objectives here, Mr. Shand. Certainly not later than Sunday morning.'

'Are you sure old Parts isn't putting on a public entertainment, is he? You'd need public liability insurance.'

'Sure, cool, no way. This is utterly private for one or two people.'

'Any damage incurred, the full rigours of the law will be... rigorous.'

'I appreciate that Reg. What will be taking place here is an act of worship actually. Freddie will be paying homage to a force of nature. Specifically water. That which we pass every day. If we're lucky.'

He gave me the key to the hall. It would save him having to open up in the morning.

'I like your porkpie hat. Myself, I'm partial to the old sou'wester.'

He stared at me, head tilted slightly.

'You need to see the brain mechanic, pal. Ask him to tighten the screws.'

'And you see the carpenter, Reg. Ask him to pull the nails out.'

He banged the door behind him.

Sam started bouncing up and down. He was on his way to Oxford. He'd be leaving home.

'How come you got in, Sam?'

'I did a great interview. I told you Neville was a tremendous help.'

'What did they ask you?'

'Well, one question they asked me was the difference between instinct and inspiration. A cat running up a tree at the last moment, to escape pursuit by a dog, is instinct. A man suddenly moved to climb the tree, to breath in the beauty of the world, that's inspiration.'

'Is the cat up the tree when the man climbs it?'

'It is not necessarily the same tree. You div!'

'What kind of tree is it?'

'A convenient tree.'

'A dog's urinal you mean?'

He vigorously rubbed his index fingers along his thighs. What would they say in Oxford when they saw him doing that?

'Does it bloody matter, what kind of tree, what kind of cat?'

'How did the world begin, Sam? I mean, where did time and space come from? How did something come from nothing?'

He cleaned his glasses with a big hankie, then blew his nose. Balling the hankie tightly, he struggled to ram it into his pocket, as if it were a towel.

'The explanation will be so simple. When man enters the next dimension. We're not there yet. Ants under a stone haven't got a meaning for the person who lifts the stone.'

'Do you believe in God?'

'Don't be silly.'

'Silly you do or silly you don't?'

'God is a Zimmer for the feeble of mind. To more serious matter. My mother popped into the local for a drink the other night. She overheard some builder types plotting to come round your house and duff you up. Be warned.'

I was worried. What could I do? Worry about it later.

We rigged up a black drape behind which Freddie could hide from his audience. When we hung the thunder sheet, Sam hit it a slap, testing it. A tinny yelp exploded to a roar that swelled, rumbled, rolled mightily through the hall before fading away, consumed by its own Old Testament wrath. He hit it again, harder - pleased with cause and effect. Excited, he quickly rubbed index fingers together, as if sharpening a knife. He caught me looking at him. With a magician's flourish, withdrawing a cigarette from behind an ear, he lit up, having struck a match on the sole of his shoe. He was hard to dislike. He sat on a chair in the corner made by the wall and the black drape. In an atmosphere oddly confessional, dragging deep on his cigarette, he spoke.

'When I was seven, I hid in my mother's wardrobe. It was a game I played. I'd hear them calling me. I was in there one day when she came in, unaware I was present. She undressed down to her...You know those under-drawers ladies wore in another century? She'd grown up in a military family. She wore a big pink bra. She sat at the dressing-table putting on her lipstick. Ever since, and I can't understand this, maybe you can, which is why I tell you, I've been a magnet for older women. They can't help finding me attractive. I've had ancient crones of fifty giving me the eye at bus stops. Think May. Need I say more?'

'Under-drawers? Do you mean those hefty elasticated bloomers still popular with Mrsblouse customers? Invariably complete with gusset.'

'Precisely. Bloomers.'

'What colour?'

'Red.'

'Fatal. Fatal, Sam. I understand. I fear you will, for the rest of your days, plough a peculiarly hectic Freudian furrow.'

'But why are they attracted to me, not me to them?'

'Are you sure it wasn't your father you saw in bloomers? Now that would be interesting.'

'Quiet sure.'

'In the gender blender all is confusion. When you went for the Balliol interview, who quizzed you? Men or women?'

'Men. Three men.'

'At least one of them wore bloomers under his trousers. He was instrumental in your selection.'

'Rubbish.'

'Did they see you doing that index finger rubbing routine?'

'It's just a comforting displacement exercise. Everybody does something similar. The girl who went in ahead of me carried a hot water bottle and smoked a pipe.'

'Was it a cold day?'

'Not particularly. She was accepted there and then!'

'Either one of you is certain to end up Prime Minister. If the office survives the present incumbent. If it's you, remember your old pal. By then I'll be in some cash-strapped secure unit, sharing a strait-jacket with April. I'm recording this by the way.'

'Bastard.'

By the time we'd slung the supermarket banner over the stage, Freddie arrived. He was carrying a diesel pump with the help of a man called Dickie Grimes. The pumps had fly wheels and were very heavy. Dickie Grimes had a shock of white hair sticking up in all directions as if he'd just been electrocuted. His spectacles hung round his neck on a string. Thin and wiry, he was extremely old. Freddie stood at the back of the hall, admiring his own name on his own canvas billing.

'It won't do,' Dickie Grimes said, scratching at his chin.

'Why not, Dickie Grimes?'

'It'll need supporting, mate.'

The stage was a series of collapsible platforms, the supporting frames held securely in place with hinge pins. Fine for a Sunday morning preacher but not for tanks full of water. The front two decks overlapped the frames by an inch. Dickie Grimes, having produced a measuring tape, ordered that first thing in the morning, Sam and I were to buy wood, saw it into lengths and wedge them home under this overhanging lip. These struts were to be thirty five inches by three. Freddie decided he'd only use two of the tanks, thus keeping the weight of water to a necessary minimum.

Dickie Grimes, with school-masterly seriousness, nodded at the tanks.

'Do you know how many gallons? The weight?'

'Yes, Sir,' said Sam, 'The large, six by six by four, equals one hundred and forty four cubic feet, thirty-six cubic feet to a ton, four ton exactly. The small one, about a ton and a third. I doubt you'll fill them to the rim, say five ton? Five ton.'

Dickie Grimes putting on his glasses the better to see this genius, decided he was worthy of further testing.

'Which is heaviest - sea water or tap water?'

'Sea water,' answered eager-beaver, top-of-the-class, Oxford-bound, Sam.
Dickie Grimes now turned to me.
'Why is that?'
'Sea water is invariably weighed down with seaweed or fish. And sand. And maybe used condoms. And shells.'
Freddie howled.
'What's ruddy funny, Freddie? Idiots we don't need.'
'He knows perfectly well, Dickie Grimes. He enjoys cheeking old buffers like us.'
'I know perfectly well. I enjoy cheeking old buffers like you.'
Dickie Grimes shifted his dentures, then tongued them back in position. Freddie, chuckling, followed him outside. He was easy in the company of a last old friend.

They came back in carrying coils of fire brigade hose. They also had an ordinary garden hose pipe. Dickie Grimes was a meticulous worker. His hands were still powerful. He wasn't as big a man as Freddie but his inner strength was greater. It was impressive seeing him wrestle a rusted valve, suddenly applying torque, forcing it to turn. A cigarette with a phallic curve of ash dangled from his mouth as he worked. He'd recently celebrated his eighty-fifth birthday.

He and Freddie started out together in engineering. Wearing grey flannel trousers, white plimsolls, an open-necked white shirt, he looked like a geriatric ghost strayed in from a tennis tournament played half a century before. In the past he'd courted Freddie's sister, but needing someone more exotic, she'd eloped to Jerusalem with a circus musician.

From the cold water tap, in the kitchenette at the front of the hall, they ran the garden hose to the tanks. Dickie Grimes calculated it would take forty-five minutes to fill them. Twelve hundred gallons.

The rings of nozzles, valves, spouts they attached to various pipes. The pipes they connected to a cross pipe with a fitting that married up to the fire brigade hose. The hose ran to the side of the stage area and connected to a series of controlling valves. These wheel valves were on a length of copper piping, connected by a few feet of hose to a diesel pump. From the other end of the pump hose ran back into the tank, thus completing a crude but effective circuit. Two circuits - two tanks, two diesel pumps.

For anchorage the valves were clamped to a table.

Freddie stood fondling the wheels, turning them on and off, testing them, as if in the boiler room of a battleship. The octopus tangle of hose and pipe work, the dreary hall, the dull tanks, the dangling crucifix above the stage - how could he transform them into the Gigantic Water Scena promised in the lurid legend? A drawing pin having come away, the legend was already wilting - the Gigantic now read igantic.

A big toe of the figure on the crucifix was missing.

Could Freddie, one last time, overcome quotidian tat? Did he really believe the TV bloke, who went to university with my wife, would be so knocked-out by his watery sensations, he'd get him a solo-series on the box? Sir Neville Earthy wouldn't be interested even if he liked it. Would a final crushing of dreams break Freddie's spirit? A broken dream could kill. Perhaps it wasn't his final dream. That could be me and April.

Dickie Grimes turned the tap in the kitchenette and let enough water into the tanks to test the system. He then started the diesel pumps, swinging on the crank handles with relentless sharp explosions of energy, until the engines caught and the fly wheels spun. There was much noise and more smoke. Freddie said the audience wouldn't hear the oily racket above the Strauss. The Blue Danube would drown it.

'Ready when you are, Dickie Grimes.'

Freddie pulled on a lever, turned some valves. Dickie Grimes, cigarette in the corner of his mouth, head at an interested angle, adjusted the engines. We waited.

Like a boa constrictor disturbed, the hose came to life with peristaltic urgency.

A vivid force of water whooshing, spluttering fiercely, emerged in the form of an unstoppable geyser. The crucifix dangling over the stage was hit so hard by the gush its string snapped.

Freddie howled in triumph. It worked. The dream was still intact.

When Sam fished the crucifix out of the tank, it was minus the other big toe.

Dickie Grimes wasn't going to be present next day. Sam and I were going to have to run the whole thing ourselves.

He told us that Freddie, in the old days, used his dancing waters for political purposes.

'He stood for election. Got me to stand as well. He'd start his water organ, then make a speech. We did Easter Monday on Wanstead Flats. Teddy Boys attacked us.'

'What party did he belong to?'

'His own party. Conservatives for Britain and Empire. It was so he could put CBE after his name. He got twenty-eight votes. I got thirty. He was arrested in the town hall at the declaration. He called the Prime Minister a gutless cuckold who gave the empire away and got nothing for it in return. England has become blingland. It's shallow.'

'Oh, I don't know. It's still got a deep end.'

Dickie Grimes was dry as sawdust.

'What's the best way to live life, Dickie?'

'Waste time in the nicest way possible. If you can afford to. Time is in our heads. The rest is technical. Freddie tells me you don't work. Normal people work.'

'Maybe I'm not normal.'

He was right. Normal people did work. I'd get a job. But what at? A century and a half of industrial revolution had petered out back in the seventies. England was now a tourist trail, a financial centre, a social security dispensation office for the world's dispossessed. The only jobs for layabouts like myself were in post-rooms or stacking shelves in supermarkets at night time. Sun-deprived jobs for aliens, youngsters, people with disabilities.

'You have no right to secretly record people like that.'

'I wasn't being secret, Dickie Grimes. I held it out towards you. You could see what it was.'

'Are you working for the government? Turn it off.'

'Tell me about April Fard.'

'There's nothing to tell. Freddie wants her to conceive immaculately. Like the Blessed Virgin. It's his dream.'

He shogged out of the hall, climbed into a clapped-out van and, right indicator flashing, drove round the corner. It was a one-way street. He should have turned left.

I stared at Freddie. April conceiving immaculately was too Gothic for words.

His dancing waters ready to go, the dream of revenge about to be realised, he was very pleased.

'I'll show 'em! Sods.'

I locked up. We went home.

Waxy druggies hung around an all-night chemist's. Some of them had prescriptions in their hands. Dying fish hooked by themselves, they looked strained, pained, the colour of death. A mini-cab office - the front window space of a derelict shop - was packed with Ethiopian drivers waiting for fares. To come so far for this...O Ethiopia!

Sam fancied a drink. The two of us left Freddie and went into the local. May instantly materialised, greeting him with a kiss, sloppy as a lick from a cow's tongue. I murdered a pint and went home.

My wife was in bed, reading.

'I'm going to get a job, darling. Knitting socks for spiders.'

'Just stop thinking you're special. Get in and go to sleep.'

'I nudge my way through the day. A street or two and this house. That's all I need. Why should I feel guilty?'

Sleep. Caterpillars started coming into my head. I imagined a cerura vinula in threat posture. It had a puss to stop your heart, with two big eye-spots and waving fangs pissing jets of poison. It looked a bit like Dickie Grimes. I worried about Freddie and April. He said she was fond of me. I worried about Miss Chats. I heard a caterpillar banging on the door. Was it her? The banging was on the internal door which gave access from the ground floor, down into our basement. A caterpillar banging on the door? My wife elbowed me awake. I sprung out of bed.

It was Rosa. Rosa hammering like mad.

'Anyone dahn there? I need 'elp! 'Elp! 'e's gorn dahn agin. 'n' this time he ain't never gettin' up. 'Elp, some bleeder, 'elp!'

She was in a long off-white nightie. Material lay round her feet like a mound of wedding dress. I followed her up the stairs and into her flat.

Gibbs lay on the floor, naked from the waist down, his flesh cold. I rested my hand on his shoulder. His tartan cap had come off. That was a bad omen. Head bare as a bullet, he looked utterly dead.

A great swathe of woodchip paper billowed down from the ceiling, the paste eaten away by a teeming army of arthopods, myriapods, arachnids. Insects were on long term tenancies beyond fear of decanting.

''e looks a gonner. It's all I bleedin' need. I just been diagnosed with breast cancer. Shall I put the kettle on?'

'You just been what, Rosa?'

'They told me I got cancer in me breast.'

Gibbs was stiffening on the floor. Rosa had breast cancer. This was the heel of the hunt and no mistake. For them.

'Phil? Are you all right? I'll phone for an ambulance.'

His bare manhood lay dead as a poisoned mouse. I covered him with a towel. He'd had another stroke. Down by the bed, the plastic milk bottle stood full.

'Phil?'

His arms were out-stretched, right knee raised a little, feet touching, chin resting on his shoulder. Another tenant crucified to the floor.

Rosa lifted his cap, rested it on his head.

'Never mind, old sausage, Joey's going to call the ambulance.'

Despite everything, the two were one. They'd been married a lifetime. They were finally succumbing.

When I first moved into the house I'd hear them singing. Friday night, as soon as they came in from the pub, they immediately set about revolving continuously forward the mirth-laden, hoop-bound wooden vessel...Praising attractive bunches of coconuts of varying sizes...Declaring all young refined females, knowing how jolly tars could be, were enamoured of same...And maybe because they were natives of the place, despite being down in the dumps, whilst going to and fro, they had a certain sensation they still loved England's capital city.

Now Gibbs looked like he didn't have long to live. Death was the ultimate caterpillar. I was scared of that word beginning with D and ending in H for heaven or hell.

I ran downstairs and phoned for the ambulance. Soon it came clattering through the night and Gibbs was carried out on a stretcher. I stood in the hallway, warning the ambulance crew not to trip on the loose Marley tiles.

Rosa, resilient as a sparrow, drank a cuppa, smoked a fag.

'Do you fink that's it for Gibbs? Will we ever see 'im agin? 'E can't last much longer, can 'e? Can 'e? What do you fink?'

I was desperate to get back to bed. To hide in, snuggle into my wife. To count myself lucky. One, two, three...to infinity.

A woodlouse hurried across the space where a short while before Gibbs lay on his cross.

Rosa hadn't even come down stairs to see him off.

'Somefing snapped inside a me a long time ago. You understand, darlin'?' It's been a long time with Gibbs. I loved 'im, love 'im. Acourse. But you know...Comes a time you can't go on anymore. I'm just not able. Who's gonna look arter me? I don't care no more. 'cos I'm not able. Me and Phil, course I loved 'im.'

They had been together for half a century. How could two people live together that long and not run out of road?

The Zimmer frame had fallen on the floor. Rosa flicked it to one side with her foot. I was only wearing a vest. I had it pulled down over my privates. Rose flicked a beady eye.

'You'll catch your death, mate.'

'Open up! Landlord here! Open in the name of the law!'

There was much scuffling about before Wally came to the door. He was in pyjamas and had newspapers stuffed down his front for extra warmth.

'Wally, come on, mate, we got things to do. We got to go to the timber yard. Me and you. And Sam. Freddie's show tonight, matey chum. Haven't forgotten, have you?'

'Yeah? What? Oh, right, yeah, cool. What's the weather like?'

'You'll love it, Wall.'

'Yeah? Cool. I'll see you in the church hall. In a minute. I was in bed.'

'Really?'

'There's going to be annuver war. I heard it on the radio. I was let down by my school. I'd like to be decanted. I been thinking about the Bozzies. It's not the same area what it used to be.'

Maybe he was on the wrong pills or took too many of the right ones.

'Get yourself dressed and I'll treat you to breakfast in the Electric.'

'Yeah? Right, cool. Did they take old whatsit away last night or what? Phil. I thought I heard carrying down.'

In the Electric he ate bacon, sausage, eggs, baked beans, fried tomato, mushrooms, fried bread, two toast, two mugs of tea. To see him polish that lot off, grease round his mouth, yoke leaking through his teeth and down his chin, was immense.

Fata the lovely waitress had left. Turkey said she was working up the High Road now.

In the massage parlour. Fata, lovely, brown-eyed Bosnian, giving manual relief...How did Turkey get her to do that?

'She didn't come all this way to work in a massage parlour, did she?'

'No one hold gun to her head.'

A new girl went in and out of the kitchen. She had black eyes, a long neck, and shiny black hair, sleek as a cormorant emerging from water. A sight for sore eyes. And mine were sore at the thought of never clapping them on Fata again.

We went round to the timber yard. Sam was waiting for us. It was a long, concreted yard, flanked on one side by a high wall separating it from railway lines and on the other by big open sheds full of lengths of timber for the building trade. You first of all had to order what you wanted in an office, then take the chit down the yard to the first available shed man. These were hardened joshers in steel-capped boots who unmercifully extracted the urine to temper boredom and cold.

'Three by one what?'

'Wood. For, ah, you know, holding up a stage.'

'Oi, Jeb! They want to hold up a stage with lengths of three by one.'

Jeb's ferret head appeared through an opening in the first floor.

'Nah, mate, you'll need a bow and arrow and a few Red Indians for that job.'

Eventually they relented, fetching three ten foots and even letting us borrow a saw with which we cut ten struts, each measuring thirty-five inches.

Back in the church hall, we banged them at intervals under the lip of the stage until we'd made a rib-cage along the front. The stage thus supported, we completed the filling of the tanks.

Sam and Wally arranged a semi-circle of chairs for the audience. I re-hung the Christ figure and stuck the G of Gigantic back up, this time using a drawing pin reinforced by a wodge of chewing gum freshly spat by Wally. The tanks filled, we walked around the stage, testing for signs of frailty.

Freddie arrived with a very old leather suitcase. His initials were imprinted on one end - F.P.

He wore a long overcoat, brown suit and brogues. He looked a man renewed, his face and ears glowing. As if his life had been a rehearsal for this day. His immense optimism made me wary. What if it all went wrong? What if life was a performance that never actually got on stage? Except the one scene that didn't need rehearsal. The death bed scene.

What if life turned out to be a long marriage to a person you no longer loved because life had worn you down?

Freddie ordered Wally to carry his suitcase. Then, leaning on my shoulder as if I were a newel post, he stepped up onto the stage. Looking out over the empty hall, he filled his chest. Nectar.

'It is Gigantic. Why give the public anything less? Who would prefer an egg cup when they could have a Grecian vase? Do you know, I had to stop and have two widdles on the way here?'

'Really? Nerves?'

'Let me hear your introductory speech. Don't be shy. Aim for the back row.'

'There isn't one.'

'Aim for it anyway.'

When I spouted the words,

'The only man. Ever to put his head. In the lion's mouth. Under water.' Wally thought we were actually going to have a lion.

'And where would we get a lion, Wally?'

'The Zoo?'

'Showbiz,' said Sam, 'is where reason and belief sink under the weight of hyperbole.'

'When you say the speech, dear boy, imagine every full stop is an exclamation mark.'

He ordered a further drape for the corner of the stage to ensure he was masked from 'his' audience.

'If they see how a thing is done it isn't magic.'

He produced a cassette player loaded with Strauss. Then three bottles of blue toilet-bowl cleaner which he poured into the smaller of the two tanks.

'Who is Annette Fischer by the way?'

'All will be revealed. Test the engines.'

First heating them with a blow torch, I eventually got them going.

Freddie was going to stay in the hall until the performance, preparing himself, building up the mood, talking to his dream, working out what to say to impress Sir Neville Earthy, Nigerian Ore, Sam's parents, May, George S. Drake. My wife was certain they were all coming.

I went home.

Nearing the house, I met Rosa mouse-hopping along with a shopping bag. I carried it for her.

'How are you? What's the news from Phil?'

'I don't know. They 'aven't told me. 'e could be dead.'

'Haven't you been to see him in the hospital?'

'I ain't got the strength, 'av I? I can't care no more, I told you.'

They had a son somewhere but he never showed up. I was pretty certain we'd never see Gibbs again. I feared for the future. His flesh was my flesh. Everyone's flesh was your flesh.

My wife was getting out of the bath. She left the water in for me. She moved about, rubbing in concoctions, drying her hair. That splendid impenetrable mass of lovely hair. You could lose your hands in it.

Putting a foot up on the side of the bath, she dried in between her toes. Lying in the bath I watched her. It was like seeing a favourite statue get down off its plinth and move about. She slipped a diamond necklace round her neck. It cost a small fortune from a fashion chancer in Kensington calling herself Pippa Paoli. Money had to be wasted in exclusive places. She slipped on a pair of knickers designed exclusively by one Ramonde. Another chancer who made it from the East End to Bond Street by designing underwear so skimpy you wondered why women bothered.

She was hard to handle. Sometimes if she was standing with her back to me, I'd stick my head between her legs, lift her up on my shoulders and prance around the room. She'd hang on, laughing, shrieking then, increasingly angry, slap at my head until I put her down. Clownish behaviour was easier for me than soul-searching.

It was only a Bible-bashing church hall, it was only Freddie, but she was going to arrive looking like a princess in complete control of fashion, money, time, space, me. And in a linen suit the price of a good second-hand cabin cruiser.

I lay in the bath wondering, should I pull a wobbly of some kind? Forget about Freddie. Just don't turn up.

The root of all creation shot up out of the water like a rogue torpedo. Her double-take was executed with mock shock and dismissive humour. Whilst blood engendered lechery, we'd chop down forests, eat animals, kill one another in wars, love one another to death. Any evolutionary advance to a stelliferous, flesh-free, pure intelligent state, was going to be a long time coming.

'I've written a poem about you.'

'Go on. If you must.'

'Thimble nipples

Fresh raspberries

Let me cream them

With my semen.'

'Prosodists everywhere, please note.'

'Pardon?'

She didn't like it.

We were all set to go. Freddie was in his draped-off corner, adjusting April's wide-brimmed summer hat. The artificial daffodil shook in her hand as if divining her nerves.

Sam was at the door welcoming the audience. The Jesus figure minus two toes hung over the stage. The tanks were full, the hose pipe ready, the diesel engines waiting, the time pushing up to eight o'clock.

"GIGANTIC Water Scena. PARTS Water Organ. Presenting The Sensational Dancing Waters."

There was no disguising the tat with lighting effects - we had none.

The minutes weighed, passed. I would soon have to start speaking. Freddie, his confidence massive, peeped out at me. When he lowered his index finger, I was to commence. The sparse audience, an indistinct jumble of limbs and faces, looked like millions.

But the instant Freddie lowered his finger - with the abrupt urgency of someone ordering an immediate execution - each one of them became clear, distinct, horribly familiar. The chap with the cheesy face and smile - Sam's dad. He'd examined up my bum. Beside him was Sam's Mum - Mrs. Tripp. She wore a Laura Ashley number that wouldn't have looked out of place covering a sofa. May, hot for Sam, leered like a gargoyle. She was wearing black and white striped tights and top, like she was some kind of fanatical Geordie with horrible taste. My wife sat between Earthy and George S. Drake. Earthy, wearing loafers, chinos, a white shirt, blonde hair slanting across his forehead, lay back on his chair, legs stretched out, his clasped hands a cushion behind his head. It was a perfect position for yawning. Near the end of the row, most astonishing sight of all, was Nigerian Ore. NO never appeared in anything other than extremely expensive suits, yet here he was in jeans and a light blue cashmere roll-neck. He'd been to Africa. You could tell. He didn't tan. His face pinked. My wife had pulling power. She looked up at me, challenging me to be normal. For once. In front of all these people...PLEASE!

Freddie was wearing his male/female attire. He was in his corner behind the table of valves, half a gent's hat cocked on one side of his head, half a tiara stuck on the other. How could I let myself be associated, in public, with such a raving loony? Plural actually - there was also April. What if she flipped, drowned herself in one of the tanks? Freddie's finger was wagging frantically.

I came out between the tanks, trying to remember what it was I was supposed to say. The words were balled up under my tongue. I'd never felt so naked in my life. Get up in public and your soul was revealed. You couldn't hide what you were.

Miss Chats and Reg Shand came in. I paused. Miss Chats wore a leather suit. Reg was in his usual flannels and blazer. And pork pie. Why had they arrived? She had a letter in her hand - a brown bureaucratic envelope. It had to be for me.

I cleared my throat and made a shy, gentle, shy, smiling, shy, nervous, shy start.

'And now ladies and gentlemen...' Laughter. That was funny?

'It gives me great pleasure!' It was a tiny house but that brought it down. Was this all it took? It explained why the world was full of comedians.

'To welcome back!' This time silence. In view of the previous two reactions, I was expecting a round of applause.

'The one! And still the only man! Ever to put his head! In the lion's mouth! Under water!'

Sam's father brayed. Mrs. Tripp had to slap him on the back. It was as if he'd never laughed before in his life and didn't know how do it properly.

Why hadn't I questioned Freddie's ludicrous claims? Could lions swim underwater? Presumably Freddie could. Why wasn't I... speaking?

My wife - Titania, the queen bee - sat with nonchalant grace but still the challenging look in her eyes and round her mouth.

Turning to where Freddie and April lurked in the corner, desperately falling into hackneyed gesture, I held my hands out to the black drape as if aiming a rifle, my intention being to give them an enormous build up.

'Mr. Freddie Parts! His protégé Miss April Fard! And winner of the Blackpool Tower Circus Souvenir medal! The gorgeous Annette Fischer!'

The way I said 'Fard', pausing before and after and rolling the 'r', elicited a high-pitched beep of amusement from Mrs. Tripp. Sam, over by the door, gave his thighs a quick rub with his index fingers. Intelligent families were the weirdest.

Nigerian Ore's name was Carter Petts-Willis. He'd very recently pulled off a massive deal in Africa with a corrupt government and was all across the quality business sections.

'Fat cat gets the cream. And a knighthood.'

I'd hardly spoken a civil word with the man. Not even to say good morning. The antipathy was essentially class based, a lamentable tribal hostility which basic good manners couldn't camouflage. Yet there he was, looking genuinely interested. Like he was witnessing a proper show. What a decent bloke, I thought.

Everybody, including NO, even Reg and Miss Chats, roared. I was shocked rigid. I hadn't done anything. Wally was looking up. They were all looking up. My wife, trying to help me, raised her eyes and her finger.

The canvas on which the lurid legend was written had come away at either end. The words - "Sainsbury's", and "Champagne", were now visible. "Sainsbury's" and "Champagne" they took to be so mutually exclusive, it was hilarious.

Trapdoors were opening and closing in my skull, with little men popping up offering fists, boots, hammers, hopeless smiles.

From the dark corner Freddie barked, 'BOY!'

His gloved, female hand, stuck out desperately, commanding me to approach the diesel engines.

I rushed to the side and, grabbing the nearest crank handle, swung madly. The engine spluttered but wouldn't catch. Having reduced me to a sweating wreck, it then decided to kick in.

Bomp-bomp-bomp-bomp...

The second engine, when I cranked it, caught no bother at all.

Bomp-bump-bomp-bump-bomp-bump...

The racket was incredible. It was like being down in the engine room of an old trawler. With a single waft of his hand Freddie dismissed me. The maestro had to be alone. The blurring fly wheels, the oily stench, the smoke, the noise, didn't worry him at all.

I scuttled over to Sam by the door.

We could see Freddie's hands manipulating the bank of valves. The water circulating, the hose pipes began to shiver. Music played - faintly at first, but gradually loud enough to be heard above the engines. The Blue Danube. The pipes, under tremendous pressure, filled to bursting.

Freddie turned a wheel valve.

A jet of water soared up and hit the first thing it met. The crucifix. Splattered so hard, it was convulsively knocked hither and thither until the frayed string holding it snapped once more. This time the crucifix avoided the water but hit the side of the tank. It flipped onto the stage, then pogoed to the hall floor. One of its plaster hands came away and spun crazily over to where Wally stood. He picked it up and smiled at everyone.

The audience found it entertaining. In a pagan democracy, a touch of sacrilege, however accidental, was always welcome.

Freddie now contrived a tiered wedding cake effect. Thick plumes of water, in ascending circles, spumed upwards to a height of six feet and, with The Blue Danube music swelling behind, it couldn't but look impressive. The water, white and foamy, appeared dense as candle-grease.

The old showman was in his element. He next turned the wheel valves controlling the water in the smaller of the tanks. Very fine flutes of blue darted to the ceiling before reducing to a height of about six inches. They looked remarkably like bluebells. A thicker, taller spume burst them asunder. We could hear Freddie's dirty laugh. This thrusting spout was the phallic effect he'd once mentioned. George S. Drake smiled. So did Earthy.

The thunder sheet crashed three times. April appeared. She looked more a daffodil than the plastic one she clutched. Watching her was like being in the presence of illness. A dangling bulb shone above her head. She looked so frail and moth-like, I expected her to fly up and flit around it. The waters danced, the music struggled against the engines but she did nothing except stare at the plastic flower. Transfixed. Terrified. Her upper lip slowly curdled, revealing the gum. The audience stared, as if witnessing a nasty accident.

Freddie's hand knocked the engines off. The Blue Danube Waltz ended. The hose pipes, so alive before, deflated as if punctured. April, in the silence, was stranded. She raised her head slightly and looked over at me.

It was a primly feral look from a body so taut, I sensed if ever I touched it, I'd be electrocuted.

A strut we'd banged in under the lip of the stage fell out.

Love Me As Though There Were No Tomorrow sung by Malcolm Vaughan began to play. April stepped down from the stage and, long-striding like a scared turkey, made for the door. Whimpering, gurgling, crackling with static, she couldn't turn the handle. Sam let her out.

Dr. Tripp turned to his wife and whispered loudly,

'Mad as a hatter.'

Freddie stepped from his corner onto the stage. He posed sideways, tense with the melodrama of his own moment. As far as anyone could see he was wearing grey striped trousers, a black jacket and a hat at a jaunty angle on his head. Craning his head dramatically, he called after April,

'When the last one loves you leaves, you know it's time for war.'

Perhaps her flight had been part of the scenario.

Twisting his head right round, he stared at the audience. Dentures visible, he snarled at them. My wife laughed. She never thought Freddie anything other than comically evil.

He spoke in a low curmudgeonly threatening voice.

'The Right Honourable Bishop of Sedgefield has sold us to Disneyland. He drinks fake blood. His sanctimonious dribblings fool only fools. His inquiries into his own wrongdoings are shams. Self-absolution is no absolution. He trots about the world whilst purposely leaving the door open for aliens. The bulldog no longer has teeth. This pulpit-licking bishop, who at heart wants to drink from his wife's Roman chalice, sends round a metaphorical collection box for the Texan Preacherman. Sedgefield Dracula and Texan Dracula don't bite clean. They have infected the world with their rabies. Haggishead will be no better than the BoS. Haggishead will be worse. This septic isle must be drained. Who is with me? Who will follow orders? What is England if she refuses to obey? Ha! Hah-hah! Annette Fischer, are you with me or against me? Your queenly lust is too apparent. Ha-hah!'

He swivelled round to reveal Annette Fischer. She had long hair, a full-length green satin dress, a red jewelled necklace, a white glove up to the elbow. The transformation was sudden and complete and couldn't be dismissed with an easy laugh. Nigerian Oil was amazed. Reg Shand looked genuinely horror-stricken. Freddie attended Bible service in this very hall. Miss Chats and my wife laughed. No costume could hide the underlying flab and wrinkles.

Annette Fischer launched into a self-mocking tirade during which she talked to herself, chastised herself.

'Annette Fischer, why have you lost yourself to so vile a man? Dear Mama scolds me so. Ah me, where is my virginity? My kingdom has been raped.'

Freddie's arm came up as if to remonstrate. But Annette Fischer pushed the hand away. An effective touch, it made you think, if only for a moment, there really were two people present. And Annette Fischer, Blackpool Tower Circus Souvenir medal winner, was the stronger.

'Unkind pervert. You were the only one to whom I freely gave myself. Not counting dear papa.'

George S. Drake guffawed. It had been nicely timed.

'I am the Queen of Hearts now. I will not bend to Lucifer. No, no, no. I am not for turning. Ah, England. They have polluted my veins.'

Perspiration gullied her thick make-up.

Filfy Wilfy arrived in from the street. He had the usual clutch of newspaper in one hand, the other out, cadging. Quickly appraising the audience - they looked prosperous - he knew if he played his cards right he'd be in for a killing. Waddling forward, he stopped dead centre in front of the stage. He had no sense of restraint or shame. I shouted at him to get out of the way.

'Old Freddie, eh? Showed you his tattoo yet? You shoulda seen him up West. In Woffington's. That right, Fred? All the toffs went up there, Woffington's. Madame Fischer ran the place. She whipped all the politicians, didn't she? The hairpins. I took Mrs. Gamm there loads a times. In the old days.'

This he said with an ingenuous air, as if everyone should have known.

Freddie swivelled again, on his face a look so dark, disdainful and threatening, Filfy scuttled to sit on a chair beside Nigerian Ore. NO crabbed quickly to another chair a few feet away.

'Out vile toe rag! Out before I throttle you!'

Filfy, cowed, mumbled truculently,

'He's me bruvver. Me muvver had him by a jockey to a gentleman. He was brought up in Croydon. He moved to Brighton later on.'

Freddie was furious. Filfy, human skunk, had lobbed a hand grenade. Everyone was looking at the pair of them, comparing the noses, the gunmetal hair, big ears, dandruff. Eyes. Freddie had airs and graces, was the nattiest of dressers; Wilfy was dung on legs; but there was a resemblance. Maybe old men looked alike the way babies did; but round the eyes they had a similarity that couldn't be explained by an accumulation of years. Wilfy, at the very least, was Freddie's shadow. A shadow was a curse.

Freddie looked a mixture of Punch and the Widow Twankey. He seemed to forget which sex he was portraying. He stood four-square, dual persona bluntly exposed.

BIG PARTS

Down the centre of his face ran the longitudinal fault line created by gender, powder, paint and liners. His gloved female hand slashed open the long dress. There was no missing the top of the nylon stocking, the glimpse of suspender belt, the frilly underwear, the muscular hairy thigh.

'Vile vulture, fed on dead opossum - out! Away! Of whose plot are you a part? You have been abandoned like tumbleweed to blow about the city. Without roots, without belief. All of you. Not him alone. Who is your God? What are you prepared to die for?'

Another strut shot out from under the lip of the stage. The plankety-plank affair I'd built for Gibbs entered my mind. It was worrying. But the rest of the struts were clearly and firmly in place.

I was wrong. Sam shouted. He'd seen it coming.

The remaining struts skittled down like bowling pins. The platforms directly supporting the tanks, with the splintering crash of a tree falling, collapsed. The big tank, plunging to the floor at an angle, the weight and roll of the water tipped it over, the contents deluging out with tsunami force right on top of the unfortunate Filfy. He was swept backwards across the floor like a drowning rat.

Nothing experienced in Monte Cassino had prepared him for this. In a twinkling he'd received the mother of all baths.

Water ripped like a fast tide over everyone's feet, all of whom were, with the exception of my wife, too slow to react. The tank, ending flat on its side, had disgorged in seconds.

Worse was to follow.

Nigerian Ore's move away, when Filfy sat beside him, had randomly placed him in the path of Freddie's inevitable downfall. The stage disintegrating under him, Freddie toppled forward like the statue of a deposed dictator. Incredibly, he somehow landed on his feet – gents shoe, ladies high-heeled slipper. But pitching at speed, unable to stop, he tottered across the floor until, brought to a halt by poor NO. Still seated, NO tumbled backwards, Freddie landing heavily on top of him. Everyone heard the sickening crack of something human breaking.

Freddie looked up accusingly at me.

'Joey, what have you done?'

The struts coming away...the collapse...it would be my fault.

'I never said I was a carpenter.'

'W + W = C,' Sam muttered, as he rushed to free the groaning NO from under the moaning but essentially undamaged sixteen stone Freddie. In his ridiculous clobber, lifting Freddie was like raising two different people. It took four of us to shift him.

Stage shattered, the hall swimming, Reg Shand, face contorted, holding the eight-toed, one-handed Saviour, stood so close to me I could smell his breath.

'You'll suffer for this. This is desecration. This is sacrilege. Police.'

'Ambulance, for God's sake. Please,' NO cried, 'I think my leg's snapped.'

My wife was already on her mobile. The way he said 'Please' was impressively civilised.

I was seriously scared of Reg. He looked mad as a ram. His sacred hall was a veritable lake. Decanting was now a certainty. How on earth were we going to get rid of all the water?

'Ah, leave it, ah, to me, Reg, it's nothing, I'll, ah, get a mop. Anyone got a mop?'

He hit me a severe blow in the stomach with his fist.

'I say, don't make matters worse,' Earthy said, jumping between us. At that moment Sir Neville was hard to dislike. Matters got worse. Wally flipped. Growling, dribbling, he launched himself at Reg, somehow landing up round his back and shoulders. To stop himself falling, he grabbed at Reg's head, then at his pork pie hat which he tore in two. Inspired, Reg executed a backwards overhead strike with the crucifix, hitting him right on the forehead, the surprise of the blow helping to loosen his grip. The women then pulled him to the floor, where he threshed about like a conger eel. Reg fled with his torn pork pie and the crucifix, now minus the Saviour's head.

In the middle of the mayhem Miss Chats, all leather and cool and smiles, handed me the brown envelope.

The ambulance arrived. NO was strapped to a stretcher. As he was carried out the door, he looked to my wife.

'Tell Dorinda she must phone the Foreign Office. Cancel Lagos. Please.'

The ambulance men, weary week-end swabbers on the middens of self-destructive man, hardly spoke a word. The sight of Freddie, monstrous, preening cock-hen, had silenced them.

Filfy Wilfy, all hope of a collection washed away, finally getting to his feet, rushed wet and screaming at Freddie.

'You 'ucking LOONTIC. If I go down with flu or som'ing, you'll be 'earing from my SOLISTOR. You shoulda been locked up YEARS ago. My muvver was right. You're MAD. Who'd vote for you? yah big hairpin. I hope you die of 'ucking bird flu!'

He scuttled out.

George S. Drake had remained throughout, calm and in control. Of himself.

'Very interesting indeed, Mr. Parts. As far as it went. Thank you.'

'Oh, really? Jolly good. You should see my six tank show.'

George S. in his big red boots exited, followed by my wife, Earthy, Miss Chats, Mr. and Mrs. Tripp and May who swooned back at Sam, wrinkling her big red lips by way of a goodbye kiss.

The show was over.

Freddie surveyed the hopeless hall, as he might a ship flung on rocks. There wasn't a chair in the place standing. The stage was in bits. The collapsible platforms had lived up to their name.

'The force of water. You see? They don't understand it.'

The smaller tank, containing over a ton of water, had gone straight to the floor but remained upright and full. We could start one of the engines and pump the water out the door.

'W + W = C, what does it mean, Sam?'

'Water plus weakness equals chaos.'

'When you've managed to reduce love to a formula, will you let me know?'

Wally was proud of the way he attacked Reg.

'Yeah, massif. I wasn't going to let 'im beat up on you, man, know what I mean?'

'Thank you, Wally. Have you ever thought of joining the police force?'

Generalissimo Gigantic Parts declared the night a triumph.

'I think we showed 'em! BBC chappie was impressed. Oh yes. He wants it. The old toe rag should be shot. Soon as he came in disaster struck. My brother? The man's mad. The mob want to be identified with power. Only I cushioned my plunge, Nigerian Ore might have been killed. He was very lucky indeed. They loved when April entered, did you notice? Fabulous. There for all to see. There for all to see.'

There was a sweeping brush in the kitchenette. We swished a lot of the water out the door. Some of it shot in under the skirting board. Out of sight, out of mind.

It only took us ten minutes to pump the small tank dry. A river ran down the side street into the High Road. In the space of an hour and a half we'd cleared the place. The tanks, the diesel pumps, hose pipes, nozzle contraptions, valves, the black drape, thunder sheet, the smashed platforms - all were dumped outside.

Freddie looked round the slimy hall.

'Thing about water, it will not be kept down. Up. In. Back. It will be free. Sooner or later. What a night! Fabulous.'

Apart from the ladies high-heel, he was still in full sartorial confusion.

'Joey, you have the saintly look of the poor student about you.'

'My name is Sidney.'

'Keep away from money, Sidney. They'll only take it from you in the end.'

Nigerian Ore had been carted away with a broken leg. Could he sue me? Could the Town Hall sue for damage caused to the hall? Could Reg Shand sue me for Wally's berserk moment?

As I locked the door behind us, an cruciform wriggler, green and hairy, hurried up and across the step and into the hall. As if it got wind, here was somewhere new and moist in which to spend a comfortable night and maybe even longer.

The water surging free from the big tank had been a six foot wide curving plunge. In shape a whale's tail.

By the door was the decapitated head of Jesus. I put it in my pocket.

'If you and your wife divorced, would you get a penny? Has her father, as yet, signed anything over to her? You see, Joey?'

'My name is Howard.'

'To dream is to be alive, Howard. Joey. Who the hell are you really?'

I read the letter given me by Miss Chats. The full powers of the landlords were being brought to bear. Bailiffs had been appointed. We had to clear off to Thatch Lane.

I smeared the letter with butter and sprinkled on sugar. I put it back in the envelope and wrote,

"For attention Miss Chats. Dear Samantha, after they evicted Lucifer, was the world a safer place?"

I heard Rosa traipsing down the stairs. I was too exhausted to get face-to-face.

'I know you're in there. Open up. He's died.'

I opened up.

'He's gorn. The police come and told me. He'll be buried Thursday week looks like.'

She wore a vest and had a towel wrapped round her waist. Her bosom sagged to her navel.

'I'm so, so sorry, Rosa. Phil was a great character. I'm so, so sad. I'll miss him.'

'Will you? It's for the best. He never recovered from the fall 'e took. When you put him on that daft bike.'

He begged me to make that frame. That dream. Where was my wife when I needed her? She'd hardly have gone off for a meal with Big Red Telly Boots?

'Phil was a remarkable man, Rosa. Not many have photographed a ghost. Defused bombs. Raced against Reg Harris on the Bath Road. Taught the police judo. But I refuse to take responsibility for his death.'

'He collected shells an' all, don't forget that.'

'I'll help in any way I can, Rosa.'

'Walk me upstairs. I'm scared a that old devil on the top floor. I sees 'im just now, coming up the stairs wearing some kinda dress. Gordelpus. He called me sauce leg. "Goodnight, sauce leg," he says to me.'

'Sauce leg?'

I'd heard him muttering one time, Rosa's saucy legs had been opened more times than Yellow Pages.

I walked her up the stairs. The cat had moved from its customary perch on the pile of newspapers and now lay curled on the bed. The plastic milk bottle was still in position. The last of Gibbs.

'I won't be at the funeral. I'm going into 'orspital Tuesday. I got to 'ave a wotsit...a masjesticky.'

She pointed a thumb at her breast. I gave her the head of Jesus.

'It's from a crucifix. It might bring you luck, Rosa.'

She stared at it. It was a long-haired head with a crown of thorns.

'Ta, darlin'.'

'Goodnight, Rosa. I'm so sorry about Phil. He will always be a hero of mine.'

I went out into the dark of the public gardens. Nigerian Ore's house was lit up like a ship. Cars, taxis, came and went. The wife, YES, greeted and goodbyed. The son from Eton arrived. Tall, good looking, he must have been the milkman's.

'Oh, Mummy, how's Daddy?' I heard him ask, as he went up the steps.

He'd only broken a leg. Phil Gibbs was dead.

A squirrel chased another squirrel round and round a tree. Catching it, teeth sunk in its neck, it mounted it with the fierceness of Wally landing on Reg. Jiggedy-jigging, like its tool was wired to a staple-gun, it eventually released its victim. It then sat, deflated. As if shattered by the mysterious force lately in its loins.

A white van pulled up. It belonged to one of the builders who worked for Cackhand & Bindweed. Two men got out. They went towards our house, mumbled, went to a house a few doors down. This was a Trust place as well. Chas and Bean the middle-class crack addicts lived in the garden flat. Chas and Bean had everything paid for - rent, social security, methadone, holidays in rehabilitation clinics, allowances of every kind for their two kids. It was a Royal existence.

Typically, Cackhand & Bindweed, the two builders were outside the wrong address. They called my name, kicked the side door, laughed. One of them pitched a dustbin through a window. They then got back in the white van and drove away. Someone had sent them to put the frighteners on me.

Chas and Bean stumbled out, wondering who'd attacked them. I shouted at them from my dark spot under the tree.

'It was a couple of builder blokes did it. Reg Shand from the Town Hall sent them.'

'Who, who's there? Who are you?'

'The beast of blackness free past midnight from the icy pit. Sent to sort out mayhem and tuck you back inside your dream. Phone the cops. Hurry.'

Chas, peering into the dark, said,

'It's that nutter, love. Along the street.'

In underpants, thin, pale, light as chaff and lit from above by a street lamp, he looked strangely ethereal. His wife Bean looked as if crack was eating her alive and hadn't much left to chew on. There were lights on at the top of our house - in April's bedroom and the kitchen. The kitchen window open, I could hear the dull clunk of pots. Freddie was cooking. Steam billowed out the window. April barked,

'Backofffuckeroll. Fuckoffbackeroll.'

Freddie was Mr. Rochester and Grace Poole combined. He sheltered her, fed her, watched over her, normalised her. He'd made a wonderland and she was Alice. He controlled her. That's what politics is. You will live as I say.

I headed for the High Road to post back the letter to Miss Chats. On the way, I stopped outside Earthy's house. In the window I could see Big Red Telly Boots, Mr. & Mrs. Tripp, Lady Hannah and my wife. They were sitting around drinking and laughing. My sense of betrayal was immense. It was a city feeling. And then some. Sometimes I'd have an urge to walk along the Thames and hang over the bridges looking down on riverboats full of laughing, drinking, dancing people. Sometimes I'd stare in at people eating in restaurants. The brain-riddler said I was alienated. And sought out the most clichéd situations, purposely, self-destructively, to develop the negative feeling.

I was trying to match myself with a significant moment. To feel dangerously alive. To feel I counted.

I should have walked on and left my wife and her friends alone. I knew that.

Up in the vast sky, Ursa Major was a supermarket trolley running down the sky. No sign of the pale mistress. The round cheese. The yellow balloon. The honeycomb. The lollipop. The shilling. The perfect orb. Oneiric ghost. Oneness. Coldness. Fullness. Skull. Full stop at the end of earth's sentence. Mushroom. Banana. Bum. Your face. Little secret of the sun. Melon. Wombman. Womoon. Cancer. Cocoon. Moon.

Dr. Tripp was on his feet, singing Mac The Knife. He shuffled rhythmically, shot his head forwards and backwards like a demented chicken, one hand held in front of him palm upwards, the other behind him palm downwards. Like he was doing an Arab sand dance. It must have been his party piece. The others were laughing. I thought of Gibbs. I went right into the front garden, which was on the same level as the window, and lowered my trousers. For a few barmy seconds I supplied the missing moon.

Tripp stopped singing. They'd seen me okay. I left them to it.

Having posted the letter I went home to bed.

I was happy. I hadn't a care in the world. I was mad in love and didn't give a damn. I was free as a bird in an open cage. I was wired to the moon.

Death is a disgrace. Old age a disgraceful state.

I had a young sister who'd died of leukaemia. The brain-riddler agreed with me that the death of my innocent sister could be one of the reasons I dug pits for myself. Shafts to fall down. Drove me at night into the gardens to sit under trees and out-stare the moon.

My wife was cosmic. She was music. She had the notes.

Sunday morning. To punish me she had slept in the spare room. The Garden of

Eden was movable. You didn't have to be banished. Eve could simply re-locate in the night.

'Mooning to our friends like that was despicably insulting.'

'It wasn't me.'

'Shut up. You asked me to invite them to that dreadful display and they came. What are you trying to do? Make a fool of me? A fool?'

'What was dreadful about it?'

'Carter has broken his leg in two places! That anile, androgynous old fascist is dangerous. I'm afraid I can't carry on in this relationship anymore. As it is now.'

'If you leave me, my stomach will be full of boiling worms. I'll die.'

'Tough titty. Do you finally understand? I want a life. A normal life.'

'There's no such thing.'

'Where I'm standing there is.'

'Why don't you lie down?'

'Daddy's coming down to-day. I've asked him to talk to you.'

'Oh. That's serious.'

'It is. I am.'

'Gibbs is dead.'

I trotted it out, hoping for some kind of softness.

'It's a blessed relief I should think, for Rosa.'

No joy there.

'Freddie likes me. He said I was a bit of a saint.'

'Which bit?'

'I don't mean anything but fun.'

'We have to leave here. The tenancy agreement you have with the Trust puts all the power on their side. Miss Chats is actually very helpful.'

'Speaking strictly ex cathedra - that's fucking rich!'

'Legal inevitabilities can't be withstood. We've got choices. We're lucky. If the newspapers found out about your capers! Unwelcome publicity I don't need. Do my zip up.'

Priceless silk closed over her cello back.

The bell on the Greek church gently rang.

I kissed the back of her neck and went out. I had the key to the hall. I had to return it to Reg. Had to pay him the final instalment too.

Freddie and April came out the front door. Boosted by the previous night's triumph, he was immaculately dressed in a dark suit, perfect shirt and tie, black shoes. His face looked slapped, creamed, powdered. This was Freddie Parts, Impresario. F. Parts, English gent. Squire Probity himself. Like something you'd see at the Cenotaph on Remembrance Sunday.

April was in her Sally Army uniform. Dark skirt, jacket, bonnet tied under the chin, black stockings, black high heels. A big white handbag rather spoiled the effect.

'Good morning. Ha-hah. Yes. Yes. Going to see God.'

Erect as a lion on its hind legs, he stomped away, swinging his brolly with pavement-tapping vim. God couldn't fail to be impressed.

In every country, splendid hocus-pocus helped keep us in line. And when we went abroad, like an internal passport, we brought our hocus-pocus with us.

Mr. Stavrou, the Cypriot, came up out of his basement. He was heading for the Orthodox Church. His sight was getting worse.

'Where have you been, Mr. Stavrou?'

'Ah, hallo. You notice? Good, good. Yes, I went back home, didn't I? To Cyprus. We were told the green line was open, you read in papers, yes? My son was with me. We crossed over anyhow, and got to my village. I told you the Turks chase us out, yes, did I? We get to our house. It is now lived in by English couple. From Bristol, yes. There was a pump in our yard. They let us drink. Oh...that was the best water I tasted since 1974. Yes, that is the way, who knows?'

He spoke with a quizzical intonation, a touch of amusement. History had rolled him over.

When I got to the church hall Reg was waiting outside with some of his congregation. Two women had mop buckets, mops and cloths. All the paraphernalia of the night before - tanks, diesel pumps, bits of smashed stage, hose pipes, valves, nozzle rings, black drape, were still where we'd dumped them. The congregation stared at them like they were instruments of the Devil. Reg clutched a Bible. I hailed him merrily.

'Good morning. Sorry to keep you waiting. Apparently you sent some builders round last night. It went horribly wrong. Have the police been to see you? How much do I owe you, Reg?'

Ostentatiously I flourished what was left of Freddie's roll.

It was clear he didn't want his congregation to know too much about our fiscal arrangements.

'The matter pertaining is not now down for discussion. See me tomorrow in the Town Hall.'

'You might be in the cop shop all day tomorrow, Reg. I'm not kidding. You know what I'm talking about.'

'The key.'

He opened up. As I went to step in, eager to see the state of the place, he bounced forward and bellied me aside.

'You let me down, sunshine. You and old Parts made horse piss of our place of worship. It's going to cost you.'

He smelled of TCP.

'Legally, Reg, you've been hit by ricochet. You were the one gave us the hall. Carter Petts-Willis had his leg broken. In two places. He is a man with governments in his back pocket. He'll sue the Town Hall. Or do you own this place? You're up to your ears in poo-poo.'

'You told me you were holding a prayer meeting.'

He bolted the door in my face.

I went home. My wife's father had arrived from Staffordshire.

He'd brought a brace of pheasants, smelling high. Spreading newspaper over the kitchen table, we started plucking them. The cock was a Ringneck, with feathers so beautiful it felt a shame to pull them. Copper reds with black tinges, grey-browns, velvet blues, greens - there were thousands of them; many so fine, no matter how carefully you put them down, they either stuck to your fingers or took off, floating round the kitchen. Plucking the breast required a delicate touch. The ripe skin tore, where it wasn't shot away. The long tail pulled out easily. The red patches and wattles round the eyes, the ivory beak, the metallic black-green head, gave it a magnificently haughty look. Brazen. It reminded me of Freddie. My wife wouldn't come into the kitchen until we'd done. Her father showed me how to gut. Fingers bloodied by the entrails, I became a Roman soothsayer. The gizzard was packed with corn and grit. If it had any meaning I couldn't find it. Close to the breast I severed the neck. Then I cut the head off. The bare, naked, singed and now shapeless body was an insult to its former glory. There was no sign it ever lived. At all. It was going to be eaten and washed down with a few glasses of claret. I picked up the head, contemplated it. The exquisite green, black and red still caught the light. My father-in-law clanked two wine bottles together, reproducing the sound made by a pheasant when alarmed and soaring for safety up over a high hedge.

'I understand you and my daughter aren't hitting it off, why is that?'

'My inappropriate behaviour.'

'That's bollocks, lad. What's the real reason? Has she met someone else?'

'Did she mention anyone else?'

'No.'

'Why ask then?'

'I understand you visit a woman along the street.'

'Hannah Earthy? She's just a neighbour.'

'Is she aristocracy?'

'No. She came from Southend. Her husband is Neville Earthy. A well known leftie 'til they gave him a sirhood. Now the Bishop of Sedgefield is a best buddy.'

'Jealousy will get you nowhere, lad.'

'Why can't she take me as I am?'

'Women hate silly, unpredictable buggers.'

My wife, sniffing for gamey smells, ventured in, sat with us at the table, took my hand, I think to cheer her father up. I never remembered her hand so cold.

'You're up against history, young man. Her mother, my wife, went off with someone else, didn't she? In the end.'

'I thought she'd died?'

'Not before she ran off.'

'When he makes a fool of himself, he's making a fool out of me. You diminish yourself. You destroy what's good about you.'

'Do I?'

The two of them looked alike. He was old, bashed about, getting jowly, but somehow boyish still. His was one of those faces that end up withered but tight. Oriental looking. Put him on a low chair, behind the counter of the local Chinese Take Away, and you'd think he owned the place. Yet he was Staffordshire as a Toby jug. My wife was like him, particularly when she was glum and sulky. You could put them either ends of a mantelpiece. She was his daughter in every way. Stubborn as a bull terrier, brave as a hunter, honest as a stone wall.

'You don't understand because you don't want to understand. This is serious. Last night was the craziest thing I have ever witnessed.'

'You're young yet, duck,' her father said, dryly.

'Nigerian Ore is in hospital! How could we have children? I couldn't trust you. I'd be worried all the time. You're too crazy. How do you think I felt when you exposed your bum? I mean...words fail me! We were all sitting in Neville's house, Daddy, and he came to the window and mooned in at us.'

'Aye? Did you?'

'I did.'

'Ruddy hell's fire.'

It worried me a little that he looked so shocked. Was mooning at friends that bad?

'I just wanted to show Earthy I didn't give a damn for his perfect kitchen. The chrome appliances, the chequer-board glass dresser, the granite tiles, the iron wine rack, the hand-made willow baskets. The string of garlic. You know.'

'It's never stopped you visiting Hannah.'

'Shut your lovely mouth.'

'Shut yours.'

We were poles apart. Everyone was poles apart. One said black, the other said white. One said Arsenal, the other said Spurs. One is company, two a crowd.

'This kitchen is just the same as their's.'

'We've got rising damp.'

'I hold the purse strings, lad. I won't loosen them unless she leaves you.'

'How very bloody generous of you, old chap.'

'No use been sarky, youth. If you're going to break up, do it quick. Move, duck. You can see the daft bugger from time to time. If you want to. And he can see you.'

This was him in blunt Potteries mode. He was trying to scare me. And succeeding. The talk was so final, I couldn't accept a word of it. Fate would protect me. Her flesh would not be able to separate from mine.

We heard approaching footsteps. For once I was pleased to see Freddie arrive. He was perturbed to see a stranger. His eyes and ears blazed with paranoia.

'My father-in-law. Freddie. Freddie. My father-in-law.'

Seeing the oven-ready pheasants, he brightened considerably.

'I say - game! I advised the gentry on culinary matters from time to time. Did I tell you that? How to get the best out of your butler, that kind of thing. Did you know I was a chef? Oh yes. I had quite a reputation. I could do the hundred main French dishes. Equal number of Italian. Various German. And the two English. I don't smoke and whilst not teetotal, drink doesn't worry me.'

The last sentence came out as if he were remembering a job application.

'About last night. My solicitor has already been informed. The despicable Carter Petts-Willis tripped me. I have to sue. No alternative. He could have broken my neck. Thank goodness you were there, my dear. You witnessed it.'

'Don't be absurd, Mr. Parts. You charged into him, fell on top of him, broke his leg in two places. I would think you are in very serious trouble. And I hope my husband is not going to be implicated. Now, if you don't mind, we're having a serious conversation here.'

'Very serious indeed, my dear. And I'm counting on you. Judges love a pretty face. I think in the opinion of everyone present, the show was an astounding success. The chap from BBC, with the pretty red boots, he adored it. I'm enormously grateful, my dear. Thank you for inviting him.'

My wife, raising her metaphorical shotgun, let the old pheasant have it right between the eyes.

'Mr. Parts, I'll be perfectly frank. George Drake, in the pretty red boots, thought it so bizarre, it could only be the product of a deranged mind. He will not be doing it on television. No one will. He told me to tell you that. So did Sir Neville.'

The thought of life without her was too painful. I made a gigantic effort to button my lip. Freddie was down, why kick him? He didn't mean to break anyone's leg. Had I been a better carpenter, it wouldn't have happened. Acting out a dream, at his age, was a flaming miracle. He had the hardest task a man could have. Living with a woman whose mind was hurting.

But my wife, having bitten the sour apple of honesty, liked the taste.

'Sir Neville Earthy thinks you should be sectioned. That dreadful play you gave him with that dreadful prop...Only someone with brain disease could have conceived it.

Pray, Mr. Parts, for forgiveness. It's what old people are supposed to do.'

Her father was looking distinctly uncomfortable. Oxford had taken his daughter's intelligence and turned her into a razor on legs. Ten per cent of the population owned ninety per cent of the brains. And they spent ninety per cent of their time letting us know. As she lambasted Freddie, she had The Times on her lap. Doing the crossword.

Freddie stood absolutely still, head up, chest puffing, right hand tight on the handle of his brolly. His knuckles were raw, drained, blunt as his cheek bones. His lips frogged, but not much; just a slight tremor, a pulse.

'You're quite right, my dear. Earthy is an utter imposter. He couldn't direct his urine. People don't realise most of this planet is water. We're water. It is calling us all the time. We're at a peculiar stage in our history. Men become millionaires by renting rooms to asylum seekers. For the first time ever, we are without proper employment. Staring at computers all day kills the male soul. The Romans gave them bread and circuses. Nowadays bread IS the circus. Is Staffordshire decadent too?'

My father-in-law blew his cheeks out, smiled.

'I lead a quiet life, I wouldn't know.'

'Surely there is one man can save us! How is your prostate?'

'Nice of you to ask. Very well, thank you.' He blew his cheeks out again, laughed shyly.

'My equipment, Joey, my tanks - get them back under the arch, will you? I have to decide what to do. I may have to stop renting that space. The television people, they'd supply me with a new place, surely?'

In his tailored, pin-striped suit, he could have been an ex-dictator or High Court judge. He had survived the personal upheavals of the best part of a century.

My father-in-law had survived bayonet charges. You couldn't tell by looking at him.

'The horse will save us. The horse, the cow, the dog. They are the only honest creatures left. If everyone had a horse and went hunting and racing, be so much less trouble in the world.'

I smiled the best smile I ever smiled. To his daughter.

'I love you, darling. I love you so much. Despite everything.'

'This decanting business is beastly,' Freddie said, 'Where is one to go?'

I bundled Rosa into a taxi and brought her to the hospital. She wore the overcoat with fur collar and carried a Sainsbury's bag containing her toiletries. Towel, a steel comb, nylon stockings, a nightdress, one slipper, a spare set of dentures. She hadn't been able to find the other slipper and neither had I. She was pleased to be in a proper taxi and looked out, proud as a dowager duchess.

'This is the life, eh?'

That she was able to say so, on the way to having as nasty an operation as a woman could have, made me want to cry. With joy. The world was saveable.

'No smoking in the cab, please,' the driver said over his shoulder.

'I'm going to the 'orspital, ain't I! I'm 'avin' a tit cut orf!'

'Oh, okay, darlin'.'

She was scared of the surgeon's knife, in case it slipped and cut her arm. Her arm was more use to her than a breast. Her face was weary and hard from battling. When we'd come out of the house a man was digging up the pavement. Over the years the paving stones had cracked or sunk dangerously. The man, working on his own, used a crowbar to prise out the slabs of Yorkshire stone and the heavy Norwegian granite kerbs. The kerbs, some of them were over five feet long, weighed a hundred weight for every foot. Lying on the ground was a beetle - a big, thick, heavy, wooden mallet. Administering batterings on a daily basis, it looked the worse for wear. Chipped, wrinkled, bruised, worn, it had turned the colour of dusty stone. But it was serviceable still and indestructible. Like Rosa's face. Her face was the colour of wet sandstone. So were her nicotined fingers and thumbs.

'Will you see to it that Gibbs gets buried?'

This was Tuesday morning. He'd died on Saturday.

'Have you any next-of-kin?'

'Next to wha'?'

'Children? Family?'

''e won't turn ahp. He's in Guildford. See if I care.'

'Was he insured? I mean, funerals cost, Rosa.'

'Him, on the corner, 'e'll do it. Dracula.'

Dracula, the local undertaker, with his long pale face, watery eyes, long black coat, always looked in need of a good feed of blood. He ate his lunch in the Electric caff. No one who recognised him sat at his table.

Everyone in the streets, as we taxied past, seemed to be talking on mobile phones.

We saw Filfy Wilfy emerge from Euston Square underground. A scruff of newspaper in his hand, coat tails flapping, he hurried along like a sick magpie trying to get airborne.

'Rosa, did Wilfy have a relationship with you? I mean, when he was young...and a lot cleaner...I presume.'

'When he come back from the war, he was proper smart. 'e tried to get me into doing vice. Oneathem vice gels. In a garage at the back of Mrs. Gamm's. Mrs. Gamm was a lady. Her wardrobe and hats was a well known feature. I used to scrub her back.'

'Why?'

'Why? 'cos she was a lady!'

She flicked her cigarette end out the window.

'I think my wife wants to leave me, Rosa. I'm sad. In fact, sad doesn't describe it.'

'Let her. She'll come back. Who cares? Don't forget to feed pussy.'

In her damp kitchen a pyramid of tins awaited daily opening.

'You don't really think I was responsible for Phil's death, do you, Rosa?'

'I do. I bleeding do. You'll break a lot of hearts you will. Some men have women queuing up to be broken. Like that Filfy.'

'Filfy Wilfy?'

'Gussie Ogdon - she died for him, the bleeder.'

We reached the hospital. I took her to reception and sat with her until a nurse came.

'Rosa, Phil's funeral, you can't miss that, can you?'

Somewhere in the bowels of the hospital, her husband lay on a mortuary slab.

'What difference would it make me being there? The old sausage is gorn and that's it. I'll be under the knife, won't I, 'ow could I go?'

A big nurse came and took her away along a dark corridor. A cat walking a mouse.

I decided to go and see the brain-sifter.

He was just getting out of his car. His face, a practised professional blank, expressed no surprise at all when he saw me loom up.

'By appointment only, I'm afraid.'

'I don't lie in bed all day. Unless there is someone nice to accompany me. Our multi-faceted weather has no effect on me at all. Neither am I afflicted with worries about mortgage repayments, the congestion charge, the Middle East, GM foods, Avian Flu, the Euro, is there oil on the moon? Water on Mars? Is total normality my problem, would you say?'

He took out his pipe and looked deep into the bowl.

'I now deal only with those suffering from narcotics. And who are trying to give them up.'

'Mrs. Gibbs thinks I killed her husband. I need help. I need to be forgiven.'

'Forgive yourself. And tell your wife to call me, will you?'

'Is death a waste of time? Or time a waste of death?'

'Death is the face of the clock. Behind the face is time. The clock itself, the cogs, wheels, spring, the mantle on which the clock sits, they are time's itch. The air we breathe. All is time.'

'That's bloody depressing.'

Walking backwards he went inside and shut the door on me. When the riddler started running from the riddle, that was bad. Did I feel any better? I couldn't say I felt any worse.

I went round to the New Building Trust offices. Miss Chats was in the reception area, talking to a party of visiting delegates from a New York housing project. They had bright breezy badges with their names and details hanging round their necks. They greeted me warmly.

'Hi. You joining us? Nice to meet with you. Ross Donner.'

'Io. I'm Joey. But you can call me Sidney. Miss Chats is trying to decant us.'

Her black leather jacket, black T-shirt, black tight skirt, black stockings, black high heels, were on the sexy side of funereal.

'Someone exciting die, Miss Chats?'

Even her finger nails were painted black. The stud in her ear was black.

'Miss Chats, I apologise for smearing your letter with butter and sugar. I hope you can take it in the anarchic spirit intended. I would love to make it up to you. Can you imagine the fun, Samantha?'

A few of the visiting delegates laughed.

Miss Chats was on her mobile in a flash.

'Police!'

Time to go. Gone. Swift as a hare. Fields lay under the concrete. Farmers had ploughed them on spring mornings before the industrial revolution was born.

Back at the hospital I met Filfy Wilfy. He was lurking at the entrance with professional intent.

'Is it true, is 'e gorn? Gibbs? I 'eard 'e was. 'ucking 'ell. He was no age at all. He still 'ad years left. What was he? Couldn't have been more than seventy-nine. I 'eard he fell off a 'ucking bicycle. 'e couldn't get on a 'ucking bike! She's on her Jack Jones now, 'nt she? Rosa. Good luck to 'er. I don't wish no harm on 'er. I coulda put her on the map. In the fifties. I had dealings wif 'er.'

Generously deciding to mark my card, he opened a newspaper. I held my tape recorder up to him. Right up to his mouth.

'There you are, see? There you are, look. Run Up The Flag. Sillas Stalker. Sillas Stalker. Run Up The Flag. Train Dart. Big Triffle. Triffle. Riverside Boy. You listening? Days of Deceit. D-E-C-E-I-T. You wanna git em all in an accumulator. You get eight up, you want about a fifteen horse accumulator.'

His sudden shifts of tone were hypnotic. A residual anger underpinned his words. So many of his selections had a history of failure. His stratagems were Talmudic conundrums. His theories on political conspiracy were never far below the surface. They were a currency to purchase attention.

'Scotland Yard can tape the lot. The words that leave your mouf, they can get them. They can retrieve them from the air. All your words spoken, they can never be destroyed. They got em clocked, mate. Your voice. And who can you complain to?'

Such was his Ancient Mariner inward stare, he didn't appear to notice my microcassette.

'My neighbours, they pick fights with me. Why? Jealousy? 'cos I don't git up in the morning?'

'I don't get up in the morning.'

'They got your number. The tahn 'all. You're in right trouble there, mate.'

I had him verbatim. A London street, day, date, time certain. There was another history happening before our eyes. I even got the gurgling sound when the flow of his urine met the gutter. That was history too. Gurtricklesplishhh.

I gave him the very last slice of Freddie's roll. He wasn't even moderately grateful.

'I coulda been drowned. You put 'im up to it, didncha? That's what, that's what they're saying round the tahn 'all. The tahn 'all. You're in right trouble I should say.'

I was. I was in trouble. Anyone in love was in trouble. Anyone not confirmed by at least one other person was in trouble.

I headed for The Electric. I walked the whole way. I wanted to see Dracula.

What did I own? A spoon and a silver ring. The spoon was a long-handled silver spoon I'd bought for my dying sister. A guy in prison gave me the silver ring. He called himself, Trevor Miles Tudor-Houston. He got done for robbing a stately home. When I left prison, determined to start anew, I dumped books, clothes, electric razor, toothbrush, the lot. Didn't even own a suitcase. I intended being a holy fool. A pilgrim.

I was a fool okay. But was I holy?

In the caff I plonked myself down at Dracula's table. In his customary suit of solemn woe, he sat alone. His demeanour was carefully downbeat. The bereaved needed assurance. They didn't want a joke merchant. They wanted solemn respect, calmness. That they got from Dracula.

Watching him eat was witnessing geometry in motion. The fork described the same slow parabola to his mouth every time. When he chewed, it looked like he was counting. Cutting a piece of bread on a side plate, he held the slice in place with a very firm hand, whilst methodically sawing away with his knife. As if working on a corpse.

Something fell from his lap onto the floor under the table. I picked it up. It was a mucky mag. On the front cover a big-boobed lass coyly pretended she was hiding her pubic gifts from the camera. Dracula put the mag back on his lap and masticating slowly, stared at me.

'Did you ever fuck a dead person?'

'It's called necrophilia.'

'What if that lass on the cover turned up on your slab?'

'She did.'

I no longer felt so cocky.

He stirred his cup of black tea thirty times. I told him Rosa had asked me to see him about Phil's funeral. It was already in hand. The hospital had given him the details, death certificate obtained, time and place of internment decided. The service would be in St. Michael's, in three days time. Internment in Kensal Green to follow. Meanwhile Gibbs would lie at rest in Dracula's parlour.

'Can I pop in and see him? It.'

'I don't entertain anarchists in my rest home.'

His hands were scrubbed white as detergent could make them. I didn't feel like eating. A corpse on a slab, food on a plate...My morbid mind.

'Who's paying for the funeral?'

'Remains to be seen.' He must have been aware of the pun.

'I'll pay for it.'

'I'm in touch with Social Services.'

'Can I add extra for a decent coffin?'

'A box is a box. Why get carried away?' Another pun?

He looked at a newly installed clock above the counter. The black second-hand circled swiftly. Every time you looked it seemed to be going past the twelve. The magazine fell on the floor again. Turkey came out from behind the counter and picked it up. The face on the cover looked familiar. Fata. Fata the waitress. Fata. The porny pose was confusing but it was definitely her. She was dead. Dracula said she'd been on his slab. And it wouldn't have been a natural cause put her there.

'Fata, right, Turkey?'

'Don't be dickhead. This not Fata. Fata don't have boobs like that, innit? Her boobs pear-shaped. This one dead. Fata in High Road relax parlour. She makin' good. She be in here in a minnit for eat. Sure. Getouttaere, this not Fata. Fata? No way. This cow ready for milkin', innit?'

He laughed.

I wasn't convinced. It was impossible to tell what Dracula was thinking. There wasn't a speck of dust on him. For all that, he looked shabby. His red eyes had seen much. He was full of death.

Turkey was full of life. His curly black hair gleamed. His brown neck was short and thick. He was fighting his way up. Not many would stand in his way. Food and sex - that's where the money lay.

I left the caff. Dracula paid for my tea.

I'd get a job. A job was eight hours guaranteed boredom and diversion. With eight hours sleep, all you had to worry about was eight hours. Instead of sixteen. Sixteen was a long time messing around in your head. Mass unemployment was scary. That's why governments had armies.

I walked up the High Road and without really meaning to, went in the police station. Toby Turfe, our community copper, stuck his head out the reception hatch. He listened to me like a priest in a confessional.

He pressed a buzzer. A door unlocked.

'Pop through,' he said affably.

There was a table and three chairs in the room. Toby came in. He was in plainclothes. I told him about Fata. I wanted to know, was she still alive. 'I'm glad you popped in as it happens. I think you're in a spot of bother, my friend. Reg Shand, you know him, right? He says you're spreading malicious stories about him.'

'I'm not here about Reg Shand. I'm here about Fata.'

'Whoever it was chucked the dustbin through Mr. and Mrs. Hall's window the other night was seen doing it. The witness says the bloke what did it, was male, white, in his twenties, over six foot. Wearing trendy, hand-crafted shoes, black William Reid trousers, blue shirt, a dark jacket, must have cost a mint. Now that sounds to me like a description we can work on. Know anyone fits the picture?'

'No.'

'See, I can't odds it. That's what you're wearing, 'n'it?'

I was so surprised I actually looked down at my clothes. It was a cop tactic. Take you by surprise. Ruffle you. Put the light on you. He had the clever cop, easy-going trick of pretending to be dead slow. You didn't notice them walking you into it.

'Who was the witness?'

'You're the one in bother, not the witness.'

Mr. And Mrs. Hall - Chas and Bean, the drug addicts.

Toby's face showed as much emotion as a slate.

'How do you know my trousers are William Reid?'

'I'm wearing a pair myself.'

I smiled as much as I could. I felt queasy. I was in the cop shop and P.C. Turfe was crafty.

'No, I can't odds it. Reginald wants to help you. And the other tenants in your house. But you won't have it, seems like. You're against peaceful decanting.'

'I heard Reg Shand, perhaps it's a lie, wants our house for a property deal.' I hadn't. But I had a hunch it was true.

Toby Turfe stood up. Carefully, with methodical purpose, he edged his rump onto the table edge. Opening his mouth wide, he popped in a Tic Tac. He beckoned me towards him with his trigger finger. I could smell his pepperminty breath.

'People are getting fed up with you, I'm being straight with you.'

'Thank you, Toby, for taking me seriously. I do too.'

'Come again? You all but killed old Phil Gibbs. You threw a work of art into the

Thames. You had a major hand in breaking Sir Carter Petts-Wotsit's leg. I really can't odds it. Do you think we don't notice? That tape recorder in your breast pocket? Turn it off. Or I'll smash it.'

He clicked his tongue at the back of his teeth. He raised his eyebrows as if I should know what was to come. I didn't.

He hit me a slap on the side of the face so hard and sudden, it made inside my head feel like Bells On Sunday. He opened the door and his hand on the knob, stood politely aside, waiting for me to leave. Had I a tail it would have been between my legs.

Physical humiliation cut to the quick. You were a beaten dog.

There was no come back. There was no building so firmly constructed it couldn't be tumbled. The mind was a flimsy shack. It could collapse without a moments notice. The tape recorder in a cop shop was a mistake.

I remembered a similar feeling from home. One day I came in from school to find my mother going crazy. A starling flew madly round the room. The wretched thing flittered round and round, crashed through a paper lamp shade, landed on the curtains, flapped crazily, tore at the window glass as it desperately tried to escape. It had come down the chimney. My mother took it as a bad omen. Some misfortune was going to happen us. I got the window open and the stupid creature eventually found its way out. My mother sunk down, panting, terrified. Like she was having a nervous breakdown. I had never seen her in such a state. I made a cup of tea. She tried to pull herself together. I was shocked. The pillar of my life had quaked before my eyes. All over a ball of feathers with a beak. Something had snapped within.

Three days later my father ran off with another woman. That was the misfortune. For her. And the other woman. Not me.

Often when I looked at April, I thought of my mother. The brain was a card-sharp.

I went up to Freddie. Did I throw his book in the river? Or did he? He must have told the police about it.

Pretending to be normal in his long dress, he had a letter in his hand which he'd just composed.

'Did you tell P.C. Turfe I threw your book in the river?'

'I had to, dear boy. In case it had hit a barge captain way below. The compensation would have been enormous. I had to cover our tracks, Joey.'

The police station had taken over from church. People dropped in with their sins. They craved forgiveness.

His letter was intended for Nigerian Ore. It was meant to be conciliatory, even apologetic, but he couldn't resist including self-defeating blustering threats. The room was practically white with talcum. Like it had been hit by a blizzard. He insisted on reading the letter aloud.

' "...It was of course a tragic accident. And no one is more deeply wounded than myself. It had an immediate deleterious affect on my performance and on my prostate. BBC will confirm this. Your leg will of course knit speedily. You are still a youngish man. There is, I insist, no need for the law to enter in. Why, when you saw me precipitated in your direction, did you fail to get out of my way?..." '

'You were the one fell on NO. The stage collapsed because your friend Dickie Grimes miscalculated. I am not taking the rap. Wally, Sam and me - we were only doing what we were told. What has your prostate got to do with the price of onions by the way?'

'It is causing concern.'

'Who to?'

'Who to? Me, for Christ's sake! Who else? You are the most infuriating boy. Very charming. But you try to be tough. Try to be a nuisance. As it is I'm prepared to wrestle you, right now. First man pinned to the bed, count ten. I'm trying to save you, don't you see? Wrestling is wonderful therapy at any age.'

I wasn't going to wrestle him. For a start, I'd witnessed the damage he'd done to Nigerian Ore, merely by falling on him.

'My mother taught me never to wrestle with men over eighty.'

'You've got to beat the lawyers to the punch. What do you think?'

He meant, what did I think of the letter - so far.

'Maybe we should allow them decant us. Go to the other end of the borough. Away over there access to us would be positively hazardous for anyone attached to a briefcase.'

'I have been doing one too many wee-wees of late. You may have noticed.'

'It's not something I've been especially keeping an eye on.'

'I went to our friend along the street. Dr. Tripp. You should have seen the queue outside his hospital door. Who would have thought there was millions to be made from men's mickeys? Christ! What a country! I am worried. If anything happened to me, where does that leave April?'

An asylum?

More worryingly, he told me he'd heard rummaging noises coming from Rosa's flat. He was convinced someone had broken in. Would I go and check?

Perhaps the noise he'd heard was the cat rampaging for food.

April stood by the landing window, leaning on the tapless sink. On the floor beneath was a watering can, a roll of canvas and empty picture frames. In the sink was a painting of an angular dandified man. It had two names boldly printed at the bottom. Ezra Pound one side, Wyndham Lewis the other. At the very bottom was Freddie's signature - F. Parts-Rinser. It must have been his copy of an original. A picture of Ezra

Pound by Lewis. Pound had a walking stick. When you looked hard at the hand, you realised it was a skull. There was intricate writing in black, red and blue. One side read,

"MagicMysteryEffect", the other - "GiganticWaterScena".

April stared into the sink. Freddie came out of his room.

'All this talcum powder, sprinkled everywhere. Why?'

'It blocks spy equipment. Oh yes. Scientific fact. The house could be full of bugs. Your wife works in Westminster, no? You see? Ha-hah. Hm-hm.'

The house was full of bugs okay. But most of them had six legs.

Rosa's flat was unlocked and when I went in the first thing I saw was the cat happily eating a saucer of meaty gunge. Someone had fed it, which meant someone else had a key. The plastic milk bottle was still in place on the floor by the bed. A woman stepped out of the kitchen, revealing her presence dramatically, as if she'd caught an intruder.

It was Miss Rudge, a local Health Visitor, who worked for Social Services and various housing associations. We'd met previously when I asked help for Mrs. Baum, the American lady next door, who had descended into Alzheimer hell.

'What are you doing here?'

'Me? Oim moving in 'erell.'

'Pardon? This is Rosa's flat.'

'Old Rosa ain't coming back 'erell. She's gorn into the 'ome. My own flat's been flooded, so they've put me in 'ere, tempry. I'm gettin' rid of this furniture, this chairell.'

There was something fishy about Miss Rudge, made all the more so by her aggressiveness.

'You're not supposed to be in 'ere'll. You live in the garden flat. I'm busy. So if you don't mind - bog off.'

She wore a white body-hugging zippy tracksuit which just about held in her considerable charms. Her high-heeled boots had studs and leather whangs. Neatly tattooed on her neck was a blue and red butterfly. She was small, thirty and as neat a definition of trailer-trash as you could wish to meet.

'I like your butterfly, Miss Rudge.'

'I don't care what you like. Bog off, I said.'

'Your name, Miss Rudge - was there a bicycle in your family?'

Turning on her C&W heels, she went into the kitchen and slammed a tape into a cassette player. Hot music boiled over. She was moving in all right. And her level of noise was sure to drive Freddie demented.

The cat sauntered across the room. The music didn't perturb it in the least.

Before I bogged off, Miss Rudge shouted that Rosa was in The Farm Home - a refuge for OAP's for whom alternatives had run out. It was under the aegis of the town hall.

When I told my wife about the strange way Miss Rudge pronounced words ending in 'r', she said it was lambdacism - an affliction affecting inflection in the more native inhabitants of Bristol. From the Greek letter for 'l'.

I sauntered round to The Farm Home. Constructed in brutal concrete and kinder brick, with its generously proportioned entry doors, carpeted reception, bright blue and yellow paint-work, it looked welcoming. Every door in the place had wheelchair access and steel tubing for people who needed something to hang on to. A plaque proclaimed that the place had been formally opened two years before by Alderman Reginald Shand.

There didn't seem to be anyone on duty in reception. Peering through a small window in a thick door, I saw a gaggle of elderly women sitting in a circle, most of them in wheelchairs. A nurse was trying to get Rosa to drink tea. Rosa was more interested in her cigarette. The nurse tried to spoon tea into her mouth but the ciggy always got there first. The nurse, exasperated, thumped her on the upper arm. Not a huge thump but a thump nonetheless. Rosa swallowed the tea.

The circle of fading women chilled me to the bone. It was like looking at a battlefield after a fight had ended. Some of the women were all but out of it. Their heads lolled, their dribbling mouths gaped, their tongues hung out. They were luckier than the ones who knew they were trapped. The ones who noticed me peeping in. In days to come, would I end up in such a circle of despair? Dante's rings of hell never convinced me. This did. This was real and no one could better real. I walked right in and all charm, up to Rosa's nurse.

She was taller, older, than Miss Rudge, but had the same tough face. Social welfare was rough. Old folk could be buggers. You had to show them who was boss. The place whiffed of urine. The room was clean, bright, with big curtained windows and shiny surfaces, but it couldn't outsmart incontinence. It could have done with a scattering of Freddie's talcum powder. I was perturbed seeing Rosa getting a thump. But was I prepared to change places with the nurse? I was.

'You feed someone else, I'll help Rosa. We're friends.'

'Who said you could walk in just like this?'

'No one.'

Rosa started wheezing, winding herself up to laughter.

''e's okay. He's from down below. Daft sod.'

The nurse was happy enough to leave me holding the tea and biscuits.

'How come you're here, Rosa?'

'The surgeon couldn't operate me. He says it's too complicated at the moment. I asked to be put in here. What's the point me going 'ome? How's pussy?'

'Someone's moved into your flat, Rosa.'

'That's okay. What do I need it for now?'

'What about all your stuff?'

'Do you want it?'

She took the cup from my hand and drank. Then she nibbled a biscuit, dunked it in the tea. The soggy end collapsed. She drank it down. They'd given her a dressing gown and slippers. Her hair needed combing. I got a brush and dragged it over her incredibly thick, crackling, wiry mop. The static could have lit a bulb. When I'd done, the hair at the front stuck up, making her look like a nutty comedian.

'I'm afraid I've made you look like a nutty comedian, Rosa.'

She lit a cigarette with a very steady hand. Smoking was the last thing she'd do well. I told her I saw the nurse thumping her.

'I kicked her on the shin.'

'What would Phil say if he saw you in here?'

''e's gorn. I'm gorn too. Soon as I can. No, son, there comes a time. Look at it. Look. Gordelpus.'

A lot of the women had begun to snore. Great billowing snores rolling up like thunder. One lady at the far end was doing a Wilfy. The nurse moved towards her with a mop. The world spent billions on weaponry. All this place needed was a few more nurses. Who were all these women? What had they done with their lives? Who was Rosa? Until recent years, she was the person sang 'Maybe It's Because I'm A Londoner', every Friday night, round the local, by request of the landlord. A prelude to last orders. What a beautiful thing to have done! Better than telling lies to bomb a country.

'Rosa, a copper clocked me. It's left me feeling shook up.'

She laughed. Lit another fag.

'Has she left you yet? She will.'

If you murdered someone you could never forget your victim. Love was like that. It could never be forgotten. But with love the victim stayed alive.

'What about your son, Rosa. You've got a son, haven't you? Has he been informed?'

'Fuckim and double-fuckim. Dracula - he'll bury Phil. Poor old sausage. God be good to 'im.'

'Do you believe in God?'

'Who else can help me now?'

She puffed her cigarette. She grinned at me. Her skin was the colour of buttercups.

On the way out I came across a mop bucket and mop. I washed the floor. The stern nurse chased me out.

I never saw Rosa again.

Back at our house Wally was sitting outside on the wall. He'd dyed his hair red. He looked distinctly odd. Miss Rudge was driving him mad. Her music boomed through the walls into his head and when he knocked on her door she refused to answer. Freddie was adding to the noise. From down in the street, he could be heard shouting.

'You fucking cow! You've been sent to force us out! You're a lesbian!'

'I'll have you for sexual harrallment! Plonker! Bog off!'

The plonker came out with a trail of 'I's'. Plonkerlll. Was he right though? Had they sent her round to drive us mad?

'Man, I gotta move, man. I can't put up wif this no more.'

'You can't move. You can't let them win. I need you here, Wally. You're part of the furniture.'

'That's annuver thing. My bed's mashed. I can't sleep in a broken bed. It does your 'ead in.'

I doubted they'd decant him to the house at the end of the borough. Was he capable of living on his own in an otherwise empty house?

The caterpillar, intrepid creature, skirts the precipitous edges of strange leafage in its perpetual quest for food and reproduction. It's rare to see one moving slowly. It's either fast or stop. So many legs are incapable of sauntering. They are in constant hurry. The thought - the action.

I had to get to the town hall quick. Reg Shand. I phoned him and told him I wanted to arrange decanting terms. I also told him we could be rich, if only he would agree to meet me. He was willing to see me straightaway.

When I got there, in the foyer a cleaning woman trailing an electric flex polished the tiles, the revolving brushes floating over the surface smooth as curling stones on ice. Another woman buffed the heavy oak furnishings and brasses. A uniformed commissionaire padded quickly round a corner and stood very close to me. He looked ex-police. He walked me the whole way to Reg's office.

'Just bear in mind, when you're in with Mr. Shand, I shan't be far away.'

A short distance from Reg's door was a window seat. The commissionaire sat down as I knocked. He'd be there all the time, ready to spring into action if required.

Reg sat back in his chair. This time there was no sign of the Bible money box. There was a starting handle on the desk. Another wasp was dying in the cone-shaped lampshade above our heads. The starting handle looked like half a swastika.

Reg's fingers drummed as he waited for me to speak. I hesitated.

'Our legal team has been fully informed and are considering all options. About the matter pertaining. You've 'ad it, chum. I'm sorry I tried to help you. Why did you want to see me?'

'Reg, Reg...May I call you Mr. Shand? I've just been to The Farm Home, which you had the honour of formally opening, right? It's understaffed. My plan is this. I know the Health Service is short of cash. Because people are living longer, there are more and more gummy eyes and snorers about. They live, for the most part, pretty useless lives. Their days are done. Their families have dumped them or circumstances, whatever.

They put an intolerable strain on the public purse. Agreed? Looking after them costs a fortune, as you know. Agreed? All that money could be used to buy more fighter planes, landmines, nuclear subs to deter refugees, build new Domes, Wembleys. There's a whole new clutch of young royals coming on the scene. You see what I'm driving at?'

'No.'

'Doesn't matter. This is my idea, Reg. How about converting all these old people into dog and cat food? Most of them in their lives owned a pet, right? Man's best friend and all that. Well, for a change, man could become the pets' best friend. The pets could bite the hands that fed them and no harm done. No old person would object to feeding their cat or dog from beyond the grave, so to speak, in the most personal way possible. As pet food, they'd be a lot more useful than they are in an old folks home. You see what I'm driving at, Reg? Turn these homes into pet food factories. When an old person can no longer look after him or herself, a swift injection and bingo! Process them, put them in cans. Wouldn't you buy a tin of Pedigree Mum instead of Pedigree Chum?'

Reg gripped the starting handle.

'What's the population - sixty million? More and more of us are living to be ancient. A complete drain on the country. Millions. Millions. That's a lot of cat food, Reg.'

'I was prepared to give you the benefit of the doubt. Concerning the matter pertaining to you and old Parts.'

Gripping his upper lip inside his lower teeth, he stared at me.

Jumping up, starting handle in hand, he shouted,

'George! George!'

The commissionaire burst into the room and crashed down on top of me like I was a rugby ball. He had me pinned to the floor, face down. Reg went to work on my legs with the starting handle, welting me on the calf muscles in a methodical manner, hurting without breaking bones.

'Give it to him in the giblets, Reg.'

'Backofffuckeroll. Fuckoffbackeroll.'

'Get his tape recorder, George.'

He couldn't.

'Murder. Murder. Help. Rape. Rape. Reg Shand's a Bible-punching pig. Help. Get off me yah fucking hump. Get off me you thick bastard. Reg Shand is on the take. His Bible box is full of money. Stop it. Let go. Bastards. Let me up. Agh. Help. Murder. Rape. My wife knows the Bishop of Sedgefield.'

Reg was sweating. So was the commissionaire. They let me up.

Panting hard, we stared at one another.

'You're a very lucky man, Mr. Shand,' the commissionaire said, 'he could have killed you. You had every right to do him. Self-defence.'

Running his hand through his ruffled hair, breathing hard, he looked at me. He burped loudly.

'You're bang to rights for GBH, minimum. If not attempted murder.'

Reg, still gripping the starting handle, stumbled to his seat.

'I tried to help you, I really did. Away you go, away you go now, pal...Afore it gets nasty.'

Breathing hard, he wiped his bubbling brow. His hand trembled round his face. He anchored it down on the desk, steadying it, worried. He wasn't in control. I'd given him a good workout. I was a gym on two legs. No ridiculous weights and other contraptions needed.

If you ever want to do it again, just let me know. Three sessions a week? We went somewhere just now, didn't we, Reginald?'

He looked worried. Had he taken a load on his back? Was I going to lurk round every corner? Had he bought into a piece of unreal estate?

I smiled sweetly and left. Went to the nearest boozer to steady my nerves. The first few whiskeys I couldn't even feel.

My wife, when she arrived home, burned bright with pride, though she tried to hide it. Her photo was in the evening paper. She'd been at a Euro bash posing with the BoS and other cod socialists. She looked gorgeous. I told her about my episode in the Town Hall.

She stroked my head. So tenderly. She kissed my brow. I was putty in her healing hands.

'I want to entertain people here. But I can't. Because I can't trust you to behave. I have to do all my entertaining in restaurants and clubs.'

'Freddie could get us membership of Woffington's.'

'That's more of it. Do you expect me to believe that someone in the Town Hall beat you up with a starting handle, for no reason? There's a big cloud descending. Can't you see? You're failing all the tests.'

'Life isn't an exam.'

'Don't you believe it, buster.'

I wrestled her to the table. She wasn't going to be pleased when she discovered I'd been pressing her onto a pound of butter. Her new bottle green suit with a sequin trim was going to be ruined. She kicked like a horse and landed me on the floor but I managed to grab an ankle and haul her down and dirty. It was merry. We rolled in under the table and when I got between her legs she lifted the table with her feet, upending it. There was the most incredible avalanche of cutlery and dishes. A fillet steak landed on the floor. For fun I stuffed it in my mouth. The force of sex is the force of war. It catches you and shakes your brains out. And afterwards leaves you limp and often guilty. Until the next time. No one would do what I was doing unless compelled to do so by the ultimate unstoppable urge to reproduce the world. It's the only thing makes Time jealous.

'This suit cost two thousand! You're dead.'

'Forgive me all my sins.'

'Don't pretend you have a conscience. You have ruined my suit. You can't get rid of butter.'

'Keep the butter, get rid of the suit.'

'I asked myself last night what I saw in you. Your eyes are like those envelopes with transparent windows through which you see the address, but can't read the contents within. Or like a person, who on seeing a lighthouse at dusk in a calm sea, takes it as the centre of peace and tranquillity. Only to find out later it is mostly the centre of storm, wreck and disarray. I'll always love something about you. But I don't know what the something is anymore.'

'Compared to the circle of the aged in the old folks home, Dante's Inferno is kindergarten stuff.'

'That's another thing - get a digital handycam. Tape recorders are so out of fashion.'

'The word's the thing. I'm looking for the healing word.'

The coffin containing the mortal remains of Phil Gibbs looked a frail craft in the vast sea of the church. Not counting Dracula and his merry men, there were seven of us at the service. We looked pretty frail too. The vicar, however, was as full of vim as a butcher's dog. My wife in her ridiculously expensive black suit, coat and hat, would have done justice to a nobler gig in St. Paul's.

The seven mourners were me and my wife, Filfy Wilfy at the back of the church, Julia, Wally, Lady Hannah and Phil and Rosa's son - Beaver. He was the same height as Gibbs, same build, same face, same Charlie Chaplin moustache, in fact a spooky carbon copy of his father. Gibbs hadn't died at all. He'd hopped out of the coffin, rejuvenated in the body of his son.

'Beaver? As in "he wore his beaver up."?'

'Pop was known as Beaver when he was on the mat.'

'Mat who?'

'The judo mat. You can call me Beaver.'

'Okay, Beaver.'

In his shiny dark suit and brown loafers, he looked like Phil must have looked in the fifties. A Chaplinesque, London Gas Board accounts clerk, escaped from an office, blinking in the light of lunch-hour freedom.

'You never came to see your parents, Beaver.'

'I've been domiciled in Hong Kong. And Guildford. Pop was a difficult man. Sometimes.'

The vicar from the ornately carved pulpit spoke about Gibbs. It was a strange conglomeration of facts no one who knew him recognised.

'Philip Clive Gibbs was a native of this part of London. He and his beloved wife, Rosa, had a host of friends. Many of whom are now passed on. Phil was baptised in this very church. He and Rosa were married in this very church. Philip was a great soldier. He was a good shot. His prowess at Judo was legendary. He once had the honour of throwing the Duke of Edinburgh. Beaver to his friends, he won many titles. Reg Harris was one of his many victims. On the Bath Road. Though punctured he still won...a black belt.'

Most likely, Beaver had given the vicar a garbled account of his father's life. My wife, like a tickled girl, shook with suppressed laughter. Leaning against me, she vibrated with mirth.

'Perhaps his single most celebrated achievement was when he won the Battle of Waterloo. In the Military Club. With toy soldiers he painted himself. Against General O'Cock....'

My wife laughing uncontrollably, tried to hide behind her hankie.

After the service we mingled in the church yard. Lady Hannah wore green high heels. She had a tongue like a whisky-stained dishcloth. When Wilfy came shuffling up to us, she sent him packing.

'Your services are not required here. Go away. And take your pong with you.'

Beaver Gibbs was last out of the church. He came over and wiping his eyes, said,

'You got to cry. On occasions like this.'

The delivery was uncannily like his father's. A flat delivery from the back of the throat with as much feeling as he could muster. Not much. It sounded exactly like Gibbs in calmer moments. He asked me, could he come round to the house later? I didn't mention Miss Rudge.

Dracula and his team wheeled the coffin out and slid it into the hearse. Dracula was immaculate. His clean-shaven face, red eyes, pale hands, were misery incarnate. It looked as if he had been up all night crying. Just for Gibbs.

'Are you all coming to the cemetery? We have laid on a car. If you please.'

A black mourning car purred to a halt.

'Who's paying for all this?'

'It's on the house. Out of respect for Mrs. Gibbs.'

'You knew Rosa well, did you?'

'We had kind dealings over the years.'

Rosa had mentioned dealings with Filfy Wifly. Filfy Wilfy mentioned dealings of the nylon kind with Rosa after the war. Who, what had Rosa been? Who, what had Dracula been? Perhaps he had orchestrated sexual dealings in a previous career. Before the short jump to dealings in death. I left him to arrange the one small wreath on the coffin. A single word in white flowers - BEAVER.

The six of us piled into the mourning car and followed the hearse to the cemetery. Lady Hannah squashed up beside me. She let her hand dangle comfortably over my thigh.

'I believe you were intimately assaulted by a starting handle. Is it true?'

'I took my lumps.'

She whiffed of expensive perfume and Glenmorangie.

'You are determined to upset all your apple carts. Why is that?'

I didn't reply. I wanted to enjoy the funeral. Besides, my wife was nudging me to be quiet.

Beaver Gibbs, head erect, sat beside Julia. He was giving the impression he knew how to act dignified.

''ave you a family of your own, sir?' Julia asked him.

'Not at the moment,' he replied, the words gurgling lazily from the back of his throat, 'but there's more fish in the sea than one fat old bass.'

Lady Hannah laughed and, in a gesture of covert mirthful solidarity, squeezed my testicles. Not hard. I roared in surprise. The driver was so startled he pulled in along the kerb for a moment.

'It's okay, mate. Lady Hannah stood on my corn.'

'Honestly, you two!' my wife said.

I sang Maybe it's because I'm a Londoner.

My hymn for Gibbs. It went down well with Beaver. At the end, he wiped his eyes.

Wally hadn't said a word all morning. Wearing a surprisingly good Burberry raincoat, he sat in the front beside the driver. His newly dyed hair in the confines of the car looked shockingly red. A bit louder than if talking to himself, he expatiated on the passing scene.

'It's nice this Kensal Green. Kensal Rise. They got good facilities. Did you see that car breakers yard? I brung a Volkswagen in there one time. The bloke who owned it had scrap rights to all this part of London. That Ladbroke Grove ain't far you know. All sorts live there. My Mum and Dad - they had thirteen kids. Yeah. I was one of them. Scrap rights. Yeah, scrap rights.'

The cemetery was hemmed in by the Grand Union Canal, gas works, breaking yards, engine sheds, the busy Harrow Road. In the distance, away over a forest of headstones, was Wormwood Scrubs prison.

My wife and Lady Hannah, standing conspiratorially close together, gave me odd looks. As if they were afraid I was going to do something extreme by the open grave.

'Think I'm going to jump in, do you?'

I was feeling lucky. It was somebody else going under.

Gibbs was ready to be lowered back into the heavy London clay that made him. O Kensal Rise! Cos no one else will!

The sky was blue. A few high sandy clouds. It was like the seaside.

Gibbs was a man I'd known. I'd felt his flesh. I'd seen him at his lowest. I lifted him. Now he was gone. I'd go too.

The Vicar hadn't arrived. He was snarled in traffic. Dracula handed a book to my wife. In beautiful, clear, dulcet tones, she read a prayer for the dead. I couldn't see any grave-diggers about. Dracula told me it was in hand.

It was odd to walk away leaving the coffin resting on the ground beside the open grave. I glanced back at it. I felt we'd abandoned him. It was a cheap coffin too. A Dracula special. The lone wreath of white flowers sat on top of the mound of earth.

BEAVER.

We knew as soon as we arrived home Miss Rudge was in. Her music, underpinned by the crucifying walloping of Freddie's hammer, blared at decibels far beyond animal tolerance.

I charged into the house and phoned the Trust. My complaints were stonewalled from one extension to another, until at last and surprisingly, Miss Chats came on. She insisted that they hadn't re-let Rosa's flat. She knew who Miss Rudge was but had no idea what I was talking about. Rosa wasn't decanted. Hadn't I caused enough trouble? They had already instructed their legal department to issue proceedings against me on a whole raft of matters. I held the receiver out the window so she could hear the racket. When I got back on the phone the line was dead.

Beaver Gibbs arrived. He followed me up the stairs. I was going to confront Miss Rudge. The door to the flat was open. The wall of music would have covered the approach of an army.

'Turn it down yah daft bitch! Or I'll chuck it out the window.'

'What did you say?'

'Turn it down yah daft bitch! Or I'll chuck it out the window. My last job was in the diplomatic service.'

She wore a blue housecoat and had a duster in her rubber-gloved hand. Most of the Gibbs' furniture had now been piled high on and around the bed and the old carpet ripped up.

'Just as well you called, like. I'm 'avin' a movin' in party. I've told that old bastarlld upstairs. It'll go on all night.'

'What will?'

'My party.'

Beaver had started rummaging in a cupboard.

'What precisely do you mean - all night?'

'All night till mornin', I shouldn't wonder.'

Up in a ceiling corner a black gobbet of cobweb snotted down. Miss Rudge attacked it with a broom.

Beaver found what he was looking for - a battered suitcase filled to the brim with tiny lead soldiers. English, Prussian, Austrian, French, Spanish men and horse, all jumbled and tangled in a symbolic confusion of war. The red, green, blue, grey, black uniforms were faded from lying discarded, gathering years, at the bottom of the dark cupboard.

'He hand-painted them hisself. They can be put to rights. I got the essential equipment for it,' Beaver said.

'There's another souvenir.'

He looked down at the plastic bottle by the bed.

'All the best, mate, and ta for keeping an eye on the pair of 'em.'

He went out and down the stairs, gripping the suitcase, the lid held shut with his index finger. The hall door banged goodbye.

Miss Rudge stood poised, alert, silent, challenging. Sexy as a ripe plum.

'I suppose a kiss would be out of the question?'

''ow did you guess?'

Her bosom, epic poetry, filled her housecoat to bursting. She looked like she'd done A-levels in Kick Boxing.

I didn't tempt fate.

Outside, an ambulance drew up. Nigerian Ore was arriving home. The ambulance men wheeled him to the steps and carried him up into his house. A massive Nigerian bodyguard accompanied them. NO's plastered leg stuck out comically straight.

He exploited a good chunk of Africa but apart from that, what did I really have against him? He lived in a massive semi-detached and bought the adjoining house so he didn't have to have neighbours. Which is as anti-social as one could get. On the other hand who'd want neighbours like us?

I rang Freddie's bell and went up to see him. What, if anything, was he going to do about the arrival of Miss Rudge? Would I be part of another of his schemes? I was an enabler. I dug the foundations for other men's dreams. The trench usually collapsed in on top of me.

He sat on the edge of the bed, staring at a Financial Times. He smelled like he'd just had a shave.

'The Stock Exchange. It's the centre of the sewer.'

'What about your own sewer?'

'That bitch is having a party. She belongs to a clique plotting to bring the country to its knees. Using drugs and jungle music. I called the police. They hate the fuzziewuzzies. Oh yes. They told me. How can April and I stay here? How can we tolerate it?'

'What are you going to do?'

'Get out.'

'You're going to let them win?'

'Just for the night of the party. She belongs to an organisation called U.R.N. Uhuru Right Now. You know what that is, don't you? Oh yes. If you hear of any organisation getting together a programme to fight them, do let me know. The Asians - they're the worst. They ruin your country with wealth. Ruin their own with poverty.'

'They haven't ruined me.'

'The Trust is doing it purposely.'

'I don't think so. Miss Chats isn't the kind of person to pull something like that. When all is said and done, they are accountable to the law. I really don't know how to fight this one, Freddie.'

'You must practice hate, dear boy.'

'You're mad, mate. You've lived a long life and never gone without a square meal, right? I no longer wish to know you. That's what I came to say.'

'Youth never thinks old age will happen to them. My bones. Your whole life aches. The pain is criminal.'

Around the edge of the carpet was a tidal mark of talcum. On the wall by the window was a damp patch. The brickwork needed re-pointing. There was a damp patch on the ceiling.

'We're finished here. The house is dying.'

'I like to think you and April could start a whole new line. Her purity and innocence, combined with your strength - which you undoubtedly have - and that streak of madness necessary for adventure, something you possess in abundance, is perfect. You are practically certified, Joey. April has uncontrollable passion for you.'

Had his dancing waters forever topped the bill, perhaps it might all have been different. He might have eased into harmless avuncular old age. Whatever it was he'd craved had avoided him. Perversely, his one triumph was April. April Fard. If he hadn't taken her on, what thumps would she be receiving, in what kind of state-run institution? If he wasn't the actual cause of her screaming, he was heroic. He was saving the world for her. She was purity incarnate. She had to be protected. The dark outside was a constant threat to island sanctity. But the old house was rotting all around him.

The very idea of starting anything with April...The sight of her snagged upper lip would put a stallion off its oats.

'Threesomes are all the rage nowadays. It was in my time too. Wednesdays in Woffington's were not to be missed.'

'I got an idea, Freddie. Put on your costume and have a threesome with yourself.'

He looked genuinely hurt.

'April. Me. You. This isn't about squalid engagement, boy. You are aware of the phenomenon of virgin birth? It is far from an outmoded possibility, a religious conceit. Especially in these days of test tubes and seriously bent medicos. But my method is the real thing.'

A blast of music engulfed the house. Miss Rudge, piloting her C&W noise machine, was bombing us with musical napalm. Freddie scrambled to his knees and commenced whacking a six-inch nail with a hammer. The nail was in a joist running as far as the fireplace. The floor juddered, the gas fire shook.

'There is your proof. They use African music to drive us from our homes.'

'It's white trash music, actually.'

Miss Rudge retaliated from below, attacking the ceiling with the handle of a brush. April, having come in, sat by the fire, staring at her toes. The place was a mad house. Gibbs had died, Rosa was gone, life had moved on. A tornado swept the land. New rules were in place. Silent certainties abolished. Noise ruled.

'Haggishead - when he takes over from the Bishop, he'll be worse.'

'Have you a cogent alternative, Freddie? Come up with one decent political insight and I might decide you're not completely nuts after all.'

I helped him up off the floor.

'Have I told you about my mickey trouble?'

'I beg your pardon?'

Sweat bubbled on his brow. He had to shout to be heard.

'I may have to be hospitalised.'

'Really?'

Miss Rudge turned her music down. The relief!

'I don't trust hospitals, as you know. They kill.'

His face was raw with fearful emotion.

'Freddie, I have to go. I'll strangle Miss Rudge on the way down.'

He howled immoderately.

Miss Rudge stood in her doorway, wearing knickers and bra and a towel turbaned on her head. She'd washed her hair. Runty, stout-legged, lovely shoulders, skin lightly tanned, she looked healthy as a Charolais heifer. Her hands were up fiddling with the turban, tucking at it. If the government taxed breasts by size, they'd make a fortune out of girls like Miss Rudge. I dived my hand between her legs.

'I'm reporting you.'

'I thought you were glad to see me.'

'Bog off!'

She slammed the door shut.

I went down stairs, put on some Dvorak and lay listening. There was magnificence in the world but what strange delightful engines fired it up! Flesh was all. I'd rather be a butterfly than a moth. I was resting, my wings shut high.

My wife came in wearing shorts. She'd been in the gym with all the other fit and svelte. Not a bit of flab or wrinkle between the lot of them. All on treadmills, walking and running to nowhere. People who wanted to be perfect wanted you to be perfect as well.

I thought of the first time...That sunny day in Hanley. The breeze shifting her dress and tugging it through her legs. We strolled through all the Pottery towns. The golden angel on Burslem Town Hall gleamed. Walking up Hartshill hand in hand, we paused and kissed. It would be hard to let those memories go. In fact I couldn't. It was through me like the sweet red ribbon in a stick of seaside rock. The Potteries really hadn't been potteries for a long time. We walked along the Etruria canal. All the undeveloped waste ground had dumps of broken crocks. The place was dead. There was one smokeless bottle-shaped kiln remaining.

And a museum. Where there's no smoke there's no fire.

I was Stoke, she was Staffordshire. My grandparents' people had been miners, gilders, designers. They made the stuff my wife's people could afford to buy. The fault lines between us sexy love made invisible. In the beginning.

I watched her in the kitchen watching the kettle boil. She had a mole on the right side of her neck. She fingered it lightly. So lost in thought, she might have been doing an April and I might as well have not existed.

'What are you thinking?'

'Civilisation may be a veneer but it is vital. Veneer is society. Do you want us all to go back up the trees?'

'Yes.'

'Fool. We can't evolve backwards.'

'Beaver Gibbs never mentioned anything at all about his mother being in a home. Rosa. Does he know? If he did he never said. That's some veneer.'

'Someone like you can't afford to be an anarchist. If that's what you are. Anarchists are middle-class. Anarchists read books. You need a more apt definition of yourself.'

'We all do.'

'The brain-sifter, as you call him, phoned me. He says you need to make your mind up. Or your mind will make you up.'

'Make my mind up about what?'

Miss Rudge's party started at seven in the evening. A constant procession of men in hats and high-heeled boots tripped up the stairs and into a wailing wall of battering music. Miss Rudge certainly had pulling power. It was like she was presiding over a mixed-race cowboy convention. The house shook under decibels of sound, way off the scale. The flat, too small to contain the numbers, the party spread out onto the landing and down the stairs to the hall door which was left wide open. Popular Miss Rudge had a hysterical laugh which, from time to time, penetrated the mayhem. She was having a ball.

The joint was jammed. Every man had a bottle in one hand, a spliff in the other. Wally was sitting on the garden wall.

'It's not on, mate. We'd be better off out of it. We'd be better off dead.'

If Miss Rudge was somebody's idea to get shot of us, it was a bloody good one. The sense of shock and outrage at being invaded was intense. Quite simply, you didn't count.

Wally went off somewhere. Probably the pub or a park bench.

Up the stairs something was happening. The crowd pressed back against the walls and banister.

Freddie and April were coming down. He faced the mob immaculately dressed in his brown suit and Oxfords. Head held high, he epitomised defiance. April, in a Mrsblouse concoction - reds, yellows and white - cowered behind him. She looked genuinely frightened. Freddie had probably scared her witless with stories of the horrors to come. One fellow raised a bottle to them in a gesture of good will. When Freddie reached the top of the outside steps he paused, as if relieved to have survived the gauntlet. He glanced behind, checking April was still with him.

'Come along, sweet-sweetie.'

He gave me a look implying that surely now I realised everything he'd said about the state of England was true.

'They've driven us from our homes. What is to stop them driving us from our country?'

They headed off to a Bed & Breakfast in Kings Cross. There they'd spend the night in exile. It was pitiable. Freddie, for all the pride he took in his wardrobe, looked like an old rooster over whom someone had thrown a bucket of water. April, clutching her handbag under her bosom, sneaked a look at me. Her upper lip contracted, revealed her teeth. She had something in her hand. It was a solid glass object which normally sat on top of the piano. When shaken, snow swirled round a country cottage in a secure sealed liquid world of folksy fantasy. She needed something to comfort her in the strange surrounds of a Kings Cross B&B.

They walked away along the street like Adam and Eve evicted from Eden. Freddie no doubt felt pleased to be a victim. He was vindicated. All the stuff in his head was proven true. Aliens had driven him from his home. He'd ignore all the whites among them, and Miss Rudge he'd see as a silly stooge in their power. It would be pointless mentioning Wally had to get out as well.

As they trudged out of sight they looked lonely and scared. The tables had turned in their favour. A panto moment. Freddie the Demon King had become hero. He was a very old man and April was in his care and she wasn't well. You couldn't but feel for them. There was always sympathy for the devil.

Miss Rudge hung out her window. She was laughing and waving to newly arriving guests. Seeing me, she stuck up the middle finger of her right hand.

My wife phoned to say because of the party she was going to stay with friends for the night.

I was on my own on an ocean of noise. Facing the music.

I had become a wayward vector in my wife's algebraic equations. She was preparing to discard me. I had to face that fact. If she left, what then? If she stayed? My body was an empty suitcase. I didn't feel I had anything left to pack. Marriage was a bird cage. Sooner or later one or the other wanted the door to open. Why try and stop them? Leave the door open and they might come back. She had spent the night away from me. That was betrayal. I was sick. Ill with unhappiness. Next day, when she came in from work, she told me a solicitor had visited her. He was acting on behalf of the Town Hall.

'They believe they have a case against Freddie. But they see you as a key player.'

'I have never played a key in my life.'

'Oh stop it, darling.'

'Who did you spend the night with? Big Red Telly Boots?'

'What? Don't be ridiculous. Liability has to be established and apportioned. It is felt you misled Mr. Shand. You intimated you needed the hall for a prayer-meeting, did you not?'

'Did I knot? Always when my shoes had laces.'

'Oh stop it, darling. See, see, you don't care.'

I was in bed. She stood in all her strength, looking down at me. I caught a glimpse of myself in the mirrors. Disappearing into an infinity of images.

'I'm sad, babe. You're casting me adrift. I see it in your eyes.'

'Darling, I'm sad too.'

Freddie came banging at the door.

'Better show him in. Please.'

'Why do all these nutcases think they can buttonhole you any time they feel like it? Think about it. Your anomic state must be brought to an end. I'm going out.'

I pillowed myself up and like a reclining duke received Freddie with a gracious sweep of the arm. The Town Hall lawyer had visited him. He had been sent packing, after first being subjected to a forensic tirade, proving conclusively that he, Freddie

Parts-Rinser, was the victim of the incident in the hall and not the perpetrator.

' "Don't talk to me," I said, "about law. Lex talionis? Like for like? The law of retaliation?" He was astounded. You see I read law, during my engineering days. You do know that, don't you? One had to prepare oneself for the crooks in control. Ha-hah. Oh yes.'

He was casually dressed in slippers and his long brown dress.

'How did you and April get on in the B&B?'

'Ghastly. Men knocked on our door all night. They thought April was for hire. I had to give her sedatives. She was like a terrified bird tearing at the bars of its cage. At one point she cried out your name. "Sidney. Sidney." That means she trusts you. If anything happened to me. You see?'

'My name's Joey.'

'I do wish you'd make your mind up. Who are you really?'

'Jason.'

He looked at me as if he'd just noticed I was in bed.

'Need tucking in? Hm-hm, ha-hah.'

'What was all that stuff about me and April? And virgin birth or something? I'll be honest with you, Freddie. I'm sorry about this. It looks like I'm going to be out of here soon. Various reasons.'

'I'm troubled. My mickey problem seems not to be getting any better. I purchased an enema and wish to return it. I thought maybe you could drive me. It's near Euston you see.'

The thought of getting him into my wife's Porsche 911 made me wince. Low slung models weren't for large ancient folk. He had hard enough a job getting into a bus. I could hear my wife's Lady Bracknell tone - "Returning an enema?"

'An enema? That dangly thing, with a bulb and a plastic end for sticking up your bum?'

'You need, at my time of life, constant irrigation. You do know that, don't you? I bought one in that chemist's in the High Road. Coombes? It proved a hopeless device. I sent April to another chemist further afield. Again - useless. She's easily put upon, April. She's not much help to me now.'

He noticed his reflection in the wardrobe mirror. Mouth frogging, chin tilted, he studied himself unflinchingly. Somewhat subdued, he let his gaze fall away.

'Finally I bought one at Euston. Hopeless, hopeless. I want my money back. I must return it.'

He was amassing quite a collection of dud enemas. He referred to at least thirteen.

He was a sinking hulk and I was moored alongside.

'Why, Sidney, why does everything go wrong.'

Next morning my wife gave me the car.

'Returning an enema?'

It upset me she agreed so readily. She was afraid I'd do something desperate if refused.

Freddie was waiting for me at the car. He was dressed like he was going to a city boardroom. Trying to get him into the low-slung front seat was a major effort. He contrived to get his bum down and right leg in but his left leg refused to follow. It stayed rooted to the pavement. Complicating the operation was the dud enema in one hand and a white plastic bowl in the other. As if it was going to help, he placed the bowl under his arm like it was a rugby ball. Why did he need a bowl? The enema looked okay to me. A brown bulbous rubber for squeezing...a dangling bit...the plastic end...

I had to manhandle his left leg in, forcibly bending the knee. It was about as yielding as an oak beam.

'Christ! Hm-hm. This country!'

When we pulled up outside the Euston chemist, the manoeuvre with his leg had to be done all over again, in reverse. The traffic on Eversholt Street was awesome. I had to hunt for meter change before going into the chemist's which was an utterly ordinary looking establishment. A shop bell above the door gave warning of our arrival with a healthy old fashioned tang-tingle.

The chemist, a respectable Englishman, was serving an elderly lady. He was, according to Freddie, the last white chemist in London. That he was already serving someone else made no difference at all. Stomping to the counter, holding the enema aloft, Freddie dangled it about so that it couldn't fail to be seen. Lips pulsing madly, he waited for the chemist to admit his guilt, angry he hadn't immediately done so. The outrage in his head was so clear to him he couldn't understand why the wretched man was failing to confess.

Eventually he spluttered,

'You sold it me. Some days ago. Fraudulently. It's a defective syringe. You knew that.'

The chemist was genuinely surprised. As if he didn't believe his ears. He looked at Freddie, then proceeded in his dealings with the woman. He wanted her out of the way before he could grapple with the strange interloper of the throbbing lips.

'It is a fraudulent enema. That much is clear. I demand my money returned.'

The chemist, stung by the accusation, now studied him closely. A tall gentleman, wearing a laundered white coat, poplin shirt, tweed tie, he was solid and old-fashioned as his shop. His various certificates were displayed behind the counter. The last of old England, this was a man you could trust.

His words when they came were weighed and measured.

'I have been in business here, nigh on twenty-five years; I retire next May as a matter of fact. My father was here before me. I speak for him too when I say, never in all our time, have we ever sold anything fraudulently. Do you understand that? Now. If you repeat your declaration, you will not be given your money back. Even if the article in question was bought here, which I doubt, and even if it is defective which, as yet, remains unproven. Do I make myself abundantly clear?'

'The receipt is very clear, hm-hm, hah, what, what?'

The elderly customer, shoving her bag of pills in her pocket and looking sideways at Freddie, hurried out, the bell ting-tangling a merry farewell.

On the chemist conceding the receipt was indeed his, Freddie plonked the plastic bowl forward. The chemist, puzzled, looked at it, looked at me. He was wondering how to proceed. Freddie, lips dancing, stared at him, as usual assuming his unspoken commands were clear as day.

'I've been in water you know? You may have heard of me.'

You could see the chemist beginning to wonder - was the man the full shilling?

'I beg your pardon?'

'The bowl. Water. Try it. Proof.'

I winked. Reassured, the chemist went out the back, returning with the bowl three-quarters full of water. Picking up the syringe - it felt like cabbage leaves - I handed it to the chemist. He squeezed the bulb and stuck the plastic end in the water. When he let the bulb go water was sucked in. The bulb part at least worked.

'Ingesting is not the problem. Hm-hm. We know that.'

The chemist squeezed the bulb. A spurt of water pulsed into the bowl.

'What exactly is your problem?'

'That is a useless jet. It has no power.'

The chemist tried again. The jet seemed to have perfectly acceptable force - to him and to me.

'You see? Ha-hah. Inadequate. An inadequate jet.'

'It's a syringe. Not a garden hose.'

Next to a National Health wig, there is nothing odder than an enema. It looks like a plucked bird crossed with a beetroot. Having Freddie anywhere near one was positively music hall. The chemist, squeezing the bulb several times, churned the water to bubbles. He appealed to me.

'Tell him it's working, for Christ's sake.'

'I know water. BBC is interested.'

The chemist now held the limp, dripping enema in his hand, rather like he'd just shot it.

'I'm at a loss how to proceed. I'm sorry.'

'When inserted and pressed there is no pressure at all. Without pressure there can be no relief. Higginsons were always the best. Give me my money back.'

The mention of Higginsons impressed the chemist. Banging an old till until it slid lazily open, he firked about in its entrails. Retrieving some coins, he handed them to Freddie.

'I hope I never ever see you ever again. Ever.'

Freddie looked at him, mortally offended.

'If an enema can't shift the load, to my mind it is not an enema of worth. Think if Martin Luther had had a Higginsons.'

The chemist puzzled this historical insight.

'Gigantic Water Scena? Does the name Parts...? No? Good day. Thank you.'

Picking up his bits and bobs he smiled graciously to the chemist and headed for the door.

Outside he emptied the water into the cobbled gutter. It took an age to get him back in the car. I could see the chemist peeping at us. He had the look of a man who had survived an encounter with a Martian.

'Congratulations, Freddie. You are public enema number one.'

We drove around until we came to a pharmacy in Mornington Crescent. Another busy street with lorries thundering about like prehistoric creatures on drugs. And mobiles. Freddie got out, the bowl under his arm. I sat on in the car. I didn't want to get a parking ticket. Especially outside a massage parlour. A few minutes later he staggered back, looking awful.

'An Asian. Didn't understand a word I said.'

His left leg still on the pavement, I had to get out, go round and manhandle it into the car. It hadn't got any easier with practice.

We drove to another place, this time in Archway. And this time I went in. The chemist was very nice and smiling...and didn't sell enemas. I went back to the car.

'Christ! Indian was he?'

'I was looking for an enema not a bow and arrow.'

'The Church of England is being taken over by female vicars. Not one of them a virgin. You see? This is where April comes in.'

Wedged in, his thigh constantly flopping over the gear lever, his whole frame mocked the space. The tight leather interior was not designed for anyone over thirty or ten stone. His head was so far back his nose touched the roof. He couldn't see out.

'Look, listen to me for a change. My wife is talking about leaving me. Can you advise me? And don't mention April.'

'She has intelligence but no insight. Is she aware of England's plight? No. Men will paw her of course. With those looks, money, breeding, oh yes. Sexual jealousy eats a nation's soul. Wise women do live with fools. But you're an exception. Where are we? I can't see out. This roof should have a window. Love? I loathe self-deluding fools. Who cares for us? Care - that's the thing. Care.'

'But what do you do when your stomach churns with feeling? When your blood is screaming. When you can't eat. Can't sleep. When the future is downright nightmarish.'

'I'm lucky. I have not that within. You and April - perfect. Hm-hm? Have you considered? April is your future.'

Twisting his cramped neck he squinted at me. I had such an alarming view up his hairy nostrils I almost crashed into a bus.

I pulled up outside yet another shop. A place bluntly calling itself Drug Store. Chas and Bean emerged as we went in. They were so strung out they didn't even notice us. As well as the illegal stuff they trafficked on the streets, they got legal stuff free on prescription. I was beginning to think Freddie was right - the country was snookered. Middle-class layabouts got sorted from cradle to grave. They didn't have to lift a finger. The aristocratic way of life had spread downwards wholesale.

The chemist in the Drug Store was yet another smiling Asian. He willingly fetched dozens of enemas, all in neat boxes and most of them rejected by Freddie straightaway. The counter was strewn with boxes, tissue, rubber. It was remarkable how many of the enemas proved useless. In half of them the bulb was split along the seam. Perhaps they had lain in the boxes so long, the rubber perished.

'Good Lord! You see. You see. If our enemas are so useless, think of the state of the roads!'

'Pardon, please?'

'Do you know about the prostate? If one leaks, one must keep oneself clean. You see? It is important to keep the bowel pristine, thus reducing your overall problems by at least one. How long have you been in this country?'

'The rubber is not always correct. Squeeze again.'

They communicated through alternate testing of the bulbs. If the gush had force, the chemist smiled hopefully at Freddie. If the gush was weak, Freddie scowled at the chemist like he was part of a plot.

'I designed a enema, you know.'

The chemist didn't know and was wise enough not to inquire.

'Why did you use the broken down form of the indefinite article, Freddie?'

'What? What? Good Lord! At last. One that works. Ha-hah!'

He held an enema by the neck, dangling it about, giving it a final once over. In his hands it was an English joke with a serious purpose.

When we got back to the car, a parking warden was securing a notice under the windscreen wiper. He looked Chinese. Freddie couldn't understand what he was doing. I explained.

'Good Lord. At home all they've got is rickshaws. Over here they administer power.'

We arrived outside our house. We were greeted by the amazing sight of Miss Rudge being evicted by Miss Chats and various housing officers. Bulging cardboard boxes were dumped on the pavement along with tea chests bunged with records, tapes, CD's, speakers, turntables and amplifiers.

Miss Chats explained that Miss Rudge had used her inside knowledge of the system to occupy Rosa's flat illegally. Brazen as a cuckoo, she had simply moved in and would have carried on paying the rent in Rosa's name without anyone in the Trust noticing. It was the all-night party did for her. My complaints had been ignored but when NO's wife phoned them, they took notice and investigated.

Miss Rudge, angry as an ant, went in and out of the house, up and down the stairs, fetching her remaining personal belongings. She was helped by a fatalistic West Indian friend, who shrugged and smiled and got on with the job of loading all the stuff into his car.

Miss Rudge protested she'd only moved in on Rosa's behalf... to help her...to look after the place whilst Rosa was 'recoopurratin"...She had no intention of staying...It wasn't fair...Now where was she going to go?

'I can recommend a Bed & Breakfast in Kings Cross,' Freddie said.

The wheel of fortune had so quickly turned. Miss Rudge had gambled and lost. If she'd simply refused to go and used the court system to delay the inevitable, Miss Chats would have brought criminal charges and had her sacked from Social Services. She had no alternative but to sling her hook.

As she was driven out of the street she glowered back over her shoulder and stuck her tongue out at us. I held up the stiff middle finger of my right hand. In ways I admired her brazen pluck. And she was a corker to look at and imagine.

Freddie went up to his flat, to gauge in privacy the efficacy of his newly purchased enema.

Miss Chats wore a leather overcoat, a fur cap and purple lipstick.

'Care to come in for a cuppa, Samantha? I'd like to record your life story. And maybe photograph you.'

'You're a fool. We are not going to decant you. We are going to evict you.' She flashed her gappy smile and walked away.

I went round to Miss Jackpots to buy an evening newspaper. A notice on the door in yellow crayon, read,

"Customer. We are now closed now. For all time. Neighbour smash party wall. Police no good. Rent to high. Goodbye all customer."

Our slow horses finally overtake us.

We lay embracing. Her waist and her stomach were warm. She cried for both of us. She was gentle. Her head was warm. Her hair was warm. How could I ever forget her?

Even her elbows were warm.

I went round to the job shop and got myself a job. In a chicken factory. In the killing room. They gave me a white coat, rubber boots and a plastic cover for my head. The bloke in charge was wary when I said I'd work in the killing room. He didn't believe me. But the money was better.

When I opened the door and went in, I thought I'd fallen into a mad house. Dead chickens hung from an overhead conveyor belt. Men were dunking unplucked chickens into a tank of water. A bloke got a chicken and squeezed it in such a way its shit shot out and splattered my coat. I was bouncing on a wall of laughing faces. I fled. I'd lasted fifteen seconds. All the men in there were Eastern European. The bloke in charge wasn't surprised I was leaving. He said he was hoping he'd get a week out of me.

Back in the street, two men, deep in conversation, leaned on a parked car. The two men I'd overheard at the bus stop discussing Ted Seegar. Definitely them. One of them wearing the same cap and plastic mac he'd on when first I saw them.

' Some time ago, I heard you talking about a man called Ted Seegar. Ted Seegar?'

They exchanged puzzled looks.

' You were eating fish and chips. You said - "Ted Seegar. I saw him play. A few years ago. In goal." You replied - " I thought he wur in Preston?" "No, he wur goalkeeper," you answered. Then you said...I remember exactly - "You couldn't have. He quit yonks ago. You insisted - "I did. I saw him. In goal. He wur a small man." And you answered... and this is why..."That's right. Because he kept a pub in Macclesfield after."

They stood still as snowmen. Had I really imagined the whole thing?

' Can't you remember? At all?'

' No, mate. Not us. That satisfy you?'

I walked away. I phoned my wife.

' Darling, logic and language don't run parallel all the time. We know this. The brain may be a computer but it has to work in flesh. Thoughts are quick. The tongue is sometimes slow catching up. Of all the things to get yourself worked up about. If it wasn't this, it would be something else. If a person wants to hang himself, he'll always find a bit of rope. Just calm down.'

' I could swear blind it was the two of them.'

' Perhaps. But they pretended they weren't.'

'Why would they do that?'

' Playing a game? You have little to worry about. Go home to bed.'

' I don't like going to bed on my own.'

'You may have to get used to the idea.'

I went home.

All evening I lay on the sofa, looking out at the sky. I thought of my wife. How would I go to bed without her?

I thought of Fata, the waitress. Was she dead or alive? I'd seen her dance one London night, wild music playing, a tree of stars above her head, the banana moon reclining, her belly full of dark.

Freddie pushed a note through our letter box.

"Dear boy, it's vital we proceed. April is prepared. As soon as you can! Urgent! Freddie."

Later on I heard him clattering down from his attic and doing something at the hall door. I could hear him muttering to himself, occasionally exclaiming, 'Christ!' I couldn't imagine what he was up to. When he went off along the street I went round the front of the house to check it out.

A blue rope ran out of the letter box and down the steps. I tugged at it but it seemed to be secured to something the other side of the door. It definitely wasn't the letter box flap holding it. When I opened the door it was to discover the rope was knotted to a length of timber serving as anchor. No one but Freddie could have rigged it. When he eventually arrived back he was carrying a transistor radio which he'd left in for repair. He was told it wasn't worth doing.

He was out of breath. It was a very hot day. He laughed when I asked him the meaning of the rope.

'The steps you see, no handrail, it's getting more and more difficult, so!'

Taking the rope in his hand, he used it to pull himself up to the hall door. It was part demonstration but mostly necessary. The invention was both ingenious and daft.

'...Two...three...four...Christ. He's no help. Five...The dollar, the euro - we're going to be crushed between them. Rotten. Rotten. Which came first - Aids or BSE? I think a human bit a monkey. Not the other way about. Evil. Man is evil. Seven... Eight... At last.'

The strain on the rope as he pulled on it was tremendous. As if he was in a tug-of-war with his own being.

To a postman, looking for a claim, that rope was a better bet than a cross dog.

'No skin off your nose. You live in the basement. I have to go into hospital. For tests. I refuse to go to Gower Street. That place is a prelude to Kensal Green. With what did your father die?'

'With a prostitute. He'd consumed a massive curry and a bottle of brandy. It was fairly glorious ending to an inglorious life.'

'I must see you this evening.'

'Why? What's this about April being prepared? Prepared for what?'

'I phoned my sister yesterday. First time we spoke in forty years. "Hello," I said, "Freddie here." "Who?" she said. "Freddie. You once had a brother." She asked me, did we have children? "Children? Christ, no! They're all right for the first year or so. Then they turn treacherous!"'

Presumably the "we" referred to him and April. Another pretence at normality. The venom in his words was awesome.

'Why did you phone your sister?'

'Our mother was ninety-six when she died. The old bitch had surgery to every part of her anatomy. My father...dear gentle soul. I love him still.'

That night I went up to him. I presumed he was going to ask me to look after April while he was in hospital. I sat on a low chair by the window. He sat on the bed. He was wearing pyjamas and munching a ginger biscuit.

'The Archbishop of Canterbury has a beard for Christ's sake!

'So had Christ.'

'The disposable razor hadn't been invented then.'

April came into the room as if she'd been hanging around outside awaiting a cue. She wore the most amazing nylon garment. It was half cloak, half nightie. Red in colour it looked a bit like Little Red Ridinghood's cape. Minus the hood. Trimmed with fur, it barely came down to her knees. The neck was ringed with a collar of feathers. Designed by Freddie, material supplied by Mrsblouse. Her limbs were naked. She sat on the bed beside Freddie. Closing her legs, she sloped them prettily to one side. Her hair was in plaits. Alice in a public housing wonderland.

Above the mantle, hanging in ecclesiastical mock splendour, was the nameless cardinal.

'I have not much time left. We must start again. Now. One last time. Pregnancy is possible without penetration. The seed can take root in other ways. It must be kept at a certain temperature, that is all. Seed, for instance, can be passed by means of fellatial and cunnilingual devising. At the very least they can be told a miracle has occurred. Deiparous is the word. They won't know any different. The mob must always be kept a distance from the truth.'

Dei was God and the 'parous' part had to do with birth. I checked my tape recorder was running. I wanted proof he existed and what he said exactly as he said it.

'We inform them April has immaculately conceived. Sensation. I need your help, Sidney. Joey. Divert them away from the old beliefs. Build anew.'

He was in thrall to his own sense of failure. Had he devoted his energy to painting, a space to himself might have been his in the Tate Modern. However, if for his final trick he orchestrated a virgin birth, his name would live forever. Well, until he was found out.

April looked round at me. She had the smile of a buck rabbit dying.

'Bring some tea, dear.'

The plaits hung down her back as far as her bum.

'In a nut-shell, dear boy, we stage an event. First we plant the rumour. Soon it becomes a truth.'

An enema looped over the back of a chair.

'Dickie Grimes will drive the lorry.'

'What lorry? What are you talking about?'

'You and April will be on the back of the lorry. There has to be a parade around the streets, you see. Flowers, incense, candles, bells. Old women to start with. Sauce leg - get her and her friends. Big Julia and her walking stick. May next door. She can be a hand-maiden. Oh yes. Word spreads like wildfire. I tried it in Macclesfield once. Marvellous.'

' Didn't know a Ted Seegar there, did you?'

'Was he a parson?'

In the kitchen, April rattled cups and saucers. Like she was trying to break them.

'The miracle of April would put us in a powerful position. The first thing you need, when attaining power, is a whip.'

His vehemence was Miltonic.

'The humping of beasts, two-legged or otherwise, is ludicrous and base. Pornography is its direct product. It cannot be helped. But it must be controlled. There is a God only if you decide to be one. My plan is clean, pure, visionary. An absolute fortune awaits us.'

'It's a con, right?'

'The purpose is salvation of the nation. For life. For art. That I do believe, Joey.'

'What's the difference between life and art?'

'Life is art without the fun.'

The door opened. Emptiness. Then she appeared, wobbling towards me, her ghostly tea spilling into the saucer. Something greeny-blue floated on top. Poison? A drug? The fur trim was now nearer her crotch than her knees. This was bedlam. A circus in an attic. 'Freddie, let me be blunt. I want no part of your virgin scena. I'm out of here.'

'April needs you. If anything happens to me.'

She sat on the bed, her knees apart an inch or three.

Hands on his big knees, Freddie lowered his head as if collapsing, depressed. His thick hair tumbled forward. The way he crouched, he looked like an aging goalkeeper peering out at the goings-on further afield. He was a Captain Ahab marooned in a London attic.

I wanted to be with my wife. I wanted to wash the dishes. Sweep the kitchen floor.

Watch telly. Anything but Freddie's attic. He was peering at me through his hair.

'Reg Shand has admitted defeat, you do know that, don't you? Oh yes, rather. My legal team heard from the Town Hall. And Nigerian Ore has hobbled back to Lagos. Isn't that wonderful? At last the wheel begins to turn. Good Lord - I must pee. Drat. It could be a scybalum in the bowels pressing on the prostate. What do you think?'

It was hard to turn on him. A slab of life that size couldn't be ignored. The big frame, chunky knees, hairy arms, waxy head, rancid eyes, begged to be confirmed. To be so old and yet have such manic drive was a kind of wonder. At that age you had earned the right to hate or love the world. He still thought he could re-create it in his own image. His delusion was immense.

At the end of the bed was a clutter of old shoes - male and female. There must have been twenty pairs. Picking up a towel from a pile of junk he headed for the loo.

Out on the landing by a chest of drawers was a bulky object covered with a purple cloth. I hadn't noticed it before. About six foot high, I assumed it was a stack of boxes or a step-ladder or a painter's easel and canvasses. Freddie whipped the cloth away. A coffin.

'Made from reinforced cardboard, apparently. It's the way it's going, you know. A prebendary clergyman delivered it. In a mini-cab.'

'Would you fit into it?'

'April tried it out.'

As if from sleep she screamed -

'Backofffuckeroll. Fuckoffbackeroll.'

I shot out of my skin. Most of my tea slopped onto the floor. I could see it seeping through the talcum powder. I made for the door. Freddie was disappointed.

'Going already?'

'You can hardly be surprised.'

On the floor by the door was a newspaper. It was open on a page depicting the latest car-bomb in Baghdad.

'When your wife leaves you, there's April. I have money, you know that, don't you, Richard? Sidney. Joey. Who are you, for Christsake? My immaculate pageant, if handled correctly, will never be forgotten. Wait and see. I am offering you a key to Paradise, Joey.' '

The inexplicable meaning of existence, as you searched for an answer, drove you barmy.

'Paradise I have found. It's this house. I don't want to lose it. Cheerio, Freddie.'

Wally burst out of his room when he heard me on the stairs.

He stood four-square before me, squat, strong, belly heaving, in his pyjamas. He was steaming angry.

'Why did you dye your hair red, Wally?'

'Nah, nah, I don't want to know. This time no excuses, I'm not taking it. The constant noise. I've put up with it long enough. I don't want to know. You people. Don't give me this, man, I ain't having it. I just want to live and let live. I don't do nuffing. I just live my life in there. I don't get in anyone's way. The constant noise, like a hammering. It goes on all the time. I'm very angry. I'm very angry. I'm going to do the person what's doing it. Nah, nah, don't try it. You people. I'm not listening to you anymore.'

His hand opened and closed as he spoke, going from fist to claw, as if itching to punch or choke.

'I can see you're very cross.'

'Cross? Yeah. I'm very cross. I've never been crosser. 'cos of it.'

Cross could have been a word from childhood. It seemed to get through to him.

'This old house, Wally...a mouse sounds like a rat. Rain on the window like someone breaking in. You mentioned hammering. Is it Freddie? April maybe?'

'It's not from up there, man, no. It's not that. It's definitely ...you know.'

As he calmed he got vaguer.

'Where is it from?'

'That's what I don't know. I got an iron bar in here. If I catch anyone, I'll do time for him, I will.'

'Why do time for it, Wally? We're doing time all the time.'

His pyjamas were silky. He had them pulled up his legs, revealing his ankles. He looked like an overweight jockey.

'Why do you spend so much time upstairs with that old crackpot?'

'Because he's an old crackpot. I like real people.'

'Romantic tosh. All people are real people. We were invited to dinner with the French Ambassador. I couldn't get in touch with you.'

'What are you doing?'

She was packing clothes into a big suitcase. The bed was covered with dresses, suits, denim and leather jackets, shoes.

'I'm sorting out my wardrobe. I'm getting rid of these to Christian Aid.'

Suitcases worried me. I was sick in the pit of my stomach with regret and longing. I dived suicidally at her across the bed. She happened to step aside at the vital moment and I crashed down on a spoon-backed chair. An antique. It disintegrated. She looked down at me, amazed. Lying on the splintered chair, I looked up at her. I knew she tasted plum-perfect. Her breasts were veiny delicate, like the wings of a damsel fly.

She held me in her arms, consoling me, as if she'd just given me medicine. It was the moment I knew I was doomed. I'd fired the retro-rocket but I'd be forever lost in space.

'We can't go on. You've just proved it.'

'Sure, sure, no, no, it'll be okay, trust me. I'm sorry, I just don't know what happened me there. Sorry about the chair. We can work it out. We love each other, that's the thing. The main thing.'

'Yeah?'

'Are you seeing anyone else? You are, aren't you?'

'Like who?'

'Like anyone.'

She carried on packing the suitcase.

'I may go up to Staffordshire for a bit.'

'A bit of what?'

She didn't answer. It sounded like she was getting ready to go for good. I hoped it wouldn't happen.

I helped her pack, carrying the gorgeous rags from the wardrobe to the bed. They'd fetch enough to fund a truck-load of weapons for Rwanda. A black kite-print georgette wrap dress cost her five hundred. A pair of nude suede boots over six hundred. They were in the bottom of the wardrobe, practically unused.

'Trying to dive on me like that! Why run up Everest? Why not walk?'

'In case it melts before I get there.'

I told her about Freddie's latest. His virgin birth schema. I shouldn't have mentioned it.

'I have funded your aberrancy long enough. The Trust are right to decant you all. I'm so sad for us. We had something wild and pure. Wild and pure.'

She said she was tired defending me all the time to the people along the street. Her work colleagues. Friends from university.

'What? George S. Drake? Big Red Telly Boots? Him? Him? Who cares what he thinks? I'll kill the bastard.'

'See? See what I mean?'

On the dressing table were her sunglasses. I placed them on my tackle. My pecker a nose, the ensemble looked like Yasser Arafat. She stared at me deadpan, refusing to laugh.

A bit unforgivable that.

I went round to the local launderette with a pillow-case full of dirty shirts. It was a smallish place and, despite getting an occasional lick of paint, always worn and tatty looking. There were enough poor and students around to keep it going. The walls were covered with quaint-sounding price lists,

"Ironing Service King size Quilt cover - 3.00p. Bed sheet - 1.00p. Shirt, Trouser, T-Shirt - 0.70p."

"Spin Dryer One 20p Coin In The Slot Please."

Its one great attraction was a warm seat at the far end, tucked in by the driers and behind an old-fashioned tub dryer. You could sit undisturbed there, almost undetected. In behind the driers, fluff and dust lay inches thick. There was a cat, lying snug, eyeing a hole in the skirting.

Filfy Wilfy shuffled in, pausing by the door, quickly working out the lie of the land. He'd chosen a good moment - the Asian couple who ran the place weren't about. The husband was always in a bad temper.

There was a table on which people folded clothes after taking them out of the driers. Filfy leaned on the table edge with the aplomb of a Prime Minister at the Dispatch Box.

'They tried to put an anti-social behaviour order on me. Outside the Tube. I don't drink I says. Never smoked, neiver. That's what I owe me longevity to. I fought for my country, I says. Leave off I says. They 'ad to let me go, didn't they?'

'Wilfy, don't you ever get fed up going round all day like a blocked toilet?'

He opened a racing paper.

'Fingers. Away The Lads. Blissful. I can't see anyfing else. Put, you put 10p, a treble see, you put 20p to be on the safe side, you double it up with number seven in the 3rd, Doncaster, nuffing else got a chance, no chance, you go for a 20p accumulator, put in She's Got It, are you with me?'

'No.'

'Old Parts, you 'eard he's got another Immaculate Virgin ready to go?'

'What do you mean another one?'

"e's done it before, 'asn't 'e? He's going to parade her round the streets. Candles and all that. Oh yes. Come an' get it. Bring your wallet. Man must have a new beginning. I will lead you to a new Jerusalem. Me God, you all silly buggers. Same as ever. He's not healthy, Partsy. You seen him lately? He's pissing a lot. He's pissing ninety. I saw him shoot into a telephone box the other day and he wasn't making no call. How do we know she's conceived immaculate?'

'Where do you sleep at night?'

'They're saying you're involved. They're saying you're pulling the strings.'

The warmth of the place made him smell worse. His stink was beginning to bake.

'Did you see where they can get your DNA and breed off it? They can turn it into another you. You'll try and give the missus one and 'e's already done it for you. He can tell the police exactly what you're finking. That's the real point of it. England will be one big prison. And who can you complain to?'

He went from machine to machine checking the coin slots. Disgruntled, he returned to the table.

'They're cloning horses an' all. How could you have a ten horse accumulator? You couldn't 'UCKING odds it.'

In the room above the launderette we heard a thud, then the noise of feet descending. Filfy Wilfy shot out the door like a weasel into a wall. The pock-marked proprietor of suds was on his way. When he came through the door leading from his flat he sniffed the air. He could tell Wilfy had been in.

'Bastard.'

On the way back to the house I met Sam Tripp. He was down from Oxford for the weekend. He looked happier than a snail on a cabbage.

'Hi, hi. Yeah, cushdy. Yeah, super.'

He wore brown shoes, brown cords that looked fifty years out of date and his familiar black leather jacket. He was minus facial ironmongery. Pinned on a lapel was a badge - "? + ? = 2A".

'What does it mean?'

'There is no meaning as such. I saw your wife getting into a car just now with Sir Neville.'

Just because she got into a car with Earthy didn't mean...On the other hand... Earthy? A dud establishment talent with a knighthood to prove it. I could see his manicured fingers cup her breasts. His plummy tongue in her mouth. How could she? For Christ's sake he wore moonboots! Was I going to let her go without a fight? My legs were jelly. Like there was an earthquake rumbling under the pavement. It threatened to de-nail my shoes.

When I got home, Freddie was outside the house, hauling himself up to the front door with the aid of the blue rope. It was a ludicrous sight beyond pity. Comic too. A Wagnerian clown. If there is such a thing. From the crook of his arm hung a shopping bag laden with tins and packages. A bunch of celery and a French loaf stuck out the top. The weight, the strain was visible in his blue grey face. He paused on the third step.

'Give me the bag, Freddie.'

'No, quite all right, dear boy. Christ. This country.'

April was at her upstairs window, staring down. Even three floors up it was a scary, dead physiognomy, shrouded in a nun's wimple of faded curtain.

He forced a foot up onto another step then, with tremendous effort, pulled himself level.

With the Sainsbury bag he was both Sisyphus and the stone.

'I woke up in agony, dear boy. Called the sawbones. He says I'm bleeding internally.'

He leaned back on the rope when he said this; taking a breather. He was a man sensing fate had shot him an arrow, warning of much worse to come. Internal bleeding was a mere front-curtain divertissement, as the heavy stuff was being dragged into place behind.

'That's dreadful, Freddie. You shouldn't be out and about like this, you should be in bed.'

'The ambulance is on its way. I had to get provisions for April. Will you keep an eye whilst I'm absent? My pageant I've had to postpone. I've informed Dickie Grimes.'

He'd stomped out to the supermarket, trudged round the shelves, queued to pay, stomped home again, all the time bleeding internally.

'I refuse to allow them take me to UCH. A knacker's yard, that place. You do know that, don't you?'

For certain the internal bleeding had something to do with the prostate.

'Did you see the Bishop in this morning's Telegraph? Why ruin our breakfast? I have written to the Editor.'

Hatred of the Prime Minister anaesthetised his pain. It was a benign side-effect of politics.

'When I'm away, April would be entirely happy if you placed her under your wing. Oh yes.'

He struggled on up the stairs to his attic. I was convinced next time he came down, he'd be in the coffin given him by the vicar. He was seriously ill and the house - the hallway - shadowed him. The wallpaper ruckled from the walls and high up in a corner above the door was a patch of blue-mould. The paper was so old, so faded, it was impossible to tell what colour it had been originally. The stairs hadn't been swept in months.

My wife was in Earthy's car. Was she under his wing?

She arrived home an hour later.

'Why Earthy's car? Why not your own?'

'He was on his way to the West End. He dropped me off at Oxford Circus. An agency wondered would I model for them. We chatted but I decided not to. Honestly, darling.'

'I don't believe you. You're having a thing with Earthy.'

'Oh, don't be ridiculous. What shall we have to eat?'

I had no proof but feelings. And I had far too many of those.

I'd watched her in Staffordshire, jumping reinless, bareback, gripping the horse with thighs only. She was the toughest woman I ever met. And the most beautiful. She made you weep like the Rembrandt in Kenwood or a bee going into a hive or a Thierry Henry shot from outside the box. I had planted acres of kisses on her face. I was afraid of her. I wasn't afraid of Earthy.

'I'm going round to Neville. I'm going to punch his lights out.'

'A - he's not there. B - you slept with his wife. N'est ce pas?'

I hated domestic rows. That's the way a marriage re-created childhood.

'I'm too tired to argue. I keep wakening in the night just to have the pleasure of looking at you when you're asleep. Stay with me so we can laugh at old age together. Please.'

'Good looks are out of fashion.'

'Oh come on! A good face is never out of fashion.'

The door bell rang. The ambulance had arrived for Freddie. I shouted to him and he eventually came down, wearing pyjamas and a woollen dressing gown. The ambulance men - two West Indians - expertly weighed him up.

'Hallo Guv'nor, okay?'

'If I was, you wouldn't be here. Hm-hm.'

The men were middle-aged, well-built, smilingly calm. Plastic identity tags hung from their necks like pectoral crosses.

'You're in your eighties, that right, Guv'nor? How come you lasted so well, Guv?'

Freddie paused on the bottom step, hand on the banister, looking down at them along his nose, pretending he was still in control.

'I had thirty pro fights before I was twenty-one. I fought the British Champion.'

The ambulance men were impressed. They looked as if they'd fought a British Champion or two themselves.

Freddie allowed one of them to take his elbow.

'What is this rope for?' the other one asked.

'It's the Trust's new communal service,' I said, 'Tenants may hang themselves, free of charge.'

The men guffawed - no doubt they had landlords of their own. Freddie, wary as an old lion, stepped up into the back of the ambulance. He paused to finger his long gun-metal grey hair. Standing at the back of the ambulance for a moment, he turned full circle, like an animal testing the direction of the wind.

Lips pulsing, fearing the worst, he looked at the men as if they ought to know precisely what was on his mind. One of them turned to me.

'We was told you were good to the old folk. You was caring for them. That's what we were told along the street.'

I was surprised. I was pleased. But I was losing my wife.

'Where are you taking him?'

'U.C.H. Guv.'

Freddie sat down, his world instantly constricted. The door shut. Old lion, old clown, he was driven away.

I heard shuffling. April was standing right behind me, gnawing at the first knuckle of her right hand. Her face, her eyes, every bit of her, was screwed up and terrified. Her hair was matted with powder.

'Are you okay, April?'

Silly question for a start.

She ran back to the bottom of the stairs, then back to me, then back to the stairs, gnawing at her knuckle and whimpering. She looked like a middle-aged woman behaving like a bare-legged school girl. She tumbled towards me again. She tried to get out the door without first opening it. She rammed flat against it. Freddie going to hospital, his absence, meant something. She ran half way up the stairs and back down again. Her dress was so stiff with starch it crackled like wings against wire. To release the pressure I opened the door, hoping she'd rush out. She stopped dead. As if surprised by the day light flooding in on top of her. She calmed down. As if the light had hit a mirror in the back of her mind. Blinding her hysteria. I closed the door. She went back up the stairs. Later I heard howling.

'Noooo. Aghhhh.'

Her shrieking could wither trees. One day I saw her looking down at our pear tree. Leaves started falling.

What if she came at me with a breadknife? What if she attacked my wife? Or Wally? He was in his room, lying on his broken bed.

Love was the cement that held the bricks together. If it crumbled, the edifice fell down.

I met April in the street.

'How's Freddie? Any news?'

In a dead, disconnected voice, she answered,

'Oh, he's all right.'

There was little humanity in her tone. It was impossible to be sure what she meant.

Next morning he phoned from the hospital. He wanted me to collect him. He was discharging himself.

I drove to the hospital in my wife's car. It was a Sunday, a wet penitential Sunday. I parked off Gower Street. I could see him waiting by the entrance. He was in his pyjamas, dressing gown, slippers. A nurse shouted to him.

'You mustn't Mr. Parts-Rinser. Come back.'

Freddie - no rope necessary - hurried down the steps and stomped towards the car. It was pelting out of the heavens. He didn't care. The rain was so heavy I could see it sinking into his grey hair. The nurse gave up.

'A shambles in that place. The whole country's rotten.'

'What did they do for you, Freddie?'

'Tests. Tests. The results are not yet in.'

He made it sound like his body was the subject of an electoral count. I managed to get him into the car. His face was about two inches from the roof. I placed the tape recorder on the dash board. His head was so far back, he couldn't see it. Relieved to be free, he spoke with tremendous energy.

'All barmy men in my ward. Another few days and I'd have been the same. One patient was a doctor. A sick doctor. He kept getting into other people's beds. An old geezer hit him on the head with a plastic piss-bottle, knocked him to the floor. He tried to get under my blankets, daft sod. "Can't you see, I'm in here," I said. His relatives were sent for. They took him away. An ex-doctor! He came from Surrey. A lot of mad people, you know, in Surrey. Oh yes. Rather. Another old sod, opposite, must have had a relationship with a Norma. He kept calling out - "Norma." "NORma." "NorMA." "Nor-Ma." Incredible the variations he got on it. A nurse said to him,

"I'm not Norma. You wouldn't like if I called you Bert, would you?" "Wouldn't mind," he says, "Bert's a nice name." It was fabulous. Hell. A complete circus.'

Baring his dentures, he laughed. He was happy to be going home. To his attic. To April.

When we got to the house I tried unbunging him. Earthy happening along, I asked him to lend a hand. Wary at first, he could see there was a genuine problem. Freddie was stuck like a cork in a bottle. We eventually dragged him out. It was only then Freddie recognised him.

'Hm-hm, ah-hah. You? Hm. I was telling the top man, my surgeon, my consultant, the senior man, in the hospital you know, about my play. Fanny by Gaslight. He cannot understand why you refuse to produce it. He agrees there is no justice.'

He fixed Earthy with an expectant stare, all the while pulsing his lips. Earthy, now regretting having stopped to help, twitched his cheeks by way of an understanding smile. Freddie, wet, tired - still bleeding internally? - turned away and, taking hold of the blue rope as if it was the most normal thing in the world, began an assault on the Everest of steps leading up to the front door.

'Christ. He's no help. One...A nation that refuses to be led, is dead. Two...'

Earthy couldn't help but watch. It was an extraordinary sight.

'Three, four...Religious fakery is now the real thing. The Bishop of Sedgefield tells you he knows he's right and that's it. God is his Commander-in-Chief. Poor England. Agh. Christ. Hm-hm - He's no help at all.'

He paused, panting on each step. The few days lying in hospital had weakened him.

Earthy looked at me.

'I am not having an affair with your wife. Understand? Not!'

'I read that thing you wrote in the paper the other night. About Alice Millar and childhood. You referred to your parents as "Mimsy" and "Pimsy". We're poles apart, mate.'

He hurried away. It started pelting down again. Freddie got to the door. Upstairs, April was framed in the window, her fingers horribly stuffed in her mouth. He rang the bell - he didn't have his key. The rain danced off the steps, delighted to be causing so much misery. It was no weather for an old sick man. A sudden malicious squawk of wind whipped a hank of hair forward and down over his eyes. No longer proudly leonine, he was more a wet broiler. Cities were caged jungles.

The empire was there when he was young. Maybe all that manifest destiny stuff had infiltrated his brain.

Two days later, he phoned. Could I come up? It was most urgent. He needed to talk in private. Please. As soon as I could. Very urgent indeed.

I went up expecting an "I need to get my affairs in order" chat. I'd have to run him to his solicitor or some such. Or maybe it was something to do with taking April under my wing. A connubial manoeuvre about as attractive as war.

He was wearing a long green silk dress and reclining on the bed. He looked ill. The up-ended coffin was still outside on the landing. I gave him a transistor radio, since his was still broken.

'Freddie, please, I insist, let me take you back to hospital.'

'Come closer, Joey. This is most private.'

I squeezed onto the bed edge. I felt if I laid a finger on him he'd disintegrate - like the old car under the railway arch. The scuff of dandruff along his forehead was rust. He had rusted away and was held together by habit alone, and darkness. A Pharaoh in his tomb, as soon as light and air got in, he'd crumble.

'I believe April is poisoning me. With arsenic.'

Head-riddlers, brain-sifters, policemen, clergy - no one has a clue what goes on in someone's mind.

'She never came to visit me. Not once. Until I phoned up from my ward. "Where are you, you fucking sod?" I slammed the phone down. Half an hour later she was there.'

Dentures bared, eyes glowing, ears red, lips pulsing angrily, he waited for his words to sink in.

'She's been acting strange.'

'Really? April?'

'My cup of tea - she always serves it to me at 5 p.m and it's always piping hot. Yesterday it was coldish and afterwards I vomited again. And am I not losing my hair? I said it to her - "Are you poisoning me?" "No." Just like that - "No." Flat. No emotion. "No." You know about mad people do you? "Oh, so they've caught onto that, have they? This should be interesting." A brain such as hers cannot be re-wired. It can only burn out. Oh yes.'

When he mimicked her voice he demeaned her horribly. Far from us having a private chat, the door was wide open and so was April's. As if reading my thoughts he said,

'I don't give a fuck if she's listening. I want her to know. See my paintings?'

They were all around the walls. A bejewelled thieving hand hovering over a bowl of fruit...The Mad Hatter's endless tea table...A carriage and horse outside the Cafe Royal...A brightly coloured pen and ink sketch of a smug bird flying over a field of butterflies and bees, wasps and snails, and in the middle of a long yellow pathway running through the field, what looked like a hive or a table...There was also one of a cat with a pink mouse in its teeth and another of two skulls in a basket. The cardinal above the mantle was the biggest canvas and the most troubling. They were the fruits of a life.

The bit about him losing his hair was ridiculous. His hair was dense as a truss of hay.

'Why would she want to poison you, Freddie?'

'Were I to pop off, my plays, my novels, my paintings, with me out of the way, she'd have it all.'

The idea of April being sold poison by anyone, apart from the apothecary in Romeo and Juliet, was just too ludicrous.

'Well, she goes out every morning for two, three hours. I don't know where she goes, do I? Anyone could be using her.'

I think he sensed the end coming and was trying to destroy her in his mind. He couldn't bear to contemplate how she'd cope without him in a hostile world. If he killed her image, he could die without torturing himself with thoughts of her confinement in a mental home, or abandoned.

'You see the horns of my dilemma? If I report her to the police, they'll take her away. Lock her up. But were I to go on living and she's not here anymore - I'm on my own. And the money I get for her, you see - gone. Oh yes, there's money in madness. It's a maddening quandary. What am I to do?'

The clock bonged Greenwich Mad Time.

'I want to do one more magnificent painting. The older you grow the more you see how substantial light really is. It's thicker than fog you know. It's water and air actually. It will take a large canvas. The cardinal expresses all I feel about authority. Its evil essence. The way it connives at the destruction of the flesh. Power. If you haven't power, you are a mere insect. You've read history, yes?'

He seemed to have forgotten about April poisoning him.

'The Daily Telegraph is run by the Vatican to convert the Royal family. Oh yes.'

From under his pillow he rooted out the copy of a letter of complaint he'd sent to the hospital.

"The doctor in question was a glossily garmented medico, with a delusion of omnipotence out-matched by an incompetence testing credulity."

He howled with laughter as he read. The nurses he fulsomely praised,

"The nursing staff, of various races and colours were, without exception, superb."

'You should still be in hospital, Freddie.'

'If I am to pop off...I have to face that. Death. Yes, let's say the ghastly word. My paintings will put her in considerable funds. If they decant you and April, will you, will you care for her, Howard? Joey.'

'Yes,' I lied, 'And Howard agrees with me.'

My wife was in the kitchen, eating toast and pate.

'I love you.'

'Do you?'

'I do. Now you say it.'

'I love you.'

'Do you?'

It was either me or Earthy. Instead of concentrating all my attention on her, I had been running up and down to Freddie and the others, a pandar at my slow demise. Freddie asking me to get involved with April cracked the pretence it was all a joke, safely kept at arm's length.

I looked out at our pear tree. Could we not be as simple as that? No matter the weather, it got on with the business of supplying every autumn ripe fruit. No matter the season, jays, magpies, pigeons, blackbirds, thrushes, sparrows, robins flitted in and out its branches. It survived everything London could fling at it, including the punk tree-surgeon. Sometimes I'd rise early and watch the first beam of sunlight hit it a sidewinder belt of gold. We were pregnant with ourselves and spent life trying to get born. I was still awaiting my butterfly moment.

Love was a pain. It stabbed you in the guts. It poisoned the air. It took away your taste for food. It took away sleep. It took the alcohol out of booze. It made the sound of laughter hideous. Money couldn't buy it.

I was in trouble. Just like Freddie, April, Wally. I hadn't the strength to walk away. Even if it was what my wife wanted. The streets I loved walking, I hated now. I wandered aimlessly about. I met Filfy Wilfy. He was leaning against a warehouse wall, lost in thought. Isolated. Normally you wouldn't see him where there wasn't a throng of people. His black overcoat hung open. His white shirt was open down to the belly button so you could see his hairless chest, pinky-white as a side of bacon. He wasn't wearing socks. His ankles were bloodless as parsnips. He clicked his long, filthy, fingernails. I often wondered where he slept at night. I asked him once but he dodged telling me.

'Wotcher, Wilfy.'

'China and the USA are ganging up on the rest of the world. Can't you 'ucking see it? Money isn't like the weather you know. It don't happen by accident. All that sterling against the dollar and that - it's orchestrated. And who can you complain to? Is your lovely mother still alive? Cuppatea?'

A one-legged Scottish dosser in a wheelchair, scooted towards us. Ratted with drink, he veered wildly. He took two cans of beer from his cardigan pockets. Gripping the ring-pull of a can between his teeth, he pulled. Froth burbled. He licked the top of the tin. The other tin he held out to Wilfy.

Wilfy stared at him, absolutely unblinkingly still. The dosser wanted to be friendly, generous, magnanimous.

'I got it ferye, Wilfy. Take it, man.'

The left side of Wilfy's upper lip curdled. He didn't drink. The dosser's leg was amputated above the knee. He wasn't pleased Wilfy was refusing his hospitality. Putting the cans down on the ground, he dived out of the wheelchair onto the pavement, ending up lying flat out. The slap of his hands and body on the concrete couldn't be louder if he'd done a kamikaze from a top window. I thought he'd died. The trouser leg containing his stump was folded up and safety-pinned in place. His head was right beside Wilfy's shoes...not the most hygienic place in the world. He started doing press-ups, using one arm only. After about twenty of these, he dragged himself back into the wheelchair. He was an alarming-looking wiry fellow with a rubbery face, twisting and grimacing all the time. Through his thick, cropped hair, a deep scar circumnavigated his skull.

There'd be no holds barred with him. His one-legged, one-armed press-ups threatened as much as astonished.

'Canadian Air Force. I did it all. Aye, I know, Wilfy. I KNOW him. Up there. Painter see. My friend my brother and no other. My mother sister to me no bother. I follow through across the air. Yes I know I see them there. Don't let me be disappointed in you, Wilfy. 'cos it's ferye. FerYE.'

As he spoke he pointed at the sky, the can in his hand. It was a good day, a blue sky. A few more beers and his brain would be so fuzzed he wouldn't know his own name and the sky by then would weigh a ton.

His head pitched to his chest, like he'd been coshed. Wilfy scuttled away.

I pushed his wheelchair into the side so he was facing the wall.

'Michelangelo...I knew him...come back, come back Sistine. Scobie.'

I switched my microcassette off. I was pleased I had him taped.

Angrily spinning back from the wall, he shot the wheelchair to the edge of the pavement. It tipped over, sprawling him into the road. I left him bawling at the sky. It was that easy to be cruel.

Is that what she wanted?

The strange creatures were like rats. If you saw one out in the open you could take it for granted there were a dozen out of sight. They were behind closed doors, watching television, eating olives, taking calls, making calls, doing things to someone's body, or not doing anything at all.

Freddie rang. He asked me to run him to hospital. Immediately.

'I'm preparing to die. The doctors have all but given up on me, apparently. Remember some time ago the business regarding April poisoning me? Well, it wasn't true. You know we attack the one we love, you know that, hm?'

'I do.'

I'd been right. There was real pain in his words. The old magus was in a bad way. You didn't have to be a doctor to see it.

I drove him to hospital. It was way much easier being decent.

A week later he phoned from the ward. He'd had a prostate operation and was once more discharging himself. They wanted to give him a catheter but he refused to have it attached.

'I will not wear a bag strapped to my knee.'

'Other than that, was the operation a success?'

'Instead of urinating every hour, now it's every half hour. When the surgeon knew I knew all about it, he was furious. He couldn't experiment with me, you see. Oh yes.'

He walked slowly beside me along Gower Street. I'd parked in a side street. It was morning rush hour. Cars, buses, vans, lorries smashed into the day. The pavements were packed with students and office workers. Freddie, wielding his umbrella, strode through them all in his pyjamas, slippers, dressing gown.

'Democracy is dead. They've split each country fifty-fifty. So no party can rule. They keep in charge. Who is to grasp the nettle? Power is rather like an ant hill. That's where the ants are. In the ant hill. Downing Street. Clear them out first. Attack Downing Street. So bloody simple.'

It was rough wedging him into the car. He was in pain.

'Freddie, is this wise? You've just had a serious operation. You shouldn't have discharged yourself again. They'll blame me for enabling you.'

'If it was a serious operation, successfully enacted, I wouldn't be dribbling, would I? I'm dribbling. Dribbling.'

He shouted this, angrily chomping his false teeth.

'Nobody in there knew who I was. They thought I was a Mr. Seegar. "Seegar," I said, "who the hell is Seegar? I'm here because my mickey's dribbling. Is that the case with this Seegar?" She looked at my chart. It seems this Seegar character was in for kidney dialysis. From Edenbridge in Kent, apparently.'

When I got him to the house and up the steps - with the help of the rope - I had to fetch a chair so he could rest in the hallway. Before attempting the climb to the attic. It was a painful struggle.

A few days later April came to our kitchen door. We had the blinds drawn. Her knocking was more like scratching. At first I thought it was a dog.

She stood outside, haunted, speechless, her jaw moving in circles, as if she were trying to snare words. She pointed upwards, finger jabbing the air. She eventually got his name out - 'Freddie.'

This time I was convinced he'd popped his clogs. I went up the stairs, nervous about seeing a dead body.

'Come in, dear boy, you must do something for me.'

The coffin was on the bed but he wasn't in it.

'You look surprised.'

He was wearing the trousers of his brown suit, braces hanging down over his rump and a woollen vest. He stood in the middle of the room, sharpening a pencil with a safety blade. Above his head the tasselled bulb shade touched his hair.

Why wasn't he dead? Red ears aglow, head cocked belligerently, he looked like he could go on forever. He was lining the coffin with red velvet.

'Why are you doing that, Freddie?'

'Do it up a bit, I thought, sell it! Why not? I called Dracula. He said he'd be interested.'

April came into the room and sat by the gas fire. She was knitting. The needles clicked a lot. Next time I looked, I could see they weren't in fact attached to the ball of wool in her lap.

'I need a bicycle wheel inner tube. Can you get me one? I'm finding it impossible to get out lately. The High Road - it's so depressing. All those foreigners.'

'You're a Little Englander to the end, Freddie.'

'I'm a Big Englander. When Big England ruled, the world kept its place. Now, alas, the world is small and we are smaller. The best of America is still English. They love our Royalty.'

'They also love Mickey Mouse.'

'Corruption is the blood of politics. We understand that. But hypocrisy is the death of the soul. Have you a soul?'

'What's it got to do with the inner tube of a bicycle wheel?'

'I will not have a bag attached to my personage. Dribbling has continued. So I have invented a device.'

He slapped sheets of paper down on the coffin lid. On one sheet was the sketch of a penis with a tube attached to the working end. An arrow bearing the legend - BICYCLE TUBE - pointed confirmation. The other sketch was of a trousered leg, a pavement and, just visible, a bicycle tube as it protruded from the bottom of the trouser. Another arrow, another legend - CONCEALED BICYCLE TUBE.

'It enables the dribble to emerge onto the pavement without being seen. Who would notice? In our climate. I have written to Higginsons. They are interested. It's so simple. Higginsons have intimated they will, on my instructions, come up with a watertight device for men who dribble from their cocks. We will have freedom to go out, escape our wives, pets. Visit our solicitors. Play cricket. Travel by bus. I'll pay you of course.'

'To travel by bus?'

'For the tube.'

'You want me to go by tube?'

'Christ! Is there something wrong with you, boy? The inner tube. Bicycle. I have an engineering background, as you know.'

He never had ordinary tittle-tattle conversation. Everything he said or was interested in was almost unbelievable. The more ordinary you seemed the more extraordinary you were. There are no small parts in Reality TV.

He lifted a fresh-smelling canvas leaning against the leg of his writing desk. It was a new painting. A butterfly. It had one colour only - purple. Clubbed antennae, proboscis, legs, face - all were in purple. The mouth had teeth, giving it a vicious appearance. He tapped the butterfly with his finger.

'That's what you want to be, yes? You are a reduced version still of the complete article we all sooner or later must become. Or die. Charming news, by the way. April is without doubt, with child. You must spread the word. The Aztecs could impregnate a woman with a bowl of dust. The son of such union grew to be a warrior. The greatest of all warriors was the warrior of revenge. I could have saved my country. I could have led. Revenge me. Revenge me until death. Your death. April can replace the princess in the hearts of the people. She can become the first real English saint since Diana Dors. I kissed her.'

'April?'

'No. Diana Dors.'

All this time the potential St. April sat dumb as stone. Her face and teeth were the same whitey-yellow colour. I could glimpse the top of her ample bosom. That was whitey-yellow.

'Agghh! I'm going to shoot myself. Agghh!'

Without warning, the scream had curdled out of her, like she was in a Punch and Judy show. Or the Devil had her by the throat. Freddie pretended normality.

'Yes, sweet-sweetie, there you are. She loves butterflies, oh yes. Don't you?'

She didn't answer. She didn't hear.

He bent over the coffin and stuck more red velvet inside it with Copydex. The rubbery smell joined the cloying sweetness of too much talcum and the rotten water in a vase of dead daffodils.

'Get to my state and nothing much can help. Not the moon. Not the stars. I feel the tide. For the first time in my life, I feel the tide pulling. This life. Each one of us has been put in the dock. Yet each one of us is unfit to plead.'

We were decanting ourselves. Our asylum was crumbling from within.

Out on the landing I took a quick peep into her room. The most noticeable thing was a heavy armchair with wide wooden armrests and chains attached. Stout chains.

'The shackles I designed myself. Oh yes, rather. The chains are secured to the frame. There is enough play to allow movement. If necessary. Leg irons. They snap round the ankles. Maximum restraint, minimum discomfort. Absolutely. Scotland Yard were very impressed. They considered ordering a job lot. I heard they gave the contract to a Polish firm instead. You can't trust the Poles, you do know that, don't you? Oh yes.'

The politicians had closed the asylums and dumped the inmates on the streets. Freddie had his own cottage industry. Complete with shackles. Whenever April became too impossible he just banged her into the armchair, shackled her legs and left her to it. He'd have the radio on at full blast, drowning her mania.

He showed me a key hidden on a hook at the back of the piano.

'This unlocks the shackles. If anything ever happened to me, you now know what to do.'

He smiled and raised his eyebrows up and down several times. If he were to die, I was to carry on shackling April.

'I wouldn't be able to incarcerate anyone, Freddie. I'd be too scared.'

'Oh, nonsense. They go like lambs eventually. As long as you show the strong arm first. They can waste your time. That is what madness is - a waste of time.'

'You admit she is mad?'

His arms were strong. He clenched his big fists.

'Are you mad just because someone says so? Madness and genius and beauty are close aligned. Madness is an industry like any other. Employs thousands. Makes millions. Freud was really a banker at heart.'

'My wife is definitely leaving me, Freddie. She doesn't come out and say it straight to my face. But I sense it. The pain, even as we speak, is boiling my guts.'

'Poor boy, you do look unhappy. Pale as a daisy. But you'll be free without her. There are other butterflies out there. I was married very briefly. I can't even remember what she looked like. I remember her mother. A mock saint with a club foot and a face like a cracked plate.'

I went off to buy the bicycle tube.

Coming back down the High Road I met my wife. She gave me a chilling look. I had the tube wrapped round my neck. For fun.

'You said you were turning over a new leaf. It's not funny.'

'Freddie's dying.'

'You promised you'd stay away from him. He's an old fascist. He probably drove that poor woman insane.'

'You don't know that. You spend your days in Westminster, smoothing chairs for plonkers.'

'Say what you like, you did something I didn't think possible - you killed my love for you. Think about it. This is it. We're through. Finito.'

I saw some hope in the 'Finito.' Did anyone who said it ever mean it? I hoped there was hope in it. My mistake was wearing the inner tube round my neck. It was an ordinary bicycle tube - 27 X 1 1/4. I had twisted the tube into an eight and doubled it over so it fitted fairly tight round my neck. It might have looked normal in a swimming pool.

I gave it to Freddie. He gave me his hat by way of payment. I wouldn't accept money.

My wife wasn't at home. I waited for her to return. When it grew dark, I went searching. I walked along the street looking in the windows. Those who weren't eating off Smallbone ash tables were watching widescreen tellies. Even the dogs and cats were watching.

She was in Earthy's house. He and Lady Hannah sat back whilst my wife, glass of red in hand, regaled them with some tale or other, making them laugh. At me? How could she laugh at this time?

'Heh, darling! Do you fancy going go-karting?'

Lady Hannah jumped up and head ducking about, peered out, trying to see where exactly I lurked.

I'd never been go-karting in my life. The headlights of a car swept round the corner. I quickly dashed into the public gardens through a hole in the fence. Earthy had called the cops. My wife had called the cops.

Two uniformed men got out and looked up and down the street. Neville came to the door.

'Thank you for coming. And so promptly.'

'Can't say as I see anyone about like. Loitering.'

'He's most likely cleared off. Thank you. It's okay officer.'

They drove away. My wife, cool as ice the whole time, had never left her chair. It was finito okay.

Sam Tripp's parents told me I'd sat against a tree for hours. Until dawn. I couldn't remember. I'd fallen down the shaft again. There was a pool of disturbance inside me. I drowned every so often. I was drowning in her eyes.

I went to the brain-riddler. She had phoned him. She knew I needed him. He had her credit card number.

'She's left me. The pain is such my stomach feels full of boiling worms.'

'You keep saying that.'

'My soul is cold. My brain is damp. I saw her come out with a suitcase. She got into her car and drove away. She left me this note saying she'd be in touch. To stay calm. How can I?'

I showed him the note. Her hand-writing was clear, round, exact. Perfect. Written in red ink.

'The hounds of logic have caught the hare of unreason.'

He meant I couldn't have it both ways. All the time I spoke he was cleaning a shotgun. He belonged to a gun club. I sensed, even then, I was just playing at being a loose cannon. I was acting out a life instead of living it.

'You have one great advantage,' he said, 'life is the only drug you get high on. Well done.'

'I feel like Adam having to leave Eden.'

'Adam was banished. You forced Eve out. She was tempted by the snake because you gave her no other alternative.'

He aimed his shotgun at an imaginary target.

There was Eden. Then The Fall. Would there be The Rise?

'The Fall, The Rise, it's just the sex-drive in parable, yeah?'

'Words get in the way. I prefer listening to birds. That's pure sound. That Freddie character you've mentioned...Think what he's thinking when he wears his frock. Not what he says. It's time you put away your microcassette.'

'I won't show you mine if you don't show me yours.'

I saw Freddie in the Post Office, eyes coldly regarding the common multitude with whom he had to stand in line. Though he himself was cashing a giro, he gave the impression that queuing was so beneath him they were extremely honoured he was witnessing this aspect of their quaintly inferior lives.

An inch of bicycle tube protruded from his trouser leg. Only the most gimlet-eyed would have spotted it against his black shoe. When the queue moved on, he'd left a dribble behind.

This was the man who wanted to announce that the virgin April was going to have a baby and it was going to save the world? I felt like crying for the old sod. Death was heading towards him fast. If, by some miracle, he attained power before then, he'd surely be the first man to rule his country an inner tube tied to his mickey.

My wife had gone. The house was silent without her...Those formidable high-heels jabbing the kitchen floor...Her laughs when on the phone...The Sunday dinners... Her splashings in the bath...Her fierce concentration when she sat quietly doing the crossword...Most of all, lying in bed listening to her breathing, the occasional rumbling in her tummy.

Now the house was so dead it was noisy. I had to listen to myself. We'd fallen in love but were poles apart. That was the rock bottom truth. I had to face it.

One morning when I went up to the hallway to collect the mail, I happened to notice the naked bulb, yellow with fly dung, dangling from the cracked ceiling. It filled me to the brim with loathing. I jumped up and punched it. I had bits of glass in my hair all day.

The morning we'd first met in Hanley played on a loop in my mind. That glorious sunny day. That shaft of light and air creaming her skin. That quick look in her eyes telling me I had a chance.

I vowed never to go near Freddie again. I blamed him for her leaving me. It wasn't true. The old bastard. When he knocked I wouldn't answer. The worst pain is soul pain. She phoned me from time to time.

'Of course you're hurting, darling. But it will pass. Honest.'

She sent money. Some times I laughed happily. Mostly I lay low.

One morning Dickie Grimes pulled up outside the house in a lorry. It was an ancient Ford, brightly painted in greens and blues and reds. A circus vehicle.

He told me Freddie had arranged a procession. One night soon. A remarkable miracle had occurred, apparently. Miss Fard was pregnant, apparently. Immaculately so. Apparently. The people were going to process after her in the streets around the public gardens. Miss Fard was going to be seated on a golden throne. I had noticed on the back of the lorry a sheet of canvas covering a bulky object. It had to be the throne.

'It's a complete con, right?'

'Maybe.'

Dickie Grimes was a wiry, weird old man. His spectacles on a cord dangled round his neck.

'The time in the Church Hall, didn't you say you'd be eighty-six next birthday? Has it happened?'

'Yes.'

'Happy Birthday.'

'Thank you for remembering.'

'Are you allowed to drive at your age?'

'What are they going to do with me?'

'What can you tell me about Freddie and April?'

'I first met him in the ring. Billy 'The Hammer' Bates, ran the Brighton gym. Everyone knew him. We weren't inside the ropes twenty seconds when he grabbed me by the ice-cream.'

'Billy 'The Hammer', grabbed you?'

'Freddie. We formed a lifelong friendship there and then.'

Cigarette ash snapped and fell into his lap.

'Politics was always what he was best at. He had the guts for it. But after the war they cleaned it up a lot and he was left out on a limb. He could have been a top man in the Conservatives. He told Macmillan what he thought of him. I was there. Right to his face. That's why he was respected.'

'What did he say?'

'He invited Macmillan to Woffingtons. He wouldn't go. "You've less balls than a eunuch", Freddie says to him.'

'What about April?'

'She came from Macclesfield. That's all anyone knows about the Fards.'

He clammed up. Then drove off to fill up with petrol.

I went round to the Electric. The first thing I noticed was Freddie's painting hanging on a wall. The cardinal. I couldn't believe it. Freddie had given it to Turkey to see if he could sell it.

'How much does he want for it?'

'Whadchoo offerin', my fren?'

I was amazed. A man who knew meat and massage parlours - what would he know about art? Hm. Everything. Under the cynical gaze of the prelate the Electric had shrunk to what it was - an Asian Minor version of a greasy spoon. There were two men at a table talking football. Every now and then they glanced up at the painting. The cardinal had more space here to deploy his cruel grimace. The canvas hanging higher than in Freddie's room, the small skull by the feet had greater prominence. There was more light to brighten the silver buckles on the black patent-leather shoes. The vast Vatican costume looked in need of a good brushing. The Papal ring was a skull and crossbones on a golden cross. The head was powerful, the hair under the biretta gun-metal grey. The visible ear was red and big as a saucer. It was a self-portrait okay.

If you wanted to bend minds you had to confront people. Scare them, boss them, then rule them.

Was I going to let my wife walk away, our separation as arbitrary as our meeting? On the other hand though, there was something pure about living alone.

I got on a bus and headed for Whitehall. I'd walk right in to her office and just for starters scream the place down. I realised it would be a hopeless gesture. You can't force someone to love you. But she said she did love me. She just couldn't live with me.

In Gower Street a family boarded the bus. They were heading for the London Eye. Down from Staffordshire their accents straightaway hit home. The two men were so alike they had to be twins. They were dressed identically in denim shirts and shabby denim jackets. They wore small ear rings. Both were unshaven. Their concave faces were like spoons. They had three women with them and three boys, aged about seven, six and five. There was a baby in a buggy. The men wrestled the buggy flat as soon as they boarded the bus.

'Bloody 'ell, this thing.'

'Give it 'ere. Out of bloody road.'

When they'd stowed it on the luggage rack they joined the women. Their energy level was so high they seemed to have commandeered half the bus. The boys were attacked verbally all the time. A non-stop assault somewhere between deadly and humorous.

'Wheer's Eye, Dad?'

'End of my fist if you're not careful.'

One of the boys ran up to the front of the bus.

''eer, cum 'eer. Afore I brek your ruddy neck.'

The three women laughed. One of them was attractive with jet black hair. The lot of them had ceramic-pale faces. The Londoners on the bus smiled at the antics but quickly realized getting involved, however tangentially, could be risky.

'Mam, 'ees on platform now, 'ees goin' ter fall off, Mam.'

'Good. Hope so.'

'Cum away from theer, daft sod. Don't swing on that ruddy pole. You'll fall off. Who cares.'

'When will we be there?'

'It's shut. They 'eard we were cummin' and buggers got heart attack.'

''owdoduck? Awreet?'

The attractive woman with short black hair was pregnant. She laughed, then chuckled for a few seconds. As if she'd become self-conscious. Pleased, the John character pressed his face to the window and shouted to a pedestrian.

'Comin' to the big whale wi' us, missus? Hopaboard, duck. We'll get you whome in time for tea.'

One of the women was small, blonde and looked nervous. Especially when the baby was poked vigorously in the back and told to look out the window. The two men, ferrety quick in movement, heads bobbing, darting all the time, were utterly without restraint.

'Tell thee summat, driver must be bloody drunk. 'e damn near crashed inta back that truck. Daft bugger - slow down! Afore I brek tha' bloody neck!'

'Would you brek 'is neck, John, would you?' One of the boys asked eagerly.

'I'd brek yours an' ah. Sit down.'

When the bus turned towards the river they caught a glimpse of the big wheel in the distance. Men and boys erupted from their seats. The baby buggy was attacked with such gusto it was a marvel it didn't disintegrate.

'Bloody 'ell, this ruddy buggy, 'ow does eet bloody work? Daft bloody thing. Put bloody baby in it then, go on.'

The baby, a pale pudding of a thing, was handed round like a frozen chicken.

When they finally got off, they stood in a silent clump - gobsmacked. A short distance away was the London Eye. It was everything they'd hoped. Magnificent, awe-inspiring, peculiar, so out of the ordinary, it was worth every inch of the journey from Stoke-On-Trent. I got off as well. They were from home. They were real as lumps of clay.

"ell's fire, 'ow does it stand up? It's like a ruddy great bicycle whale.'

'Are them spokes, John?'

'It's like the insides of a big umbrella, 'n't it?'

'Can we go up on eet, Dad?'

'Why doyer think we bloody cum all this way, daft bugger? Cum on.'

The older boy took the man's hand and they rushed ahead of the others. The women looked round shyly, moved off, the three of them pushing the buggy, hanging on to it. They had fear in their eyes. The men looked daft as brushes.

I watched them mill about the wheel, shouting, gesticulating, being terrifically interested in how it DID stand up.

'It's on an axel that big, 'nt it? Must be, there you are, see. Must be biggest whale in tworld.'

The way they clunked close together, face to face, jabbering, moving, they might have been a tribe of badgers come up for air. I was that tribe. Their accents in the big city made me lonely. For myself. It was going to cost them a packet to get on the Eye. They thought children were free. I paid for the kids. They looked at me like I was nuts. I was the weirdo, not them.

'Ta, youth.'

One of the boys nibbled a chocolate biscuit. It smeared his face, crumbed down his cardigan. I could smell it, smell back to when I was his age. Aged five, nibbling an oatcake in bed, waiting for my parents to come home at half-pissed twelve. The cold of a Potteries winter piercing through the thin blue bricks, the damp of the night defying sleep. The under sheet full of crumbs, bits of toe nails, navel fluff.

Licking an ice cream cone, I walked to Whitehall. The massive cut-stone buildings, cement mixed with the blood of nations, were more intimidating than the big wheel. She was in there somewhere. Her office was down a snug side street, a private yard. Security let me as far as reception but reception wouldn't allow me further.

'I'm her husband.'

'We're sorry, but we've strict instructions. Your name isn't on the list. Sorry.'

They'd tell her I'd called, of course they would, oh yes, absolutely. Which would give her plenty of warning. She'd dodge out a back way or something. She'd know my form - I'd hang around till the crack of doom. The receptionist did let slip she'd a lunch appointment. I told them I couldn't wait, pretending I'd an urgent appointment elsewhere.

She'd done a neat job of leaving me. I'd hardly noticed her slither off.

I hung about in the foyer of a theatre. Out on the street a police car sped along, cut in front of a BMW, forcing it to stop. A flurry of cops erupted. They pulled the driver out and pinioned him to the pavement. The man, young, black, well dressed, protested, wincing as his arms were twisted behind his back.

'Please. Can I phone my solicitor?'

People gathered round. Five cops on top of one man. In the eyes of everyone watching the scales of justice prejudicially tipped every which way.

I saw her, definitely her, coming towards me. She couldn't see me from the crowds. There was someone with her. It wasn't Earthy. As they came bobbing towards me along the packed lunch-hour street, it was hard to be definite but I vaguely recognised the bloke. It was Big Red Telly Boots. He was wearing an exceptionally smart suit and overcoat and carrying a briefcase.

I jumped out in front of them. Breathing madness.

'George S. Drake, I declare. What are you doing with my wife?'

I should have scared the life out of them. But they were prepared. My wife wore her tired, forgiving smile. Big Red Telly Boots stood strong.

'Your wife and I work in the same building. I've left television.'

'Darling, don't create a scene. Please. Not here.'

I flew at Big Boots, grabbed him by the lapels and half tried to nut him, hit him, knock him to the pavement. He proved a solid customer. I swung out of him, trying to tumble him. People scattered, shrieking. Soon we had a whole chunk of Whitehall to ourselves. As I of him, he had a firm hold of me. Tugging, pushing, spinning we were like a pair of drunks in a Highland bothy. A big lady in a burkha got felled. You couldn't see much of her but could she shriek! My wife was cool as champagne from the fridge. I was so weak with passion I knew if Big Red Telly Boots didn't drop in a second I wasn't going to be able to do whatever it was I was trying. I subsequently learned the bugger had played rugger. I had too, but whereas I disappeared down space-holes, time-traps, even as I scored, he had trotted out for England schoolboys.

Ignominiously, I began to slide down his nice overcoat. Were those my knees on concrete? Jesus, he was laying me down like I was dead. Was that his arm expertly across my neck? This wasn't what I...how the hell had this happened? Now there were four arms holding me stiff and stern.

Undercover cops. Whitehall was full of them. By the time they hauled me to my feet and pinned me against Portland stone, my wife and George S. Drake had vanished. One of the cops was on his mobile, checking me out. They wanted to be on the safe side. Had they anything political on me in Scotland Yard? I had to give my name, date of birth. No, nothing, I was clean.

'Look, we're letting you go. This time. Just keep away from your wife.'

'Is that how your marriage works?'

I'd gathered a goodly crowd. The real theatre was in the streets.

I'd lost a shirt button. It wasn't a high price to pay. The cops had pinned me to the wall like I was a butterfly on a setting board. When they discovered my tape recorder they switched it on. Freddie's voice boomed out,

'My cock is giving trouble, you know that, don't you, Sidney?'

I walked the whole way home, the sound of my feet reminders of my shame. I'd been whupped. I had no sense of myself. I'd been trying to slip through life, unseen. Yet at the same time throwing up obstacles.

I went round to Hannah's. I had to talk with someone. I begged her to take me in. I promised I'd behave. She had music playing - Jim Diamond singing Sugarolly Mountains. When I told her about my wife and Big Red Telly Boots, she laughed.

'Don't be ridiculous. It's not George. It's Neville. She and Neville have been an item for some time. They are going to live together. You fool.'

'Why don't you seem to mind?'

We were in the sitting room. In a corner I spied a pair of green high-heels. I picked them up. My wife's. I smelled them to be certain. Hannah laughed and poured herself another shot of whiskey. The way she poured, it was a shot. You could hear the explosion as it hit the rocks in the bottom of the glass. Her marriage to Sir Neville, England's greatest living or dead director, was over. They were being very civilised about it. No shrieking, no lawyers, everything sorted.

'How about Zoe?'

'She's going to Benenden.' Settled.

My wife and Earthy holding hands...Lying down together...Earthy on top of her? Her? Earthy? The pain of broken love is the pain at the centre of the universe. There is no other pain like it. Not even a mouth ulcer. Hannah and Neville were very modern. Pain could be blocked. By money. But could it? I remembered Freddie saying pain was like water. It couldn't be blocked, shut out, kept in.

'You see, Joey,' Hannah said, 'your wife and Neville - same class. Same class.'

'Am I supposed to let it go, just like that?'

'It's gone. They've gone. An hour ago. Did you not know Neville comes from very near her home? Uttoxeter. The Earthys. Very well known. They know each other's families.'

'She never mentioned it.'

'You can bed down here if you wish.'

'That's bloody kind of you, Hannah.'

'It is, isn't it?'

'I'll never accept it. Him and her.'

'The landed gentry keep one another in reserve. For emergencies. Then you suddenly find you're up against it.'

'Aren't you gentry?'

'Gentrified. My father was a banker.'

'Mine was a wanker.'

Her hair was now blonde. Beauty parlours camouflaged well. But you could see lines tracing her face under the make-up and when she needed to dial a number she had to put on glasses. Earthy had traded her in for a younger model.

'Yes. I've been put out to grass.'

She'd heard Freddie was going to parade April round the streets. People were very curious. April had healing hands apparently. Big Julia was walking better since she'd been touched by her. Had I impregnated April by any chance?

'It's a concept I couldn't imagine outside the back of a circus tent.'

'Mr. Parts-Rinser is a circus.'

'The circus is life.'

'You have a gentle soul, Joey, which is why you've been crushed. I have a gentle soul. I'm still a girl at heart. I've lost a stone in three weeks. It makes me feel good. So much happier. What do you think of my figure? Is my bottom too fat?'

'Better to have a fat bottom than a fat head.'

'You're so annoying. Love is your problem. It can ruin sex. Your feelings get in the way. This is the twenty-first century.'

'I don't know what you mean.'

The music played. I danced with her slowly.

"I lived my dreams out on the Sugarolly Mountains

While looking down on No Mean City way below

So many dreams up on the Sugarolly Mountains

One day I'd be a rock'n'roll singer

The next I'd be building boats..."

She was sad, she said. She wanted to visit Scotland.

I went home. Eventually. Freddie beat on my door most of the night but I wouldn't answer. I took pills and got to sleep.

The following evening I could hear something happening outside the house. It had to be, it was - Freddie's pageant.

A good deal of Dickie Grimes' lorry was draped in white sheets and April was up on the back, ensconced on a golden throne. She wore a long white dress and a medieval wimple complete with veil. Freddie, flanked by two young crew-cut men, stood on the back of the lorry. The two crew-cuts wore leather jackets and gave the distinct impression they were more Roman than Galilean.

When Freddie saw me he was angry.

'I knocked. You didn't open. The moment has come. The pause called the end.'

Big Julia, May, Miss Jackpot, Filfy Wilfy, Mr. Stavrou - the half-blind Greek man and some women I recognised from walking their dogs in the public gardens were the extras in Freddie's charade. Neighbours stood at their doors or watched through front windows. Even Nigerian Ore - still on a crutch - and his wife watched.

Dickie Grimes started the engine. The crew-cuts fired two Guy Fawkes rockets, the explosions and shower of coloured stars making a powerful impact for about one and a half seconds. The lorry moved off, Freddie gripping the side to steady himself.

An ancient battered loudspeaker sticking out the passenger window crackled loudly, then blared out Jerusalem.

Filfy Wilfy sidled along, cackling, nails clicking.

'He offered me a job, old Partsy, if he gets to power. Starting the Grand National every year.'

Julia, who carried a burning candle, told me April had cured her arthritis. Not by the laying on of hands but by just looking at her.

'You can see for yourself, look, I ain't got no stick, have I?'

Going past Mr. Stavrou's house, the door opened and his wife emerged carrying a proper big Greek candle, her hand cupped about the flame. She waved cheerfully.

Every now and then the crew-cuts, with two ordinary flash-lamps, lit Freddie up.

There were similar moments in European history but with greatly superior wattage.

Miss Jackpot appeared alongside me, head bowed, troubled.

'What's up, Muzie?'

'I have sold. All is sold. I am gone out of it.'

Jerusalem finished playing. Dickie Grimes brought the lorry to a halt under a street light. Awash in amber, the moment had come for Freddie. The last throw of the dice. The old magus would merge reality and myth or die a failure. How had he the nerve to do what he was doing?

A dog barked. A magpie flitted from a tree.

Freddie raised his arms. He looked cranky. April, clutching her handbag to her bosom, looked a mixture of Elizabeth I, Mrs. Thatcher and Alice.

Freddie dropped his arms. His voice was powerful.

'We salute you, O England. I feel your sadness and am come to bring you hope.'

'Cuppatea, Guv?'

The crew-cuts shone their torches in Filfy's sour milk face.

"ucking 'ell,' he muttered, 'that's out of order.'

'The poor are poor because they have no money. So give them money. A man with money in his pocket wants to make more. That's how the rich got rich. Close down the House of Lords. It is the place where God created aids. Take pity on foreigners - send them home. Our climate doesn't suit them. Hang murderers. Ban cars in the cities. No cars - no car bombs. Could anything be simpler?'

'Right, yeah,' Julia said.

Freddie, mesmerising himself, continued.

'We need new rulers, new symbols, new queens. That much is obvious. Man is dead. We let our Gods kill him. Build anew. Yes. New. New. I give you April Fard.'

She sat on the throne, lifeless as a piece of monumental sculpture. Freddie raised his arms in her direction. Perhaps he was back in the urgent thirties when ruthless men wore black shirts and their leaders Savile Row suits.

'Singled out by Divine Will, there has been an exchange of celestial ointments of creation, the fruits of which will shortly, immaculately, manifest itself for all to see. The poor at last can live in hope. Those who are rich and of good breeding shall not be turned away. You do know I have an engineering background? Oh yes, rather.'

The loudspeaker, sticking out the passenger window, parted company with whatever held it in place. Hitting the road with a tinny clatter, swivelling playfully, it finally rolled in under the lorry.

'I 'ave late night and I set clock bee-SIDE my ear to go off the bloomin' ting at heh quarter to the hour so I get to Ladbroke at right time enough. How do I avoid doubtful matters? You see?'

Muzie looked at me. The street light sparkled on his spectacles.

Life was a place where nobody listened to nobody.

Freddie continued, his emotions shocking.

'She is the symbol of England. She will be a blue plaque on the wall of our history. Beauty, purity, innocence...April has never harmed a person in her life. Help her. Please. Why should she be decanted? Why should anyone be decanted? We all of us inherited this other Eden.'

He was placing her in the care of those who knew her. Before he died. I couldn't see him living longer than a month. He was bleeding internally. He had a bicycle tube attached to his water-works.

'Freddie, come down before you fall down. I'll look after her. I promise.'

He peered into the harsh night, trying to locate me. Chest heaving, he could no longer continue.

I helped the crew-cuts man-handle him to earth.

Had his life been a rehearsal for this pathetic parade? A charade. A pantomime. Was it really only about April? Would I really look after her? Cook for her? Cash her giro for her? Buy clothes for her in Mrsblouse?

The house that night as I lay in bed was unusually still. Even the woodlice wore slippers. There wasn't a squeak, a creak. I couldn't hear the tube trains rumble below. I listened for any sound to drown the beatings of my heart. Eventually, a police siren bludgeoned a hole in the dismal silence and, speeding along the High Road, let the dawn in.

I sat on the edge of the bed wondering what to do. That radio edge where the BBC returns from serving the world. 5.20 am. She was gone. With Earthy. Anyone else on earth more unlike me didn't exist. How was I ever going to trust again? A fly buzzed out from behind the wardrobe, bounced off surfaces, zipped at my head. At that time of morning it was noisy as a dog with fits. I got it with a shoe. Splat.

I'd follow her. I'd chase them down. I wasn't going to be an idiot fly.

Eight o'clock. I made a cuppa. I heard footsteps on the stairs. It had to be April's scattery-slappy feet.

I could hear her whimpering, gasping. What had he done to her? I opened the door.

'Freddie's died.'

The words were flat, bald; her white face, eyes, never so devoid of feeling. She looked dead as a clock with broken hands.

'Freddie? Dead? Are you sure? How do you know?'

She was wearing a white nightdress and a pink bath cap. Perhaps she was so upset she couldn't speak. Whatever their set-up, Freddie had been her lifeline.

'How are you, April?'

'I'm all right.'

Again the words came out flat, but the pronoun took a slight hit, matching the pronoun in my question. I told her to leave the attic door open and I'd come up in a minute after I dressed. I was bollock naked. She hadn't noticed.

He was dead alright. Lying on the bed. April sprinkled round him with talcum powder. A shower of it went across my Gucci toes. Big and bulky in his woman's dress, he was dead as the lion I saw dumped at the back of a circus in Longton. The bicycle tube dangled from his hand. I eased it from him and slung it across the back of a chair. I phoned Dracula, reminding him a coffin was not needed. I waited in the room, trying to read in Freddie's face a word or two of wisdom. The flaky forehead, the strong nose, the thick grey hair, the blue lips, his marvellous square chest, they were so him, yet so baffling in their emptiness. The big ears were no longer red. As if they'd been switched off. He was dead as a January Christmas tree. I was glad his eyes were shut. What did he mean by the pause called the end? Was death a pause? Did he believe in a continuing life? April came back into the room with a carpet sweeper. One of those old-fashioned items you were supposed to roll over and back. She used it noisily, like it was a carpet-beater. She seemed not to care that Freddie was dead. Every time she hit the leg of the bed, or some other bit of furniture, she gave a frustrated squeal. Her hair hung down over her shoulders, some of it reaching the small of her back.

Piled on the shelves to the right of the gas fire were dozens of manuscripts. The pinstripe suit he wore during his pageant hung neatly on a clothes-hanger on the back of the door. He'd changed into his frock before going to bed.

Dracula arrived, accompanied by a doctor. Freddie had been his patient round the Health Centre.

They stood for a few professional moments observing the corpse. April beat about with the carpet-sweeper, then went out. The doctor looked at me. I shrugged. I was alive, that's all I knew. Lifting Freddie's hand, he felt the wrist for a pulse he knew he wouldn't find. Placing a stethoscope to his chest, he listened for the beat he knew had fled. With his thumb he opened each eye.

'Mr. Parts is no longer with us.'

He knew Freddie's case history. No inquest needed. Turning to Dracula he said,

'He's all yours really.'

Dracula examined the coffin, now leaning against the mantle. He was intrigued with the ruched velvet lining.

'It's a handy bit of work this. Waste of money though.'

Simultaneously they both took out mobile phones.

April was in the kitchen. I went in and, leaning against the fridge, watched her. With a breadknife she stabbed at a digestive biscuit. When she saw me, she raised the knife protectively before her, then lowering it, stepped closer. She wanted something from the fridge. I was in her way.

'If you want me, I'll be downstairs, April.'

Buffaloing in between me and the fridge door, she knocked me flying. Saucepans and a colander fell from a shelf. She had the wet yeasty look and total strength of insanity. A force of nature askew. Armed with a knife. Gurgling animal noises swelling in her throat, hand rumbling round inside the fridge, she located a packet of butter. Throwing it down on the table, she swiped at it with the knife.

Dracula stopped me on the landing. Freddie had to be coffined, then carried down to the hearse. It was a two-man job. I wouldn't be needed at the funeral parlour - he had a man there. A Bosnian. They weren't scared of death. Nor thought it beneath them. They were used to it. Death was all around.

Freddie would lie in state in the funeral parlour until arrangements were finalised. The doctor, scribbling in a notebook, asked,

'Was it his custom to wear a dress?'

'Not all the time.'

'They say he was a Lordship,' Dracula said. 'Lord Rinser. He's left a lot of money

- that I do know. He was a transvestite performer during the war. They say the Lord Chamberlain ordered him to stop. I'm not burying him in female attire.'

'Why not? You'd look well in a short skirt.'

'Not me. Him. You birk. He requested a horse-drawn hearse.'

An Edwardian touch. On the long schlep up to Kensal Green he'd have a final audience.

'What about April?'

'Miss Fard? He's left her a fortune.'

'Who'll look after her? Freddie said she had recently immaculately conceived. In an exchange of sacred ointments, celestially introduced.'

The doctor exchanged looks with Dracula.

'He's a sardine short of a full tin, Doctor. So was old Parts.'

The doctor looked round the room at the trail of powder...the laden shelves, the table with the word processor...the hand-painted wardrobe...the nail sticking up from a floorboard, a hammer alongside...the bicycle tube across the back of a chair. Intrigued, biro flicking against his bottom lip, he tried to work it out. The two bits of yellow ribbon attached to one end of the tube had him stumped.

'What was that for?'

'His mickey.'

'What's all that? Powder? Or dust?'

'Dust is life.'

'Was he a writer?'

'He had a poltergeist in his inkwell. But he never let it out.'

Making a final note, taking a final glance at Freddie, a final one at me, he finally left the room.

'Goodbye, gentlemen.'

Dracula undressed the corpse. Buttoned down the front, the dress was easily removed. Dracula's speedy hands soon had the body naked. Freddie looked like a side of meat on a butcher's table. So quickly lifeless. He'd been freshly knocked to the canvas for a count of infinity. His lust for power was counted out. He looked like a monstrous plucked turkey. He was a democrat at last. Part of the great majority. His lips had shrunk. His false teeth no longer fitted his mouth. The upper ones peeked out. He looked a bit like Freddie Mercury.

Dracula, bundling him over on his side, rammed a wad of tissue up his bum. Had he done the same thing to Fata?

'You ah, ah, don't really ah, need me, do you?'

'Hand me that suit.'

He pulled the trousers from the hanger.

'They don't tailor 'em like this no more. Lord Rinser of Rainow or some such.'

April came in with a cup of tea. Who was it for? Freddie? Blankly, she stared in the direction of his naked corpse. Her face screamed silently. Even Dracula watched, Freddie's trousers dangling in one hand, the jacket still on the hanger in the other. The saucer and cup rattled. Shivering teeth. At this time every morning she probably brought Freddie a cuppa. An elevenses - could anything be more normal? Dracula stared at the tea. Was it meant for him? Smart, trim, slim, all in black - even his shirt - he blinked nervously.

April didn't move. A growl swelled her neck. It sounded as if she had swallowed a dog. Opening her mouth wide, some kind of spiritual boil burst within.

'Blaghughyeekacksssshhruckkbackofffuckerollfuckoffbackerollaghhaghhpisshahjah. Jah.'

The saucer, cup and contents flew out of her hand, hit the ceiling, splattered down on top of the corpse, the bedclothes, the floor, Dracula.

Dropping Freddie's suit, he rugby-tackled her to the floor. Tumbled beneath him, helpless, gasping, fiercely engulfed, his fist squashed down hard on her forehead. Subdued, he dragged her out the door.

'What are you doing? She's harmless now.'

'Get out of the road.'

His moves were professional. He knew how to handle bodies. He bundled her into her room, dumped her in the armchair, expertly shackled her ankles.

'Now then, you daft bitch!'

Having coughed a demon she looked utterly spent. She didn't seem to mind what Dracula had done to her. In time she'd swell again with other demons. Perhaps the same one. Insanity was repetition.

An inability to break the circle.

'Was that necessary?'

'Old Parts showed me the drill. Told me about you too.'

He brushed at the dust and tea-stains on his clothes.

The saucer had landed upside down over Freddie's right nipple.

'Daft bugger,' Dracula said. He meant Freddie. As if in death the old clown had placed the saucer on his pectoral for comic effect.

Dracula, retrieving the suit from the floor, dragged the trousers up Freddie's legs. The obstruction that was no longer his privates he tucked out of the way the better to ease the garment to the belly. It was said Dracula handled more cocks in a week than the Royal Family on the first of November.

Catching the corpse by the wrists he hauled it into a sitting position. Efficiently he got the shirt on, a tie, then the jacket. As he buttoned the jacket he ordered me to slip on the shoes. Freddie's bloodless toe nails were long and turning upwards. The feet were powerful. Great hooves, they'd never clatter on the stairs again. He must have weighed the best part of sixteen stone. Would the environmentally-friendly coffin contain him?

We struggled down the stairs, Dracula going first, taking most of the burden. When we got outside the hearse had been given a parking ticket. Dracula, outraged, circled about looking for the traffic warden. There was no one in sight. Breathing deeply, a cold black mask of a man, he spoke with quiet intensity.

'He might have been right, you know, old Parts. No respect left.'

When he drove away the sense of emptiness was immense. That was it. Freddie was gone. The pause called the end had come out of the blue.

Space was the black and white hole in which we revolved. Time was the stuff we inhaled. And it was killing us.

In the gardens, women walked their dogs. A jumbo piked across the sky. All the doors along the street were shut. No one knew Freddie was dead. I looked up at April looking down. She had enough chain to move to the window. The armchair was heavy and Freddie had nailed a long length of timber to the back legs, making it impossible for her to drag it out the door. Once shackled, she was trapped in her room. Until released.

I pulled the blue rope in and, from hand to elbow, coiled it.

I went back up to April. She was at the window, her back to me. Retrieving the key from behind the piano, I knelt by her ankles and set her free.

She made me feel normal. That took some doing.

The loss of my wife weighed heavier than Freddie's coffin. I phoned her to tell her the news. Any excuse to hear that voice. The receptionist put me through from one person to another. They all said she wasn't at her desk.

'Yah bunch of lying toads.'

Without her the flat was emptier than if someone had stolen every stick of furniture. I lay down. On the floor by the bed was a hair brush, a crocodile skin handbag and a pair of boxer shorts. Hers.

Out on the communal stairs I heard the clattering of sandals slapping loosely on the steps. It had to be April. As if she was dragging something down the stairs. I peeped out the window. She was dumping black plastic rubbish bags by the dustbins. Freddie barely cold, she was already getting rid of his stuff.

'They have no feelings - you know that, don't you? No emotions.'

She slapped up and down, time and time again, with yet more bags. I nipped out to take a closer look.

Freddie's clothes bulged the sacks. His suits, coats, jackets, shirts, waistcoats, ties, cravats, Oxfords and the half-man/half-woman costume. Besides the clothes he had a life time of personal effects. It took her hours to dump it all. Her energy was unflagging.

When I went back out later, an old bald-headed totter was poking through the vast pile. He examined an outsize pair of sequined falsies with a broad elastic band at the back. They could only have fitted Freddie. The wizened totter spent his days nosing round the streets pushing a pram. He had seen it all. The fag-ends of lives.

'Don't worry, Guv, I'll tidy up after me. I'll get rid of it all for you, Guv.'

He didn't want the sequined falsies. Trading instincts rather than moral scruples.

'You have 'em, sir.'

'Not my size.'

I threw them in behind the bins.

By nightfall she was dumping Freddie's manuscripts. I found a rolled up copy of Fanny by Gaslight and inside it a drawing of the essential. Earthy had the real thing.

Next morning Freddie's word processor and Adler Electric 21D were on the pile. Along with fountain pens, pencils, watering can, pots, brushes, an easel and much else.

Peculiarly, she didn't touch his paintings. He'd drummed into her they were beyond price. On the other hand, she was in most of them. Mental illness was ego gone mad. The other thing she didn't throw out was the clock. It was the only friend she had. Apart from me.

The bags by the bins were a mountainous testimony to a self-regarding life. He'd hoarded himself into everything he touched. There must have been twelve sacks of Daily Telegraphs. Ten sacks of mucky mags. Three sacks of personal letters. A sack of photographs had split open.

A younger Freddie's romantic image lay on the pavement. It had already been walked on. There was a copy of a letter he'd written to the Bank of England -

"...This device will end S & G (smash & grabs) for all time... Incidentally, my safe is gunpowder proof with an unpickable lock..."

It took the totter and his pram two days to clear it all away.

'Who was he, Guv? Mustabeen a wealthy man.'

The only thing left was the out-sized sequined bra.

April was ruthless. Did she hate him so much she couldn't wait to get rid of everything belonging to him? Was she clearing the decks for a new life?

A few days later she shoved a note in my door. Written in pencil, in big letters, two or three words to the line, it read,

"Freddie's funeral is at 12 o clock next Monday. A car is coming to pick me up, father Jones is coming to at 11.15".

I still have that note.

She was getting on with it. Why couldn't I? Mostly, I sat around punishing myself. That laughing face, the intelligent eyes and forehead, the tumble of wheaten hair...how to live without them? I checked the mail each day. April ignored letters addressed to Freddie. I insisted on knocking on her door and delivering the bills into her hand, pointing out which was the electric bill, the gas bill or the phone bill. I knew Freddie paid the rent by standing order. That would have to be sorted.

I phoned Miss Chats. My news didn't phase her.

'He lived long. A peaceful end. Thank you.'

'Samantha, I'm here on my own now. Would you like to come round? We could play dressing up.' Phone slam.

There were only two tenants left to be decanted. Me and April. Wally I hadn't seen for weeks, nor had his rent been paid. I worried about April. She was up there in the attic on her own, barking every day and rarely going out. I followed her one morning to Sainsbury's. She loaded two shopping bags with biscuits, sponge cakes, bars of chocolate, tins of spaghetti, bread, boxes of tea bags, hair dye, talcum powder. She didn't speak to a soul.

The flat, since she emptied it, was extremely cold. When I went up one day with the mail, she was inside Freddie's room, beating the clock with a hammer. I got out fast. Later, she dumped the clock in the bin.

My wife wrote me a letter telling me she had loved me, had learned so much from me (what?), still cared for me but the time was right to move on, the pain of parting would be bearable after a year and a day, the future was bright...And to keep taking the tablets. What tablets? I didn't take tablets! If God had meant us to take tablets we'd have been born with a prescription.

What if I became like April? End up with no feelings as a way to protect myself.

Miss Chats and a Cackhand & Bindweed operative came round to talk me out of the house. I refused to open the hall door. I deliberately put my mouth to the letter-box so they could see nothing but my lips and teeth.

'Oh come on, open up. Please. You must admit the house is seriously in need of a complete overhaul and now is a good time to do it.'

'How's that, Miss Chats?'

'Do you really have to talk to us through the letter-box? Come on, it's ridiculous.'

'Not from where I'm standing.'

'It would be no great inconvenience for you and Miss Fard to move at this time.'

'I can smell your perfume, Samantha. Thank you for wearing it.'

'Look sunshine, if you don't open up, we'll break the door down. You got that?'

He rang the doorbell.

'We're not in.'

I got enough of a glimpse of Miss Chat's retreating leather mini-skirt for my heart to skip a beat. Where there was life there was...a slap on the face.

I met young Zoe in the street. She was outside her house, slopping about in a pair of high-heels. Green ones.

'My Daddy and your Mammy are friends. They're on holiday.'
'She's not my Mammy. She's my wife, Zoe.'
'No. I'm Zoe.'
I handed her my tape recorder and showed her how to use it.
'Speak, Joey.'
'Have a look there, Zoe. Can you see wings?'

Freddie's funeral. I went round to Dracula's parlour. A few locals, hearing it was to be a horse-drawn affair, gathered to watch. No prayers by order of the deceased, the cortège was going direct to the cemetery.

Standing across the street I saw Reg Shand. Had he come to make sure Freddie was dead? Nipping home I retrieved the sequined bra from behind the bins. Putting it in a big envelope, I addressed it to Mr. Reginald Shand, marking it PERSONAL. Back again to the High Road and in very mournful, respectful mood, approached Reg. He was lurking in the door of the pub across from Dracula's. As usual, he was dressed like a Territorial Army Corporal on a day out - porkpie hat, a blazer with shiny metal buttons, grey flannel trousers, a white shirt and a regimental tie. He was wary about accepting the bulky envelope.

'I know you and Mr. Parts-Rinser had your difficulties. But in a genuine desire for forgiveness, Freddie willed this gift to you. He was concerned, even on his death bed, that it be safely delivered. Personally. Freddie admired you for your work in local politics but most especially because you were, like him, a committed Christian.'

Reg's skin was light-deprived. Thirty years in a town hall office made it look like he'd spent his life in an enclosed order of nuns. In the excitement and confusion of the arrival of the horse-drawn hearse, he accepted the package.

The glass-sided hearse was drawn by two black horses. In shiny black harness, topped with black plumes, they looked the part. Their backs were covered in decorated black mourning cloth. An elderly driver in bowler hat and overcoat sat high on a seat, hands gripping the reins and a long stiff whip. A younger man walked beside the nags, hands on the bridles, reversing before them, guiding them to a halt along the busy street. The elderly driver came down from his perch with arthritic deliberation.

'Where's old wotsisname?'

'Here,' said Dracula, stepping from the funeral parlour.

He'd honoured the occasion by wearing a ceremonial mourning suit and top hat.

'Gor blimey,' said the watching Julia, impressed.

Two young Bosnians, less ostentatious but suitably attired in dark suits, wheeled the coffin out to the hearse.

'Mind out,' said the elderly driver as they slid the coffin inside, concerned they might damage his museum-piece. His young partner kept the bevelled glass panel raised until the coffin was secure and Dracula had placed two wreaths on top of it. They were large affairs in floral lettering. One read - FREDDIE; the other - WOFFINGTONS. How did Woffingtons know?

'I'm a member,' Dracula said.

A funeral car pulled up behind the hearse. April was in it. Her hair was piled on her head in a bun. She was wearing a white plastic raincoat. I opened the door and told her I'd join her a little later, if that was okay. I wanted to walk after the horses for a while. She made no move nor even looked at me. Julia and a few other women crowded round the car. They tapped the window and waved in.

"allo darlin', you all right, luv?'

They were hoping for miracles. A touch from her hands. A sign. One of the women was so old she had a pronounced beard. One carried a plastic bag full of bingo sheets, pools coupons, lotto entry forms. Julia, red-faced with enthusiasm, back on her walking stick, leg heavily bandaged, knocked at the funeral car window. April ignored her request for a lift to the cemetery.

As Dracula brought the traffic to a halt and the horses were driven out onto the crown of the road, I glanced over at Reg Shand. He was just in the act of pulling the sequined bra from the envelope. Even at a distance it looked a big item.

The horses were two Friesian stallions. Straining either side of the pole shaft, the undercarriage creaking, traces slapping, chains rattling, hooves clopping, spoked wheels blurring, reins flapping on flesh, they followed after the resplendent stiff-backed Dracula who led the way up the High Road. The pavements were packed with shoppers, the street lined with cars forced to stop. A multitude of eyes were riveted on the dancing black plumes and the magnetic graceful arched necks of the horses. Stallions kept their black colour better than geldings. On the high seat, the two bowler-hatted men sat tense, alert, keeping up a gruff non-stop chatter to the horses.

'On there, Gunner.'

'Stop that, Laddie.'

The older man's gloved hands were full. With pulling on the reins one moment, flicking the whip urgently the next, looking angrily at double-decker buses, tipping his hat to policemen who guided him through red lights, he looked anything but relaxed. You could never count on horses. Even in the uncluttered world of fields they shied. A leaf blowing in a breeze could do it. A bird. On the High Road there were a dozen winking distractions every few yards. Dracula knew the score - he kept glancing back over his shoulder. Each time he did, the older driver grunted,

'Okay, Guv'nor, okay.'

Dracula answered his mobile phone. Straitlaced, perfectly funereal, he just about tolerated the intrusion. Presumably someone else had died.

Filfy Wilfy emerged out of a side street. Munching a sandwich, a bundle of newspapers under one arm, he shuffled alongside me.

'Told you, didn't I, 'e was someone? Old Partsy. 'ucking funeral! Must be the biggest 'ucking funeral since they buried Lady Di. Come right out of the blue, didn't it? He wasn't old. Ninety's young nowadays. The Queen Mum, she's gorn an' all.'

A pestilential stink rising from him, he was more of a corpse than the one in the box. I was tempted to suggest he hop in the hearse and get a free ride to the grave. Trying to shake him off, I was slightly ahead of the hearse. But he kept with me. When he'd finished vulturing his sandwich, he scrunched the paper bag it came in. Casually tossing it away, it landed out in the middle of the road, where it bounced a few times...right in front of the horses.

Up went Gunner's hooves, in a perfect panic, and Laddie, not to be outshone, reared even higher. The look on the faces of the people along the pavements, in the cars, on the buses, was as nothing compared to the fear in the horses' eyes. The driver tried with all his might to stop them plunging wildly across the street and onto the footpath. Shoppers scattered, screaming in every direction. Pulling like crazy on the reins, bowler-hat managed to get the show back on the road. But the horses then decided to gallop dead straight up the High Road like it was a race track or open country.

The younger of the men pulled desperately at the hand-brake but the wooden block fell off. The hearse swayed so much it looked as if it was going to split apart. With Freddie on board, it weighed the best part of a ton. Cars shot down side streets. Buses pulled over. The funeral car driver, taking advantage, accelerated onwards. April looked out, her upper lip wriggling like she was a big rabbit being taken for a drive. I ran as fast as I could to keep up with the mayhem. It was certainly the kind of divertissement stopped you thinking about yourself. By the tube station, for no apparent reason at all, the headlong flight came to a stop. The stallions, meek as lambs, nuzzled each other and looked about as if calmly awaiting further instructions. The older man, now minus his hat, was breathing so heavily he might have been the one bolting. Reins gathered tightly in his hands, face dripping, he showered curses on his charges.

'Bastards! You wait! Fucking pair of gits! That's it, you've 'ad it! Bad boys. Just you wait! Bad boys.'

The younger man, white-faced, gripped their bridles and reversing before them, got the procession going again, at dead slow pace.

'You okay, Squire?'

'As long as the corpse didn't part company, 'sall I was worried about.'

'If I get my hands on that toerag! He was the one spooked 'em.'

Apart from the brake block coming away, no damage was done.

Now the horses high-stepped along in perfect order, their lovely plumed heads bobbing, touching. The younger man, still holding their bridles, walked backwards for a considerable distance.

Dracula, having run hard to catch up, collapsed into the front of the funeral car beside the driver. He had summoned the police. A motorbike cop sped up and rode ahead, warning the traffic out of the way. The younger driver, deciding the horses were settled, jumped up beside his mate. I hopped into the funeral car and sat beside April.

She was gurgling, grinding, growling, looking like any moment she was going to outdo the horses in the terror stakes. Focusing for a moment on my face, the demon seemed to leave her. What had she seen in my eyes?

Dracula, breathing heavily, complained bitterly.

'The police, they'll charge for such service. What if the corpse had appeared to the public? Can you imagine the local rag? That old geezer, filthy skunk. He spooked the nags.'

'He threw a paper bag.'

'By the way - Reg Shand phoned me. Passing the Abbey National. You compromised him with a dubious garment, it seems. Did you? I think it's time you went back up north. I mean it, mate. It's where you come from, isn't it? This town is filling with strangers. They got guns. What if one of them started pointing at you?'

Sounded like a threat to me.

'You've been getting away with it because you're young. That's the only reason. Your wife is not around anymore to protect you, is she?'

April's coat and skirts were above her knees. There was a lot of startling flesh on view.

Not so long ago, Freddie said to me,

'You don't understand what dying means, do you? The end. Nothingness. Finito. Of course you don't.'

The car hit a red light and a lorry swinging out from a side street blocked our progress. We stopped momentarily beside a pub. There was a sign in the window.

"Wanted Barman".

Quietly opening the funeral car door I got out and as quietly closed the door behind me. One hand on the top rail, I sprung across a pedestrian barrier and strolled into the pub. The funeral car moved on.

I wanted to snap out of it. The torpor. The pain. You could change. Swop one life for another. Get my wings.

The Guv'nor looked me up and down.

'Have you worked behind a bar before? Don't bother me if you're a time waster.'

'At university, I worked the Student Union bar for two years. I was a cellar man in

Woffingtons one time.'

'Can I trust you? What kind of bloke would you say you are?'

'I'm the kind of bloke who was homesick living at home.'

'When can you start?'

'Tomorrow morning?'

'You won't come wearing that suit, will you? Frighten all my tosspots.'

Spur of the moment, my life had changed. I had a job. A job was a future.

April returned from the funeral, went alone up to her room and for weeks no one came near her, spoke to her, inquired after her. Except me. For April Fard, social intercourse minus Freddie was double-minus all the way. The pub paid me cash every night. I didn't need cash. I didn't need anything. Except my wife. Missed her every minute of the day. I didn't want freedom. Freedom was meaningless without the naked touch.

Eventually someone sent someone round to see April. A bloke on crutches. He looked in need of help himself. About forty, a Geordie, wispy moustache, he struggled up the stairs and spent the best part of the morning with her. He knocked on my door on the way out. He wanted to liaise with me and to thank me for keeping an eye on her.

'It's what society's all about, mate.'

'Is it? So why are you trying to decant us?'

That wasn't his department. If she persisted in not picking up her mail, I was to call him.

'An illness like hers, it can be handled. Don't worry, mate.'

I never saw him again. The mail piled up in the hallway.

I opened a letter one morning addressed to Freddie. It had been sent from Guernsey. It was a bank statement in April's name. The account was healthily in the black. She was a sitting duck for exploitation.

She began adding new words to her repertoire. One morning I stuck my head in the downpipe shaft the better to listen.

'It's not fair, it's not fair. Please, John, leave me alone. Leave me alone. Now look at all the fucking trouble you've caused. Don't, please don't. No, no. I don't want it. I don't want it. Fuckoffbackeroll.'

Radio 2 belted out chatter and love pop. She knew how to turn the radio on and off. I hoped she was as capable with the gas fire. Freddie's death had thawed her tonsils. She seemed to be in the company of a crowd of tormenting spirits.

One evening she came looking for me. It was my day off from the pub and I'd gone to bed early. The knocking on my door was so fierce I thought it was the police and the Trust trying to break in. Then I heard the familiar dog-whimpering. Angry gusts of sound too intense to bother with the weight of words.

'My door. I can't do it. It's. It's. I can't stand it.'

She'd come out of her flat onto the communal staircase and shut the door after her. When she tried to get back in, she couldn't. Sticking between the door and the far wall was the three foot length of three by two. As I tested the door, trying to work out how I was going to get in, she stood beside me, trembling with temper and impatience. She'd put on weight since Freddie died. All those sponge cakes. She was swelling into a heap of danger. And she was beside me. I could smell her. Talcy electric.

Turning her key in the Chubb lock, I managed with all my might to force the door open a little. But not enough to get my arm in and over to the length of wood.

'Don't worry, April, we'll manage it.'

I was wearing a short silk dressing gown. I felt vulnerable. She started throwing herself at the door, smashing into it with her shoulder. The stairs shook. The floor shook. She bullocked so frantically, she forced the inside length of wood through the door panel. The door was cheapo-cheapo Trust stuff, but even allowing for that her strength was prodigious. Eventually I managed to get in. Soon as I did, she burst past me and charged up the stairs like a rogue elephant. She went into the kitchen and started throwing pots and pans around. Like she was fighting with someone who was throwing them back.

'Let go. Please. I'll bonk your face, Charlie.'

I set about botching a repair on the door. Cackhand & Bindweed came naturally. With a hammer, tacks and a square of plywood I covered the hole in the panel.

Up in her flat all had gone eerily silent. Maybe there wasn't anything left to throw. I went up to see was she okay.

The stairs to the landing and the landing itself were now even tattier. The dumping of Freddie's stuff, the elimination of the familiar clutter that makes a home, had starkly exposed the barrenness of the place. What had once been whacky and warm was now a shocking emptiness. Talcum had been walked to a slush on the scraggy carpet. The top of the skirting board was a roadway for silver fish and woodlice. Dirty grey spits of cobweb hung round the door to Freddie's room. Apart from the bed and his paintings, the room was bare. I peeped into the kitchen - she wasn't there. Crockery, pots, pans, cutlery, tins of baked beans, spaghetti, a sweeping brush were strewn about with such calamitous abandon it wouldn't have looked out of place in Tate Britain.

The bedroom door was open but I couldn't see her. She definitely wasn't in the kitchen, the bathroom or Freddie's room. Where was she?

Tight in the angle between a wall and door-frame, was a smudge of what looked at first like grey web. It was a cocoon. Secure inside half a mile of silk, was the pupa of a moth. A creature like myself awaiting amazing change.

I listened for breathing. An impish urge taking over I called out,

'Sweet-sweetie!'

I ventured into her room. She wasn't to be seen. The big armchair and shackles were there, the pink bedclothes, the pink wallpaper...Had she fallen down the other side of the piano? All I could see was a pile of empty talcum containers and enema boxes dumped on the floor between the piano and the wall. I was about to peer under her bed when I heard a strangulated gasp for air.

From the corner of my eye I just had time to glimpse her hurtling towards me. Screaming, she landed on my back, her fingers tightly round my neck. The impact of her weight alone winded me. The psychological blow was worse. Had she exploded from real or was this imaginary stuff? It had to be real. She was doing her best to choke me.

'I can't stand it. Let me go. I'll kill you, Jack. Don't, don't.'

She'd been lurking behind the door. I grabbed her wrists. She was so strong I could hardly breathe. The pressure across my windpipe made me gag. My tongue stuck out. I felt ashamed, even as I thought I was dying. Whimpering, she desperately tried to finish me off. Raising my foot to the piano keyboard, I pushed backwards with the little strength I had left. We crashed across the room and onto the bed. Her head clunked the wall. She let go. I rolled away to the floor. She lay panting, dazed, legs wide open. I scrambled to my feet.

Her hands began to hover before her face, like she was expecting me to jump on her. And she was only going to make a half-hearted effort to stop me. My neck hurt. I'd come close to choking. Death had shook my hand.

My dressing gown hung open but I didn't care. Grabbing one of the shackles I quickly snapped it round her ankle. She jumped up, arms flailing. I roughly pushed her back down into the armchair. Stunned for a second she sat dumb. I snapped the second shackle into place.

'Stay there and calm down, April.'

I sweated fear. A cat came into the room and nimbly sprung onto her lap. It was Rosa's cat. I'd forgotten all about it. Had April taken pity on it?

She seemed composed now, her hands lying along the armrests. She could have been a dotty queen on a low throne, legs askew, puzzled. As if she couldn't work out whether I'd just performed a sexual duty or was just about to.

'I'll set you free later. Don't be afraid. You probably miss Freddie. In your own way.'

I had felt when she attacked me peculiarly wingless. Like she was a big bird frantically tearing at me with her beak. Breaking into my cocoon. My skull.

I hadn't thought of my wife, not for a second. The struggle for survival had set me free. For a minute or two anyway.

I was limping as I went down the flight of stairs from the attic. In the desperate tussle I must have hit my foot against something. Pulling the door out after me, relieved to be alive, I let it slam. The length of wood I felt sure had again fallen down and into place. I'd have to deal with it later.

I phoned the social worker's mobile. There was a recorded voice,

'Out of the office. Please leave a message.'

I did.

'April Fard just tried to kill me. Please come round.'

Totally exhausted, I fell asleep. I dreamed I was alive. Great. I could feel wings. Are these wings? "Are you ready to fly, Sir?" "No. No, I'm not Sir. I'm Joey. I'm me."

It was a brilliant double-rainbow world.

I jolted up in the bed. Was there a caterpillar on my neck? Sleep fogged my brain. Like smoke. I heard a plap down on the pillow, right beside my ear. A moth? Water? A muffled plap. Water dripping on the bedclothes. Four times already we'd been flooded. Wally, coshed by welfare pills, kept forgetting to turn his taps off. Plap-plap. Hitting the pillow, yes. On my face. Dreamy fear. Wait a sec...I hadn't seen Wally for ages. I struggled to tell reality from sleep. I was down a deep shaft inside myself. The bedside radio... The World Service...A war in Africa...That's real enough. I'm awake.

I put on the light. The switch clicked like I'd walked on a cockroach. The cracked plaster on the ceiling had torn the lining paper. The room was in the cold grip of an English summer night. What was I thinking? It wasn't water. The pillow was dry. I hadn't cried that night. No flood. No Wally. Only April.

I put my ear to the boxed cavity behind the bed. The pipes ran from the top of the house all the way down. Maybe she had flushed the loo. That's what had woken me. She was up there, alone, all day, every day. And nights most of all. I heard crackling. Sometimes, in the small hours, I'd hear desperate hawkish cries. But this was some kind of crackling. Getting louder. Seals munching lobsters. Wings beating.

There was only the two of us left. From attic to basement, we possessed the house.

I scrambled around for something to wear. Dopey with sleep, I grabbed a pair of boxer shorts. I found my keys, my mobile phone. I went upstairs to the communal hallway. A scattering of unopened mail lay on the floor. On the stair treads the lino was worn to linseed wisps. Unhappy feet were heavy feet. The balusters, undercoated in a previous age, had never been glossed.

I listened at April's door. Definitely crackling of some kind. Like a terrier in brushwood. Smoke seemed to be seeping out the door. Was I really awake? Fire. Had to be. I could smell it. Fire. I'd feared it more than loneliness. I shoulder-charged the door. Shouted her name.

'April. April.'

The anti-burglary device was in place. My fault? I'd never be able to burst the door in.

'April. April. Fire.'

She wouldn't heed voices outside her own head. The irony of fire destroying the last of Freddie's fleshy liquidities. Unless I could do something. Our house was burning. My cocoon.

I ran into the street. Flames antlered out the upstairs windows and up over the roof parapet. Black smoke in evil billows choked the air. The faded net curtains and the blanket on the kitchen window were alight. Crackling. Like the time we walked on the beach at Brighton and our feet crunched across shell and shingle. In my mind I could see the tattered carpet, the piano, the old furniture, talcum powder, canvasses, all twisting, melting to black threads. The flames hit out hard, shimmying the trees, splitting the dark. An angry crow, disturbed, rattled blackly. How was April going to get out alive? I dialled 999.

Three o'clock in the morning, coffin-cold, the houses all around were sleeping, the useless dogs dreaming bones.

April appeared in her window, her hair burning, her face in silent scream, hands whirling about her head as if flailing at wasps. Right to the end her torments stayed inside her. The flaming pain sizzled her skin. Anaesthetised by schizophrenia, she never made a sound. There was nothing I could do.

Hours before, had I slammed that door? I called her name.

Like a sick bee crawling from the hive, she had managed to clamber out onto the window sill. Her days filled with screaming voices, now at death's door, she'd clammed shut. As if the flames consumed her tongue. Her last few seconds, she became a burning bush.

I could tell she was going to jump. She'd hit our basement garden four floors below. Under intense heat a window shot out. She jumped. She never reached the ground. This wasn't nightmare. This was real. She was dangling in the burning night, crackling. Neither flying nor falling. As if hit by gunshot, another window shattered. She dangled in space because she couldn't hit the ground. The shackles. The armchair. She was anchored to the room. I'd shackled her. I knew where the key was. But I couldn't get in. How had she set herself alight? Flame was a magnet for madness. Some think they are holding the sun.

She'd made it to the window and jumped, but the armchair was too big to follow through. She dangled upside down, burning before my eyes. Her flaming dress fell round her neck. Her clawed hands twitched before finally hanging down, not moving at all.

Once Freddie had been taken to Kensal Green, something like this was inevitable. I watched powerless. Poor April. Was this my fault too?

The fire-brigade at last came hurtling down the empty High Road. They'd cut her down and pump the house full of water. April and water - the only loves in Freddie's life. Our house destroyed by both. Books, records, manuscripts, love letters, paintings, furniture - everything that staked out life - all would be ruined.

She was dead. It wasn't murder but a crime nonetheless. I had begged them to take her away and look after her. She didn't fit in with official policy.

'Chaos In The Community,' Freddie had called it.

You could hang burning from a top window and no one in the street would notice. Had it happened a few doors down would I have noticed it myself?

In the dark, the fire-fighters hurried about, the scatty moon polishing their helmets. What was left of the window glass was blown to smithereens by a jet of water so powerful it knocked lumps of plaster from the parapet.

April still hung upside down.

A fireman sped up a ladder and attacked her chains with a bolt-cutter. Another man, managing to get her across his shoulder, carefully carried her down. Her shoes fell off.

Soon there would be nothing much left to decant us from. Decant me from. The Trust had won.

I was standing over by the public garden fence. A caterpillar dropped on my bare shoulder from an overhanging tree.

A hand gripped the back of my neck. Police.

'All right, Scobie, you're under arrest.'

'My name's not Scobie.'

'It's an offence to appear naked in public.'

'I'm not naked.'

'Arsonist!'

'Me? I called the fire brigade.'

'Course you did. It's what arsonists do.'

April's charred remains were placed in an ambulance.

I was shoved into a police van.

Three o'clock in the morning, wrapped in a grey cell blanket, I wasn't alone. For company I had two West Indians, three Nigerians, four drunks - one of whom was the one-legged Scot in a wheelchair. His lips were smeared with fresh blood. Two strips of thick elastoplast crossed on his forehead. An eye, raw as liver, bulged over a cheek-bone.

A door opened. A uniformed arm shunted in Miss Jackpot. Muzie. His brown eyes were tired, his body listless. He stared at us like we were characters in a dream. He edged onto the corner of my chair.

'Today I miss jackpot. I 'ave all bloomin' eight hawses, the bet vos placed, yeah? ve-well the dawkit vos ritten out an' everting an' I have to place bet by two p.m. o'clock...'

'Why have they arrested you, Muzie?'

'...I 'ave late night and I set clock bee-side my ear to go off the bloomin' ting at heh quarter to the hour so I get to Ladbroke at right time enough...'

He had the addicted face of a saint.

I was wearing boxer shorts and a blanket. A Vivienne Westwood/Big Issue number. No one noticed.

Toby Turfe, our custody officer for the night, looked in.

'You.'

He beckoned me out. Standing by the reception window, eating late night fish and chips, he looked me up and down. He told me they were letting me go. I was nervous in case he hit me another slap on the face.

'We know where to find you.'

'More than I can say myself.'

'You put old Parts up to all them scams. Flooding the church hall. The Blessed Virgin racket.'

'No one put Freddie up to anything.'

'Why are you only wearing women's shorts?'

'I had to get out quick. They were the first thing to hand.'

'You look like a tart.'

As I went out the door he grabbed the blanket. Property of the Met. But for the shorts I was naked.

Thankfully the High Road hadn't a sinner save myself. It started raining. On the clock above Dracula's funeral parlour, the big black hand fell half a minute to 5.30.

A coconut clatter of horse hooves erupted from the foggy gloom. I darted into the doorway of Mrsblouse - the outsize shop for outsize ladies. Torso models displayed jumpers, blouses, frocks, suits. They had either high, tight, sticky-out pointed breasts, aimed at the younger set or stout rounded mother-hen bosoms, for the maturer patron. This was where Freddie bought April's clothes. He liked the wide, flouncy dresses, the screaming fabrics, the arcane under-the-counter items for the cognoscenti. Bloomers with gussets. Suspender belts.

The spacious shop entrance had black and white tiles. I was a pawn caught between night and morning.

A troop of cavalry on early morning manoeuvre came clattering down the road. There were at least fifty men and more horses - some of the troopers had two in hand. The men wore green overcoats, caps and black riding boots heeled with blunt spurs. They were young, tight-muscled, pale, edgy. Most of the horses were gleaming caviar-black. Jangling harness, shouted commands, cluc-clupping hooves filled the street in sea-shell uproar. They were ceremonial ghosts in a cold dawning. Eastwards over the rooftops the day was creeping in.

Under the road, I could hear a hidden river flowing its secret miles to the Thames.

By the Greek church, a thin bearded dosser hunkered into the studded double-doors. Thinking I was coming to halve his hopes, he spat at me with surprising malice.

I made for our street. The morning my future wife first moved in, I knelt for luck beside her suitcase and kissed the pavement between her feet.

As I approached the burnt wreck of the house, big Julia was in her front garden.

'Coming from a party, sir?'

'From the police station. There was a fire last night and April's...ah...dead.'

She was more interested in my boxers.

'I wouldn't mind them panties, sir, when you're finished with 'em.'

'They're not panties as such. I doubt they'd fit you.'

With practised gormlessness she ignored the remark.

'They'd make a nice duster.'

'I'm sentimentally attached to them. Good morning.'

'Bleeding blighter. No wonder she left you, sir. Your lady wife.'

Pretending she'd shot a dart after me, clutching my bum, I hopped in the air.

A police tape cordoned our house. The parapet above the top floor was scorched black, the paint-work blow-torched, the cement-work burnt bare. There wasn't a single window-pane intact. Glass littered the steps, shards spiked the garden. The smell of fire was thick, wet, evil.

April dangling, burning, upside down...how would I ever bank that image down?

I went through the side door and into our basement. A squirrel shot out from the open kitchen door. Grey scavenger without conscience. In the kitchen the ceiling bellied down, visibly swelling, ready to give. I stabbed at it with my finger. Gallons of water smashed over me. I didn't even jump out of the way. Sloshing my way to the bathroom, I gathered my clothes, picked up the hat Freddie had given me. I went into the bedroom and looked at the double-bed one last time. I bought it second-hand in Jimmy Satwick's shop. The second-best bed is the best bed. Love before money.

I sat on the bed thinking what to do. I had neither love nor money. I heard a noise up the stairs somewhere. Presuming it to be a slosh of water breaking through a ceiling, I ignored it. This place had been my cocoon and when you left the cocoon the cocoon was smashed. You flew on, let the wind play you up the sky.

'Heh, man, are you there? Sorry, like you know. Cool.'

Wally. It was Wally. He'd disappeared long ago. But it had to be him.

He stood on top of the communal stairs. In his pyjamas, solid as a rock. I almost cried to see him.

'Wally, Wally, what's up, mate? You okay? Where have you been? I thought you'd gone.'

He indicated the water puddles in the hallway, the water glistening down the walls, the wet stairs. The fire-brigade had left the house looking like we were under the sea. Wally thought it was all his fault.

'Sorry, man, this time bang to rights. The sink, the tap, man. Sorry. I said sorry. The valve went, see, seems like. Don't go on about it. The plumber turned it off, then it came on. I'll get a mop in a minute. Massif. Cool.'

He must have lain in his room, pilled to the top of his loaf. Somehow he'd managed to sleep through the conflagration. And the ensuing water scena. He'd often flooded us. The one and only watery calamity he wasn't responsible for, he now happily claimed.

'No, no, man, it was me. I'm not trying to get out of it. The tap you see. The Trust - it's their tap. They're the ones what really done it. I'm let down by it.'

There was a brown envelope lying on the floor. I opened it. It was one of the Trust bulletins. There was a headline, congratulating themselves, on receiving a rating of 90% for their own office reception area.

'And didn't you hear the fire engine, Wally? The police siren. The flames, the dancing water? Me?'

'You kidding?'

'Wally, don't let anyone ever say your pills aren't the best. What a country! What a great country! What great pills! What great reception areas!'

Clinging to each other, we laughed like drains.

As I left the shell that was once my home, I walked right into a gloating Reg Shand, a smirking Miss Chats and cocky Cackhand & Bindweed labourers, lump hammers ready to hand.

No one beat them. In the end. In the pause called the end.

'If you had gone when you were ordered, all this would never have happened. You got away with it, 'cos your wife was protecting you.'

'Thank you, Reg. Miss Chats - I'm going to buy a video camera. I'd like to film you. As yourself. All you'd have to do is...BE. Shall I ring you, Samantha?'

I wasn't really seeing them. In my mind were the jets of water shooting right over the top of the house. Like the firemen were saluting Freddie.

I ran down the side of the house and into our garden. In a panic they rushed after me, ready with the lump hammers.

The tree, undamaged, in the rising sun, dazzled. There would be pears again come